SPEAKING OF
LUST
Stories of Forbidden Desire

SPEAKING OF

LUST

Stories of Forbidden Desire

Edited by Lawrence Block

The seven DEAdly Sins series

Cumberland House
Nashville, Tennessee

Published by Cumberland House Publishing, Inc., 431 Harding Industrial Drive, Nashville, TN 37211

Cover design: Gore Studio, Inc.

Library of Congress Cataloging-in-Publication Data

Speaking of lust: stories of forbidden desire / edited by Lawrence Block.
        p. cm. -- (The seven deadly sins series)
    ISBN 1-58182-153-0 (alk. paper)
    1. Erotic stories, American. 2. Psychological fiction, American. 3. Lust --Fiction.
    I. Block, Lawrence. II. Series.

PS648.E7 S64 2001
813'. 01083538--dc21

                                                                2001017266

Printed in the United States of America
1 2 3 4 5 6 7—05 04 03 02 01 00

CONTENTS

BEFORE WE BEGIN...

Lawrence Block

ONE OF THE DUTIES of an anthologist is to provide some prefatory remarks for the stories he has collected. All things considered, this has to be as much a make-work project as anything ever dreamed up by the WPA. If the assembled stories are any good at all, what do they need with an introduction? And, if they're not good enough to stand on their own, what good will an introduction do? And why collect them in the first place?

Well, put your mind at rest. The stories I've rounded up for you, all centered on that exceedingly deadly sin we call lust, are not just good enough to stand before you unintroduced—they are, I must say, outstanding.

Nevertheless, I'm going to say my piece. Because, you see, I need to do something to justify having my name on this volume, and on my royalty checks. The hard work of anthologizing has been done by my worthy partner in this enterprise, the inestimable Marty Greenberg. It is he who has shuffled paper and secured permissions, while I get to hang around and take credit. If writing an introduction is a make-work project, well, that only seems fair. I ought to have work made for me, and I'm honor-bound to do it.

And, as luck would have it, I have Something To Say.

Not about lust. (Well, I have no end of things to say about lust, but they're none of your business.) And not about the stories, either, because they need my blessing like a moose needs a hatrack—or, more in keeping with this book's theme, like a mink needs Viagra.

No, this introduction will be about my own story, the original novelette "Speaking of Lust" written especially for this volume.

In a sense it doesn't need an introduction, either; you'll like it or you won't, irrespective of anything I might tell you about it ahead of time. What I want to tell you, though, is less about the story than about the circumstances of its writing. You may find it instructive. Lord knows I do.

Lust, the handsome volume you hold in your hand, is the first of a projected series, seven volumes in all, one for each of the seven cardinal sins. (Or deadly sins, as you prefer. "Deadly" has, alas, a double meaning, and thus carries the connotation of *boring* along with that of *lethal*; "cardinal" is more apt to put me in mind of Stan Musial and Mark McGwire. Never mind.)

The series concept was a natural, no question. But I tried to figure out what my own contribution might be. Oh, I'd write an intro, one always has to write an intro, but could I do something else with the goal of making the book a little bit special?

Maybe, I thought, I could write an original story for each book.

Hmmm.

Maybe the stories could be somehow linked.

Hmmm again.

Maybe they could all have the same lead character. But I wouldn't want to use any of my existing series characters, so, uh, maybe I could develop a new character or characters specifically for the series of anthologies.

And maybe these stories would be a little more substantial than, well, mere *stories*. Longer, that is to say. Quite a bit longer. Novelette length, say. Or, well, novella length.

Everybody liked the concept. Everybody agreed it was a terrific idea. And then I woke up one morning and realized I'd committed myself to the task of dreaming up a brand-new series and writing seven novellas featuring this as-yet-unimagined cast of characters. What kind of hell had I made for myself?

Well, go know. I had as much fun writing "Speaking of Lust" as I've had with anything in years, and if you enjoy it half as much as I did you'll be happy indeed. As I already know you'll be happy with all the other stories in the book.

For my part, I look forward to the other six volumes. And right about now the one I'm most looking forward to is *Sloth*.

—Lawrence Block
Greenwich Village

CRACK

James W. Hall

Wʜᴇɴ I ꜰɪʀsᴛ sᴀᴡ ᴛʜᴇ sʟɪᴛ ᴏꜰ ʟɪɢʜᴛ ᴄᴏᴍɪɴɢ ᴛʜʀᴏᴜɢʜ ᴛʜᴇ ᴡᴀʟʟ, I halted abruptly on the stairway, and instantly my heart began to thrash with a giddy blend of dread and craving.

At the time, I was living in Spain, a section named Puerto Viejo, or the Old Port, in the small village of Algorta just outside the industrial city of Bilbao. It was a filthy town, a dirty region, with a taste in the air of old pennies and a patina of grime dulling every bright surface. The sunlight strained through perpetual clouds that had the density and monotonous luster of lead. It was to have been my year of *flamenco y sol*, but instead I was picked to be the Fulbright fellow of a dour Jesuit university in Bilbao on the northern coast where the umbrellas were pocked by ceaseless acid rain and the customary dress was black— shawls, dresses, berets, raincoats, shirts, and trousers. It was as if the entire Basque nation was in perpetual mourning.

The night I first saw the light I was drunk. All afternoon I had been swilling Rioja on the balcony overlooking the harbor, celebrating the first sunny day in a month. It was October and despite the brightness and clarity of the light, my wife had been darkly unhappy all day, even unhappier than usual. At nine o'clock she was already in bed paging aimlessly through month-old magazines and sipping her sherry. I finished with the dishes and double-checked all the locks and began to stumble up the stairs of our two-hundred-fifty-year-old stone house that only a few weeks before our arrival in Spain had been subdivided into three apartments.

I was midway up the stairs to the second floor when I saw the slim line of the light shining through a chink in the new mortar. There was no debate, not even a millisecond of equivocation about the propriety of my actions. In most matters I considered myself a scrupulously moral man. I had always been one who could be trusted with other people's money or their most damning secrets. But like so many of my fellow Puritans I long ago had discovered that when it came to certain libidinous temptations I was all too easily swept off my safe moorings into the raging currents of erotic gluttony.

I immediately pressed my eye to the crack.

It took me a moment to get my bearings, to find the focus. And when I did, my knees softened and my breath deserted me. The view was beyond anything I might have hoped for. The small slit provided a full panorama of my neighbors' second story. At knee-high level I could see their master bathroom and a few feet to the left their king-size brass bed.

That first night the young daughter was in the bathroom with the door swung open. If the lights had been off in their apartment or the bathroom door had been closed I might never have given the peep-hole another look. But that girl was standing before the full-length mirror and she was lifting her fifteen-year-old breasts that had already developed quite satisfactorily, lifting them both at once and reshaping them with her hands to meet some standard that only she could see. After a while she released them from her grip, then lifted them on her flat palms as though offering them to her image in the mirror. They were beautiful breasts, with small nipples that protruded nearly an inch from the aureole, and she handled them beautifully, in a fashion that was far more mature and knowing than one would expect from any ordinary fifteen-year-old.

I did not know her name. I still don't, though certainly she is the most important female who ever crossed my path. Far more crucial in my life's trajectory than my mother or either of my wives. Yet it seems appropriate that I should remain unaware of her name. That I should not personalize her in any way. That she should remain simply an abstraction—simply the girl who destroyed me.

In the vernacular of that year in Spain, she was known as a *niña pera*, or pear girl. One of hundreds of shapely and succulent creatures who cruised about the narrow, serpentine roads of Algorta and Bilbao on loud mopeds, their hair streaming in their wake. She was as juicy as any of them. More succulent than most, as I had already noticed from several brief encounters as we exited from adjacent doors onto the narrow alley-streets of the Old Port. On these two or three occasions, I remember fumbling through my Spanish greetings and taking a stab at small talk while she, with a patient but faintly disdainful smile, suffered my clumsy attempts at courtesy. Although she wore the white blouse and green plaid skirts of all the other Catholic schoolgirls, such prosaic dress failed to disguise her pearness. She was achingly succulent, blindingly juicy. At the time I was twice her age. Double the fool and half the man I believed I was.

That first night, after a long, hungering look, I pulled away from the crack of light and with equal measures of reluctance and urgency, I marched back down the stairs and went immediately to the kitchen and found the longest and flattest knife in the drawer and brought it back to the stairway, and with surgical precision I inserted the blade into the soft mortar and as my pulse throbbed, I painstakingly doubled the size of my peephole.

When I withdrew the blade and applied my eye again to the slit, I now could see my *niña pera* from her thick black waist-length hair to her bright pink toenails. While at the same time I calculated that if my neighbors ever detected the lighted slit from their side and dared to press an eye to the breach, they would be rewarded with nothing more than a static view of the two-hundred-fifty-year-old stones of my rented stairwell.

I knew little about my neighbors except that the father of my pear girl was a vice-consul for that South American country whose major role in international affairs seemed to be to supply America with her daily dose of granulated ecstasy.

He didn't look like a gangster. He was tall and elegant, with wavy black hair that touched his shoulders and an exquisitely precise beard. He might have been a maestro of a European symphony or a painter of romantic landscapes. And his young wife could easily have been a slightly older sister to my succulent one. She was in her middle thirties and had the wide and graceful hips, the bold, uplifting breasts, the gypsy features and black unfathomable eyes that seemed to spring directly from the archetypal pool of my carnality. In the Jungian parlance of my age, the wife was my anima, while the daughter was the anima of my adolescent self. They were perfect echoes of the dark secret female who glowed like uranium in the bowels of my psyche.

That first night when the bedsprings squeaked behind me, and my wife padded across the bedroom floor for her final visit to the bathroom, I allowed myself one last draft of the amazing sight before me. The *niña* was now stooped forward and was holding a small hand mirror to her thicket of pubic hair, poking and searching with her free hand through the dense snarl as if she were seeking that tender part of herself she had discovered by touch but not yet by sight.

Trembling and breathless, I pressed my two hands flat against the stone wall and shoved myself away and with my heart in utter disarray, I carried my lechery up the stairs to bed.

The next day I set about learning my neighbors' schedule and altering mine accordingly. My wife had taken a job as an English teacher in a nearby *instituto* and was occupied every afternoon and through the early evening. My duties at the university occupied me Monday, Wednesday, and Friday. I was expected to offer office hours before and after my classes on those days. However, I immediately began to curtail these sessions because I discovered that my *niña pera* returned from school around three o'clock, and on many days she showered and changed into casual clothes, leaving her school garb in a heap on the bathroom floor as she fled the apartment for an afternoon of boy-watching in the Algorta pubs.

To my department chairman's dismay, I began to absent myself from the university hallways immediately after my last class of the day, hurrying with my umbrella along the five blocks to the train station so I could be home by 2:55. In the silence of my apartment, hunched breathless at my hole, I watched her undress. I watched the steam rise from her shower, and I watched her towel herself dry. I watched her on the toilet and I watched her using the sanitary products she preferred. I watched her touch the flawless skin of her face with her fingertips, applying makeup or wiping it away. On many afternoons I watched her examine herself in the full-length mirror. Running her hands over that seamless flesh, trying out various seductive poses while an expression played on her face that was equal parts exultation and shame—that peculiar adolescent emotion I so vividly recalled.

These were the times when I would have touched myself were I going to do so. But these moments at the peephole, while they were intensely sexual, were not the least masturbatory. Instead, they had an almost spiritual component. As though I were worshiping at the shrine of hidden mysteries, allowed by divine privilege to see beyond the walls of my own paltry life. In exchange for this gift I was cursed to suffer a brand of reverential horniness I had not imagined possible. I lusted for a vision that was forever intangible, a girl I could not touch, nor smell, nor taste. A girl who was no more than a scattering of light across my retina.

Although I never managed to establish a definite pattern to her mother's schedule, I did my best to watch her as well. At odd unpredictable hours, she appeared in my viewfinder and I watched the elder *niña pera* bathe in a tub of bubbles, and even when her house was empty, I watched her chastely close the bathroom door whenever she performed her toilette. I watched her nap on the large brass bed. And three times that fall in the late afternoons, I watched her slide her hand inside her green silk robe and touch herself between the legs, hardly moving the hand at all, giving herself the subtlest of touches until she rocked her head back into the pillow and wept.

I kept my eye to the wall during the hours when I should have been preparing for my classes and grading my students' papers and writing up their weekly exams. Instead, I stationed myself at the peephole, propping myself up with pillows, finding the best alignment for nose and cheek against the rough cool rock. I breathed in the sweet grit of mortar, trained my good right eye on the bathroom door and the bed, scanning the floor for shadows, primed for any flick of movement, always dreadfully alert for the sound of my wife's key in the front door.

After careful study, I had memorized her homecoming ritual. Whenever she entered our apartment, it took her two steps to reach the foyer and put down her bag. She could then choose to turn right into the kitchen or take another step toward the stairway. If she chose the latter, almost instantly she would be able to witness me perched at the peep-hole, and my clandestine life would be exposed. In my leisure, I clocked a normal entry and found that on average I had almost a full twenty seconds from the moment her key turned the tumblers till she reached the bottom of the stairs, twenty seconds to toss the pillows back into the bedroom and absent myself from the hole.

I briefly toyed with the idea of revealing the peephole to her. But I knew her sense of the perverse was far short of my own. She was consti-tutionally gloomy, probably a clinical depressive. Certainly a passive-aggressive, who reveled in bitter non-response, bland effect, withdrawing into maddening hours of silence whenever I blundered across another invisible foul line she had drawn.

I watched the father too, the vice-consul. On many occasions I saw him strip off his underwear and climb into the shower, and I saw him dry himself and urinate and brush his teeth. Once I saw him reach down and retrieve a pair of discarded briefs and bring the crotch to his nose before deciding they were indeed fresh enough to wear again. He had the slender and muscular build of a long-distance runner. Even in its slackened state his penis was formidable.

On one particular Sunday morning, I watched with grim fascination as he worked his organ to an erection, all the while gazing at the reflec-tion of his face. And a few moments later as the spasms of his pleasure shook him and he was bending forward to ejaculate into the sink, the *niña pera* appeared at the doorway of the bathroom. She paused briefly to watch the vice-consul's last strokes, then passed behind him and stepped into the shower with a nonchalance that I found more shock-ing than anything I had witnessed to that point.

Late in November, the chairman of my department called me into his office and asked me if I was happy in Spain, and I assured him that I most certainly was. He smiled uncomfortably and offered me a glass of scotch and as we sipped, he told me that the students had been complaining that I was not making myself sufficiently available to them. I feigned shock, but he simply shook his head and waved off my pretense. Not only had I taken to missing office hours, I had failed to return a single set of papers or tests. The students were directionless and confused and in a unified uproar. And because of their protests, much to his regret, the chairman was going to have to insist that I begin holding my regular office hours immediately. If I failed to comply, he would have no choice but to act in his students' best interest by calling the Fulbright offices in Madrid and having my visiting professorship withdrawn for the second semester. I would be shipped home in disgrace.

I assured him that I would not disappoint him again.

Two days later after my last class of the day as I walked back to my office, all I could think of was my *niña pera* stripping away her Catholic uniform and stepping into the shower, then stepping out again wet and naked and perfectly succulent. I turned from my office door and the five scowling students waiting there and hurried out of the building. I caught the train just in time and was home only seconds before she arrived.

And this was the day it happened.

Breathless from my jog from the train station, I clambered up the stairs and quickly assumed my position at the slit, but was startled to see that it was not my *niña pera* beyond the wall, but her father, the diplomat in his dark suit, home at that unaccustomed hour. He was pacing back and forth in front of the bathroom, where a much shorter and much less elegant man was holding the head of a teenage boy over the open toilet bowl. The young man had long stringy hair and was dressed in a black T-shirt and blue jeans. The thug who was gripping him by the ears above the bowl was also dressed in black, a bulky black sweatshirt with the sleeves torn away and dark jeans and a black Basque beret. His arms were as gnarled as oak limbs, and the boy he held was unable to manage even a squirm.

The vice-consul stopped his pacing and spat out a quick, indecent bit of Spanish. Even though the wall muffled most conversation, I heard and recognized the phrase. While my conversational skills were limited, I had mastered a dozen or so of the more useful and colorful Spanish curses. The vice-consul had chosen to brand the boy as a pig's bastard child. Furthermore, a pig covered in its own excrement.

Though my disappointment at missing my daily appointment with the *niña pera* deflated my spirits, witnessing such violence and drama was almost fair compensation. My assumption was that my neighbor was disciplining the young man for some botched assignment—the most natural guess being that he was a courier who transported certain highly valued pharmaceutical products that happened also to be the leading export of the vice-consul's country. The other possibility, of course, and one that gave me a particularly nasty thrill, was that the boy was guilty of some impropriety with the diplomat's daughter, my own *niña pera*, and now was suffering the dire consequences of his effrontery.

I watched as the vice-consul came close to the boy and bent to whisper something to him, then tipped his head up by the chin and gave some command to the thug. The squat man let go of the boy's right ear, and with a gesture so quick I only caught the end of it, he produced a knife and slashed the boy's right ear away from his head.

I reeled back from the slit in the wall and pressed my back against the banister and tried to force the air into my lungs.

At that moment I should have rushed downstairs, gotten on the phone, and called the militia to report the outrage beyond my wall. And I honestly considered doing so. For surely it would have been the moral, virtuous path. But I could not move. And as I considered my paralysis, the utter selfishness of my inaction filled me with acid self-contempt. I reviled myself even as I kept my place. I could not call for help because I did not dare to upset the delicate equipoise of my neighbors' lives. The thought of losing my *niña pera* to the judicial process, or even worse to extradition, left me lifeless on the stairway. Almost as terrifying was the possibility that if I called for the militia, a further investigation would expose the slit in the wall and I would be hauled out into the streets for a public thrashing.

For a very long while I did not move.

Finally, when I found the courage to bring my eye back to the crack in the wall, I saw that the thug had lifted the boy to a standing position before the toilet, and the vice-consul had unzipped him and was gripping the tip of his penis, holding it out above the bloody porcelain bowl, a long steak knife poised a few inches above the pale finger of flesh.

The vice-consul's arm quivered and began its downward slash.

"No!" I cried out, then louder, "No!"

My neighbor aborted his savage swipe and spun around. I watched him take a hesitant step my way, then another. His patent-leather shoes glowed in the eerie light beyond the wall. Then in an unerring path he marched directly to the wall where I was perched.

I pulled away, scooted backward up the stairs, and held my breath.

I waited.

I heard nothing but the distant siren wail of another supertanker coming into port.

I was just turning to tiptoe up to the bedroom when the blade appeared. It slid through the wall and glittered in the late-afternoon light, protruding a full five inches into my apartment. He slipped it back and forth as if he, too, were trying to widen the viewing hole, then drew it slowly out of sight. For a second I was in real danger of toppling forward down the flight of stairs, but I found a grip on the handrail and restrained myself on the precarious landing.

Though it was no longer visible, the knife blade continued to vibrate in my inner sight. I realized it was not a steak knife at all, but a very long fillet knife with a venomous tapered blade that shone with the brilliance of a surgical tool. I had seen similar knives many times along the Algorta docks, for this was the sort of cutlery that saw service gutting the abundant local cod.

And while I held my place on the stairs, the point of the knife shot through the wall again and remained there, very still, as eloquent and vile a threat as I had ever experienced. And a moment later in the vice-consul's apartment I heard a wet piercing noise followed by a heavy thunk, as if a sack of cement had been broken open with the point of a shovel.

A second later my wife's key turned in the front-door lock and she entered the apartment, shook her umbrella, and stripped off her rain gear and took her standard fifteen seconds to reach the bottom of the stairs. She gazed up and saw me frozen on the landing and the knife blade still shimmering through the wall of this house she had come to despise. For it was there in those four walls that I had fatally withdrawn from her as well as my students, where I had begun to match her obdurate silences with my own. In these last few months I had become so devoted to my *niña pera* that I had established a bond with this unknown juvenile beyond the wall that was more committed and passionate than any feelings I had ever shown my wife.

And when she saw the knife blade protruding from the wall, she knew all this and more. More than I could have told her if I had fallen to my knees and wallowed in confession. Everything was explained to her, my vast guilt, my repellent preoccupation, the death of our life together. Our eyes interlocked, and whatever final molecules of adhesion still existed between us dissolved in those silent seconds.

She turned and strode to the foyer. As I came quickly down the stairs, she picked up her raincoat and umbrella and opened the heavy door of our apartment and stepped out into the narrow alley-street of the Old Port. I hurried after her, calling out her name, pleading with her, but she shut the door behind her with brutal finality.

As I rushed to catch her, pushing open the door, I nearly collided with my succulent young neighbor coming home late from school. She graced me with a two-second smile and entered her door, and I stood on the stoop for a moment looking down the winding, rain-slicked street after my wife. Wretched and elated, I swung around and shut myself in once more with my utter depravity.

I mounted the stairs.

There was nothing in my heart, nothing in my head. Simply the raging current of blood that powered my flesh. I knelt at the wall and felt the magnetic throb of an act committed a thousand times and rewarded almost as often, the Pavlovian allure, a need beyond need, a death-hungering wish to see, to know, to live among that nefarious family who resided only a knife blade away.

I pressed my eye to the hole and she was there, framed in the bathroom doorway wearing her white blouse, her green plaid skirt. Behind her I could see that the toilet bowl had been wiped clean of blood. My *niña pera*'s hands hung uneasily at her sides and she was staring across the room at the wall we shared, her head canted to the side, her eyes focused on the exact spot where I pressed my face into the stone and drank her in. My pear girl, my succulent child, daughter of the devil.

And though I was certain that the glimmer of my eye was plainly visible to her and anyone else who stood on that side of the wall, I could not pull myself from the crack, for my *niña pera* had begun to lift her skirt, inch by excruciating inch, exposing those immaculate white thighs. And though there was no doubt she was performing under duress and on instructions from her father, I pressed my face still harder against the wall and drank deep of the vision before me.

Even when my succulent one cringed and averted her face, giving me a second or two of ample warning of what her father was about to do, I could not draw my eye away from the lush expanse of her thighs.

A half second later her body disappeared and a wondrous flash of darkness swelled inside me and exploded. I was launched into utter blankness, riding swiftly out beyond the edges of the visible world, flying headlong into a bright galaxy of pain.

And yet, if I had not passed out on the stairway, bleeding profusely from my ruined eye, if somehow I had managed to stay conscious for only a few seconds more, I am absolutely certain that after I suffered the loss of sight in my right eye, I would have used the last strength I had to reposition myself on the stairway and resume my vigil with my left.

In the following months of recuperation and repair, I came to discover that a man can subsist with one eye as readily as with one hand or leg. For apparently nature anticipated that some of us would commit acts of such extreme folly and self-destructiveness that we would require such anatomical redundancy if we were to survive. And in her wisdom, she created us to be two halves co-joined. So that even with one eye, a man can still see, just as with only a single hand he may still reach out and beckon for his needs. And yes, even half-heartedly, he may once again know love.

THE GIRLS IN VILLA COSTAS

Simon Brett

T HERE WAS ONLY ONE GIRL WORTH LOOKING AT IN THAT PLANELOAD. I'd been doing the job for two months, since May, and I'd got quicker at spotting them.

She was tall, but then I'm tall, so no problem there. Thin, but the bits that needed to be round were good and round. Dress: expensive casual. Good jeans, white cotton shirt, artless but pricey. Brown eyes, biscuit-coloured hair pulled back into a rubber band knot, skin which had already seen a bit of sun and just needed Corfu to polish up the colour. (Have to watch that. With a lot of the girls—particularly from England—they're so pale you daren't go near them for the first week. Lascivious approaches get nothing but a little scream and a nasty smell of Nivea on your hands.)

The girl's presence moved me forward more keenly than usual with my little spiel. "Hello, Corforamic Tours, Corforamic Tours. I am your Corforamic representative, Rick Lawton. Could you gather up your baggage please, and proceed outside the arrivals hall to your transport."

I ignored the puffing English matrons and homed in on the girl's luggage.

It was then that I saw the other one. She looked younger, shorter, dumpier; paler brown hair, paler eyes, a sort of diluted version, as if someone had got the proportions wrong when trying to clone from the dishy one.

They were obviously together, so I had to take one bag for each. They thanked me in American accents. That in itself was unusual. Most of the girls who come on these packages are spotty typists from Liverpool.

But then their destination was unusual, too. The majority of the Corforamic properties are tiny, twin-bedded apartments in Paleokastritsa and Ipsos. But there's one Rolls-Royce job near Aghios Spiridion—converted windmill, sleeps eight, swimming pool, private beach, live-in maid, telephone. And that was where they were going. They'd booked for a month.

I read it on their labels. "Miss S. Stratton" (the dishy one). "Miss C. Stratton" (the other one). And underneath each name, the destination—"Villa Costas."

By six I'd seen all the ordinary punters installed, answered the questions about whether it was safe to drink the water, given assurances that the plumbing worked, given the names of doctors to those with small children, told them which supermarkets sold Rice Krispies, quoted the minimal statistics for death by scorpion sting, and tried to convince them that the mere fact of their having paid for a fortnight's holiday was not going automatically to rid the island of mosquitoes.

Villa Costas was a long way to the north of the island. I'd pay a call there the next day.

I drove to Niko's, on the assumption that none of my charges would venture as far as his disco on their first evening. You get to value your privacy in this job. I sat under the vine-laden shelter of the bar and had an ouzo.

As I clouded the drink with water and looked out over the glittering sea, I felt low. Seeing a really beautiful woman always has that effect. Seems to accentuate the divide between the sort of man who gets that sort of girl and me. I always seem to end up with the ugly ones.

It wasn't just that. There was money, too, always money. Sure I got paid as the Corforamic rep., but not much. Winter in England loomed, winter doing some other demeaning selling job, earning peanuts. Not the sort of money that could coolly rent the Villa Costas for a month. Again there was the big divide. Rich and poor. And I knew which side I really belonged. Poor, I was cramped and frustrated. Rich, I could really be myself.

Niko's voice cut into my gloom. "Telephone, Rick."

She identified herself as Samantha Stratton. The dishy one. Her sister had seen a rat in the kitchen at Villa Costas. Could I do something about it?

I said I'd be right out there. Rats may not be dragons, but they can still make you feel knight-errantish. And, as any self-respecting knight-errant knows, there is no damsel so susceptible as one in distress.

Old Manthos keeps a kind of general store just outside Kassiope. It's an unbelievable mess, slabs of soap mixed up with dried fish, oil lamps, saucepans, tins of powdered milk, brooms, faded postcards, coils of rope, tubes of linament, deflated beach-balls, dusty Turkish Delight, and novelty brandy bottles shaped like Ionic columns. Most of the stock appears to have been there since the days of his long-dead father, whose garlanded photograph earnestly surveys the chaos around him.

But, in spite of the mess, Manthos usually has what you want. May take a bit of time and considerable disturbance of dust, but he'll find it.

So it proved on this occasion. With my limping Greek, it took a few minutes for him to understand the problem, but once he did, he knew exactly where to go. Two crates of disinfectant were upturned, a bunch of children's fishing nets knocked over, a pile of scouring pads scattered, and the old man triumphantly produced a rusty tin, whose label was stained into illegibility.

"Very good," he said, "very good. Kill rats, kill anything." He drew his hand across his throat evocatively.

I paid. As I walked out of the shop, he called out, "And if that doesn't work . . ."

"Yes?"

"Ask the priest. The Papas is sure to have a prayer for getting rid of rats."

It was nearly eight o'clock when I got to Villa Costas, but that's still hot in Corfu in July. Hot enough for Samantha to be on the balcony in a white bikini. The body fulfilled, or possibly exceeded, the promise I had noted at the airport.

"Candy's in bed," she said. "Shock of seeing the rat on top of all that travelling brought on a migraine."

"Ah. Well, let's see if we can put paid to this rat's little exploits," I said, in a business-like and, to my mind, rather masculine manner.

"Sure."

I filled some little paper dishes with poison and laid them round the kitchen floor. Then I closed the tin and washed my hands. "Shall I leave the poison with you, so you can put down more if you want to?"

She was standing in the kitchen doorway. The glow of the dying sun burnt away her bikini. Among other things, I saw her head shake. "No, thanks. Dangerous stuff to have around. You take it."

"Okay."

"Like a drink?"

She was nice. Seemed very forthcoming with me, too. But I didn't want to queer anything up by moving too fast.

Still, when she asked where one went for fun on the island, I mentioned Niko's disco. And, by the time I left—discreetly, didn't lay a finger on her, play it cool, play it cool—we'd agreed to meet there the next evening.

And as I drove back to my flat in Corfu Town, I was beginning to wonder whether maybe after all I was about to become the sort of man who gets that sort of girl.

When I arrived at nine, there were quite a lot of people at the disco. But no tall, beautiful American girl. Come to that, no less tall, less beautiful American girl.

I could wait. Niko signalled me over to where he was sitting, and I ordered an ouzo.

The group drinking at the table was predictable. Niko's two brothers (the one who drove a beer lorry and the one who rented out motorscooters) were there, along with his cousin the electrician, and Police Inspector Kantalakis, whose relaxed interpretation of government regulations about overcrowding, noise and hygiene always ensured him a generous welcome at the bar.

There was also a new face. Wiry black hair thinning on top, thick black moustache draped over the mouth, healthy growth of chest hair escaping from carefully faded denims. Solid, mid-thirties maybe, ten years older than me. "Rick, this is Brad," said Niko.

He stretched out a hairy hand. "Hi." Another American. "We were just talking about Niko's wife," he said with a grin.

They all laughed, Niko slightly ruefully. Whereas some people have bad backs or business worries to be tenderly asked after, Niko always had wife problems. It was a running joke and, from the way Brad raised it, he seemed to know the group well. "How are things at home, Niko?" he continued.

The proprietor of the bar shrugged that round-shouldered gesture that encompasses the whole world of marital misery.

Brad chuckled. "Sure beats me why people get married at all."

Inspector Kantalakis and the others gave man-of-the-world laughs, siding with him and conveniently forgetting their own tenacious little wives. The American turned to me. "You married?"

I shook my head. "Never felt the necessity."

"Too right. There is no necessity."

The married men laughed again, slightly less easily. Brad called their bluff. "Now come on, all you lot got wives. Give me one good reason why, one argument in favour of marriage."

Inspector Kantalakis guffawed. "Well, there's sex . . ."

"You don't have to get married for that," I said.

The Inspector looked at me with distaste. For some reason he never seemed to like me much.

"Come on, just one argument for marriage," insisted Brad.

They looked sheepish. Faced by this transatlantic sophisticate, none of them was going to show himself up by mentioning love, children, or religion. They wanted to appear modern, and were silent.

"You think of any reason, Rick?"

"Money," I said, partly for the laugh I knew the word would get, but also because the idea had been going through my mind for some years. Marriage remains one of the few legal ways that someone without exceptional talents can make a quick and significant change in his material circumstances. I reinforced the point, playing for another laugh. "Yes, I reckon that's the only thing that'd get me to the altar. I'm prepared to marry for money."

As the laugh died, Brad looked at me shrewdly. "If that's so, then you ought to set your cap at what's just arriving."

I turned to see the girls from Villa Costas getting out of a hired car. "Those two," Brad continued, "are the daughters of L. K. Stratton of Stratton Petrochemicals. When the old man goes, the elder one gets the lot."

I was feeling sore. The two girls had joined us at the table and had a couple of drinks. Seeing them together again had only reinforced my previous impression. Miss S. (Samantha) Stratton was not only beautiful, but also poised and entertaining. Miss C. (Candice, to give her full name) Stratton was not only drab in appearance, but mouselike and tentative in conversation. I waited for a lull in the chat, so that I could ask Samantha to dance. If she had needed any recommendation other than that body, Brad's words had just supplied it.

But the minute I was about to suggest a dance, damn me if Brad, who seemed to know the girls quite well, didn't say, "C'mon, Sam, let's bop," and lead her off into the flashing interior of the disco. The way they started dancing suggested that they knew each other *very* well.

Within minutes, Niko and his relations and Inspector Kantalakis had melted away, leaving me in a role I had suffered too often in double dates from schooltime onwards—stuck with the ugly one.

And what made it worse was that I gathered in this case she was also the poor one.

I stole a look across at her. The sun had already started its work on her pale flesh. The nose glowed; in a couple of days the skin would be coming off like old wallpaper.

She caught my eye and gave a gauche little smile, then looked wistfully to the thundering interior.

No, no, I wasn't going to be caught that way. That terrible old feeling that you *ought* to ask a girl to dance. Hell, I was twenty-six, not some creepy little adolescent.

Still, I had to say something, or just leave. "Your big sister seems to be enjoying herself," I commented sourly.

"Half-sister, actually. And only big in the sense that she's taller than I am."

"You mean you're older than she is?"

"Two years and four months older."

"Would you like to dance?"

***

Candice was very shy and I played her with exemplary tact. Met her every evening for most of the next week. Picked her up at the Villa Costas and took her down to Niko's. She was too shy to go there on her own, and Sam and Brad (who turned out to be engaged, for God's sake) seemed anxious to be off on their own most of the time.

So I courted Candice like a dutiful boy-next-door. Looked at her soulfully, danced close, kissed her goodbye, nothing more. I was the kind of young man every mother would like their daughter to meet—serious, respectful, with intentions honourable even to the point of matrimony.

And, once I'd written off any chance with Samantha, Candice really didn't seem too bad. Not unattractive at all. Any personal lustre she lacked I could readily supply by thinking of her father's millions.

The fourth night, as I kissed her goodbye with boyish earnestness, I explained that a new planeload of tourists was arriving the next day and I wouldn't have time to pick her up. She looked disappointed, which showed I was getting somewhere. Rather than not see her, she agreed to go under her own steam to Niko's, meet me there at nine. That was a big step for her. I promised I wouldn't be late.

By the middle of the following afternoon it was clear I was going to be. The flight from London was delayed by an hour and a half.

Never mind. Still the dutiful, solicitous boy-next-door, I rang the Villa Costas. Brad answered. Sorry, would he mind telling Candice I couldn't get to Niko's till half-past ten? Either I'd see her there or pick her up usual time the next evening.

Sure, Brad'd see she got the message.

When I saw her face at ten-twenty that night at Niko's, it was clear she hadn't got the message. She was sitting at the same table as, but somehow not with, Niko's relations and Inspector Kantalakis. And she looked furious.

It didn't surprise me. Greek men don't really approve of women, even tourists, going to bars alone, and that lot wouldn't have made any secret of their feelings. I moved forward with smiling apologies on my lips.

But I didn't get a chance to make them. Candice rose to her feet. "I only stayed," she spat out, "to tell you that I think you're contemptible, and that we will not meet again."

"Look, I left a message with Brad. I said I'd be late and . . ."

"It's not just your lateness I'm talking about. Goodbye." And she swept off to the hired car.

I sat down, shaken. Inspector Kantalakis was looking at me with a rather unpleasant smile. "What the hell did you say to her?" I asked.

He shrugged. "I may have mentioned your views on marriage."

"What? Oh shit—you mean about marrying for money?"

"I may have mentioned that, yes."

"But when I said it, it was only a joke."

"You sounded pretty serious to me," said the Inspector, confirming my impression that he didn't like me one bit.

But that evening wasn't over. I started hitting the local paint-stripper brandy. I was furious. The Inspector and the others sauntered off, as if satisfied by their evening's destruction. I gazed bitterly across the black sea to the few mysterious lights of Albania.

"Rick." I don't know how long had passed before the sound broke into my gloom. I looked up.

It was Samantha. And she was crying.

"What's the matter?"

"It's that bastard, Brad . . ."

"Oh. I've got a bone to pick with him too. What's he done?"

"Oh, he's just . . . It's always the same. He treats me badly and he goes off with some other girl and always reckons he can just pick up again as if nothing has happened and . . . Well, this is the last time, the last time . . ." She was crying a lot by then.

"Can I get you a drink or . . . ?"

"No, I just want to go back to the villa. I was looking for Candy. I wanted a lift. Brad's driven off in his car and . . ."

"Candy's gone, I'm afraid."

"Oh."

"I'll give you a lift."

When we were in the car park, she was seized by another burst of crying and turned towards me. Instinctively my arms were round her slender, soft, soft body and I held her tight as the spasms subsided.

"Doesn't take you long," said a voice in Greek.

I saw Inspector Kantalakis' sardonic face in the gloom.

"Mind your own business," I said. At least, that would be a paraphrase. The expression on the Inspector's face showed that I was making great strides with my colloquial Greek.

"She's upset," I continued virtuously. "I'm just comforting her, as a friend."

But I wasn't, I wasn't.

Amazing how quickly things can change. Actually, since by "things" I mean women, I suppose it's not so amazing.

I got to know a lot more about Samantha on that drive back, and I discovered that appearances can be distinctly deceptive. For a start, the great engagement with Brad was not, as it appeared, the marriage of true minds, but a kind of possessive blackmail exerted on an unwilling girl by a selfish and violent man. She had been trying to break it off for years.

Also—and this was the bit I enjoyed hearing—the reason for the quarrel of that night had been her admitting she fancied someone else. Me.

"But if you're so keen to get rid of him, why did you mind his going off with another girl?"

"Only because I know he'll be back. He never stays away for long. And then he thinks he can just pick up where he left off."

"Hmm. But he couldn't do that if he found you'd got someone else."

"That's true."

The car had stopped outside Villa Costas. We were suddenly in each other's arms. Her body spoke its clear message to mine, while our tongues (when free) mumbled meaningless nothings. Yes, she wanted me. Yes, I was the only man who she'd ever felt like that about.

But no, I'd better not come into the villa now. Because of Candy . . . And she didn't really fancy the beach. Tomorrow. Tomorrow afternoon at three. She'd see that Candy was out. And then . . .

The way she kissed me, and where she kissed me, left me in no doubt as to what would happen then.

I arrived sharp at three the following afternoon in a state of . . . well let's say in a predictable state of excitement.

But things weren't initially as private as I had hoped. Theodosia, the live-in maid, was sitting on the verandah under the shade of an olive tree. (Corfiots, unlike the tourists, regard sun as a necessary evil, and avoid it when possible.) She grinned at me in a way that I found presumptuously knowing.

And then, as if that wasn't enough, Candice Stratton appeared from the villa and stood for a moment blinded by the sun. She wore a bikini in a multi-coloured stripe that accentuated her dumpiness; she carried a box of Turkish Delight that would no doubt, in time, accentuate it further. The other hand held a striped towel and an Agatha Christie.

When her eyes had accommodated to the brightness, they saw me, and an expression of loathing took over her face. "You bastard! I said I never wanted to see you again. So don't think you can come crawling back."

Any intentions I might have had to be nice to her vanished at that. "I didn't come to see *you*," I said, and walked past her into the villa. I felt Theodosia's inquisitive eyes follow me.

Samantha was on the balcony in the white bikini. Momentarily I played the aggrieved lover. "I thought you were going to see Candy was out."

"Sorry, we got delayed. Brad came round."

I hadn't reckoned on that.

"Don't worry, Rick. I sent him off with a flea in his ear." She looked at me levelly. "I haven't changed my mind."

I relaxed. "How'd he take it?"

"Usual arrogance. Said he'd be back. Even tried his old trick of making up to Candy to make me jealous. Brought her a big box of Turkish Delight and all that. He ought to know by now it doesn't work."

"On you or on her?"

"On me, you fool." She rose and put an arm round my waist.

Together we watched Candy across the little private bay, settling on her towel for further ritual peeling.

I looked into Samantha's brown eyes, screwed up against the glare of the sun. I was aware of the tracery of fine lines around them as her body pushed against mine.

"Candy be out there for some time?" I murmured.

"You betcha. She'll eat her way right through that box of Turkish Delight. Always eats when she's unhappy."

My hand glided up the curve of her back and gave the bikini strap a gentle twang. "Shall we go inside?"

There was a double bed (a rarity in the world of Corforamic, another luxury feature of the Villa Costas). We lay on it and I reached more purposefully for the strap.

"Oh damn," said Samantha.

"What?"

"Candy didn't take her drink."

"Hmm?"

"There's a large Coca-Cola in the fridge. She was going to take it with her."

"So?" I shrugged.

"So . . . if she hasn't got it, she'll be back here as soon as she's thirsty. And the Turkish Delight's going to make her very thirsty."

"Ah."

"You take it over to her."

"But she doesn't want to see me. . . ."

"Then we won't be disturbed." There was a kind of logic in that. "Go on, Rick. And while you're away, I'll slip out of these heavy clothes."

When I got back, Samantha had slipped out of her few milligrams of clothes. She had on nothing but a bottle of Remy Martin and two glasses on the flat table of her stomach.

Candy had been predictably annoyed to see me, but had accepted the bottle of Coke wordlessly. And Theodosia's beady little eyes had followed me all the way across the beach and back.

But I soon forgot both of them. Samantha's body would have

cleaned out the memory bank of a computer.

With the body and the brandy, time telescoped and distorted. We caressed and made love and dozed and caressed and made love and dozed. . . . Sam's hands had the softness of a mouth and her mouth the versatility of fingers, so that after a time I ceased trying to work out which bit was doing what and succumbed to the bliss of anatomical confusion.

Darkness came and we didn't notice it. Through the sea-breathing blackness our bodies found new games to play, and as dawn started its first grey probings, we still found the possibilities had not been exhausted.

I didn't hear whether Candice came in or not. Quite honestly, I had other things on my mind. Not only on my mind, either.

Sleep eventually claimed us, but in my dreams the ecstasy seemed to continue.

It was therefore an unpleasant shock to be woken by the sight of Inspector Kantalakis at the foot of the bed, and by the sound of his voice saying, in English, "Still furthering your marriage plans, Mr Lawton?"

We both sat up. Samantha raised a sheet to cover her breasts, and I was pleased about that. I felt a proprietary interest; they weren't here to be drooled over by Greek policemen.

She was still half-asleep. "Marriage?" she echoed. "You did mean it, Rick, what you said last night, about wanting to marry me?"

"Uh?" I was still pretty much asleep too.

"I have bad news," said Inspector Kantalakis.

We looked at him blearily.

"Miss Stratton, your sister was found this morning on the beach. Dead."

"What?"

"She appears to have been poisoned."

I don't know if you've ever been involved in a murder inquiry in Greece, but let me tell you, it is something to be avoided. Questions,

questions, questions, endlessly repeated in hot concrete police cells. And expressions on the cops' faces that show they don't subscribe to the old British tradition of people being innocent until proved guilty.

I was with them for about twenty-four hours, I suppose, and the first thing I did when I got out was to go up to the Villa Costas. Sam looked shaken. She'd had quite a grilling too, though some connection of her father's had pulled strings through the American Embassy in Athens and it hadn't taken as long as mine.

"And now the bastard's disappeared," were her first words.

"Who?" My mind wasn't working very well.

"Brad."

"What do you mean?"

"Brad must have poisoned her."

"Why?" I couldn't catch up with all this.

"Because of the money."

"Uh?"

"He wanted me *and* Daddy's money. With Candy dead, I inherit."

"Good Lord, that never occurred to me."

"Well, it's true."

"But how did he do it?"

"Obvious. The Turkish Delight."

"Are you sure?"

"The Inspector says he hasn't had the forensic analysis yet—everything takes that much longer on an island—but I'd put money on the results."

"Brad'll never get away with it."

"Oh, he'll have sorted out some sort of alibi. He's devious. He will get away with it, unless we can find some proof of his guilt."

"But it will all have been for nothing if he doesn't get you."

"Yes." She sounded listless.

"And he hasn't got you, has he?"

She pulled herself together and looked at me with a little smile. "No, he hasn't. You have."

"So that's all right."

She nodded, but still seemed troubled. "The only thing that worries me . . ."

"Yes?"

"Is that he does still have power over me when I see him."

"Then we must ensure you don't see him. If he's disappeared, that doesn't sound too difficult. Anyway, as soon as the analysis of the Turkish Delight comes through, the police'll be after him."

"But suppose they're not. Suppose he's sorted out some kind of alibi. . . ."

"Don't worry." Suddenly I was full of crusading spirit. "If the police won't do it, I'll prove myself that he poisoned Candy."

"Oh, thank you, Rick. Thank God I've got you."

I tried all the contacts I had on the island, but none of them had seen Brad. I didn't give up, though. I wanted to do it for Sam, to prove Brad's crime and see to it that he was put behind bars where he belonged.

It was the next day she told me she was going to have to fly back to the States. Her father, L. K. Stratton, had had a mild stroke when he heard the news of his elder daughter's death, and the younger one had to fly back to be by his side. Inspector Kantalakis had cleared her from his inquiries, and she was free to go. Apparently, he was near to an arrest; just needed the results of the forensic analysis to clinch it.

Though I was depressed about her going, the news of the investigation was promising. The police were obviously near to nailing Brad, just needed proof of the poison in the Turkish Delight.

All they had to do then was find him.

Unless I could find him first.

I arranged that I'd see Sam off at the airport.

It was less than two weeks since I'd first seen her when I kissed her goodbye. A lot had happened in less than two weeks. When I first saw that splendid body I hadn't dared hope that it would ever be pressed to mine with such trust and hope.

"I'll come back as soon as I can, Rick. Really."

"I know. Let's hope you're back to give evidence at a murder trial."

"I will be. Don't worry."

Her baggage was checked in through to Kennedy via London. There didn't seem much more to say. Our togetherness didn't need words.

Not many, anyway. "And then, Sam, we'll get married, huh?"

She nodded gently and gave me another kiss. Then she turned and went off towards the Departure Lounge. Tall, beautiful, and mine.

Not only mine, it occurred to me, but also very rich. Suddenly I had got it all, suddenly I was the sort of man who got that sort of girl.

I watched her into the Departure Lounge. She didn't turn round. We didn't need that sort of clinging farewell.

Suddenly I got a shock. A dark, denim-clad figure had appeared beside her in the Lounge.

Brad.

I couldn't go through ticket control to save her. I had to find the police. And fast.

I was in luck. As I rushed into the dazzle of sunlight, I saw Inspector Kantalakis leaning against my car, with his hands behind his back.

"The man who murdered Candy—I know who it is," I panted.

"So do I," said the Inspector.

"He intended to marry Sam, but he wanted the money too, so he poisoned Candy."

"Exactly."

"Well, why don't you arrest him?"

"I've been waiting for a forensic report for final proof. Now I have it. Now there will be an arrest."

"Good. He's in the airport building. The plane leaves in half an hour."

"Yes." The Inspector made no move.

Fine, he must have the place staked out. We could relax; there was plenty of time. I grinned. "So the poison *was* in the Turkish Delight."

He shook his head. "No."

"No?"

"It was really a very straightforward case. Our murderer, who made no secret of his intention to marry for money, tried first with the older sister, the heiress. Unfortunately they quarrelled, so he took up with the younger one. But she would only inherit if her elder sister died. So . . ."

He shrugged.

"I didn't realize Brad had ever made a play for Candy."

"He hadn't. Nor did he kill her. After he saw the girls in the Villa Costas, he spent the rest of the day of the murder with me."

"Then who are we talking about?" I asked blankly.

Inspector Kantalakis drew one hand from behind his back. It held a rusty tin, a tin which had been bought from Manthos' shop. "I found this in the trunk of your car."

"Yes, I bought it to deal with the rats at the Villa Costas."

"Really? It was this poison that killed Candice Stratton. It was put in the bottle of Coca-Cola."

"The Coca-Cola!"

"Yes. The Coca-Cola you gave to the murder victim. Do you deny you gave it to her? The maid Theodosia saw you."

"No, I gave it all right. I see! Brad must have dosed it, knowing Candy'd drink it sooner or later. He must have fixed it when he came round that morning with the Turkish Delight. Sam may have seen him go to the fridge. Ask her."

"I have asked her, Mr. Lawton. According to Miss Samantha Stratton, there never was any Coca-Cola in the Villa Costas. Nor, incidentally were there any rats," Inspector Kantalakis added portentously.

Then he arrested me.

And I realized that, after all, I wasn't the sort of man who got that sort of girl.

I don't know. Maybe I'm just stupid.

I'm Not That Kind of Girl

Marthayn Pelegrimas

I READ ONCE that loneliness is the bond uniting twentieth century adults. Thousands and thousands of people so desperate for anyone to share a meal with, hold in the night. Don't touch, I warn. Why won't they listen? It's infuriating, predictable and boring.

Men approach me, smug, playing their games, directed by lopsided rules, making private decisions when to disconnect. The pattern is maddening—always the same. Mid-life has left cautious survivors. Wiser, they think naivete was packed away, long ago, with virginity and hope. So vain, so stupid. I warn I'm different. But they've seen it all through myopic, contact lensed eyes. Tyrannical dwarfs ruling the minute kingdom of their diminutive brain.

He watches me, smiles, lifts a half-filled glass: the prelude to a hundred similar scenes. What energizes his gestures? Loneliness or the life weary baggage he lugs from city to city?

He's typical, like all the others: six feet, covered in three pieces of a matching pinstriped suit; he strives to blend in the executive world. Divorced, he's fathered 2.3 children and is now bitter. Love screwed him over, royally. Never again, he's learned that women are bitches, cock-sucking, money-hungry bitches. He's out for a good time now. There's nothing real about him, not even the name he'll introduce.

What the hell. He's in Midwest USA for this one evening. He's deodorized, stylized and working on his third scotch and water.

I just want to listen to the band, drink my vodka in the cool dimness. I want to be left alone in a world of desperate joiners, organizers and fanatics. I have no cause, no passion burns inside my heart for inhumanities suffered throughout the world. I crave time to relax, don't want to be cordial, sociable or extend myself.

He smiles again, hoping to snag my attention from his bar stool. I look away. Maybe it's the indifference that attracts. I know him without the benefit of physical contact. He ate dinner alone: a steak, well done, small dinner salad, no roll, no butter, watching his cholesterol count. He lays in the sun, by the pool of his singles apartment on weekends. His eyes never miss a pair of twenty-year-old breasts bobbing under bikini pouches. His shoes are imitation leather, his watch a genuine Rolex knock-off and the pinkie ring, a six-diamond, fourteen karat gold bargain, was purchased through the cousin of a friend.

He comes over to my table. "Mind if I join you?"

"Yes." Not an insult, the truth. "Yes, I do."

He laughs, they always do. His brain long ago deciphered the mysteries of womankind. His father educated that females always mean yes when they scream no. They all want to be raped, son. The American dream.

I look to the stage, concentrating on a red-haired drummer. He beats the skins with vicious force. I feel the man standing at my back, wrestling between anger and dejection. He'll try charm—phase one.

"I didn't mean to offend you. It's just that I saw you sitting here, alone. Has anyone ever told you you're a dead ringer for Grace Kelly?"

"Yes." I don't bother to turn around. Why can't he feel the chill from my cold shoulder? Where's his pride?

"Ahhh, I'm new in town; don't know a soul. Maybe we could have a drink, talk?" His hands go up displaying smooth palms. "I don't bite, honest." Phase two—sympathy.

He won't leave. They never do, even after I warn them. Why prolong the discomfort of his hovering, shifting from leg to leg? "One drink."

Beaming. His face lights up like it's Christmas, for chrissake. "Look, I meant it. I can tell you're a lady. I just want someone to talk to."

They always say "to" when they mean "at." I can't even pretend interest as he explains the complexities of computers, his hopes for a military contract. He speeds on, his tongue has shifted into third gear. He mistakes my nod for attention.

"I have to warn you . . ." I start. But they always interrupt.

"I know, I know." He touches my hand. "You're not the kind of girl who picks up strange men in bars."

"No, I wasn't going to say that."

"Well, maybe not in so many words, but I can tell. I could see from across the room that you're a lady."

It must be the blond hair. Inside, I'm dark, seething with yearnings never fulfilled. Outside I appear frosted over with calm. "I'm trying to explain . . ."

"Don't worry; I won't hurt you," he assures.

"I wasn't worried."

"Good. I'm one of those old-fashioned, honest type guys. And you're shy, sheltered and trusting. Have to protect yourself. Take it from one who's been around, quite a few times, it's tough out there."

"I know."

"Do you?" he asks, mocking, unbelieving the jade flecks scorching my eyes as anger heats the water filming over.

"Yes."

Phase three: All-Knowing-World-Traveler lectures Sweet-Young-Thing.

He has no hint of my age, wouldn't believe I'm older than the fantasy his hormones dictate to his crotch. He wants me innocent, sees me through his retarded time warp.

The scotch breeds familiarity. Closer, I smell his breath while he snakes an arm across the back of my chair. "You live in a small town."

"I'm not from here, originally."

"Whatever, it's not where you're from, you're alone . . ."

"By my own choosing."

"No. No woman wants to be alone. You want a man, children, a home."

"Who told you this?" Why don't I leave? He'd only follow, apologize, cajole, and patronize.

"Like I said, I've been out there. A woman wants a man, forget all this equality bullshit. Keep 'em barefoot and pregnant. The old timers knew the secret."

"Stop it." No more. I can't handle this another time. I stand, knocking over the low cushioned chair. "I have to go."

"I'm sorry. I didn't mean to cuss. I'm sure you're not accustomed to such language."

Assuming his words offended strictly for their grammatical value, not content, I warn one last time. "You don't know what I'm accustomed to. You don't know anything about me, not one goddamn thing!"

"You're right." He pats me on the head with condescending words. "I don't know you, personally. But I do know women like you, in your position. Look, I didn't mean to come off rude. Can I buy you another drink, please?"

He bends down, sets my chair upright. "Here." Swiveling it around to accept my bottom. "Sit," commanding like an animal trainer. I want to scratch his face.

We're gearing up for phase four—second to the last. He's so desperate, worrying only for his comfort on a long night in a strange town.

"One more drink."

He's shallower than the others. Insincerity is his second skin. I've tried warning him. I am a fair person. And truthful—painfully truthful. But this would be a public service. Maybe I do have a cause, a reason to react.

I sit.

"Come here often?" He begins again.

It's difficult not laughing at his lack of imagination.

"No."

"The band's okay, for a local group."

"How do you know they're local?"

"Playing in a place like this, they'd have to be."

"Oh, I forgot, you've been everywhere. You know all there is to know about women, music. . . ."

"Not exactly. I just know about life."

Oops, back step to phase three, another lecture, I intercede. "I don't even know your name and here you are educating me about life. I'm Mary." The name fits his needs, he'll eat it up. I smile at my improvisation.

"I knew it." He nods, lower lip extended in a contemplative gesture. "A sweet name for a sweet lady. Glad to meet you, Mary. I'm Stephen." He offers a hand. Polite. "Steve."

I shake glad-to-meet-you. "Now, you were going to tell me about life."

Wouldn't it be wonderful if Steve What's-His-Last-Name? reflected for a moment, turned and said, "I don't think you need anyone to tell you about life." No, I forgot, he knows my type.

"Oh, right. I don't want to upset you, Mary, but things aren't always what they seem to be."

"Really?" I'm going to rip the mustache off his face.

"Really. People are mean and crazy."

"I know, Steve, for God's sake, do you think I just dropped out of the sky? I do have a life, been around myself, several times."

Phase four—he apologizes, again.

"I'm sorry. I just don't think you grasp my meaning."

"It's not that difficult. You are speaking English. I have excellent hearing. And your I.Q. is certainly not comparable with that of Einstein's. What's not to grasp?" Holding in the majority of my anger, he's only receiving surface irritability.

"I'm saying that people are devious, calculating. I've met more than my share."

"Who hasn't?"

"A girl like you? Pretty, sweet, pampered, used to getting what she wants."

"Some things come easily, others have to be worked for."

"But, someone like you must not have to work too hard and long for what she really wants."

"Ahh, you're so wrong. I want to be left alone and would you believe all the trouble and work I have to extend just for peace?"

"A piece?" He smirks, insulated in the soundproof booth between his ears.

"I'm leaving."

"So soon?"

"Yes, so soon." I'll kill him if I stay another minute, looking into those imbecilic eyes. I stand.

"Can't I walk you to your car, at least?"

"Why?" No more warnings; he's begging for it.

He reaches inside his pocket for bills to pay the tab. "You never know who's out there."

"Yeah, maybe someone waiting to make me barefoot and pregnant." A joke. He doesn't laugh.

"Trust me, the world's crawlin' with freaks and doped-up loonies."

"And we wouldn't want any of them to violate a girl like me."

"No way, sweetheart."

We turn toward the door. Two fraternity brothers take time from chugging their beer as I pass the bar. My dress is cut low in the back; I sense their eyes feeling me up.

"I can find my own car."

"Let a man take care of you, enjoy." He grabs my hand, kisses the tip of each finger.

Phase five.

His touch disgusts me, his sexual, rehearsed nibbling squeezes bile from my stomach into my mouth. He's been warned. I've tried being truthful and honest. He deserves it.

"If it'll make you feel better." Coy now, I'll play the game. "My car's over there."

A smile slimes over his lips, evening wind tries ruffling his hair-sprayed cut as we walk across the black-topped parking lot.

"What a coincidence, we're parked alongside each other." This insignificant detail delights him. "I assume that's your car next to my Mercedes."

My cue to be impressed. "Gee, my old Toyota looks like trash compared to your car." Opening eyes wide, I look up, allow him to gloat.

"Do you have to go right home? I'd like to buy you breakfast."

"I really shouldn't." Act hesitant, that ensures they'll beg.

"Please, just a cup of coffee if you're not hungry."

"Well, I do have work tomorrow."

"Awww." Now it's his turn to stare wide-eyed, con. He's almost as good as I.

"All right. There's a place around the corner."

Opening the passenger door of his red car, he commands, "Hop in."

This is too easy, no challenge, why expend the energy?

"I can take my own car."

Then, he touches again. Nudges me onto the leather seat with his cologned body. "Hey, babe, ride in style. Come on, let Steve take care of you."

The heavy door slams, almost catching my shoe. I vibrate with anger, fury induced by his artificial concern. God, I laugh to myself, this one's too easy.

He lets himself in the driver's side, positioned behind the steering wheel, he leans, kisses me, taking me by surprise. I feel his tongue dart into my mouth. "No."

"I couldn't help myself. You're so beautiful."

Poor, pathetic Steve. He hasn't got a chance at the competition he's entered. I always take first place. I'm the undefeated champion. A song lyric repeats in my head, "pretty girls just seem to find out early, how to open doors with just a smile."

It never surprised me when the butcher gave me candy every time I wore that yellow sundress, tied my hair back in a bow. My first evening gown, realizing I had the boys wrapped around the crook of my pinkie.

In college, professors promised grades for favors. I warned them, I tried telling them, but they were scholars. Dean Chadwell knew all about life, too. Just like good ole Steve. I used to fight against my femininity; now I make it work for me. The intelligence camouflaged under fluffed hair, behind emerald eyes, allows me to manipulate these morons.

"Can we go now? Suddenly, I'm starved."

His eyebrows rise with his hopes. "For what?" He won't give up.

"Breakfast." I play dumb. I'm the champion, remember?

"Whatever your little heart desires." Gallant, he thinks he's scored and is on the field heading for a touchdown.

"First," I insist, "buckle your seatbelt. We don't want anything to happen to you, do we?"

"That's cute." He pats my cheek. "I usually don't bother with the damned thing, messes up the suit. But for you . . . anything."

I purr, "Thank you, Stephen."

Suddenly he whips the silver clasp, striking me along the left temple. "Slut! How much of your shit am I supposed to swallow?"

Don't panic, don't panic. I reach to ease the ache inside my skull. Blood warms a trail toward my ear.

He twists my wrist, pulls me toward him. "Where the hell do you get off thinking you're so goddamn special?" His teeth clamp my lower lip in a vicious kiss. "I'll just have to teach you about the real world, the real threats to your precious little ass."

Not yet, I've been through worse. Hold on, must save myself to win, ensure victory.

Perspiration soaks through his monogrammed shirt; I smell his excitement. He grunts. Shoving me, pulling my legs, he rips off my shoes, throwing them into the back seat. "Now you'll get it. You'll beg for it. Beg. Come on, bitch, start begging."

He's in a frenzy to thrust his hatred inside me. My pantyhose shred as his raging fingers tear through the flimsy material.

I kick, clench my knees together, my purse serves as a weapon. I beat his head with its studded front.

"You're nothing but a goddamn whore. You deserve everything you're gonna get. What kind of lady sits in a bar?"

I struggle as he forces his hand between my legs, turns and wedges his knees inside my thighs while his other hand unzips his pants.

"I knew you were garbage from the first piece of crap outta your mouth." Trying to distract him, I continue to taunt, slapping his face. "Come on, Stud. Think you got what it takes?"

"You'll never forget tonight," he spits.

Crouched over me, his manicured nails scratch into my panties. He looks surprised, they always do—at first. Later on, toward the end, they look stunned. But, at this moment, Steve recoils with a surprised scream that falls from his mouth as my penis unfolds from its black lace binding.

Yanking the blond wig from my head, I scream, "Surprise! Welcome to the REAL world, Stephen, darling."

"Freak!" He presses himself into the driver's seat. "Holy shit!"

I don't realize it's a pen. The cold metal attracts my hand as I claw myself upright. His eyes bulge with the first stab. Bull's-eye! Straight to the heart.

"Oh God!" He looks to verify the pain shooting through his chest.

I'm quick. Five more stabs into his shirt before he can react, much less open the door. The steering wheel pins down his flailing legs.

"You wouldn't leave me alone, would you?"

Stab!

Ten more times. Blood spurts across the dashboard, dribbles down the windshield.

"Dear God!" He doesn't know where to grab first. He's a frantic Dutchboy trying to plug erupting holes with his fingers.

Stab!

He tries wrestling the pen from my hand. Undefeated, I stab again.

"You . . . are . . . so . . . smart." I plunge with each syllable. "You've seen it all. Right, Stephen, baby? Seen any loonies or crazy people lately, huh? ANSWER ME! Seen any whores or blond bitches? SPEAK UP STUD!"

"Please. Why?"

I punch holes along his thigh. Up and down. The car flecks with red dots, his slacks paisley into a bloody maroon. He's quiet, heaving against the seat.

I whisper, "Stephen. Oh, Stephen."

He lunges, revived with terror.

"Good! Man to man—mano a mano—a fair fight." I bend back a little finger until it cracks then gouge his palm.

His hands go to his face, shielding. "What? Jesus Christ! What do you want? Why are you doing this?"

I giggle, digging the sticky pen into his cheek, an unprotected area. "To show you, to make a point." Laughing, I take a Kleenex from my purse, wipe the instrument designed for writing. "Come on, keep up with me." I yell into his ear, jerk his head forward and release it banging into the window.

He whimpers.

Why did I clean the pen? Have to dot my exclamation points.

"I've suffered insulting remarks from bastards like you for too many years. I've tried reason. I've run through years of patience. It's always the same. You won't listen. The whole world is divided by your rules, into two groups: normal and freak. I warned you to leave me alone. I've warned you all.

"But you laughed when I told you to go away. Remember? You, the great sage. Well, I think this is what we call behavior modification."

I stab three short times to his ear. "Can you hear me?"

He's unconscious. Damn. I knew he wouldn't be a challenge.

"Stephen," I grab his hair. A flicker of life ripples beneath his eyeballs. "You were right about the world being populated by crazies. One final lesson . . . one last word of advice: Listen. Shut your goddamn mouth long enough to listen."

I stab into his neck. Air hisses through the puncture like a tire pierced with a rusty nail. "Next time, listen when someone warns you. See what a pleasant evening you would've had if only you'd believed me when I told you I'm not *that* kind of girl."

THE END OF IT ALL

Ed Gorman

SOMETIMES THE ONLY THING WORSE THAN LOSING
THE WOMAN IS WINNING THE WOMAN.

–French saying

EMBRACE YOUR FATE.

–French saying

I GUESS THE FIRST THING I SHOULD TELL YOU ABOUT is the plastic surgery. I mean, I didn't always look this good. In fact, if you saw me in my college yearbook, you wouldn't even recognize me. I was thirty pounds heavier and my hair had enough grease on it to irrigate a few acres of droughted farmland. And the glasses I wore could easily have substituted for the viewing instruments they use at Mt. Palomar. I wanted to lose my virginity back in second grade, on the very first day I saw Amy Towers. But I didn't lose my virginity until I was twenty-three years old and even then it was no easy task. She was a prostitute and just as I was guiding my sex into her she said, "I'm sorry, I must be coming down with the flu or something. I've got to puke." And puke she did.

This was how I lived my life until I was forty-two years old—as the kind of guy cruel people smirk at and decent people feel sorry for. I was the uncle nobody ever wanted to claim. I was the blind date women discussed for years after. I was the guy in the record shop the cute girl at the cash register always rolls her eyes at. But despite all that I somehow managed to marry an attractive woman whose husband had been killed in Vietnam, and I inherited a stepson who always whispered about me behind my back to his friends. They snickered mysteriously whenever they were around me. The marriage lasted eleven years, ending on a rainy Tuesday night several weeks after we'd moved into our elegant new Tudor in the city's most attractive yuppie enclave. After dinner, David up in his room smoking dope and listening to his Prince CDs, Annette said, "Would you take it personally if I told you I'd fallen in love with somebody?" Shortly thereafter we were divorced, and shortly after that I moved to Southern California, where I supposed there was plenty of room for one more misfit. At least, more room than there had been in an Ohio city of 150,000.

By profession I was a stockbroker, and at this particular time there were plenty of opportunities in California for somebody who'd managed his own shop as I had. Problem was, I was tired of trying to motivate eight other brokers into making their monthly goals. I found an old and prestigious firm in Beverly Hills and went to work there as a simple and unhassled broker. It took me several months, but I finally got over being dazzled by having movie stars as clients. It helped that most of them were jerks.

I tried to improve my sex life by touring all the singles bar that my better-looking friends recommended, and by circumspectly scanning many of the Personals columns in the numerous newspapers that infest L.A. But I found nothing to my taste. None of the women who described themselves as straight and in good shape ever mentioned the word that interested me most—romance. They spoke of hiking and biking and surfing; they spoke of symphonies and movies and art galleries; they spoke of equality and empowerment and liberation. But never romance and it was romance I most devoutly desired. There were other options, of course. But while I felt sorry for homosexuals and bisexuals and hated people who persecuted them, I didn't want to be one of them; and try as I might to be understanding of sado-masochism and cross-dressing and transsexualism, there was about it something—for all its sadness—comic and incomprehensible. Fear of

disease kept me from whores. The women I met in ordinary circumstances—at the office, supermarket, laundry facilities in my expensive
apartment house—treated me as women usually did, with tireless sis-
terly kindness.

Then some crazy bastards had a gunfight on the San Diego freeway,
and my life changed utterly.

This was on a smoggy Friday afternoon. I was returning home from
work, tired, facing a long, lonely weekend when I suddenly saw two
cars pull up on either side of me. They were, it seemed, exchanging
gunfire. This was no doubt because of their deprived childhoods. They
continued to fire at each other, not seeming to notice that I was caught
in their crossfire. My windshield shattered. My two back tires blew out.
I careened off the freeway and went halfway up a hill, where I smashed
into the base of a stout scrub pine. That was the last thing I remember
about the episode.

My recuperation took five months. It would have been much shorter,
but one sunny day a plastic surgeon came into my room and explained
what he'd need to do to put my face back to normal and I said, "I
don't want it back to normal."

"Pardon me?"

"I don't want it back to normal. I want to be handsome. Moviestar
handsome."

"Ah." He said this as if I'd just told him that I wanted to fly. "Perhaps we need to talk to Dr. Schlatter."

Dr. Schlatter too said "Ah" when I told him what I wanted, but it
was not quite the "Ah" of the original doctor. In Dr. Schlatter's "Ah"
there was at least a little vague hope.

He told me everything in advance, Dr. Schlatter did, even making it
interesting, how plastic surgery actually dated back to the ancient
Egyptians, and Italians as early as the 1400s were performing quite
impressive transformations. He showed me sketches of how he hoped
I'd look, he acquainted me with some of the tools so I wouldn't be
intimidated when I saw them—scalpel and retractor and chisel—and he
told me how to prepare myself for my new face.

Sixteen days later, I looked at myself in the mirror and was happy to see that I no longer existed. Not the former me anyway. Surgery, diet, liposuction, and hair dye had produced somebody who should appeal to a wide variety of women—not that I cared, of course. Only one woman mattered to me, only one woman had ever mattered to me, and during my time in the hospital she was all I thought about, all I planned for. I was not going to waste my physical beauty on dalliances. I was going to use it to win the hand and heart of Amy Towers Carson, the woman I'd loved since second grade.

It was five weeks before I saw her. I'd spent that time getting established in a brokerage firm, setting up some contacts and learning how to use a new live phone hookup that gave me continuous stock analysis. Impressive, for a small Ohio city such as this one, the one where I'd grown up and first fallen in love with Amy.

I had some fun meeting former acquaintances. Most of them didn't believe me when I said I was Roger Daye. A few of them even laughed, implying that Roger Daye, no matter what had happened to him, could never look this good.

My parents living in Florida retirement, I had the old homestead—a nice white Colonial in an Ozzie and Harriet section of the city—to myself, where I invited a few ladies to hone my skills. Amazing how much self-confidence the new me gave the old me. I just took it for granted that we'd end up in bed, and so we did, virtually every single time. One woman whispered that she'd even fallen in love with me. I wanted to ask her to repeat that on tape. Not even my wife had ever told me she loved me, not exactly anyway.

Amy came into my life again at a country club dance two nights before Thanksgiving.

I sat at a table watching couples of all ages box-step around the dance floor. Lots of evening gowns. Lots of tuxedos. And lots of saxophone music from the eight-piece band, the bandstand being the only light, everybody on the floor in intimate boozy shadow. She was still beautiful, Amy was, not as young-looking, true, but with that regal, obstinate beauty nonetheless and that small, trim body that had inspired ten or twenty thousand of my youthful melancholy erections. I felt that old giddy high school thrill that was in equal parts shyness, lust, and a romantic love that only F. Scott Fitzgerald—my favorite writer—would ever have understood. In her arms I would find the purpose of my entire existence. I had felt this since I'd first walked home with her through the smoky autumn afternoons of third and fourth and fifth grade. I felt it still.

Randy was with her. There had long been rumors that they had a troubled marriage that would inevitably disintegrate. Randy, former Big Ten wide receiver and Rose Bowl star, had been one of the star entrepreneurs of the local eighties—building condos had been his specialty—but his success waned with the end of the decade and word was he'd taken up the harsh solace of whiskey and whores.

They still looked like everybody's dream of the perfect romantic couple, and more than one person on the dance floor nodded to them as the band swung into a Bobby Vinton medley, at which point Randy began dancing Amy around with Technicolor theatrics. Lots of onlooker grins and even a bit of applause. Amy and Randy would be the king and queen of every prom they ever attended. Their dentures might clack when they spoke, Randy's prostate might make him wince every thirty seconds, but by God the spotlight would always find its ineluctable way to them. And they'd be rich—Randy came from a long line of steel money and was one of the wealthiest men in the state.

When Randy went to the john—walking right meant the bar; walking left meant the john—I went over to her.

She sat alone at a table, pert and gorgeous and preoccupied. She didn't notice me at first, but when her eyes met mine, she smiled.

"Hi."

"Hi," I said.

"Are you a friend of Randy's?"

I shook my head. "No, I'm a friend of yours. From high school."

She looked baffled a moment and then said, "Oh, my God. Betty Anne said she saw you and—oh, my God."

"Roger Daye."

She fled her seat and came to me and stood on her tiptoes and took my warm face in her cold hands and kissed me and said, "You're so handsome."

I smiled. "Quite a change, huh?"

"Well, you weren't that—"

"Of course I was—a dip, a dweeb—"

"But not a nerd."

"Of course a nerd."

"Well, not a complete nerd."

"At least ninety-five percent," I said.

"Eighty percent maybe but—" She exulted over me again, bare shoulders in her wine-red evening gown shiny and sexy in the shadow. "The boy who used to walk me home—"

"All the way up to tenth grade when you met—"

"Randy."

"Right. Randy."

"He really is sorry about beating you up that time. Did your arm heal all right? I guess we sort of lost track of each other, didn't we?"

"My arm healed just fine. Would you care to dance?"

"Would I care to? God, I'd love to."

We danced. I tried not to think of all the times I'd dreamed about this moment, Amy in my arms so beautiful and—

"You're in great shape, too," she said.

"Thank you."

"Weights?"

"Weights and running and swimming."

"God, that's so great. You'll break every heart at our next class reunion."

I held her closer. Her breasts touched my chest. A stout and stern erection filled my pants. I was dizzy. I wanted to take her over into a corner and do it on the spot. She was the sweet smell of clean, wonderful woman flesh, and the even sweeter sight of dazzling white smile against tanned, taut checks.

"That bitch."

I'd been so far gone into my fantasies that I wasn't sure I'd heard properly.

"Pardon?"

"Her. Over there. That bitch."

I saw Randy before I saw the woman. Hard to forget a guy who'd once broken your arm—he'd had considerable expertise with hammer locks—right in front of the girl you loved.

Then I saw the woman and I forgot all about Randy.

I didn't think anybody could ever make Amy seem drab, but the woman presently dancing with Randy did just that. There was a radiance about her that was more important than her good looks, a mixture of pluck and intelligence that made me vulnerable to her even from here. In her white strapless gown, she was so fetching that men simply stood and stared at her, the way they would at a low-flying UFO or some other extraordinary phenomenon.

Randy started to twirl her as he had Amy, but this young woman—she couldn't have been much more than twenty—was a far better dancer. She was so smooth, in fact, I wondered if she'd had ballet training.

Randy kept her captive in his muscular embrace for the next three dances.

Because the girl so obviously upset Amy, I tried not to look at her— not even a stolen glance—but it wasn't easy.

"Bitch," Amy said.

And for the first time in my life, I felt sorry for her. She'd always been my goddess, and here she was feeling something as ungoddess- like as jealousy.

"I need a drink."

"So do I."

"Would you be a darling and get us one, then?"

"Of course," I said.

"Black and White, please. Straight up."

She was at her table smoking a cigarette when I brought the drinks back. She exhaled in long, ragged plumes.

Randy and his princess were still on the dance floor.

"She thinks she's so goddamned beautiful," Amy said.

"Who is she?"

But before Amy could tell me, Randy and the young woman deserted the floor and came over to the table.

Randy didn't look especially happy to see me. He glanced first at Amy and then at me and said, "I suppose there's a perfectly good reason for you to be sitting at our table."

Here he was flaunting his latest girlfriend in front of his wife, and he was angry that she had a friend sitting with her.

Amy smirked. "I didn't recognize him, either."

"Recognize who?" Randy snapped.

"Him. The handsome one."

By now I wasn't looking at either of them. I was staring at the young woman. She was even more lovely up close. She seemed amused by us older folks.

"Remember a boy named Roger Daye?" Amy said.

"That candy-ass who used to walk you home?"

"Randy. Meet Roger Daye."

"No way," Randy said, "this is Roger Daye."

"Well, I'm sorry, but he is."

I knew better than to put my hand out. He wouldn't have shaken it.

"Where's a goddamned waiter?" Randy said. Only now did I realize he was drunk.

He bellowed even above the din of the crowd.

He and the young woman sat down just as a waiter appeared.

"It's about goddamned time," Randy said to the older man with the tray.

"Sorry, we're just very busy tonight, sir."

"Is that supposed to be my problem or something?"

"Please, Randy," Amy said.

"Yes, please, Dad," the gorgeous young woman said.

At first I thought she might be joking, making a reference to Randy's age. But she didn't smile, nor did Roger, nor did Amy.

I guess I just kind of sat there and thought about why Randy would squire his own daughter around as if he were her new beau, and why Amy would be so jealous.

Six drinks and many tales of Southern California later— Midwesterners dote on Southern California tales the way people will someday dote on tales of Jupiter and Pluto—Randy said, "Didn't I break your arm one time?" He was the only guy I'd ever met who could swagger while sitting down.

"I'm afraid you did."

"You had it coming. Sniffing around Amy that way."

"Randy," Amy said.

"Daddy," Kendra said.

"Well, it's true, right, Roger? You had the hots for Amy and you probably still goddamned do."

"Randy," Amy said.

"Daddy," Kendra said.

But I didn't want him to stop. He was jealous of me and it made me feel great. Randy Carson, Rose Bowl star, was jealous of me.

"Would you like to dance, Mr. Daye?"

I'd tried hard not to pay any attention to her because I knew if I paid her a little I'd pay her a lot. Wouldn't be able to wrench my eyes or my heart away. She was pure meltdown, the young lady was.

"I'd love to," I said.

I was just standing up when Amy looked at Kendra and said, "He already promised me this one, dear."

And before I knew what to do, Amy took my hand and guided me to the floor.

Neither of us said anything for a long time. Just danced. The good old box step. Same as in seventh grade.

"I know you wanted to dance with her," Amy said.

"She's very attractive."

"Oh, Jesus. That's all I need."

"Did I say something wrong?"

"No—it's just that nobody notices me anymore. I know that's a shitty thing to say about my own daughter, but it's true."

"You're a very beautiful woman."

"For my age."

"Oh, come on now."

"But not vibrant, not fresh the way Kendra is."

"That's a great name, Kendra."

"I chose it."

"You chose well."

"'I wish I'd called her Judy or Jake.'"

"Jake?"

She laughed. "Aren't I awful? Talking about my own daughter this way? That little bitch."

She slurred the last two words. She'd gunned her drinks—Black and White straight up—and now they were taking their toll.

We danced some more. She stepped on my foot a couple of times. Every once in a while I'd find myself looking over at the table for a glimpse of Kendra. All my life I'd waited to dance like this with Amy Towers. And now it didn't seem to matter much.

"I've been a naughty girl, Roger."

"Oh?"

"I really have been. About Kendra, I mean."

"I suppose a little rivalry between mother and daughter isn't unheard of."

"It's more than that. I slept with her boyfriend last year."

"I see."

"You should see your face. Your very handsome face. You're embarrassed."

"Does she know?"

"About her boyfriend?"

"Uh-huh."

"Of course. I planned it so she'd walk in on us. I just wanted to show her—well, that even some of her own friends might find me attractive."

"You felt real bad about it, I suppose?"

"Oh, no. I felt real good. She naturally told Randy and he made a big thing over it—smashed up furniture and hit me in the face a few times—and it was really great. I felt young again, and desirable. Does that make sense?"

"Not really."

"But they got back at me."

"Oh?"

"Sure. Didn't you see them tonight on the dance floor?"

"Pretty harmless. I mean, she's his daughter."

"Well, then you haven't had a talk with good old Randy lately."

"Oh?"

"He read this article in *Penthouse* about how incest was actually a very natural drive and how it was actually perfectly all right to bop your family members if it was mutual consent and if you practiced safe sex."

"God."

"So now she walks around the house practically naked, and he rubs her and pats her and gives her big, long squeezes."

"And she doesn't mind?"

"That's the whole point. They're in on this together. To pay me back for sleeping with Bobby."

"Bobby being—"

"Her boyfriend. Well, ex-boyfriend I guess."

Kendra and Randy came back on the floor next dance. If any attention had been paid to Amy and me, it was now transferred to Kendra and Randy. But this time, instead of the theatrical, they embraced the intimate. I was waiting for Randy to start grinding his hips into Kendra dry-hump style, the way high school boys always do when the lights are turned down.

"God, they're sickening," Amy said.

And I pretty much agreed with her.

"She's going to try to seduce you, you know," Amy said.

"Oh, come on now."

"God, are you kidding? She'll want to make you a trophy as soon as she can."

"She's what? Twenty? Twenty-one?"

"Twenty-two. But that doesn't matter, anyway. You just wait and see."

At our table again, I had two more drinks. None of this was planned. Handsome Roger would return to his hometown and beguile the former homecoming queen into his arms. Technicolor dreams. But this was different, dark and comic and sweaty, and not a little bit sinister. I could see Randy touching his nearly nude daughter all over her wonderful body, and I could see Amy—not a little bit pathetic—hurtling herself at some strapping college student majoring in gonads.

Jesus, all I'd wanted to do was a little old-fashioned home wrecking . . . and look what I'd gotten myself into.

Kendra and Randy came back. Randy abused a couple more waiters and then said to me, "You having all that plastic surgery—surprised you didn't have them change you into a broad. You always were a little flitty. Nothing personal, you understand."

"Randy," Amy said.

"Daddy," Kendra said.

But for me this was the supreme compliment. Randy Big Ten Carson was jealous of me again.

I wasn't sure where Kendra was going when she stood up, but then she was next to me and said, "Why don't we dance?"

"I'm sure Roger's tired, dear," Amy said.

Kendra smiled. "Oh, I think he's probably got a little bit of energy left, don't you, Mr. Daye?"

On the floor, in my arms, sexy, soft, sweet, gentle, cunning, and altogether self-possessed, Kendra said, "She's going to try to seduce you,
you know."

"Who is?"

"Amy. My mother."

"You may not have noticed, but she's married."

"Like that would really make a difference."

"We're old friends. That's all."

"I've read some of your love letters."

"God, she kept them?"

"All of them. From all the boys who were in love with her. She's got
them all up in the attic. In storage boxes. Alphabetized. Whenever she
starts to feel old, she drags them out and reads them. When I was a
little girl, she'd read them out loud to me."

"I imagine mine were very corny."

"Very sweet. That's how yours were."

Our gazes met, as they like to say in novels. But that wasn't all that
met. The back of her hand somehow passed across the front of my
trousers, and an erection the goatiest of fifteen-year-olds would envy
sprang to life. Then her hand returned to proper dancing position.

"You're really a great-looking man."

"Thank you. But did you ever see my Before picture?"

She smiled. "If you mean your high school yearbook photo, yes, I
did. I guess I like the After photo a little better."

"You're very skilled at diplomacy."

"That's not all I'm skilled at, Mr. Daye."

"How about calling me Roger?"

"I'd like that."

I wish I had a big capper for the rest of the evening at the country
club, but I don't. By the time Kendra and I got back to the table, Amy
and Randy were both resolutely drunk and even a bit incoherent. I
excused myself to the john for a time, and as I came back I saw Amy
out on the veranda talking to a guy who looked not unlike a very successful gigolo, macho variety. Later, I'd learn that his name was Vic.
Back at the table good old Randy insulted a few more waiters and
threatened to punch me out if "I didn't keep my goddamned paws" off
his wife and his daughter, but he was slurring his words so badly that

the effect was sort of lost, especially when he started sloshing his drink around and the glass fell from his hand and smashed all over the table.

"Maybe this is a good time to leave," Kendra said, and began the difficult process of packing her parents up and getting them out to their new Mercedes, which, fortunately, she happened to be driving.

Just as they were leaving, Kendra said, "I may see you later," leaving me to contemplate what, exactly, "later" meant.

After one shower, one nightcap, most of a David Letterman show, and a slow fall into sleep, I found out what "later" meant.

She was at the door, behind a sharp knock in the windy night, adorned in a London Fog trench coat that was, I soon learned, all she wore.

She said nothing, just stood on tiptoes, wonderful lips puckered, waiting to be kissed. I obliged her, sliding an arm around her and leading her inside, feeling a little self-conscious in my pajamas and robe.

We didn't make it to the bedroom. She gently pushed me into a huge leather armchair before the guttering fireplace and eased herself gently atop me. That was when I found out she was naked beneath her London Fog. Her wise and lovely fingers quickly got me properly hard, and then I was inside her and my gasp was exultant pleasure but it was also fear.

I imagine heroin addicts feel this way the first time they use—pleasure from the exquisite kick of it all but fear of becoming a total slave to something they can never again control.

I was going to fall disastrously in love with Kendra, and I knew it that very first moment in the armchair when I tasted the soft, sweet rush of her breath and felt the warm, silken splendor of her sex.

When we were done for the first time, I built the fire again, and got us wine and cheese, and we lay beneath her trench coat staring into the flames crackling behind the glass.

"God, I can't believe it," she said.

"Believe what?"

"How good I feel with you. I really do."

I didn't say anything for a long time. "Kendra."

"I know what you want to ask."

"About your mother."

"I was right."

"If you slept with me only because—"

"—because she slept with Bobby Lane?"

"Right. Because she slept with Bobby Lane."

"Do you want me to be honest?"

I didn't really, but what was I going to say? No, I want you to be dishonest. "Of course."

"That's what first put the thought in my mind, I guess. I mean coming over here and sleeping with you." She laughed. "My mom is seriously smitten with you. I watched her face tonight. Wow. Anyway, I thought that would be a good way to pay her back. By sleeping with you, I mean. But by the end of the evening—God, this is really crazy, Roger, but I've got like this really incredible crush on you."

I wanted to say that I did, too. But I couldn't. I might be a new Roger on the outside but inside I was strictly the old model—shy, nervous, and terrified that I was going to get my heart decimated.

By dawn, we made love three times, the last time in my large bed with a jay and a cardinal perched on the window watching us, and soft morning wind soughing through the windbreak pines.

After we finished that last time, we lay in each other's arms for maybe twenty minutes until she said, "I have to be unromantic."

"Be my guest."

"Goose bumps."

"Goose bumps?"

"And bladder."

"And bladder?"

"And morning breath."

"You've lost me."

"A, I'm freezing. B, I really have to pee. And C, may I use your toothbrush?"

In the following three weeks, she spent at least a dozen nights at my place, and on those nights when one or both of us had business to attend to, we had those lengthy phone conversations that new lovers always have. Makes no difference what you say as long as you to hear her voice and she gets to hear yours.

Only occasionally did I pause and let dread come over me like a drowning wave. I would lose her and be forever bereft afterward. I was suffused with her tastes and smells and sounds and textures—and yet someday all these things would be taken from me and I would be forever alone, and unutterably sad. But what the hell could I do? Walk away? Impossible. She was succor, and life source, and all I could do was cling till my fingers fell away and I was left floating on the vast, dark ocean.

The eighth of December that year was one of those ridiculously sunny days that try to trick you into believing that spring is near. I spent two hours that afternoon cutting firewood in the back and then hauling it inside. Fuel for more trysts. On one of my trips inside, the doorbell rang. When I peeked out, I saw Amy. She looked very good—indeed, much better than she had that night at the country club—except for her black eye.

I let her in and asked her if she wanted a cup of coffee, which she declined. She took the leather couch, I the leather armchair that Kendra and I still used on occasion.

"I need to talk to you, Roger." She wore a white turtleneck beneath a camel hair car coat and designer jeans. There was a blue ribbon in her blond hair, and she looked very sexy in a suburban sort of way.

"All right."

"And I need you to be honest with me."

"If you'll be honest with me."

"The black eye?"

"The black eye."

"Who else? Randy. He came home drunk the other night and I wouldn't sleep with him so he hit me. He sleeps around so much I'm afraid he's going to pick up something." She shook her head with a solemnity I would never have thought her capable of.

"Does he do this often?"

"Sleep around?"

"And hit you."

She shrugged. "Pretty often. Both, I mean."

"Why don't you leave him?"

"Because he'd kill me."

"God, Amy, that's ridiculous. You can get an injunction."

"You think an injunction would stop Randy? Especially when he's been drinking?" She sighed. "I don't know what to do anymore."

This was the woman I'd come back to steal, but now I didn't want to steal her. I didn't even want to borrow her. I just felt sorry for her, and the notion was disorienting.

"Now, I want you to tell me about Kendra."

"I love her."

"Oh, just fucking great, Roger. Just fucking great."

"I'm know I'm a lot older than she is but—"

"Oh, for God's sake, Roger, it's not that."

"It isn't?"

"Of course it isn't. Come over here and sit down."

"Next to you?"

"That's the general idea."

I went over and sat down. Next to her. She smelled great. Same cologne Kendra wore.

She took my hand. "Roger, I want to sleep with you."

"I don't think that would be a good idea."

"All those years you were in love with me. It's not fair."

"What's not fair?"

"You should have gone on loving me. That's how it's supposed to work."

"What's supposed to work?"

"You know, lifelong romance. We're both romantics, Roger, you and I. Kendra is more like her father. Everything's sex."

"You slept with her boyfriend."

"Only because I was afraid and lonely. Randy had just beaten me up pretty badly. I felt so vulnerable. I just needed some kind of assurance. You know, that I was a woman. That somebody would want me." She took both my hands and brought them to her lips and kissed them tenderly. I couldn't help it. She was starting to have the effect on me she wanted. "I want you to be in love with me again. I can help you forget Kendra. I really can."

"I don't want to forget Kendra."

"Deep down she's like Randy. A whore. She'll break your heart. She really will."

She put two of my fingers in her mouth and began sucking.

She was quite good in bed, maybe even better technically than Kendra. But she wasn't Kendra. There was the rub.

We lay in the last of the gray afternoon and the wind came up, a harsh and wintry wind suddenly, and she tried to get me up for a second time, but it was no good. I wanted Kendra and she knew I wanted Kendra.

There was something very sad about it all. She was right. Romance—the kind of Technicolor romance I'd dreamed of—should last forever, despite any and all odds, the way it did in F. Scott Fitzgerald stories. And yet it hadn't. She was just another woman to me now, with more wrinkles than I had suspected, and a little tummy that was both sweet and comic, and veins like faded blue snakes against the pale flesh of her legs.

And then she started crying and all I could do was hold her and she tried in vain to get me up again and saw the failure not mine but her own.

"I don't know how I ever got here," she said finally to the dusk that was rolling across the drab, cold Midwestern land.

"My house, you mean?"

"No. Here. Forty-two goddamned-years old. With a daughter who steals the one man who truly loved me." A gaze icy as the winter moon then as she said, "But maybe things won't be quite as hunky-fucking-dory as she thinks they'll be."

Later on, I was to remember what she said vividly, the hunky-fucking-dory thing, I mean.

Kendra appeared at nine that same night. I spent the first half hour making love to her and the second half trying to decide if I should tell her about her mother's visit.

Later, in front of the fireplace, a wonderful old film noir called *Odds Against Tomorrow* on cable, we made love a second time and then, lying in the sweet, cool hollow of her arms, our juices and odors as one now, I said, "Amy was here today."

She stiffened. Her entire body. "Why?"

"It's not easy to explain."

"That bitch. I knew she'd do it."

"Come here, you mean?"

"Come here and put the shot on you. Which she did, right?"

"Right."

"But you didn't—"

I'd never had to lie to her before and it was far more difficult than I'd imagined it might be.

"Things get so crazy sometimes—"

"Oh, shit."

"I mean you don't intend for things to happen but—"

"Oh, shit," she said again. "You fucked her, didn't you?"

"—with all the best intentions, you—"

"Quit fucking babbling. Just say it. Say you fucked her."

"I fucked her."

"How could you do it?"

"I didn't want to."

"Right."

"And I could only do it once. No second time."

"How noble."

"And I regretted it immediately."

"Amy told me that when you were real geeky-looking that you were one of the sweetest people she ever knew."

She stood up, all beautiful, brash nakedness, and stalked back toward the bedroom. "You should have kept your face ugly, Roger. Then your soul would still be beautiful."

I lay there thinking about what she said a moment, and then I stalked back to the bedroom.

She was dressing in a frenzy. She didn't as yet have her bra on completely. Just one breast was cupped. The other looked lone and dear as anything I'd ever seen. I wanted to kiss it and coo baby talk to it.

Then I remembered why I'd come in here. "That's bullshit, you know."

"What's bullshit?" she said, pulling up the second cup of her bra. She wore panty hose but hadn't as yet put on her skirt.

"All that crap about keeping my face ugly so my soul would remain beautiful. If I hadn't had plastic surgery, neither you nor your mother would have given me a second glance."

"That's not true."

I smiled. "God, face it, Kendra, you're a beautiful woman. You're not going to go out with some geek."

"You make me sound as if I've really got a lot of depth."

"Oh, Kendra, this is stupid. I shouldn't have slept with Amy and I'm sorry.

"I'm just surprised she hasn't managed to tell me about it yet. She's probably waiting for the right dramatic moment. And in her version, I'm sure you threw her on the bed and raped her. That's what my father told her the night she caught us together. That I was the one who'd wanted to do it—"

"My God, you mean you—"

"Oh, not all the way. They had one of their country club parties, and both Randy and I were pretty loaded and somehow we ended up on the bed wrestling around and she walked in and—Well, I guess I tried very hard to give her the impression that we'd just been about to make it when she walked in and—"

"That's some great relationship you've got there."

"It's pretty sick and believe me, I know it."

I felt tired standing in the shadowy bedroom, the only light the December quarter moon above the shaggy pines.

"Kendra—"

"Could we just lie down together?" She sounded tired, too.

"Of course."

"And not do anything, I mean?"

"I know what you mean. And I think that's a wonderful idea."

We must have lain there six, seven minutes before we started making love, and then it was the most violent love we'd ever made, her hurling herself at me, inflicting pleasure and pain in equal parts. It was a purgation I badly needed.

"She's always been like this."

"Your mother?"

"Uh-huh."

"Competitive, you mean?"

"Uh-huh. Even when I was little. If somebody gave me a compliment, she'd get mad and say, 'Well, it's not hard for little girls to look good. The trick is to stay beautiful as you get older.'"

"Didn't your dad ever notice?"

She laughed bitterly. "My father? Are you kidding? He'd usually come home late and then finish getting bombed and then climb in bed next to me and feel me up."

"God."

Bitter sigh. "But I don't give a shit. Not anymore. Fuck them. I come into my own inheritance in six months—from my paternal grandfather—and then I'm moving out of the manse and leaving them to all their silly fucking games."

"Is now a good time to tell you I love you?"

"You know the crazy goddamned thing, Roger?"

"What's that?"

"I really love you, too. For the first time in my life, I actually love somebody."

On the night of 20 Jan, six weeks later, I went to bed early with a new Sue Grafton novel. Kendra had begged off our date because of a head cold. I'm enough of a hypochondriac that I wasn't unhappy about not seeing her.

The call came just before two a.m., long after I was sleeping and just at the point where waking is difficult.

But get up I did and listen at length to Amy's wailing. It took me a long time to understand what the exact message her sobs meant to convey.

The funeral took place on a grim snowy day when the harsh, numbing winds rocked the pallbearers as they carried the gleaming silver coffin from hearse to graveside. The land lay bleak as a tundra.

Later, in the country club where a luncheon was being served, an old high school friend came up and said, "I bet when they catch him he's a nigger."

"I guess it wouldn't surprise me."

"Oh, hell, yes. Poor goddamned guy is sleeping in his own bed when some jig comes in and blasts the hell out of him and then goes down the hall and shoots poor Kendra, too. They say she'll never be able to walk or talk again. Just sit in a frigging wheelchair all the time. I used to be a liberal back in the sixties or seventies, but I've had enough of their bullshit by now. I'll tell you that I've had their bullshit right up to here, in fact."

Amy came late. In the old days one might have accused her of doing so so she could make an entrance. But now she had a perfectly good reason. She walked with a cane, and walked slowly. The intruder who'd shot up the place that night, and stolen more than $75,000 in jewelry, had shot her in the shoulder and the leg, apparently leaving her for dead. Just as he'd left Kendra for dead.

Amy looked pretty damned good in her black dress and veil. The black gave her a mourning kind of sexiness.

A line formed. She spent the next hour receiving the members of that line just as she'd done at the mortuary the night before. There were tears and laughter with tears and curses with tears. The very old looked perplexed by it all—the world made no sense anymore; here you were a rich person and people still broke into your house and killed you right in your bed—and middle-aged people looked angry (i.e., damned niggers) and the young looked bored (Randy being the drunk who'd always wobbled around pinching all the little girls on their bottoms—who cared he was dead, the pervert?).

I was the last person to go through the line, and when she saw me, Amy shook her head and began sobbing. "Poor, poor Kendra," she said. "I know how much she means to you, Roger."

"I'd like to visit her tonight if I could. At the hospital."

Beneath her veil, she sniffled some more. "I'm not sure that's a good idea. The doctor says she really needs her rest. And Vic said she looked very tired this morning."

The bullet had entered her head just below her left temple. By rights she should have died instantly. But the gods were playful and let her live—paralyzed.

"Vic? Who's Vic?"

"Our nurse. Oh, I forgot. I guess you've never met him, have you? He just started Sunday. He's really a dear. One of the surgeons recommended him. You'll meet him sometime."

I met him four nights later at Kendra's bedside.

He was strapping arrogant was our blond Vic, born to a body and face that no amount of surgery or training could ever duplicate, a natural Tarzan to my own tricked-up one. He looked as if he wanted to tear off his dark and expensive suit and head directly back to the jungle to beat up a lion or two. He was also the proud owner of a sneer that was every bit as imposing as his body.

"Roger, this is Vic."

He made a point of crushing my hand. I made a point of not grimacing.

The three of us then stared down at Kendra in her bed, Amy leaning over and kissing Kendra tenderly on the forehead. "My poor baby. If only I could have saved her—"

That was the first time I ever saw Vic touch her, and I knew instantly, in the proprietary way he did, that something was wrong. He probably was a nurse, but to Amy he was also something far more special and intimate.

They must have sensed my curiosity because Vic dropped his hand from her shoulder and stood proper as an altar boy staring down at Kendra.

Amy shot me a quick smile, obviously trying to read my thoughts.

But I lost interest quickly. It was Kendra I wanted to see. I bent over the bed and took her hand and touched it to my lips. I was self-conscious at first, Amy and Vic watching me, but then I didn't give a damn. I loved her and I didn't give a damn at all. She was pale and her eyes were closed and there was a fine sheen of sweat on her forehead. Her head was swathed in white bandages of the kind they always used in Bogart movies, the same ones that Karloff also used in *The Mummy*. I kissed her lips and I froze there because the enormity of it struck me. Here was the woman I loved, nearly dead, indeed should have been dead given the nature of her wound, and behind me, paying only a kind of lip service to her grief, was her mother.

A doctor came in and told Amy about some tests that had been run today. Despite her coma, she seemed to be responding to certain stimuli that had had no effect on her even last week.

Amy started crying, presumably in a kind of gratitude, and then the doctor asked to be alone with Kendra, and so we went out into the hall to wait.

"Vic is moving in with us," Amy said. "He'll be there when Kendra gets home. She'll have help twenty-four hours a day. Won't that be wonderful?"

Vic watched me carefully. The sneer never left his face. He looked the way he might if he'd just noticed a piece of dog mess on the heel of his shoe. It was not easy being a big blond god. There were certain difficulties with staying humble.

"So you know Kendra's surgeon," I said to Vic.

"What?"

"Amy said that the surgeon had recommended you to her."

They glanced at each other and then Vic said, "Oh, right, the surgeon, yes." He gibbered like a Miss America contestant answering a question about patriotism.

"And you're moving in?"

He nodded with what he imagined was solemnity. If only he could do something about the sneer. "I want to help in any way I can."

"How sweet."

If he detected my sarcasm, he didn't let on.

The doctor came out and spoke in soft, whispered sentences filled with jargon. Amy cried some more tears of gratitude.

"Well," I said. "I guess I'd better be going. Give you some quality time with Kendra."

I kissed Amy on the cheek and shook Vic's proffered hand. He notched his grip down to mid-level. Even hulks have sentimental moments. He even tried a little acting, our Vic. "The trick will be to get her to leave before midnight."

"She stays late, eh?" I said.

Amy kept her eyes downcast, as befitted a saint who was being discussed.

"Late? She'd stay all night if they'd let her. You can't tear her away."

"Well, she and Kendra have a very special relationship."

Amy caught the sarcasm. Anger flashed in her eyes but then subsided. "I want to get back to her," she said. And Mother Theresa couldn't have said it any more believably.

I took the elevator down to the ground floor, then took the emergency stairs back up to the fourth floor. I waited in an alcove down the hall. I could see Kendra's door, but if I was careful neither Amy nor Vic would be able to see me.

They left ten minutes after I did. Couldn't drag Amy away from her daughter's bedside, eh?

***

In the next six weeks, Kendra regained consciousness, learned how to manipulate a pencil haltingly with her right hand, and got tears in her eyes every time I came through the door. She still couldn't speak or move her lower body or left side, but I didn't care. I loved her more than ever and in so doing proved to myself that I wasn't half as superficial as I'd always suspected. That's a good thing to know about yourself—that at age forty-four you have at least the potential for becoming an adult.

She came home in May, after three intense months of physical rehab and deep depression over her fate, a May of butterflies and cherry blossoms and the smells of steak on the grill on the sprawling grounds behind the vast English Tudor. The grounds ran four acres of prime land, and the house, divided into three levels, included eight bedrooms, five full baths, three half baths, a library, and a solarium. There was also a long, straight staircase directly off the main entrance. Amy had it outfitted with tracks so Kendra could get up and down in her wheelchair.

We became quite a cheery little foursome, Kendra and I, Amy and Vic. Four or five nights a week we cooked out and then went inside to watch a movie on the big-screen television set in the party room. Three nurses alternated eight-hour shifts so that whenever Kendra—sitting silently in her wheelchair in one of her half-dozen pastel-colored quilted robes—needed anything, she had it. Amy made a cursory fuss over Kendra at least twice an evening, and Vic went to fetch something unimportant, apparently in an attempt to convince me he really was a working male nurse.

More and more I slipped out early from the brokerage, spending the last of the day with Kendra in her room. She did various kinds of physical therapy with the afternoon nurse, but she never forgot to draw me something and then offer it up to me with the pride of a little girl pleasing her daddy. It always touched me, this gesture, and despite some early doubts that I'd be able to be her husband—I'd run away and find somebody strong and sound of limb; I hadn't had all that plastic surgery for nothing, had I?—I learned that I loved her more than ever. She brought out a tenderness in me that I rather liked. Once again I felt there was at least some vague hope that I'd someday become an adult. We watched TV or I read her interesting items from the newspaper (she liked the nostalgia pieces the papers sometimes ran) or I just told her how much I loved her. "Not good for you," she wrote on her tablet one day and then pointed at her paralyzed legs. And then broke into tears. I knelt at her feet for a full hour, till the shadows were long and purple, and thought how crazy it all was. I used to be afraid that she'd leave me—too young, too good-looking, too strong-willed, only using me to get back at her mother—and now she had to worry about some of the same things. In every way I could, I tried to assure her that I'd never leave her, that I loved her in ways that gave me meaning and dignity for the first time in my life.

Hot summer came, the grass scorching brown, night fires like the aftermath of bombing sorties in the dark hills behind the mansion. It was on one of these nights, extremely hot, Vic gone someplace, the easily tired Kendra just put to bed, that I found Amy waiting for me in my car.

She wore startling white short-shorts and a skimpy halter that barely contained her chewy-looking breasts. She sat on the passenger side. She had a martini in one hand and a cigarette in the other.

"Remember me, sailor?"

"Where's lover boy?"

"You don't like him, do you?"

"Not much."

"He thinks you're afraid of him."

"I'm afraid of rattlesnakes, too."

"How poetic." She inhaled her cigarette, exhaled a plume of blue against the moonlit sky. I'd parked at the far end of the pavement down by the three-stall garage. It was a cul-de-sac of sorts, protected from view by pines. "You don't like me anymore, do you?"

"No."

"Why?"

"I really don't want to go into it, Amy."

"You know what I did this afternoon?"

"What?"

"Masturbated."

"I'm happy for you."

"And you know who I thought of?"

I said nothing.

"I thought about you. About that night we were together over at your house."

"I'm in love with your daughter, Amy."

"I know you don't think I'm worth a shit as a mother."

"Gee, whatever gave you that idea?"

"I love her in my way. I mean, maybe I'm not the perfect mother, but I do love her."

"Is that why you won't put any makeup on her? She's in a fucking wheelchair, and you're still afraid she'll steal the limelight."

She surprised me. Rather than deny it, she laughed. "You're a perceptive bastard."

"Sometimes I wish I weren't."

She put her head back. Stared out the open window. "I wish they hadn't gone to the moon."

I didn't say anything.

"They spoiled the whole fucking thing. The moon used to be so romantic. There were so many myths about it, and it was so much fun thinking about. Now it's just another fucking rock." She drained her drink. "I'm lonely, Roger. I'm lonely for you."

"I'm sure Vic wouldn't want to hear that."

"Vic's got other women."

I looked at her. I'd never seen her express real anguish before. I took a terrible delight in it. "After what you and Vic did, you two deserve each other."

She was quick about it, throwing her drink in my face, then getting out of the car and slamming the door shut. "You bastard! You think I don't know what you meant by that? You think I killed Randy, don't you?"

"Randy—and tried to kill Kendra. But she didn't die the way she was supposed to when Vic shot her."

"You bastard!"

"You're going to pay for it someday, Amy. I promise you that."

She still had the glass in her hand. She smashed it against my windshield. The safety glass spiderwebbed. She stalked off, up past the pines, into invisibility.

* * *

I didn't bring it up. Kendra did. I'd hoped she'd never figure out who was really the intruder that night. She had a difficult enough time living. That kind of knowledge would only make it harder.

But figure it out she did. One cool day in August, the first hint of autumn on the air, she handed me what I assumed would be her daily love note.

VIC
CHECK
FIGHT
$

I looked at the note and then at her.

"I guess I don't understand. You want me to check something about Vic?"

Her darting blue eyes said no.

I thought a moment: Vic, check. All I could think of was checking Vic out. Then, "Oh, a check? Vic gets some kind of check?"

The darting blue eyes said yes.

"Vic was having an argument about a check?"

Yes.

"With your mother?"

Yes.

"About the amount of the check?"

"Yes."

"About it not being enough?"

Yes.

And then she started crying. And I knew then that she knew. Who'd killed her father. And who'd tried to kill her.

I sat with her a long time that afternoon. At one point a fawn came to the edge of the pines. Kendra made a cooing sound when she saw it, tender and excited. Starry night came and through the open window we could hear a barn owl and later a dog that sounded almost like a coyote. She slept sometimes, and sometimes I just told her the stories she liked to hear, "Goldilocks and the Three Bears" and "Rapunzel," stories, she'd once confided, that neither her mother nor her father had ever told her. But this night I was distracted and I think she sensed it. I wanted her to understand how much I loved her. I wanted her to understand that even if there were no justice in the universe at large, at least there was justice in our little corner of it.

On a rainy Friday night in September, at an apartment Vic kept so he could rendezvous with a number of the young women Amy had mentioned, a tall and chunky man, described as black by two neighbors who got a glimpse of him, broke in and shot him to death. Three bullets. Two directly to the brain. The thief then took more than $5,000 in cash and traveler's checks (Vic having planned to leave for a European vacation in four days).

The police inquired of Amy, of course, as to how Vic had been acting lately. They weren't as yet quite convinced that his death had been the result of a simple burglary. The police are suspicious people but not, alas, suspicious enough. Just as they ultimately put Randy's death down to a robbery and murder, so they ultimately ruled that Vic had died at the hand of a burglar, too.

On the day Amy returned from the funeral, I had a little surprise for her, just to show her that things were going to be different from now on.

That morning I'd brought in a hair stylist and a makeup woman. They spent three hours with Kendra and when they were finished, she was as beautiful as she'd ever been.

We greeted Amy at the vaulted front door—dressing in black was becoming a habit with her—and when she saw Kendra, she looked at me and said, "She looks pathetic. I hope you know that." She went directly to the den, where she spent most of the day drinking scotch and screaming at the servants.

Kendra spent an hour in her room, crying. She wrote the word *pathetic* several times on her paper. I held her hand and tried to assure her that she indeed looked beautiful, which she did.

That night as I was leaving—we'd taken dinner in Kendra's room, neither of us wanting to see Amy any more than we needed to—she was waiting in my car again, even drunker than she'd been the first time. She had her inevitable drink in her hand. She wore a dark turtleneck and white jeans with a wide, sash-like leather belt. She looked a lot better than I wanted her to.

"You prick, you think I don't know what you did?"

"Welcome to the club."

"I happened to have fucking loved him."

"I'm tired, Amy. I want to go home."

In the pine-smelling night, a silver October moon looked ancient and fierce as an Aztec icon.

"You killed Vic," she said.

"Sure, I did. And I also assassinated JFK."

"You killed Vic, you bastard."

"Vic shot Kendra."

"You can't prove that."

"Well, you can't prove that I shot Vic, either. So please remove your ass from my car."

"I really never thought you'd have the balls. I always figured you for the faggot type."

"Just get out, Amy."

"You think you've won this, Roger. But you haven't. You're fucking with the wrong person, believe me."

"Good night, Amy."

She got out of the car and then put her head back in the open window. "Well, at least there's one woman you can satisfy, anyway. I'm sure Kendra thinks you're a great lover. Now that she's paralyzed anyway."

I couldn't help it. I got out of the car and walked over to her across the dewy grass. I ripped the drink from her hand and then said, "You leave Kendra and me alone, do you understand?"

"Big, brave man," she said. "Big, brave man."

I hurled her drink into the bushes and then walked back to the car.

In the morning, the idea was there waiting for me.

I called work and told them I wouldn't be in and then spent the next three hours making phone calls to various doctors and medical supply houses as to exactly what I'd need and what I'd need to do. I even set up a temporary plan for private-duty nurses. I'd have to dig into my inheritance, but this was certainly worth it. Then I drove downtown to a jeweler's, stopping by a travel agency on my way back.

I didn't phone. I wanted to surprise her.

The Australian groundsman was covering some tulips when I got there. Frost was predicted. "G'day," he said, smiling. If he hadn't been over sixty with a potbelly and white hair, I would have suspected Amy of using him for her personal pleasure.

The maid let me in. I went out to the back terrace, where she said I'd find Kendra.

I tiptoed up behind her, flicked open the ring case, and held it in front of her eyes. She made that exultant cooing sound in her throat, and then I walked around in front of her and leaned over and gave her a gentle, tender kiss. "I love you," I said. "And I want to marry you right away and have you move in with me."

She was crying but then so was I. I knelt down beside her and put my head on her lap, on the cool surface of her pink quilted housecoat. I let it lie there for a long time as I watched a dark, graceful bird ride the wind currents above, gliding down the long, sunny autumn day. I even dozed off for a time.

At dinnertime, I rolled Kendra to the front of the house, where Amy was entertaining one of the Ken-doll men she'd taken up with these days. She was already slurring her words. "We came up here to tell you that we're going to get married."

The doll-man, not understanding the human politics here, said in a Hollywood kind of way, "Well, congratulations to both of you. That's wonderful." He even toasted us with his martini glass.

Amy said, "He's actually in love with me."

Doll-man looked at me and then back at Amy and then down at Kendra.

I turned her chair sharply from the room and began pushing it quickly over the parquet floor toward the hallway.

"He's been in love with me since second grade, and he's only marrying her because he knows he can't have me!"

And then she hurled her glass against the wall, smashing it, and I heard, in the ensuing silence, doll-man cough anxiously and say, "Maybe I'd better be going, Amy. Maybe another night would be better."

"You sit right where you fucking are," Amy said, "and don't fucking move."

I locked Kendra's door behind us on the unlikely chance that Amy would come down to apologize.

Around ten, she began to snore quietly. The nurse knocked softly on the door. "I need to get in there, sir. The missus is upstairs sleeping."

I leaned over and kissed Kendra tenderly on the mouth.

We set the date two weeks hence. I didn't ask Amy for any help at all. In fact, I avoided her as much as possible. She seemed similarly inclined. I was always let in and out by one of the servants.

Kendra grew more excited each day. We were going to be married in my living room by a minister I knew vaguely from the country club. I sent Amy a handwritten note inviting her, but she didn't respond in any way.

I suppose I didn't qualify as closest kin. I suppose that's why I had to hear it on the radio that overcast morning as I drove to work.

It seemed that one of the city's most prominent families had been visited yet again by tragedy—first the father dying in a robbery attempt a year earlier, and now the wheelchair-confined daughter falling down the long staircase in the family mansion. Apparently she'd come too close to the top of the stairs and simply lost control. She'd broken her neck. The mother was said to be under heavy sedation.

I must have called Amy twenty times that day, but she never took my calls. The Aussie gardener usually picked up. "Very sad here today, mate. She was certainly a lovely lass, she was. You have my condolences."

I cried till I could cry no more and then I took down a bottle of Black and White scotch and proceeded to do it considerable damage as I sat in the gray gloom of my den.

The liquor dragged me through a Wagnerian opera of moods—forlorn, melancholy, sentimental, enraged—and finally left me wrapped around my cold, hard toilet bowl, vomiting. I was not exactly a world-class drinker.

She called just before midnight, as I stared dully at CNN. Nothing they said registered on my conscious mind.

"Now you know how I felt when you killed Vic."

"She was your own daughter."

"What kind of life would she have had in that wheelchair?"

"You put her there!" And then I was up, frantic, crazed animal, walking in small, tight circles, screaming names at her.

"Tomorrow I'm going to the police," I said.

"You do that. Then I'll go there after you do and tell them about Vic."

"You can't prove a damned thing."

"Maybe not. But I can make them awfully suspicious. I'd remember that if I were you."

She hung up.

It was November then, and the radio was filled with tinny, cynical messages of Christmas. I went to the cemetery once a day and talked to her, and then I came home and put myself to sleep with Black and White and Valium. I knew it was Russian roulette, that particular combination, but I thought I might get lucky and lose.

The day after Thanksgiving, she called again. I hadn't heard from her since the funeral.

"I'm going away."

"So?"

"So. I just thought I'd tell you that in case you wanted to get hold of me."

"And why would I want to do that?"

"Because we're joined at the hip, darling, so to speak. You can put me in the electric chair, and I can do the same for you."

"Maybe I don't give a damn."

"Now you're being dramatic. If you truly didn't give a damn, you would've gone to the police two months ago."

"You bitch."

"I'm going to bring you a little surprise when I come back from my trip. A Christmas gift, I guess you'd call it."

I tried working but I couldn't concentrate. I took an extended leave. The booze was becoming a problem. There was alcoholism on both sides of my family, so my ever increasing reliance on blackouts wasn't totally unexpected, I suppose. I stopped going out. I learned that virtually anything you needed would happily be brought you if you had the money, everything from groceries to liquor. A cleaning woman came in one day a week and bulldozed her way through the mess. I watched old movies on cable, trying to lose myself especially in the frivolity of the musicals. Kendra would have loved them. I found myself waking, many mornings, in the middle of the den, splayed on the floor, after apparently trying to make it to the door but failing. One morning I found that I'd wet myself. I didn't much care, actually. I tried not to think of Kendra, and yet she was all I did want to think about. I must have wept six or seven times a day. I dropped twelve pounds in two weeks.

I got sentimental about Christmas Eve, decided to try to stay reasonably sober and clean myself up a little bit. I told myself I was doing this in honor of Kendra. It would have been our first Christmas Eve together.

The cleaning lady was also a good cook and had left a fine roast beef with vegetable and potato fixings in the refrigerator. All I had to do was heat it up in the microwave.

I had just set my place at the dining room table—with an identical place setting to my right for Kendra—when the doorbell rang.

I answered it, opening the door and looking out into the snowwhipped darkness.

I know I made a loud and harsh sound, though if it was a scream exactly, I'm not sure.

I stepped back from the doorway and let her come in. She'd even changed her walk a little, to make it more like her daughter's. The clothes, too, the long double-breasted camel hair coat and the wine-colored beret, were more Kendra's style than her own. Beneath was a four-button empire dress that matched the color of the beret—the exact dress Kendra had often worn.

But the clothes were only props.

It was the face that possessed me.

The surgeon had done a damned good job, whoever he or she was, a damned good job. The nose was smaller and the chin was now heart-shaped and the cheekbones were more pronounced and perhaps a half inch higher. And with her blue blue contacts—

Kendra. She was Kendra.

"You're properly impressed, Roger, and I'm grateful for that," she said, walking past me to the dry bar. "I mean, this was not without pain, believe me. But then you know that firsthand, don't you, being an old hand at plastic surgery yourself."

She dropped her coat in an armchair and fixed herself a drink.

"You bitch," I said, slapping the drink from her hand, hearing it shatter against the stone of the fireplace. "You're a goddamned ghoul."

"Maybe I'm Kendra reincarnated." She smiled. "Have you ever thought of that?"

"I want you out of here."

She stood on tiptoes, just as Kendra had once done, and touched my lips to hers. "I knew you'd be gruff the first time you saw me. But you'll come around. You'll get curious about me. If I taste any different, or feel any different. If I'm—Kendra."

I went over to the door, grabbing her coat as I did so. Then I yanked her by the wrist and spun her out into the snowy cold night, throwing her coat after her. I slammed the door.

Twenty minutes later, the knock came again. I opened the door, knowing just who it would be. There were drinks, hours of drinks, and then, quite before I knew what was happening and much against all I held sacred and dear, we were somehow in bed, and as she slid her arms around me there in the darkness, she said, "You always knew I'd fall in love with you someday, didn't you, Roger?"

A THEME FOR HYACINTH

Julian Symons

Happiness, Robin Edgley thought as he felt the sun on his chest and stomach and legs, seeping through the epidermis to irradicate the blood and sinew and, yes, heart beneath; it is by pure chance that I have discovered happiness for the first time in my life. If Felix had not been laid low by influenza and been delayed leaving England for a week, Gerda would never have spoken to me and this would have been simply another holiday. Instead, it was a revelation to himself of his inmost nature.

Happiness, happiness! It was a golden body that you held in your hands on a green island beside a blue sea, but it was also—to move beyond that rather seaside-posterish conception—the inward reassurance given by his love for Gerda, the feeling of merging his identify with that of another human being, something that went beyond the possibilities of words.

Pleasurable warmth was turning into heat. Perhaps his front had been cooked sufficiently. He removed the bandage from his eyes, glanced round, and saw that he shared the terrace beside the sea with half a dozen old men and women; he turned onto his stomach and picked up the poetry anthology he had been reading. One poem, *Le Monocle de Mon Oncle* by Wallace Stevens, fascinated him. It was a middle-aged man's reflections on love:

> In the high west there burns a furious star.
> It is for fiery boys that star was set
> And for sweet-smelling virgins close to them.
> The measure of the intensity of love
> Is measure, also, of the verve of earth.

True, he thought. He felt in himself a sharpening of the senses, a deepened awareness of everything about him. But the next verse provoked disagreement.

> When amorists grow bald, then armours shrink
> Into the compass and curriculum
> Of introspective exiles lecturing.
> It is a theme for Hyacinth alone.

No, no, he cried silently. His head was silvered and not bald, but the point was that love between a mature man and a young woman could contain everything felt by those "fiery boys"—and more, much more. Was the poem not proved untrue by almost the first words Gerda had spoken to him?

He was wondering at that time, three days ago, why he had ever come. He had succumbed to the boyish eagerness of his cousin Felix, and had regretted it almost immediately. Looking sideways at him out of those dark eyes that were absurdly longlashed for a man's, Felix had said he was going away and asked why Nunky—which was his name for Robin, although they were not blood relations—didn't come too.

"I'm fed up with bloody agents, bloody producers, bloody theatre. Getting out of it, Nunky, going to look for the sun. Let them bloody ring my flat and not find me, they'll be keener when I come back. Since you're a man of leisure, why not make it a twosome?" Where was he going? He didn't know but it turned out to be Yugoslavia, the Adriatic coast, Dubrovnik. "Boiling hot, wonderful swimming, fishing, and cheap. Not that that matters to you, but it does to me. And we might find a couple of birds. If you're so inclined."

Again that sideways glance from the fine eyes that—he could admit it frankly now—always disturbed him. The disturbance came from the doubts about himself raised by such glances and by the impulse he felt at times to put an arm round the young man's shoulders, to push him playfully over onto a sofa when they had an argument. It was five years since Mary's death and he had neither remarried nor even engaged in a love affair since then. Was there something wrong with him?

Thinking of his own fastidiousness, of the care he took about the colour and fit of clothes, of his liking for picking up nice little pieces of bric-à-brac and of putting them in just the right spot in his flat, he wondered whether he could possibly be (a word he disliked using, disliked even the thought of) queer? Or was it just that the rackety life Felix lived fascinated him, shifting quarterly from flat to flat, often out of work and sometimes tremendously hard up? Occasionally Robin had lent him small sums of money which had always been returned, but he had worried even about these. Was he trying to buy affection?

He could admit all this now, since Gerda had proved that there was nothing queer about him.

So much for Felix, who had done him the best turn of his life by contracting influenza and by telephoning, in a woe-begone voice about which there was as always a hint of self-mockery, to say that he would come out as soon as he felt better. But these had not been Robin's thoughts as he took a hot bath, changed into a dashing maroon dinner jacket, and sat down to dinner alone on that first night in the hotel. Afterward he stood on the terrace leaning on his silver-headed malacca cane, and stared gloomily at the lights of the old city. He felt a touch on his arm.

"You will forgive me if I speak to you," the girl said. "But I could not help looking at you in the restaurant. You were the most attractive man in the room." She paused and made a careful amendment. "That is not quite right. I should have said the most *interesting* man."

That made it easier for him to say, "Thank you."

"My name is Gerda."

"Robin Edgley." She was young, blonde, beautiful. He felt a

moment's panic. "Shall we sit down? Would you like a drink?"

When they were sitting in chairs that overlooked the bay, drinks by their sides, he felt a little more comfortable. "You took my breath away. Do you often say that kind of thing to a strange man?"

"Never before. Please believe me." She spoke gravely, and he did believe her. She was not, he now saw, quite the dazzling beauty he had thought. Her hair was silky and her features fine, but the large mouth turned down sulkily at the corners and her blue eyes were very wide apart under their thick blonde brows. The eyes looked cold, but a kind of warmth came from her, almost as if some fire burned within her. Her English was perfect, but accented.

He asked if she was German and she nodded. "You're a very unusual girl."

"Don't talk like that. As if you were my uncle." She spoke sharply. "We are the same age, you and I."

"What nonsense. I might be your uncle. I am forty-five." In fact, he was four years older.

"I did not mean in that way. We feel the same emotions. When you look at this landscape what do you feel?"

He looked into gathering darkness and she said impatiently, "Not now. When you came."

"Romantic, I suppose."

"And subtle."

"Yes, romantic in a subtle way," he said, although he had not felt this at all.

"Young men do not feel such things. They bore me." Without taking breath she asked, "Shall we go for a walk?"

They walked in the Gradac Park, among old cypress and pine trees, above the sea. He found himself talking with unusual freedom, telling her that he had been a partner in a small firm manufacturing a new kind of air vent for kitchens, and that he had retired from it a couple of years ago. He tried to explain something of his feeling.

"Suddenly it seemed ridiculous, going into an office every day. I thought, is this all I'm going to do with my life? Of course when Mary was alive it was different, but she died five years ago."

"Mary?"

"My wife. I forgot you didn't know her. Isn't that silly?"

"Nothing about you is silly. Yes, there is one thing." She pointed to the stick. "Why use that? It is for lame men."

"Ah, but you don't realise—" With a twist and a flourish he drew the sword from its sheath. "If I am attacked."

"I think it is foolish." In her precise English it sounded very definite. "What else have you found in life?"

"I don't know. Places—all the places I haven't seen. Poetry—I always liked reading poetry. Meeting people, not just English people."

"Have you found what you hoped?"

"I don't know. Enough to be glad that I gave up business."

But as he spoke it seemed to him that something was terribly missing. He asked what she did, and she laughed deep in her throat.

"You will see." She would say nothing more. On the way back he was very conscious of her physical presence at his side. There was something animal, assured yet stealthy, about the movements of her body. Once he touched her arm and felt an almost irresistible desire to grip her shoulders and turn her to him. Then the moment was over and they were walking along again.

In the hotel lobby he was uncertain whether to suggest a drink in his room. Then that moment also passed. She said good night and was walking away, the golden hair like a cap at the back of her head.

On the following morning he woke in excellent spirits. He ate breakfast on the balcony outside his room and watched tourists going off in coaches to Mostar, the bay of Kotor, and on the Grand Tour of Montenegro. The holiday makers, mostly brawny Germans and unbecomingly sunburned English, stood about chatting until they were shepherded by energetic guides into the coaches. The voices of the guides rang out like those of schoolteachers gathering children to cross the road.

"Hurry, please. We are already five minutes late."

There was something familiar about the precision of the tone even as it floated up to him, and he identified her in a blue and white sleeveless dress, with a dark blue peaked cap on the side of her head. She looked up, saw him, touched her fingers to her lips, then jumped into the coach and was gone.

He was in the sun lounge when the travellers returned in the early evening. He assured himself that he was not waiting for her, but the thrill that went through his body at the sight of her golden hair under the peaked cap was something he had not felt for years.

She came up to him at once. Beads of moisture marked her upper lip. He asked if she wanted a drink. She shook her head. "I am not presentable. Those coaches are hot. But in ten minutes I should like a large, *large* gin and tonic."

He had it waiting for her in the bar.

"So you're a guide."

"Only for a few days, with this one party. On Sunday my husband comes out. Then we shall be on holiday." Her petulant mouth turned down. "His name is Porter, so that I am Gerda Porter. It sounds ridiculous. He is a travel agent. I thought it would be amusing to play the part of a guide, for just one party, so he arranged it."

"He sounds nice."

"Don't let us talk about him. Shall I come to your room now or after dinner?" He stared at her. "I have shocked you? You do not like women to be frank?"

He went on staring and she looked back with one thick eyebrow raised, half smiling. "Now," he said and then added, with what he felt at the time to be wretched pusillanimity, "in separate lifts. We must be careful."

They went up in separate lifts. They did not come down to dinner.

Two days later her party went home. He watched her with them, talking to the men who asked about playing at the casino where only foreign currency was permitted and about making special trips to see what they called "something of the way people really live here" (as though the Yugoslavs were another species), and with the women who engaged her in endless chats about what they could buy and what they could take home.

She handled all their queries with efficiency, courtesy and an apparently endless patience. After seeing them off at the airport she came back and sat in a chair beside him.

"I'm glad that's over. What a boring lot!"

"You handled them perfectly."

"Why not? I used to be a travel courier. I was enjoying it. But after meeting you—" She left the sentence unfinished. "We have three days."

"Three days?"

"Before my husband arrives." Her eyes were like blue marbles.

That day they explored Dubrovnik, intoxicated by the pleasure of being in a city sacred to walkers. They wandered from side to side of the Placa looking in the windows of shops that all seemed to sell the same goods, priced head scarfs and rugs in the Gundulic Square market, ate unidentifiable fish at a little restaurant in Ul Siroka, made a circuit of the ramparts. After lunch they drank coffee on the terrace of the Gradska Kafana by the harbour. Then they hired a motorboat with surprising ease, and in the motorboat discovered the island.

The Dalmatian coast is full of islands, including Lokrum, less than half a mile from the walled city, which appears to be covered with pine woods but in fact contains a park filled with subtropical vegetation and twenty small coves for bathers. Lokrum is a "trippers' haunt", but a little beyond it there are a dozen tiny islands, no more than a few hundred yards long, some almost pure rock, others covered by shrubs and dwarf trees, and with natural landing places.

It was one of these that they found, rowing in the last few yards and pulling up the boat into a tiny bay. They took off their clothes, swam naked in the clear blue water, then walked back a few yards from the beach and made love on the grass. The walls of Dubrovnik were visible less than a mile away, yet they were completely alone. The is unreal, he told himself; it has nothing to do with any life I have ever known. These thoughts were interrupted by Gerda.

"Look at me! I sweat like a pig." There was moisture on her brow and on her body. "Disgusting. Not like you—your body is dry."

"Dry with old age."

"Don't talk like that, it's stupid. My husband is an old man."

"Gerda—"

"And I do not wish you to call me Gerda, it is the name he uses. I tell you my secret name—it is Hella. You call me Hel."

"Hel, you have shown me heaven," he said inanely. "Does he look like me, your husband?"

She snorted with laughter. "You'll see." With her face half buried in grass she told him about her life. Her parents had escaped from East to West Germany, and she had gone from West Germany to England, where she worked as an *au pair* girl. She had no intention of remaining with the family, but she could not get a job without a labour permit. So she forged one and was engaged as a courier by Porter Travel Limited.

"And then you married the boss." He said it lightly, to hide the fact that her calm talk of forgery had shocked him.

"Yes."

"You say he is—my age. Did he attract you?"

"Yes, but that was not important. He found out that my permit was no good, so it was the only thing to do. When I see something must be done I do it."

"You're ruthless."

"When it is necessary. But if I had known what it would be like—" Again she did not finish the sentence, but stared at him with her brilliant marble eyes. Then she turned and ran down again to the sea. He got up and followed her.

It was on the island, the following day, that he told her he loved her. This was something he had not said to any woman, except to Mary in the early days of their marriage. She made no reply. "But you don't love me, Hel, do you?"

"I am not sure. Anyway it does not matter. It is Friday. On Sunday afternoon my husband will arrive."

"Felix too. I've had a cable." He had told her about Felix.

"When he is here it will be all over."

"I want to marry you." He had not known that he was going to say these words, but as soon as they were uttered he knew them to be true. She remained silent. "Did you hear me?"

"I heard you. It is impossible."

"Why?"

"My husband is a Catholic. He would not divorce me."

"If you left him we could live together." He was astonished to hear himself suggest it.

"He would bring a law case, drag you through the courts. Would you like that, respectable Robin? There is only one way we could be together."

"How?"

"If he were dead."

He had closed his eyes. Now he opened them. She had a towel

wrapped round her, and she was leaning on one arm looking at him. He realised at once that she meant they should kill her husband in some way. He was not even surprised, for he understood by now the total ruthlessness of her character. But he was a conventional man, and conventional words accurately expressed his reaction. "You must be mad."

She made no reply, but began to dress. They went down to the boat in silence. Then she put her arms round him. "I love you, Robin, but how can I permit myself to do so? What would be the use?"

"If you loved me you wouldn't talk like that."

"I love like a German. If I want something I try to get it. If I cannot get it I do without and don't complain. You do not have the courage to help me, so we have till Sunday. We can enjoy that much."

But Robin did not enjoy it, or not in the same way. The sensual grip she exerted on him was very powerful. He had always thought of himself as a less than average sensual man, for he had never experienced with Mary anything like the feelings that Gerda inspired in him. The intensity of his actions and reactions during lovemaking frightened him, just as in a different way he was frightened by the feeling that he existed as an instrument for her satisfaction. He told himself that he loved her, but did he feel anything more than a sexual itch? Lines from another poem came into his head:

> But at my back from time to time I hear
> The sound of horns and motors which shall bring
> Sweeney to Mrs Porter in the spring.

To think of himself as apeneck Sweeney, the image of mindless sensuality, distressed and worried him. But overriding such feelings was the longing he felt for her that made another part of himself say, "This is the first happiness you have had in your long dreary life. Are you going to throw it away?"

He held out until Sunday morning. On Saturday they went to the island but it was not a success, and on Sunday morning neither of them suggested a visit. When they found that two places were vacant on a coach expedition to Cilipi, a few miles away, to see the peasants come to church in local costume, they got in.

The scene as they approached was farcical. Dozens of coaches were drawn up along the roadside. They parked half a mile from the church square. When they reached it, the place was packed with camera-carrying tourists, taking shots of everything in sight. A few locals moved in and out of the throng, the women wearing white nunlike coifs, embroidered blouses, and long black skirts. Tourists snapped cameras within inches of their faces, asked them to hold still, climbed onto cars to get angled shots. A scrawny American with white knees showing below baggy shorts aimed his camera at a fezzed village elder who sat placidly smoking a long clay pipe.

"Excuse it, please." The American pushed Robin and Gerda aside, dropped to one knee, then suddenly flung himself flat onto the ground and squinted up at the Cilipian who stared into the distance with imperturbable dignity. Robin looked at Gerda. They both burst out laughing, then walked out of the square and the village down a rough path that led through scrub to nowhere.

"You do not have your cane." He had left it in his room ever since that first evening. He said curtly she had been right, he did not need it. She glanced at him, said nothing.

"Did you ever see anything so awful as those tourists? The Yugoslavs must think we're all barbarians."

"But I am a barbarian. You think so." Her words were like an accusation.

She leaned against a rock. "You are afraid of everything. If I said to you take me into that field, make love to me, would you do it?"

"Hel, it wouldn't be—" Two coiffed women came up the stony path. "*Dobar dan*," he said.

"*Dobar dan*." They passed on.

She said ironically, as he stumbled on the rock, "You need your cane. I think you should carry it." She wore dark glasses, but he knew that behind them her blue eyes would be cold. He could not bear the thought of losing her. "Hel, tell me what you want."

"It must be what *we* want."

"What we want." When he put his hand on her arm it seemed to burn him.

She told him in her precise English, speaking in a rapid low voice. She used sleeping tablets and would put two of them into her husband's coffee one day after lunch. Robin would take him out in the boat. In half an hour her husband would be asleep. Near the island the boat would overturn and the sleeping man would drown. Robin was a strong swimmer, he could easily reach the island. There he would wait until a boat saw him, or an expedition came looking for them from Dubrovnik.

"It would be murder."

"He would know nothing."

"I should be suspected. People have seen us together."

"Do you think the Yugoslav police will trouble about that? They are peasants, like the people here. It is obviously an accident. Probably they do not find the body. And if they do—" The sulky mouth curved upward in a smile. "I will tell you something. He cannot swim."

"*La Belle Dame sans Merci*," he said.

"What is that?"

"A poem. It means you are ruthless. And I am in thrall to you."

"I do not understand."

"Yes. It means that I say yes."

She did not reply, did not take off the dark glasses, merely looked at him and nodded. Then she took his hand and led him into the field. The pleasure that followed was intense, and almost painful.

"You're looking uncommonly fit, Nunky," Felix said. "A fine bronzed figure of an Englishman. You bear every sign of not having missed me. Discovered any female talent?"

"Don't be absurd."

"Most of them look over the age of consent to me."

"I have been out once or twice with Mrs. Porter. Her husband was on your plane. They're staying at this hotel."

"Little fat chap—I remember meeting her. A blonde piece, a bit too Nordic for me."

"She is of German origin," he said with what he knew to be ridiculous stiffness.

Felix looked at him and whistled. "You sound its if you've fallen for the fair Nordic lady. I shall have to look after you, Nunky, I can see that."

He went out with Felix in the boat that afternoon, and landed on the island. They both swam and then Felix put on his skindiving equipment and disappeared for three-quarters of an hour while Robin lay on the beach and thought about Hel. Her absence ached in him like a tooth, and when Felix reappeared and talked enthusiastically about the marvellous clarity of the water so that he could see fish swimming fifty feet below him, and said it would be quite easy to swim from the island to Dubrovnik, he heard himself becoming unreasonably snappish.

The old relationship with Felix, in which he had responded eagerly to his young cousin's coquettish facetiousness, had been replaced by a feeling of irritation. He no longer wished to be called Nunky and felt no inclination to indulge in pseudoboyish horseplay. When the young man took out a mirror and began carefully to comb his hair he felt a faint stirring of distaste.

Closing his eyes he immediately saw Hel in bed with her fat stumpy husband, forced to accept his lovemaking or—worse still—welcoming it. He got up, walked to the water's edge, began to throw stones into the sea. Felix watched him with a smiling mouth and inquisitive eyes.

She introduced him to Porter that evening. Good heavens, Robin thought, as he looked at the squat paunchy little man who shook hands with him, he's *old*! However did she bring herself to marry him? It was a shock to remember that Porter was no more than two or three years older than himself, but then there was the difference between them of a man who had kept his body in trim and one who had let it go to seed.

"Hear you've been squiring Gerda around, Mr. Edgley. I appreciate that. Not that she's had much spare time, with this crazy idea she had of being guide to one of my parties. Had to indulge her—I'm an indulgent man, isn't that so, my dear?" He patted her hand.

"From what I saw she was a most efficient guide."

"Should be. Used to do it for it living, now it's for fun. I tell you what I'd like, Robin—don't mind if I call you that, I know Gerda does—what I'd like is for you and your friend to be my guests this evening. Let's go and paint this little old Communist town red."

"Norman knows all the best places," Gerda said without smiling.

"I should, my dear, I should. The food at this place is—well, it's hotel food and that's all you can say for it. But I know a little place where—just you leave it to me." He winked one eye.

It was a terrible evening. They ate a special Montenegrin dinner which began with smoked ham, followed by red mullet and *raznici*, which proved to be a brother to *kebab*, meat grilled on a skewer. The restaurant was set in a garden, just outside the city walls.

Porter—or, as he insisted on being called, Norman—talked Serbo-Croat to waiters who responded in English. They drank slivovitz to begin with, continued with several bottles of full red Yugoslav wine, and ended with more slivovitz. Norman sent back one bottle of slivovitz with what sounded like a flow of objectionable remarks in Serbo-Croat. When the waiter shrugged and brought a bottle of another make he said triumphantly, "You see. You have to know to get the right stuff."

There was a band, and all three of them danced with Gerda. When Robin moved round, feeling the hard warmth of her body beneath his hand, he found the sensation almost intolerable. "You see what he is like," she said. "An old man. Disgusting."

"Not much older than I am."

"Do not be stupid. It is not at all the same."

"Hel, I have to see you, talk to you."

"We cannot," she said crisply. "This I told you."

"I just have to see you alone."

"Impossible. Besides, what is there to talk about? Today is Sunday. Tomorrow after lunch."

The dance was almost finished before he said, "Yes."

Felix danced with Gerda, holding her as lightly as possible, his arched nostrils slightly distended, his head held high in the manner of a horse ready to shy at what he may meet round the next corner. They seemed to exchange little conversation. Norman drank another glass of slivovitz, belched slightly.

"After this I want you to be my guest at the casino."

"Very kind of you, but—" Robin protested.

"Won't take but for an answer. Beautiful, isn't she?"

An alarming remark. Robin did not know what to say. "Very charming."

"Some men would be jealous. Not me. I like it, like her to have other friends. I understand." He drummed with his fingers on the table. Robin realised that his host was drunk. "I've never regretted any-thing—want you to know that. No regrets, no heel taps. Loveliest girl I ever saw, married her. What d'you say to that?"

Robin had no desire to say anything to it. When Gerda and Felix came back, Porter rose a little unsteadily. "May I have the pleasure?"

She said nothing, but moved into his arms. Felix seemed about to speak, then did not. Robin watched them dancing. Porter's arm was on her bare back, and he seemed to be talking continuously.

Felix, like a man who has come to a decision, said, "Nunky."

Irritation spilled over. "Once and for all, will you please understand that I do not want to be called by that ridiculous name!"

"Sorry."

There was a disturbance among the dancers. Gerda emerged from it, half supporting her husband. Porter sat down heavily, closed his eyes, and opened them again. He insisted they must all go on to the casino, but with the headwaiter's help they got a taxi and returned to the hotel. During the taxi ride Porter began to snore. At the hotel Felix and Robin each took an arm to get him into the lift. In the bedroom Gerda removed his jacket and waved them away.

"I can put him to bed, thank you. I have done it before."

Alone in his room Robin looked at himself in the glass. Below the abundant white hair his face was youthful. Calves and thighs were slightly withered but his body was supple, his stomach flat.

"With this body I thee worship," he said aloud. He picked up the malacca walking stick, drew the sword from it, made a few passes at an imaginary enemy. Perhaps he too was a little drunk, he thought, as he carried on a dialogue with himself while staring into the glass.

Robin Edgley, he said, retired director of a firm manufacturing fan ventilators, you are reaching out for happiness, and there is only one way to obtain it. Make up your mind to that. But what you are about to do is crazy, another part of himself said; you are thinking of forever but she is thinking of today and tomorrow and perhaps next year. And not only is it crazy but it is wrong, opposed to all the instincts you have lived by since youth. How can you imagine that after doing wrong you will be happy? What does that matter, the first voice said, when I have been given a glimpse of eternity. . . .

It was a long time before he fell asleep, and when he slept he dreamed. He was in the sea and Porter was with him, the boat over-turned; he was holding Porter under the water, but instead of submitting quietly the man flailed and twisted like a fish. Then Robin gripped a throat which was smooth, young, and white instead of the swollen wrinkled column he was expecting, and it was Hel's throat he was squeezing, her face that was gaspingly lifted to his own before he too started to gasp and thrash about, conscious that life was being pressed out of him. . . .

He woke with the sheet twisted round his body. The dream disturbed him. There was some element in it that he could not recall; something had happened that his conscious mind refused to register. He looked at his watch and saw that it was only two o'clock. He did not sleep again until four. . . .

In the morning Porter looked pale but cheerful. At eleven o'clock he was drinking a champagne cocktail on the terrace. "Hear you put me to bed last night, old man, very nice of you. Sort of thing that's liable to happen, you know, first night." He spoke like the victim of some natural disaster.

"How do you feel now?"

"I'm OK. Champagne with cognac always puts me right. Though mind you, it's got to be cognac, not this filthy local brandy. You're a fisherman, Gerda tells me."

"I do fish, yes."

"How about taking a boat after lunch, the two of us, eh?"

"I'm really not at all expert."

"That's all right, neither am I. We'll just trawl for mullet and bream—what do they call 'em here, *dentex*? That's a hell of a name to give a fish."

"What about your wife?"

"She wants to go to Lokrum, going to show it to that cousin of yours. I've been out half a dozen times myself, sooner do a bit of fishing. Bores Gerda, I know it does. Anyway, I want to have a quiet natter."

"All right, let's go fishing."

Later, walking round Dubrovnik with Felix, he learned a little more about the intended expedition to Lokrum. Sitting between the coupled columns in the elegant cloister of the Franciscan monastery, swinging a leg clad in tight sky-blue slacks, Felix calmly admitted that he had deliberately arranged it.

"Let's be frank about it, Porter's a slob but Hel's poison. You don't want to be mixed up with her."

"I am not mixed up, as you put it."

"Oh, come *on*." Felix could not help posing, whatever his surroundings, and now he turned away from Robin so that his fine profile was outlined against the grey stone like the head on a coin. "You follow her with your eyes wherever she goes, you treat her as though she were made of china. And believe me she's not, she's tough as old boots. I know her kind." Robin made no reply. Felix went on. "Even old slob Porter must spot it soon. So I thought I'd remove you from temptation this afternoon. And for the rest of the time we're here—well, they tell me there are lots of perfectly fascinating places to see on guided tours."

"Thank you." He knew how much Felix disliked guided tours.

"Think nothing of it. And now shall we go and look at the Museum of the Socialist Revolution? You know I've been longing to do that ever since I got here."

They visited the museum and then went round the ramparts. Coming away from them down the narrow steps Felix slipped and fell. He got up and grimaced. He had twisted his ankle. After hobbling back to the hotel he borrowed Robin's stick. "If I'm going to hobble I'll do it in style, look like a man of distinction."

He was with Gerda alone for a few minutes before lunch. She wore an op art dress in zigzags that drew a great many eyes to her. Catching a brief glimpse of them both in a glass and admiring his own dark-blue linen shirt and pale trousers, he could not help thinking they made a handsome couple. She let him buy her a drink in the bar. She spoke rapidly.

"This afternoon your cousin takes me to Lokrum, so I shall be out of the way. You will drink coffee with us after lunch."

"Hel, I don't know."

"What?" she said sharply. "What do you not know?"

"Whether I can go through with it."

She finished her drink, turned on her heel, and left him.

After lunch it was Porter who stopped by their table and suggested that they all have coffee together. Really, Robin thought, if ever a man could be called the architect of his own destruction it was Porter—but no doubt Hel had put him up to it. She smiled briefly as she waited for them at the table, with coffee already poured. Porter was jovial.

"You know what made me marry Gerda? Because she's the most honest woman I ever met."

"Is that so?" Felix made the question sound like an insult.

"You know she worked for me as a courier and I found she had a phony work permit. So when I said marry me she said, 'I might consider it; this way at least I won't have to worry about a permit.'"

"The kind of thing that other people think I am prepared to say." Gerda spoke with a touch of complacency.

"And would you believe it, she made another condition. A girl in her position, making conditions with me!" He roared with laughter. "'You're more than twice my age,' she says, 'you'll have the best years of my life. So what happens to me when you die?' She actually *said* that, mind you. So I told her I'd look after her, and I have."

"Very rash." Felix murmured the words so that Porter did not hear them, but Gerda did.

"I am a German, and Germans are realistic." Her glance at Felix was hostile. It seemed likely to be an uncomfortable afternoon for them both on Lokrum. "We will walk down to the boat with you. If you can manage that," she said to Felix.

"I'm improving rapidly." Certainly he limped much less as they went down to the harbour. Porter was carrying some fishing tackle in case, as he said, he had a chance to use it. Robin changed into clean shorts. The crisp elegance of his appearance contrasted favourably, he thought, with Porter's sweat-stained shirt and general grubbiness.

The slick young man who rented the boat indicated with a slightly contemptuous air the trawling lines fixed to it, and Porter nodded and waved his hand to indicate that he did not need to be told. He climbed in, complete with fishing tackle. Robin in the stern started the outboard, and they were away. Felix and Gerda waved from the harbour.

They skirted Lokrum and moved into the open water beyond. Porter dropped his lines, lighted a pipe, and sat back. He looked what he was—a prosperous businessman carrying too much weight. Robin stared at him, unable to believe what he was going to do.

"Tell me something." Porter's next words were inaudible. Robin almost closed the throttle, so that the boat jogged up and down on the blue water.

"What's that?"

"I like you, Robin, so I thought I ought to—" His next words were again inaudible. "Gerda," he ended.

"I can't hear properly." He closed the throttle completely, so that the motor cut out. They drifted slowly toward the island, his island, only a few hundred yards away. Porter's voice came through the stillness.

"Gerda likes to be with me. I don't say she's happy, because she's not a contented person, never would be. But don't get the wrong idea."

"I don't know what you mean."

"She likes me. She thinks of crazy things, does them sometimes. Ran away from me once, came back after a couple of weeks, no money. She needs money, that's her motive power, like the engine that runs this boat. So she always comes back."

"Why are you telling me this?" There was something wrong in the boat.

"Just wanted you to understand. I'm not a fool, Robin—I may look it but I'm not. Why do you think I let her do this crazy little job out here? Think I haven't got other couriers? I knew she wanted an affair, wanted to let off steam."

With a feeling of disbelief he saw that his cane lay just below Porter's fishing tackle. "How did that get there?" he cried.

"What? Oh the cane. Your cousin asked me to slip it in with my tackle, thought you might need it. In case the rocks were slippery, he said. He's a bit of a joker, that boy."

"I don't understand."

"About Gerda now, don't get the wrong idea, that's all. You were just a pebble who happened to be on the beach. She doesn't like men of our age. I ought to know." Porter knocked out his pipe. "OK, start her up again."

Robin tugged savagely at the cord and the outboard sprang to life. They roared through the water with the throttle wide open. When will it happen, he thought, when are the pills going to work? I can't stand much more of this. He felt weary himself, a weariness that sprang from the bad dreams and restlessness of the night.

Porter's voice seemed to come from far away and he ignored it. The island looked larger, and momentarily he lost his grip on the tiller. Porter was scrambling toward him, his face alarmed. The boat rocked. Robin began to laugh.

"Better not upset the boat when you can't swim," Robin warned.

"Who the hell told you I couldn't swim? All fat men can swim. Here, give me the tiller, I'll take the boat in. Are you ill?"

He wanted to say that he had the situation under control and that Porter's own wife had said he was a non-swimmer, but suddenly he was too tired to speak. *She's* made a mess of it, he thought, as Porter leaned over him, pushing him to the bottom of the boat in his anxiety to steer. *She put the pills in the wrong cup.* Then he could no longer keep his eyes open.

He was in the middle of a dream which was both pleasurable and disturbing. Pleasurable because he was not fighting for breath as he had been last night, nor involved in any kind of struggle. He lay on the island beach, just a few yards from the sea, the sun burning down. Concern about the boat was removed by the sight of it carefully drawn up onto the beach.

Good old Porter! All that nonsense about the boat overturning—it must have been nonsense because Porter could swim. It had been a figment of his imagination. "Figment," he said happily, but could not hear the word. When he felt more energetic he would go into the sea.

Why was he disturbed then? Well, first of all, was he dreaming or not? "Do I wake or sleep?" he asked, but again could hear no words spoken. But that was not the main thing. The main thing was that in his dream he had heard a cry. Perhaps the cry of a bird, but no bird was visible. Had the cry wakened him, or was he still dreaming?

He found it difficult to focus. The boat, like everything else, looked hazy. And now a monster appeared in the sea, vanished, reappeared briefly, then sank under the waves. What kind of monster? Dark and with nothing very distinguishable in the way of a head, a strange dark monster that writhed and splashed and vanished. The sea snake of Dubrovnik?

But surely sea snakes did not exist. I refuse to believe in you, monster, he thought, you are part of my dream. And sure enough the monster had gone—he *was* dreaming. He closed his eyes again.

When they reopened the sun was low in the sky and had lost its power. He felt cold, he knew that he was awake, and his uneasiness had increased. Where was Porter? Asleep somewhere else? It was still an effort to move, and a greater effort to think.

Had Porter gone back to Dubrovnik? There was something wrong with this idea, and he worked out what it was. Porter could not have gone to Dubrovnik or the boat would not still be on the beach.

Something else worried him, something done or said which he must try to remember. Was it perhaps that he had never even attempted what he had set out to do, that whether through his fault or hers he had failed? Oh, hell, he thought, oh, hell, oh, Hel, what is there left for us now?

And then he traced the origin of this particular uneasiness. Hel, she had said, was a special name, one that even her husband never used, and that he himself must never use in public. He had not done so. How did it happen that Felix knew the name? He remembered the conversation, which seemed long ago although it was only this morning; he even remembered the words: "Porter's just a slob but Hel's poison."

Desperately, like a man submerged trying to reach the surface, he strove to understand this but failed.

At the far end of the beach, jewels glittered. Were they diamonds? Through the haze of his mind came the thought that jewels are not found on beaches. If he was lying on jewels it would be proof that he was dreaming. He picked up a handful of sand, looked at it, saw that it was the characteristic powdery shingle of the coast. It did not shine, so why were diamonds flashing less than a hundred yards away?

Collect them, he thought, sell them, and he would be rich. He tried to get up, dropped on his knees again dizzily, and then managed it. Tottering like an invalid he approached the thing that shone. Half a dozen yards away he identified it. His swordstick, removed from its walking-stick sheath, was what glittered in the setting sun.

That was not surprising, for the sun always glittered on metal. But what was it doing here, and why did one end of it look dull? At the same time he noticed dark smears on his shirt.

He ran down to the sea, dipped the blade in the water. The stick itself lay a little farther back up the beach. He stared at it, stared again at the blade, began to shiver. The putt-putt of an engine came into his consciousness, and looking out to sea he saw a motor launch making for the island. A man in uniform stood in the bow, blasts sounded on a hooter.

Robin Edgley dropped to his knees and prayed that what he saw and felt might still be a dream. . . .

The young Yugoslav lieutenant of police and his assistant found the woman's husband without difficulty. The body lay a few yards back from the beach in a hollow, with stab wounds through the chest. The weapon was present, the swordstick which the man Edgley had been cleaning in the water.

As for the motive, the woman herself had admitted behaving badly with Edgley when she called on them to ask for police help because she was worried that the boat had not returned. The lieutenant found the situation both ridiculous and disgusting. One would not have supposed—this was the only surprise—that so fussy a man as this Englishman would have been capable of so vigorous a reaction.

He offered no resistance when the lieutenant handcuffed him. They put the dead man into the other boat, and his assistant brought it back. On the return journey the lieutenant, who was proud of the English he had learned as a second language at school, tried without success to make conversation. The Englishman said almost nothing, except when they passed Lokrum. Then he made the suggestion that a man wearing skindiving equipment could have swum from Lokrum to the island.

"It would be possible," said the lieutenant. "But what man? And my dear Mr. Edgley, how would he have obtained your sword? And why were you cleaning the sword when we came?"

"It is hopeless," Edgley said, and then after a pause, "It was all planned, of course."

Was this a kind of religious determinism, a reference to the God in whom Edgley no doubt believed? The lieutenant decided to make the situation clear. "It is hopeless to attempt to deceive. But it was a crime of passion. You will find that we understand such things. You will perhaps be only five years in prison."

The Englishman made no reply. He said only one more thing, just before they tied up in Dubrovnik harbour. The woman waited there, her gold hair visible in the dusk. A man whom the lieutenant knew to be Edgley's cousin waited with her. Edgley then said something which the lieutenant, in spite of his excellent English, did not understand. "Will you please repeat that?" he asked, a little annoyed.

"A theme for Hyacinth," Edgley said. "It is a theme for Hyacinth alone."

It made no better sense the second time.

HOT SPRINGS

James Crumley

AT NIGHT, EVEN IN THE CHILL MOUNTAIN AIR, Mona Sue insisted on cranking the air conditioner all the way up. Her usual temperature always ran a couple of degrees higher than normal, and she claimed that the baby she carried made her constant fever even worse. She kept the cabin cold enough to hang meat. During the long, sleepless nights Benbow spooned to her naked, burning skin, trying to stay warm.

In the mornings, too, Mona Sue forced him into the cold. The modern cabin sat on a bench in the cool shadow of Mount Nihart, and they broke their fast with a room-service breakfast on the deck, a robe wrapped loosely about her naked body while Benbow bundled into both sweats and a robe. She ate furiously, stoking a furnace, and recounted her dreams as if they were gospel, effortlessly consuming most of the spread of exotic cheeses and expensively unseasonable fruits, a loaf of sourdough toast and four kinds of meat, all the while aimlessly babbling through the events of her internal night, the dreams of a teenage girl, languidly symbolic and vaguely frightening. She dreamt of her mother, young and lovely, devouring her litter of bare-foot boys in the dark Ozark hollows. And her father, home from a Tennessee prison, his crooked member dangling against her smooth cheek.

Benbow suspected she left the best parts out and did his best to listen to the soft southern cadences without watching her face. He knew what happened when he watched her talk, watched the soft moving curve of her dark lips, the wise slant of her gray eyes. So he picked at his breakfast and tried to focus his stare downslope at the steam drifting off the large hot-water pool behind the old shagbark lodge.

But then she switched to her daydreams about their dubious future, which were as deadly specific as a .45 slug in the brainpan: after the baby, they could flee to Canada; nobody would follow them up there. He listened and watched with the false patience of a teenage boy involved in his first confrontation with pure lust and hopeless desire.

Mona Sue ate with the precise and delicate greed of a heart surgeon, the pad of her spatulate thumb white on the handle of her spoon as she carved a perfect curled ball from the soft orange meat of her melon. Each bite of meat had to be balanced with an equal weight of toast before being crushed between her tiny white teeth. Then she examined each strawberry poised before her darkly red lips as if it might be a jewel of great omen and she some ancient oracle, then sank her shining teeth into the fleshy fruit as if it were the mortal truth. Benbow's heart rolled in his chest as he tried to fill his lungs with the cold air to fight off the heat of her body.

Fall had come to the mountains, now. The cottonwoods and alders welcomed the change with garish mourning dress, and in the mornings a rime of ice covered the windshield of the gray Taurus he had stolen at the Denver airport. New snow fell each night, moving slowly down the ridges from the high distant peaks of the Hard Rock Range and slipped closer each morning down the steep ridge behind them. Below the bench the old lodge seemed to settle more deeply into the narrow canyon, as if hunkering down for eons of snow, and the steam from the hot springs mixed with wood smoke and lay flat and sinuous among the yellow creek willows.

Benbow suspected, too, that the scenery was wasted on Mona Sue. Her dark eyes seemed turned inward to a dreamscape of her life, her husband, R. L. Dark, the pig farmer, his bullnecked son, Little R.L., and the lumpy Ozark offal of her large worthless family.

"Coach," she'd say—she thought it funny to call him Coach—interrupting the shattered and drifting narrative of her dreams. Then she would sweep back the thick black Indian hair from her face, tilt her narrow head on the slender column of her neck, and laugh. "Coach, that ol' R.L., he's a-comin'. You stole somethin' belonged to him, and you can bet he's on his way. Lit'l R.L., too, prob'ly, 'cause he tol' me once he'd like to string your guts on a bob-wire fence," she recited like a sprightly but not very bright child.

"Sweetheart, R. L. Dark can just barely cipher the numbers on a dollar bill or the spots on a card," Benbow answered, as he had each morning for the six months they'd been on the run, "he can't read a map that he hasn't drawn himself, and by noon he's too drunk to fit his ass in a tractor seat and find his hog pens. . . ."

"You know, Puddin', an ol' boy's got enough a them dollar bills, or stacks a them Franklins like we do," she added, laughing, "he can hire-out that readin' part, and the map part too. So he's a-comin'. You can put that in your momma's piggy bank."

This was a new wrinkle in their morning ritual, and Benbow caught himself glancing down at the parking lot behind the lodge and at the single narrow road up Hidden Springs Canyon, but he shook it off quickly. When he made the fateful decision to take Mona Sue and the money, he vowed to go for it, never glancing over his shoulder, living in the moment.

And this was it. Once more. Leaving his breakfast untouched, again, he slipped his hand through the bulky folds of Mona Sue's terry cloth robe to cradle the warm ripening fullness of her breasts and the long, thick nipples, already rock hard before his touch, and he kissed her mouth, sweet with strawberry and melon. Once again, he marveled at the deep passionate growl from the base of her throat as he pressed his lips into the hollow, then Benbow lifted her small frame—she nestled the baby high under the smooth vault of her rib cage and even at seven months the baby barely showed—and carried her to the bedroom.

Benbow knew, from recent experience, that the horse wrangler who doubled as room-service waiter would be waiting to clear the picnic table when they came out of the house to finish the coffee. The wran-gler might have patience with horses but not with guests who spent their mornings in bed. But he would wait for long minutes, silent as a Sioux scout, as Mona Sue searched her robe for his tip, occasionally exposing the rising contour of a breast or the clean scissoring of her long legs. Benbow had given him several hard looks, which the wrangler ignored as if the blunt stares were spoken in a foreign tongue. But nothing helped. Except to take the woman inside and avoid the wrangler altogether.

This morning Benbow laid Mona Sue on the feather bed like a gift, opened her robe, kissed the soft curve of her swollen belly, then blew softly on her feathery pubic hair. Mona Sue sobbed quickly, coughed as if she had a catfish bone caught in her throat, her long body arching. Benbow sobbed, too, his hunger for her more intense than the hunger growling in his empty stomach.

While Mona Sue had swelled through her pregnancy, Benbow had shed twenty-seven pounds from his blocky frame. Sometimes, just after they made love, it seemed as if her burning body had stolen the baby from his own muscled flesh, something stolen during the tangle of love, something growing hard and tight in her smooth, slim body.

As usual, they made love, then finished the coffee, ordered a fresh pot, tipped the wrangler, then made love again before her morning nap.

While Mona Sue slept, usually Benbow would drink the rest of the coffee as he read the day-old Meriwether newspaper, then slip into his sweats and running shoes, and jog down the switchbacks to the lodge to laze in the hot waters of the pools. He loved it there, floating in the water that seemed heavier than normal, thicker but cleaner, clearer. He almost felt whole there, cleansed and healthy and warm, taking the waters like some rich foreign prince, fleeing his failed life.

Occasionally, Benbow wished Mona Sue would interrupt her naps to join him, but she always said it might hurt the baby and she was already plenty hot with her natural fevers. As the weeks passed, Benbow learned to treasure his time alone in the hot pool and stopped asking her.

So their days wound away routinely, spooling like silk ribbons through their fingers, as placid as the deeply still waters of the pool.

But this noon, exhausted from the run and the worry, the lack of sleep and food, Benbow slipped effortlessly into the heated gravity of Mona Sue's sleeping body and slept, only to wake suddenly, sweating in spite of the chill, when the air conditioner was switched off.

R. L. Dark stood at the foot of their bed. Grinning. The old man stretched his crinkled neck, sniffing the air like an ancient snapping turtle, testing the air for food or fun, since he had no natural enemies except for teenage boys with .22's. R.L. had dressed for the occasion. He wore a new Carhart tin coat and clean bib overalls with the old Webley .455 revolver hanging on a string from his neck and bagging the bib pocket.

Two good ol' boys flanked him, one bald and the other wildly hirsute, both huge and dressed in Kmart flannel plaid. The bald one held up a small ballpeen hammer like a trophy. They weren't grinning. A skinny man in a baggy white suit shifted from foot to foot behind them, smiling weakly like a gun-shy pointer pup.

"Well, piss on the fire, boys, and call the dogs," R. L. Dark said, hustling the extra .455 rounds in his pocket as if they were his withered privates, "this hunt's done." The old man's cackle sounded like the sunrise cry of a cannibalistic rooster. "Son, they say you coulda been some kinda football coach, and I know you're one hell of a poker player, but I'd a never thought you'd come to this sorry end—a simpleminded thief and a chickenfuckin' wife stealer." Then R.L. brayed like one of the old plow mules he kept in the muddy bottoms of the White. "But you can run right smart, son. Gotta say that. Sly as an old boar coon. We might still be a-lookin' if'n Baby Doll there ain't a called her momma. Collect. To brag 'bout the baby."

Jesus, Benbow thought. Her mother. A toothless woman, now, shaped like a potato dumpling, topped with greasy hair, seasoned with moles.

Mona Sue woke, rubbing her eyes like a child, murmuring, "How you been, Daddy Honey?"

And Benbow knew he faced a death even harder than his unlucky life, knew even before the monster on the right popped him behind the ear with the ballpeen hammer and jerked his stunned body out of bed as if he were a child and handed him to his partner, who wrapped him in a full nelson. The bald one flipped the hammer and rapped his nuts smartly with it, then flipped it again and began breaking the small bones of Benbow's right foot with the round knob of the hammerhead.

Before Benbow fainted, harsh laughter raked his throat. Maybe this was the break he had been waiting for all his life.

* * *

Actually, it had all been Little R.L.'s fault. Sort of. Benbow had spotted the hulking bowlegged kid with the tiny ears and the thick neck three years earlier when the downward spiral of his football coaching career had led him to Alabamphilia, a small town on the edge of the Ozarks, a town without hope or dignity or even any convincing religious fervor, a town that smelled of chicken guts, hog manure, and rampant incest, which seemed to be the three main industries.

Benbow first saw Little R.L. in a pickup touch football game played on the hardscrabble playground and knew from the first moment that the boy had the quick grace of a deer, combined with the strength of a wild boar. This kid was one of the best natural running backs he'd ever seen. Benbow also found out just as quickly that Little R.L. was one of the redheaded Dark boys, and the Dark boys didn't play football.

Daddy R.L. thought football was a silly game, a notion with which Benbow agreed, and too much like work not to draw wages, with which once again Benbow agreed, and if'n his boys were going to work for free, they were damn well going to work for him and his hog operation, not some dirt-poor pissant washed-up football bum. Benbow had to agree with that, too, right to R.L.'s face, had to eat the old man's shit to get to the kid. Because this kid could be Benbow's ticket out of this Ozark hell, and he intended to have him. This was the one break Benbow needed to save his life. Once again.

It had always been that way for Benbow, needing that one break that never seemed to come. During his senior year at the small high school in western Nebraska, after three and a half years of mostly journeyman work as a blocking back in a passcrazy offense, Benbow's mother had worked double shifts at the truck-stop café—his dad had been dead so long nobody really remembered him—so they could afford to put together a videotape of his best efforts as a running back and pass receiver to send down to the university coaches in Lincoln. Once they had agreed to send a scout up for one game, Benbow had badgered his high school coach into a promise to let him carry the ball at least twenty times that night.

But the weather screwed him. On what should have been a lovely early October Friday night, a storm raced in from Canada, days early, and its icy wind blew Benbow's break right out of the water. Before the game, it rained two hard inches, then the field froze. During the first half it rained again, then hailed, and at the end of the second quarter it became a blinding snow squall.

Benbow had gained sixty yards, sure, but none of it pretty. And at halftime the Nebraska scout came by to apologize but if he was to get home in this weather, he had to start now. The lumpy old man invited Benbow to try a walk-on. Right, Benbow thought. Without a scholarship, he didn't have the money to register for fall semester. *Damn*, Benbow thought as he kicked the water cooler, and *damn it to hell*, he thought as his big toe shattered and his senior season ended.

So he played football for some pissant Christian college in the Dakotas where he didn't bother to take a degree. With his fused toe, he had lost a step in the open-field and his cuts lost their precision, so he haunted the weight room, forced thick muscle over his running back's body, and made himself into a solid if small fullback, but good enough to wrangle an invitation to one of the postseason senior bowl games. Then the first-string fullback, who was sure to be drafted by the pros, strained his knee in practice and refused to play. Oh, God, Benbow thought, another break.

But God foxed this one. The backfield coach was a born-again fundamentalist named Culpepper, and once he caught Benbow neither bowing his head nor even bothering to close his eyes during a lengthy team prayer, the coach became determined to convert the boy. Benbow played along, choking on his anger at the self-righteous bastard until his stomach cramped, swallowing the anger until he was throwing up three times a day, twice during practice and once before lights-out. By game day he'd lost twelve pounds and feared he wouldn't have the strength to play.

But he did. He had a first half to praise the football gods, if not the Christian one: two rushing touchdowns, one three yards dragging a linebacker and a corner, the other thirty-nine yards of fluid grace and power; and one receiving, twenty-two yards. But the quarterback had missed the handoff at the end of the first half, jammed the ball against Benbow's hip, and a blitzing linebacker picked it out of the air, then scored.

In the locker room at halftime, Culpepper was all over him like stink on shit. *Pride goeth before a fall!* he shouted. *We're never as tall as we are on our knees before Jesus!* And all the other soft-brain clichés. Benbow stomach knotted like a rawhide rope, then rebelled. Benbow caught that bit of vomit and swallowed it. But the second wave was too much. He turned and puked into a nearby sink. Culpepper went mad. Accused him of being out of shape, of drinking, smoking, and fornicating. When Benbow denied the charges, Culpepper added another, screamed *Prevaricator!* his foamy spittle flying into Benbow's face. And that was that.

Culpepper lost an eye from the single punch and nearly died during the operation to rebuild his cheekbone. Everybody said Benbow was lucky not to do time, like his father, who had killed a corrupt weighmaster down in Texas with his tire thumper, and was then killed himself by a bad Houston drug dealer down in the Ellis Unit at Huntsville when Benbow was six. Benbow was lucky, he guessed, but marked "Uncoachable" by the pro scouts and denied tryouts all over the league. Benbow played three years in Canada, then destroyed his knee in a bar fight with a Chinese guy in Vancouver. Then he was out of the game. Forever.

Benbow drifted west, fighting fires in the summers and dealing poker in the winter, taking the occasional college classes until he finally finished a PE teaching degree at Northern Montana and garnered an assistant coach's job at a small town in the Sweetgrass Hills, where he discovered he had an unsuspected gift for coaching, as he did for poker: a quick mind and no fear. A gift, once discovered, that became an addiction to the hard work, long hours, loving the game, and paying the price to win.

Head coach in three years, then two state championships, and a move to a larger school in Washington State. Where his mother came to live with him. Or die with him, as it were. The doctors said it was her heart, but Benbow knew that she died of truck-stop food, cheap whiskey, and long-haul drivers whose souls were as full of stale air as their tires.

But he coached a state championship team the next year and was considering offers from a football power down in northern California when he was struck down by a scandalous lawsuit. His second-string quarterback had become convinced that Benbow was sleeping with his mother, which of course he was. When the kid attacked Benbow at practice with his helmet, Benbow had to hit the kid to keep him off. He knew this part of his life was over when he saw the kid's eye dangling out of its socket on the grayish pink string of the optic nerve.

Downhill, as they say, from there. Drinking and fighting as often as coaching, low-rent poker games and married women, usually married to school-board members or dumb-shit administrators. Downhill all the way to Alabamphilia.

Benbow came back to this new world propped in a heap on the couch in the cottage's living room with a dull ache behind his ear and a thousand sharp pains in his foot, which was propped in a white cast on the coffee table, the fresh cast the size of a watermelon. Benbow didn't have to ask what purpose it served. The skinny man sat beside him, a syringe in hand. Across the room, R.L.'s bulk stood black against a fiery sunset, Mona Sue sitting curled in a chair in his shadow, slowly filing her nails. Through the window, Benbow could see the Kmart twins walking slow guard tours back and forth across the deck.

"He's comin' out of it, Mr. Dark," the old man said, his voice as sharp as his pale nose.

"Well, give him another dose, Doc," R.L. said without turning. "We don't want that boy a-hurtin' none. Not yet."

Benbow didn't understand what R.L. meant as the doctor stirred beside him, releasing a thin, dry stench like a limestone cavern or an open grave. Benbow had heard that death supposedly hurt no more than having a tooth pulled and he wondered who had brought back that bit of information as the doctor hit him in the shoulder with a blunt needle, then he slipped uneasily into an enforced sleep like a small death.

When he woke again, Benbow found little changed but the light. Mona Sue still curled in her chair, sleeping now, below her husband's hulk against the full dark sky. The doctor slept, too, leaning the fragile bones of his skull against Benbow's sore arm. And Benbow's leg was also asleep, locked in position by the giant cast resting on the coffee table. He sat very still for as long as he could, waiting for his mind to clear, willing his dead leg to awaken, and wondering why he wasn't dead too.

"Don't be gettin' no ideas, son," R.L. said without turning.

Of all the things Benbow had hated during the long Sundays shoveling pig shit or dealing cards for R. L. Dark—that was the trade he and the old man had made for Little R.L.'s football services—he hated the bastard calling him "son."

"I'm not your 'son,' you fucking old bastard."

R.L. ignored him, didn't even bother to turn. "How hot's that there water?" he asked calmly as the doctor stirred.

Benbow answered without thinking. "Somewhere between ninety-eight and one-oh-two. Why?"

"How 'bout half a dose, Doc?" R.L. said, turning now. "And see 'bout makin' that boy's cast waterproof. I'm thinkin' that hot water might take the edge off my rheumatism and I for sure want the coach there to keep me company. . . ."

Once again Benbow found the warm, lazy path back to the darkness at the center of his life, half listening to the old man and Mona Sue squabble over the air conditioner.

After word of his bargain with R. L. Dark for the gridiron services of his baby son spread throughout every tuck and hollow of the county, Benbow could no longer stop after practice for even a single quiet beer at any one of the rank honky-tonks that surrounded the dry town without hearing snickers as he left. It seemed that whatever he might have gained in sympathy, he surely lost in respect. And the old man treated him worse than a farting joke.

On the Saturdays that first fall, when Benbow began his days exchanging his manual labor for Little R.L.'s rushing talents, the old man dogged him all around the hog farm on a small John Deere tractor, endlessly pointing out Benbow's total ignorance of the details of trading bacon for bread and his general inability to perform hard work, complaining at great length, then cackling wildly and jacking the throttle on the tractor as if this was the funniest thing he'd ever seen. Even knowing that Little R.L. was lying on the couch in front of the television and soothing his sore muscles with a pint jar of 'shine, couldn't make Benbow even begin to resent his bargain, and he never even bothered to look at the old man, knowing that this was his only escape.

Sundays, though, the old man left him alone. Sunday was Poker Day. Land-rich farmers, sly country lawyers with sharp eyes and soft hands, and small-town bankers with the souls of slave traders came from as far away as West Memphis, St. Louis, and Fort Smith to gather in R.L.'s double-wide for a table stakes hold 'em game, a game famous in at least four states, and occasionally in northern Mexico.

On the sabbath he was on his own, except for the surly, lurking presence of Little R.L., who seemed to blame his coach for every ache and pain, and the jittery passage of a slim, petulant teenage girl who slopped past him across the muddy farmyard in a shapeless feed-sack dress and oversized rubber boots, trailing odd, throaty laughter, the same laughter she had when one of the sows decided to dine on her litter. Benbow should have listened.

But these seemed minor difficulties when balanced against the fact that Little R.L. gained nearly a hundred yards a game his freshman year.

The next fall, the shit-shoveling and the old man's attitude seemed easier to bear. Then when Benbow casually let slip that he had once dealt and played poker professionally, R.L.'s watery blue eyes suddenly glistened with greed, and the Sunday portion of Benbow's bargain became both easier and more complicated. Not that the old man needed him to cheat. R. L. Dark always won. The only times the old man signaled him to deal seconds was to give hands to his competitors to keep them in the game so the old man could skin them even deeper.

The brutal and dangerous monotony of Benbow's life continued, controlled and hopeful until the fall of Little R.L.'s junior year when everything came apart. Then back together with a terrible rush. A break, a dislocation, and a connection.

On the Saturday afternoon after Little R.L. broke the state rushing record the night before, the teenage girl stopped chuckling long enough to ask a question. "How long you have to go to college, Coach, to figure out how to scoot pig shit off concrete with a fire hose?"

When she laughed, Benbow finally asked, "Who the fuck are you, honey?"

"Mrs. R. L. Dark, Senior," she replied, the perfect arch of her nose in the air, "that's who." And Benbow looked at her for the first time, watched the thrust of her hard, marvelous body naked beneath the thin fabric of her cheap dress.

Then Benbow tried to make conversation with Mona Sue, made the mistake of asking Mona Sue why she wore rubber boots. "Hookworms," she said, pointing at his sockless feet in old Nikes. *Jesus*, he thought. Then *Jesus wept* that night as he watched the white worms slither through his dark, bloody stool. Now he knew what the old man had been laughing about.

On Sunday a rich Mexican rancher tried to cover one of R.L.'s raises with a Rolex, then the old man insisted on buying the fifteen-thousand-dollar watch with five K cash, and when he opened the small safe set in the floor of the trailer's kitchen, Benbow glimpsed the huge pile of banded stacks of one-hundred-dollar bills that filled the safe.

The next Friday night Little R.L. broke his own rushing record with more than a quarter left in the game, which was good because in the fourth quarter the turf gave way under his right foot, which then slid under a pursuing tackle. Benbow heard the *pop* all the way from the sidelines as the kid's knee dislocated.

Explaining to R.L. that a bargain was a bargain, no matter what happened with the kid's knee, the next day Benbow went about his chores just long enough to lure Mona Sue into a feed shed and out of her dress. But not her rubber boots. Benbow didn't care. He just fucked her. The revenge he planned on R. L. Dark a frozen hell in his heart. But the soft hunger of her mouth and the touch of her astonishing body—diamond-hard nipples, fast-twitch cat muscle slithering under human skin, her cunt like a silken bag of rich, luminous seed pearls suspended in heavenly fucking fire—destroyed his hope of vengeance. Now he simply wanted her. No matter the cost.

Two months later, just as her pregnancy began to show, Benbow cracked the safe with a tablespoon of nitro, took all the money, and they ran.

Although he was sure Mona Sue still dreamed, she'd lost her audience. Except for the wrangler, who still watched her as if she were some heathen idol. But every time she tried to talk to the dark cowboy, the old man pinched her thigh with horny fingers so hard it left blood blisters.

Their mornings were much different now. They all went to the hot water. The doctor slept on a poolside bench behind Mona Sue who sat on the side of the pool, her feet dangling in the water, her blotched thighs exposed, and her eyes as vacant as her half-smile. R. L. Dark, Curly, and Bald Bill, wearing cutoffs and cheap T-shirts, stood neck-deep in the steamy water, loosely surrounding Benbow, anchored by his plastic-shrouded cast, which loomed like a giant boulder under the heavy water.

A vague sense of threat, like an occasional sharp sniff of sulphur, came off the odd group and kept the other guests at a safe distance, and the number of guests declined every day as the old man rented each cabin and room at the lodge as it came empty. The rich German twins who owned the place didn't seem to care who paid for their cocaine.

During the first few days, nobody had much bothered to speak to Benbow, not even to ask where he had hidden the money. The pain in his foot had retreated to a dull ache, but the itch under the cast had become unbearable. One morning, the doctor had taken pity on him and searched the kitchen drawers for something for Benbow to use to scratch beneath the cast, finally coming up with a cheap shish kebab skewer. Curly and Bald Bill had examined the thin metal stick as if it might be an Arkansas toothpick or a bowie knife, then laughed and let Benbow have it. He kept it holstered in his cast, waiting, scratching the itch. And a deep furrow in the rear of the cast.

Then one morning as they stood silent and safe in the pool, a storm cell drifted slowly down the mountain to fill the canyon with swirling squalls of thick, wet snow, the old man raised his beak into the flakes and finally spoke: "I always meant to come back to this country," he said.

"What?"

Except for the wrangler slowly gathering damp towels and a dark figure in a hooded sweatshirt and sunglasses standing inside the bar, the pool and the deck had emptied when the snow began. Benbow had been watching the snow gather in the dark waves of Mona Sue's hair as she tried to catch a spinning flake on her pink tongue. Even as he faced death, she still stirred the banked embers glowing in Benbow's crotch.

"During WW Two," the old man said softly, "I got in some trouble over at Fort Chaffee—stuck a noncom with a broomstick—so the Army sent me up here to train with the Tenth Mountain. Stupid assholes thought it was some kinda punishment. Always meant to come back someday. . . ."

But Benbow watched the cold wind ripple the stolid surface of the hot water as the snowflakes melted into it. The rising steam became a thick fog.

"I always liked it," Benbow said, glancing up at the mountain as it appeared and disappeared behind the roiling clouds of snow. "Great hunting weather," he added. "There's a little herd of elk bedded just behind that first ridge." As his keepers' eyes followed his upslope, he drifted slowly through the fog toward Mona Sue's feet aimlessly stirring the water. "If you like it so much, you old bastard, maybe you should buy it."

"Watch your tongue, boy," Curly said as he cuffed Benbow on the head. Benbow stumbled closer to Mona Sue.

"I just might do that, son," the old man said, cackling, "just to piss you off. Not that you'll be around to be pissed off."

"So what the fuck are we hanging around here for?" Benbow asked, turning on the old man, which brought him even closer to Mona Sue.

The old man paused as if thinking. "Well, son, we're waitin' for that baby. If'n that baby has red hair and you tell us where you hid the money, we'll just take you home, kill you easy, then feed you to the hogs."

"And if it doesn't have red hair, since I'm not about to tell you where to find the money?"

"We'll just find a hungry sow, son, and feed you to her," the old man said, "startin' with your good toes."

Everybody laughed then: R. L. Dark threw back his head and howled; the hulks exchanged high fives and higher giggles; and Benbow collapsed underwater. Even Mona Sue chuckled deep in her throat. Until Benbow jerked her off the side of the pool. Then she choked. The poor girl had never learned to swim.

Before either the old man or his bodyguards could move, though, the dark figure in the hooded sweatshirt burst through the bar door in a quick, limping dash and dove into the pool, then lifted the struggling girl onto the deck and knelt beside her while enormous amounts of steaming water poured from her nose and mouth before she began breathing. Then the figure swept the hood from the flaming red hair and held Mona Sue close to his chest.

"Holy shit, boy," the old man asked unnecessarily as Bald Bill helped him out of the pool. "What the fuck you doin' here?"

"Goddammit, baby, lemme go," Mona Sue screamed, "it's a-coming!"

Which roused the doctor from his sleepy rest. And the wrangler from his work. Both of them covered the wide wooden bench with dry towels, upon which Little R.L. gently placed Mona Sue's racked body. Curly scrambled out of the pool, warning Benbow to stay put, and joined the crowd of men around her sudden and violent contractions. Bald Bill helped the old man into his overalls and the pistol's thong as Little R.L. helped the doctor hold Mona Sue's body, arched with sudden pain, on the bench.

"Oh, Lordy me!" she screamed, "it's tearin' me up!"

"Do somethin', you pissant," the old man said to the wiry doctor, then slapped him soundly.

Benbow slipped to the side of the pool, holding on to the edge with one hand as he dug frantically at the cast with the other. Bits of plaster of paris and swirls of blood rose through the hot water. Then it was off, and the skewer in his hand. He planned to roll out of the pool, drive the sliver of metal through the old man's kidney, then grab the Webley. After that, he'd call the shots.

But life should have taught him not to plan.

As Bald Bill helped his boss into the coat, he noticed Benbow at the edge of the pool and stepped over to him. Bald Bill saw the bloody cast floating at Benbow's chest. "What the fuck?" he said, kneeling down to reach for him.

Benbow drove the thin shaft of metal with the strength of a lifetime of disappointment and rage into the bottom of Bald Bill's jaw, up through the root of his tongue, then up through his soft palate, horny brainpan, mushy gray matter, and the thick bones of his skull. Three inches of the skewer poked like a steel finger bone out of the center of his bald head.

Bald Bill didn't make a sound. Just blinked once dreamily, smiled, then stood up. After a moment, swaying, he began to walk in small air-less circles at the edge of the deck until Curly noticed his odd behavior.

"Bubba?" he said as he stepped over to his brother.

Benbow leapt out of the water; one hand grabbed an ankle and the other dove up the leg of Curly's trunks to grab his nut sack and jerk the giant toward the pool. Curly's grunt and the soft clunk of his head against the concrete pool edge was lost as Mona Sue delivered the child with a deep sigh, and the old man shouted boldly, "Goddamn, it's a girl! A black-headed girl!"

Benbow had slithered out of the pool and limped halfway to the old man's back as he watched the doctor lay the baby on Mona Sue's heaving chest. "Shit fire and save the matches," the old man said, panting deeply as if the labor had been his.

Little R.L. turned and jerked his father toward him by the front of his coat, hissing, "Shut the fuck up, old man." Then he shoved him violently away, smashing the old man's frail body into Benbow's shoulder. Something cracked inside the old man's body, and he sank to his knees, snapping at the cold air with his bloody beak like a gut-shot turtle. Benbow grabbed the pistol's thong off his neck before the old man tumbled dead into the water.

Benbow cocked the huge pistol with a soft metallic click, then his sharp bark of laughter cut through the snowy air like a gunshot. Everything slowed to a stop. The doctor finished cutting the cord. The wrangler's hands held a folded towel under Mona Sue's head. Little R.L. held his gristled body halfway into a mad charge. Bald Bill stopped his aimless circling long enough to fall into the pool. Even Mona Sue's cooing sighs died. Only the cold wind moved, whipping the steamy fog across the pool as the snowfall thickened.

Then Mona Sue screamed, "No!" and broke the frozen moment.

The bad knee gave Benbow time to get off a round. The heavy slug took Little R.L. in the top of his shoulder, tumbled through his chest, and exited just above his kidney in a shower of blood, bone splinters, and lung tissue, and dropped him like a side of beef on the deck. But the round had already gone on its merry way through the sternum of the doctor as if he weren't there. Which, in moments, he wasn't.

Benbow threw the pistol joyfully behind him, heard it splash in the pool, and hurried to Mona Sue's side. As he kissed her blood-spattered face, she moaned softly. He leaned closer, but only mistook her moans for passion until he understood what she was saying. Over and over. The way she once called his name. And Little R.L.'s. Maybe even the old man's. "Cowboy, Cowboy, Cowboy," she whispered.

Benbow wasn't even mildly surprised when he felt the arm at his throat or the blade tickle his short ribs. "I took you for a backstabber," he said, "the first time I laid eyes on your sorry ass."

"Just tell me where the money is, *old man*," the wrangler whispered, "and you can die easy."

"You can have the money," Benbow sobbed, trying for one final break, "just leave me the woman." But the flash of scorn in Mona Sue's eyes was the only answer he needed. "Fuck it," Benbow said, almost laughing, "let's do it the hard way."

Then he fell backward onto the hunting knife, driving the blade to the hilt above his short ribs before the wrangler could release the handle. He stepped back in horror as Benbow stumbled toward the hot waters of the pool.

At first, the blade felt cold in Benbow's flesh, but the flowing blood quickly warmed it. Then he eased himself into the hot water and lay back against its compassionate weight like the old man the wrangler had called him. The wrangler stood over Benbow, his eyes like coals glowing through the fog and thick snow.

Mona Sue stepped up beside the wrangler, Benbow's baby whimpering at her chest, snow melting on her shoulders.

"Fuck it," Benbow whispered, drifting now, "it's in the air conditioner."

"Thanks, old man," Mona Sue said, smiling.

"Take care," Benbow whispered, thinking, *This is the easy part*, then leaned farther back into the water, sailing on the pool's wind-riffled, snow-shot surface, eyes closed, happy in the hot, heavy water, moving his hands slightly to stay afloat, his fingers tangled in dark, bloody streams, the wind pushing him toward the cool water at the far end of the pool, blinking against the soft cold snow, until his tired body slipped, unwatched, beneath the hot water to rest.

DO WITH ME WHAT YOU WILL

Joyce Carol Oates

"Then what?"

"I got very . . . I got very excited and. . . ."

"Did she look at you?"

"Yeah. And it made me want to. . . . It made me want to go after her, you know, like grab hold of her. . . . Because she was thinking the same thing. She was afraid of me and she was thinking. . . ."

"She kept looking back at you?"

"Oh, yes, she did. Yes. Back over her shoulder. I got so excited that I just followed her. I mean I must of followed her, I don't even remember my legs going. . . .It was just her, looking back over her shoulder at me, like checking on me, and me following her, just her and me and nobody else on the street. I never saw nobody else. I just saw her ahead of me, but I didn't even see her face, I was too excited."

"When did she start to run?"

"Oh, my, I don't know, I . . . I guess it was by . . . uh . . . that drugstore there, what is it, some drugstore that. . . . Well, it was closed, of course, because of the late hour. Uh . . . some name you see all the time. . . ."

"Cunningham's."

"Oh, yes, yes. Cunningham's. But I don't know if I really saw that,

Mr. Morrissey, so clear as that . . . any place at all . . . like I know the neighborhood upward and downward, but I wasn't watching too close at the time. Because I had my eye on her, you know, to see she couldn't get away. She was like a fox would be, going fast all of a sudden, and damn scared. That makes them clever, when they're scared."

"Then she started to run? Where was this?"

"The other side of the drugstore . . . across a street. . . I don't know the names, but they got them written down, the police. They could tell you."

"I don't want any information from them, I want it from you. The intersection there is St. Ann and Ryan Boulevard. Is that where she started running?"

"If that's what they said. . . . "

"That's what she said. She told them. When she started to run, did you run?"

"Yeah."

"Right away?"

"Yeah, right away."

"Did you start running before she did?"

"No. I don't know."

"But only after she started running. . . ?"

"I think so."

"Did you? After she started running, but not before?"

"Yeah."

"Were there any cars waiting for the light to change at that intersection?"

"I don't know . . . I was in a frenzy. . . . You know how you get, when things happen fast, and you can't pay attention. . . . I . . . I saw her running and I thought to myself, *You ain't going to get away!* I was almost ready to laugh or to scream out, it was so. . . . It was so high-strung a few minutes for me. . . ."

"Did she run across the street, or out into the street?"

"She . . . uh . . . she started screaming. . . . That was when she started screaming. But it didn't scare me off. She ran out into the middle of the street. . . . yeah, I can remember that now . . . out into the middle, where it was very wide. . . . I remember some cars waiting for the light to change, now. But I didn't pay much attention to them then."

"Then what happened?"

"Well, uh, she got out there and something like, like her shoe was broke, the heel was snapped . . . and she was yelling at this guy in a car, that waited for the light to change but then couldn't get away because she was in front of the car. And . . . uh . . . that was a . . . a Pontiac Tempest, a nice green car. . . . And it was a man and a woman, both white. She was yelling for them to let her in. But when she ran around to the side of the car, and grabbed the door handle, well, it was locked, of course, and she couldn't get it open and I was just waiting by the curb to see how it would go . . . and the guy, he just pressed down that accelerator and got the hell out of there. Man, he shot off like a rocket. I had to laugh. And she looked over her shoulder at me where I was waiting, you know, and. . . ."

"Yes, then what?"

"Well, then. Then I, uh, I got her. There wasn't anything to it, she was pretty tired by then, and . . . I just grabbed her and dragged her back somewhere, you know, the way they said . . . she told them all the things that happened. . . . I can't remember it too clear myself, because I was crazylike, like laughing because I was so high, you know. I wasn't scared, either. I felt like a general or somebody in a movie, where things go right, like I came to the edge of a country or a whole continent, you know, and naturally I wouldn't want the movie to end just yet. . . ."

"But you don't remember everything that happened?"

"I don't know. Maybe. But no, I guess not, I mean. . . . You know how you get in a frenzy. . . ."

"You signed a confession."

"Yeah, I s'pose so. I mean, I wanted to cooperate a little. I figured they had me anyway, and anyway I was still so high, I couldn't come in for a landing. I wasn't scared or anything and felt very good. So I signed it."

"Did they tell you you had the right to call an attorney?"

"Yeah, maybe."

"You had the right to counsel. . . ? Did the police tell you that?"

"*Right to counsel.* . . . Yeah, I heard something like that. I don't know. Maybe I was a little scared. My mouth was bleeding down my neck."

"From being struck?"

"Before they got the handcuffs on me. I was trying to get away. So somebody got me in the face."

"Did it hurt?"

"No, naw. I didn't feel it. I started getting wet, then one of the policemen, in the car, he wiped me off with a rag, because it was getting on him. I don't know if it hurt or not. Later on it hurt. The tooth was loose and I fooled around with it, wiggling it, in jail, and took it out myself; so I wouldn't swallow it or something at night. My whole face swoll up afterward. . . ."

"So you waived your right to counsel?"

"I don't know. I guess so. If they said that, then I did."

"Why did you waive your right to counsel?"

"I don't know."

"Were you pressured into it?"

"What? I don't know. I . . . uh . . . I was mixed up and a little high. . . ."

"Did you say, maybe, that you didn't have any money for a lawyer?"

"Uh . . . yeah. In fact, I did say that, yeah. I did."

"You did?"

"I think so."

"You did say that."

"I think I said it. . . ."

"You told them you couldn't afford a lawyer."

"Yeah."

"And did they say you had the right to counsel anyway? Did they say that if you were indigent, counsel would be provided for you?"

"Indigent. . . ?"

"Yes, indigent. If you didn't have money for a lawyer, you'd be given one anyway. Didn't they explain that to you?"

"What was that. . . ? *In. . .*?"

"Indigent. They didn't explain that to you, did they?"

"About what?"

"If you were indigent, counsel would be provided for you."

"Indigent. . . ."

"Indigent. Did they use that word? Do you remember it?"

"Well, uh . . . Lots of words got used. . . . I . . ."

"Did they use the word *indigent*? Did they explain your situation to you?"

"What situation. . . ? I was kind of mixed up and excited and. . . ."

"And they had been banging you around, right? Your tooth was knocked out . . . your face was cut . . . your face swelled up. . . . So you signed a confession, right? After Mrs. Donner made her accusation, you agreed with her, you signed a confession for the police, in order to cooperate with them and not be beaten any more. I think that was a very natural thing to do under the circumstances. Do you know which one of the police hit you?"

"Oh, they all did, they was all scrambling around after me. . . . Damn lucky I didn't get shot. I was fearless, I didn't know shit how close I came to getting killed. Jesus. Never come in for a landing till the next day, I was so high. Pulled the tooth out by the roots and never felt it. But later on it hurt like hell. . . . I couldn't remember much."

"Were you examined by a doctor?"

"No."

"A dentist?"

"Hell, no."

"Let's see your mouth. . . . What about those missing teeth on the side there? What happened to them?"

"Them, they been gone a long time."

"It looks raw there."

"Yeah, well, I don't know. . . . It looks what?"

"It looks sore."

"Well, it might be sore, I don't know. My gums is sore sometimes. They bleed sometimes by themselves."

"What happened to your mouth?"

"I got kicked there. Two, three years back."

"Your mother told me you'd had some trouble back in your neighborhood, off and on, and I see you were arrested for some incidents, but what about some trouble with a girl. . . ? Did you ever get into trouble with a girl?"

"What girl?"

"Your mother says it was a girl in the neighborhood."

"Yeah."

"Yeah what?"

"Yeah, it was a girl, a girl. She never made no trouble for me. Her father was out after me, but he got in trouble himself. So I don't know, I mean, it passed on by. She was. . . . She didn't want no trouble, it was her old man tried to make a fuss. What's my mother been telling you, that old news? That's damn old news; that's last year's news."

"You weren't arrested for rape, were you?"

"No. I tole you, it was only her father; then he had to leave town."

"Before this you've been arrested twice, right? And put on probation twice? And no jail sentence."

"That's a way of looking at it."

"How do you look at it?"

"I hung around a long time waiting to get out. . . . waiting for the trial. . . . You know, the trial or the hearing or whatever it was. Then the judge let me go anyway."

"You waited in jail, you mean."

"Sure I waited in jail."

"Why couldn't you get bond?"

"My momma said the hell with me."

"According to the record, you were arrested for theft twice. You pleaded guilty. What about the assault charges?"

"From roughing somebody up? Well, uh, that stuff got put aside. There was a deal made."

"So you got off on probation twice."

"Yeah, that worked out OK."

"You were arrested for the first time when you were nineteen years old, right?"

"If that's what it says."

"That isn't bad. Nineteen years old . . . that's a pretty advanced age for a first offense. . . . And no jail sentence, just probation. Now, tell me, is all this accurate: Your father served a five-year sentence for armed robbery, right?—then he left Detroit? Your mother has been on AFDC from 1959 until the present, right? You have four brothers and two sisters, two children are still living at home with your mother, and your sister has a baby herself?—and you don't live at home, but nearby somewhere? And you give her money when you can?"

"Yeah."

"It says here you're unemployed. Were you ever employed?"

"Sure I been employed."

"It isn't down here. What kind of job did you have?"

"How come it ain't down there?"

"I don't know. What kind of job did you have?"

"Look, you write it in yourself, Mr. Morrissey, because I sure was employed. . . . I call that an insult. I was kind of a delivery boy off and on, I could get references to back me up."

"This is just a photostat copy of your file from Welfare; I can't write anything in. . . . Where did you work?"

"Some store that's closed up now."

"Whose was it?"

"I disremember the exact name."

"You're unemployed at the present time, at the age of twenty-three?"

"Well, I can't help that. I . . . Mr. Morrissey, you going to make a deal for me?"

"I won't have to make a deal."

"Huh? Well, that woman is awful mad at me. She's out to get me."

"Don't worry about her."

"In the police station she was half-crazy, she was screaming so. . . . Her clothes was all ripped. I don't remember none of that. The front of her was all blood. Jesus, I don't know, I must of gone crazy or something. . . . When they brought me in, she was already there, waiting, and she took one look at me and started screaming. That was the end."

"She might reconsider, she might think all this over carefully. Don't worry about her. Let me worry about her. In fact, you have no necessary reason to believe that the woman who identified you was the woman you followed and attacked. . . . It might have been another woman. You didn't really see her face. All you know is that she was white, and probably all she knows about her attacker is that he was black. I won't have to make a deal for you. Don't worry about that."

"She's awful mad at me, she ain't going to back down. . . ."

"Let me worry about her. Tell me: How did the police happen to pick you up? Did they have a warrant for your arrest?"

"Hell, no. It was a goddamn asshole accident like a joke. . . . I, uh, I was running away from her, where I left her . . . and . . . and . . . I just run into the side of the squad car. Like that. Was running like hell and run into the side of the car, where it was parked, without no lights on. So they picked me up like that."

"Because you were running, they picked you up, right?"

"I run into the side of their goddamn fucking car."

"So they got out and arrested you?"

"One of them chased me."

"Did he fire a shot?"

"Sure he fired a shot."

"So you surrendered?"

"I hid somewhere, by a cellar window. But they found me. It was just a goddamn stupid accident. . . . Jesus, I don't know. I must of been flying so high, couldn't see the car where it was parked. They had it parked back from the big street, with the lights out. I saw one of them with a paper cup, some coffee that got spilled down his front, when I banged into the door. He was surprised."

"So they brought you into the station and the woman was brought in also, this Mrs. Donner, and she identified you. Is that it? She took one look at you and seemed to recognize you?"

"Started screaming like hell."

"She identified you absolutely, in spite of her hysterical state?"

"I guess so."

"And you admitted attacking her?"

"I guess so."

"Was that really the correct woman, though? This 'Mrs. Donner' who is accusing you of rape?"

"Huh?"

"Could you have identified her?"

"Me? I don't know. No. I don't know."

"Let's go back to the bar. You said there were three women there, all white women. Did they look alike to you, or what?"

"I don't know."

"Did one of them catch your attention?"

"Maybe. I don't know. One of them . . . she kind of was watching me, I thought. They was all horsing around."

"It was very crowded in the bar? And this woman, this particular woman, looked at you. Did she smile at you?"

"They was all laughing, you know, and if they looked around the place, why, it would seem they was smiling. . . . I don't know which one it was. I'm all mixed up on that."

"Would you say that this woman, let's call her 'Mrs. Donner' tem- porarily, this woman was behaving in a way that was provocative? She was looking at you or toward you, and at other men?"

"There was a lot of guys in there, black guys, and some white guys, too. I liked the tone of that place. There was a good feeling there. I wasn't drunk, but. . . ."

"Yes, you were drunk."

"Naw, I was high on my own power, I only had a few drinks."

"You were drunk; that happens to be a fact. That's an important fact. Don't forget it."

"I was drunk. . . ?"

"Yes. You were drunk. And a white woman did smile at you, in a bar on Gratiot; let's say it was this 'Mrs. Donner' who is charging you with rape. Do you know anything about her? No. I'll tell you: She's married, separated from her husband, the husband's whereabouts are unknown, she's been on and off welfare since 1964, she worked for a while at Leonard's Downtown, the department store, and was discharged because she evidently took some merchandise home with her . . . and she's been unemployed since September of last year, but without any visible means of support; no welfare. So she won't be able to account for her means of support since September, if that should come up in court."

"Uh . . . You going to make a deal with them, then?"

"I don't have to make a deal. I told you to let me worry about her. She has to testify against you, and she has to convince a jury that she didn't deserve to be followed by you, that she didn't entice you, she didn't smile at you. She has to convince a jury that she didn't deserve whatever happened to her. . . . She did smile at you?"

"Well, uh, you know how it was . . . a lot of guys crowding around, shifting around. . . . I don't know which one of the women for sure looked at me, there was three of them, maybe they all did . . . or maybe just one . . . or . . . It was confused. Some guys was buying them drinks and I couldn't get too close, I didn't know anybody there. I liked the tone of the place, but I was on the outside, you know? I was having my own party in my head. Then I saw this one woman get mad and put on her coat—"

"A light-colored coat? An imitation-fur coat?"

"Jesus, how do I know? Saw her put her arm in a sleeve. . . ."

"And she walked out? Alone?"

"Yeah. So I . . . I got very jumpy. . . . I thought I would follow her, you know, just see what happens. . . ."

"But you didn't follow her with the intention of committing rape."

"I . . ."

"You wanted to talk to her, maybe? She'd smiled at you and you wanted to talk to her?"

"I don't know if . . ."

"This white woman, whose name you didn't know, had smiled at you. She then left the bar—that is, Carson's Tavern—at about midnight, completely alone, unescorted, and she walked out along the street. Is this true?"

"Yes."

"When did she notice that you were following her?"

"Right away."

"Then what happened?"

"She started walking faster."

"Did she pause or give any sign to you? You mentioned that she kept looking over her shoulder at you—"

"Yeah."

"Then she started to run?"

"Yeah."

"She tried to get someone to stop, to let her in his car, but he wouldn't. He drove away. She was drunk, wasn't she, and screaming at him?"

"She was screaming. . . ."

"She was drunk, too. That happens to be a fact. You were both drunk, those are facts. This 'Mrs. Donner' who is accusing you of rape was drunk at the time. So. . . The driver in the Pontiac drove away and you approached her. Was it the same woman who had smiled at you in the tavern?"

"I think. . . uh. . . . I don't know. . . ."

"She was the woman from the tavern?"

"That got mad and put her coat on? Sure. She walked out. . . ."

"Did all three women more or less behave in the same manner? They were very loud, they'd been drinking, you really couldn't distinguish between them. . . ?"

"I don't know."

"When you caught up to the woman, what did she say to you?"

"Say? Nothing. No words."

"She was screaming?"

"Oh, yeah."

"What did you say to her?"

"Nothing."

"Could you identify her?"

"I . . . uh. . . . That's where I get mixed up."

"Why?"

"I don't remember no face to her."

"Why not?"

"Must not of looked at it."

"Back in the bar, you didn't look either?"

"Well, yes . . . but I . . . It's all a smear, like. Like a blur."

"This 'Mrs. Donner' says you threatened to kill her. Is that true?"

"If she says so. . . ."

"No, hell. Don't worry about what she says. What do *you* say?"

"I don't remember."

"*Lay still or I'll kill you.* Did you say that?"

"Is that what they have down?"

"Did you say it? *Lay still or I'll kill you?*"

"That don't sound like me."

"You didn't say anything to her, did you?"

"When? When we was fighting?"

"At any time."

"I don't remember."

"In the confusion of struggling, it isn't likely you said anything to her, is it?—anything so distinct as that? Or maybe it was another man, another black man, who attacked this 'Mrs. Donner' and she's confus-ing him with you. . . ?"

"Uh . . ."

"Did you intend to kill her?"

"No."

"What did you have in mind, when you followed her out of the tavern?"

"Oh, you know . . . I was kind of high-strung. . . ."

"She had smiled at you, so you thought she might be friendly? A pretty white woman like that, only twenty-nine years old, with her hair fixed up and a fancy imitation-fur coat, who had smiled at you, a stranger, in a bar. . . ? You thought she might be friendly, wasn't that it?"

"Friendly? Jesus! I never expected no friendship, that's for sure."

"Well, put yourself back in that situation. Don't be so sure. If a white woman smiled at you, and you followed her out onto the street, it would be logical you might expect her to be friendly toward you. Keep your mind clear. You don't have to believe what other people tell you about yourself; you don't have to believe that you assaulted that woman just because she says you did. Things aren't so simple. Did you expect her to fight you off?"

"Don't know."

"If she hadn't fought you, there wouldn't be any crime committed would there? She resisted you, she provoked you into a frenzy. . . . But don't think about that. I'll think about that angle. I'm the one who's going to question Mrs. Donner, and then we'll see who's guilty of what. . . . But one important thing: Why didn't you tell the police that you really didn't recognize the woman, yourself?"

"Huh? Jesus, they'd of been mad as hell—"

"Yes, they would have been mad, they might have beaten you some more. You were terrified of a further beating. So, of course, you didn't protest, you didn't say anything. Because she's a white woman and you're black. Isn't that the real reason?"

"I don't know."

"There weren't any black men in the station. You were the only black man there. So you thought it would be the safest, most prudent thing to confess to everything, because this white woman and the white police had you, they had you, and you considered yourself fair game. And already you'd been beaten, your mouth was bleeding, and you didn't know you had the right to an attorney, to any help at all. You were completely isolated. They could do anything to you they wanted. . . . Your instincts told you to go along with them, to cooperate. Nobody can blame you for that: that's how you survived. Does any of this sound familiar to you?"

"Some kind of way, yes. . . . Yes, I think so."

"And the police demonstrated their antagonism toward you, their automatic assumption of your guilt, even though the woman who accused you of rape was a probable prostitute, a woman of very doubtful reputation who led you on, who enticed you out into the street . . . and then evidently changed her mind, or became frightened when she saw how excited you were. Is that it? Why do you think she identified you so quickly, why was she so certain?"

"Must of seen my face."

"How did she see your face, if you didn't see hers?"

"I saw hers but didn't take it in, you know, I kind of blacked out . . . she was fighting me off and that drove me wild . . . it was good luck she stopped, or . . . or something else might of happened. . . . You know how frenzied you get. There was a streetlight there, and I thought to myself, *She ain't going to forget me.*"

"Why not?"

"Gave her a good look at my face. My face is important to me."

HERO

Jeremiah Healy

I

FRANK ROSSI SAT IN HIS SWIVEL CHAIR by the telephone table at the gallery end of the jury box, watching the "real cop" testify from the witness stand. As a court officer, Frank was by statute entitled to police powers himself, like the right to carry the Glock 17 on his right hip. And he went to the firing range every Friday to make sure he could hit what he aimed at. Because that same statute also said a bailiff could arrest a perp if he saw something illegal go down on the street. Only problem was, any time Frank'd be on the street, he'd be wearing civvies instead of his uniform, and fat chance Angela Rossi's only son would risk his life to bring in some scumbag.

You can picture yourself as Sylvester Stallone playing Rambo, or even Rocky, but when you're more like Sly as the fat sheriff in *Copland*, who'd you be kidding, huh?

Frank liked being a court officer well enough, though, despite the low pay. After all, it was an eight-to-four job with plenty of dead space in it, and no cameras in the courtroom to catch a poor civil servant on the doze. Most of the dead space came from a trial being less like your slick, bang-bang movie and more like a theater play the actors and all were still rehearsing, with lots of stops and delays in the action. If endless testimony and truckloads of documents counted as "action." But

Frank thought the different people he got to see made up for all the bullshit.

Take this trial, for instance. *Commonwealth vs. Dennis Doyle.* Or Dennis "the Menace," which was Doyle's mob nickname. Frank actually enjoyed seeing the Irish Mafia get roasted for a change. Doyle himself was a big guy, kind of role you'd give Brian Dennehy with the broad shoulders, beefy face, and wavy hair. Every tooth in his head perfect from birth or dentistry, Doyle had to be in his sixties trying real hard not to look a day past fifty, and pulling it off. Of course, he pulled off a lot of things, running most of the rackets on the South Shore, but according to the prosecution, the Menace had made the mistake of whacking somebody by his own hand in Frank's county. Doyle claimed he was framed, which was par for the course, given that somebody had to have pumped three slugs into the victim. Frank had seen the crime-scene photos of the body when they were put into evidence and passed around the jury. Not pretty pictures, either, and even Dennis the Menace with all his money got denied bail on the charge back at his arraignment.

Which was about all the poor prosecutor had won, far as Frank could tell. Assistant D.A. Ellen Duchesne was short and fat, with a whiny voice that made her seem not exactly up to the task at hand. You'd cast her as Rhoda's sister from that old sitcom, feeling sorry for her every time she opened her mouth.

Mainly, though, you'd feel sorry for her because of the tap dance the defense attorney was doing on the prosecution's evidence. Frank had to admit, he ever got in felony trouble himself, be nice to afford Aaron Weinberg in there pitching for him. Medium height with a beard, the guy was kind of a bald Al Pacino. Sharp dresser, yeah, but sharp as a tack, too. And genuinely "courtly" to everybody, not like those assholes on O.J.'s "dream team."

Weinberg managed to look noble even when he was talking with Doyle's number-two guy, one of those thirtyish, executive types with a quarterback's build that every mob seemed to be bringing up as the next generation. Edward was his name, but Frank thought of him as just "Eddie," account of the guy reminded him of Eddie Haskell from the old *Leave It to Beaver* show. Doyle's Eddie would sit in the first row of the gallery, directly behind the defense table, though he was gone from the courtroom a lot, probably running errands for his boss. Eddie had the good fortune not to be indicted for this particular homicide, as he was driving Mrs. Doyle home from some kind of charity function at the time.

Which brought Frank to the most interesting part of the case, at least from his standpoint. Mrs. Lisa Doyle. About five-six in sensible heels, but with great legs that seemed to vibrate as she walked down the center aisle of the courtroom. She always took the gallery bench right behind Weinberg, so the Menace could see her by turning only halfway in the defendant's chair. And so the loving couple could kind of clasp hands briefly over the bar enclosure rail whenever the two other bailiffs brought Doyle to or from the defense table. Maybe thirty or so, Lisa didn't dress to show off the rest of what Frank figured to be a dynamite figure under the clothes, but she couldn't do much to hide that face, even when she was bringing a dark hankie up to it—just so— to dab at her eyes from time to time. Eyes that hung back a little above cheekbones like Michelle Pfeiffer's, only with longish black hair, like Michelle wore hers in *Married to the Mob*. Which made Frank laugh a little, he had to admit.

Here Lisa Doyle reminds you of your favorite actress in that movie, and the poor broad actually *is* married to the mob.

Then Frank Rossi caught himself staring at her because he suddenly realized she was sending him a smile. Kind of a warm, dreamy one, which Frank held on to almost too long. Almost long enough for her husband to maybe turn sideways a little and notice. Which thank Christ he didn't, especially since, with Aaron Weinberg earning his money, Dennis the Menace was probably gonna walk out of the courtroom a free man.

II

In the bailiffs' locker room, Frank changed from his uniform to a flannel shirt and blue jeans. The jeans were loose enough at the waist to let him stick the Glock over his right hip under the shirt, which his late mother always thought looked sloppy but which made Frank feel a lot more secure. After he was done changing clothes, Frank left the courthouse through the employee's entrance, thankfully spared the "anti-terrorist" arch of metal detector that visitors had to go through on the other side of the building.

Hitting the open-air parking lot, he got into the old wreck of a Buick that had been his mom's and started the usual ritual. Drive to a bar, have a few pops while catching part of a ballgame on the tube, Monday Night Football that October evening. Then stop off at the video store to return last night's selection and pick up a new one to watch later in his apartment. From bed, fantasizing the VCR was letting him pull back the sheets for the best-looking woman in the flick. Frank saw a lot of guys renting the hard-core porn tapes, but half the bimbos in them were stone-ugly, and the other half were dense as a fucking post, the way they talked, if the director let them talk at all.

No, Frank preferred the real thing, somebody with a genuine personality. Kathleen Turner in *Body Heat* or Sharon Stone in *Basic Instinct*, if he was into flashy and dangerous. Sandra Bullock for good fun, Winona Ryder for sensitive—

Whoa, boy. Pay attention to the traffic. Plenty of time to make up your mind after you're on the corner stool a while.

And it was a while, sitting on that corner stool at the bar, before Frank noticed the blonde over in the booth, all by herself. She was wearing tinted glasses and a bulky turtleneck. He watched two guys try their luck, neither getting as far as sliding onto the bench across from her. Hard to tell much about the broad with the shades and sweater, but there was something about the way she was holding her head that rang a bell. She even looked over at him, more than a couple times, almost like that—

Hey, who you kidding now? You got Doyle's wife on the brain. Go back to your ballgame.

Which Frank did, for one more beer before leaving the change on the bartop and going out the door.

He didn't recognize the voice behind him because he'd never heard her yell before.

"Frank, you want to wait up?"

He stopped and turned. The blonde, with a walk he did recognize.

Frank looked around the block nervously. "The hell you think you're doing?"

"Trying to talk with you." Lisa was less than an arm's length away now, her tone conversational. "Okay?"

Frank didn't think it was, but he couldn't tell her so.

She said, "I've been watching you in that courtroom for a week now. Found out your name, put on this wig and glasses, and followed you to that bar back there."

"Why?" was all Frank could manage.

"My husband. Aaron thinks he's going to get off on this murder charge."

Frank thought, "Aaron," not "my husband's lawyer."

Lisa said, "And I think he's right."

So did Frank, but what did that matter?

She leaned a little closer. "I can't stand being married to Dennis anymore, Frank."

He began to turn away. "You want a divorce, find your own lawyer."

Lisa touched his arm. Didn't grab it or even the shirt. Just a touch, nails long and pink. Frank felt something like electricity ripple through him.

All the way through him.

Lisa said, "I don't want to get divorced, Frank. I want to be widowed."

"You're talking crazy now."

"I'm not crazy, but I will be if I have to spend another night with Dennis. He's a pig, Frank. And I need somebody to take him out of my life."

"I don't do murder." Frank turned away. Partly to get away, sure, but partly—mostly—to see if Lisa Doyle would touch him again.

She did, and it stopped him because she picked a slightly different spot on his arm for her fingers.

Same feeling though.

Lisa said, "I can offer you money, Frank. And lots of it, once Dennis is dead."

"Okay, that's crazy just as it stands," Frank thinking he was sounding perfectly reasonable. "You expect me to kill a guy—a goddamned mobster—without being paid for it up front?"

That dreamy, Michelle Pfeiffer smile from the courtroom. "I've come up with a way to make it worth your while. I'm going to be staying at our beach house on the shore tomorrow night." Suddenly she was tucking a folded piece of paper into his shirt pocket. "That's the address, with my little diagram for parking at a shopping center five blocks away, so nobody'll notice your car. This time of year, none of our neighbors use their houses during the week."

Frank said the first thing that popped into his head. "What about your security?"

"Security?"

"That Eddie guy or his goons?"

The dreamy smile. "You watch too many movies, Frank."

Lisa Doyle walked away. Frank stood where she'd left him, following her with his eyes until she got into a silver Mercedes sports coupe and drove out of sight.

That's when he said to himself that he'd think about it. Just think about it.

But before heading north to his apartment, Frank Rossi stopped at the video store and rented a copy of *Married to the Mob*.

III

That next Tuesday, in the courtroom, Frank sat in his chair at the end of the jury box and watched Lisa Doyle. When he realized he had to stop watching her, he turned toward the witness stand and thought about watching her.

Absently, Frank felt sorry for Ellen Duchesne, her whiny voice botching the direct examination of a crime lab techie who'd run some tests on fibers found at the homicide scene. Just as Aaron Weinberg began slicing and dicing the techie on cross-examination, Eddie the number-two guy came in the courtroom, waiting until the morning recess to confer with Dennis the Menace. The two mobsters leaned toward each other above the bar enclosure like a couple of suburbanites chatting over a picket fence.

Once, when Frank turned back to Lisa, she was staring at him, mouthing the word "tonight."

That's when he turned away again, he thought for good. By the clock on the courtroom wall though, barely three minutes had passed before his eyes strayed over again. And again.

Frank Rossi found himself looking up at the clock often, thinking the hands must be moving backwards, it still seemed so long till four o'clock and quitting time.

After changing in the locker room, Frank tried to follow his usual routine. Walk to the car, drive to the bar, early hockey game on the TV over the top shelf. Midway through the first period and only one beer, though, he found himself going through the door. At the video store, Frank returned *Married to the Mob* and came out onto the sidewalk, breathing hard. Before he was behind the wheel again, Frank knew which way he was going to turn.

South. Toward the shore.

Frank did a drive-by of Lisa Doyle's address at normal speed, nothing to call attention to himself.

It was a saltbox cape with weathered shingles, backing right onto the ocean. Her silver Mercedes coupe, snugged up against a garage door, glittered like a piece of jewelry. Frank could see a couple of lights in the cape, one downstairs, one up. The windows of the surrounding houses stood dark, though, and there were no cars in front of them.

Continuing along the street, Frank found the little shopping center right where Lisa's diagram put it. If nobody else was using the shore houses, enough other folks must be year-rounders, because the lot seemed nearly full, and his Buick could kind of hide in the crowd.

Frank turned off the ignition and sat for a while. Sat until he thought a guy alone in an old wreck might look suspicious.

Then realized that wasn't the reason he wanted to get out of his car.

Frank opened the driver's side door and heaved himself to his feet. After locking up, he started walking the five blocks back toward the house. Started huffing, too, and consciously slowed down.

Hey, you don't want to faint on her stoop, right?

At the cape, Frank moved up the path, the Mercedes to his right now catching some moonlight, the same moonlight that twinkled off the ocean water beyond. He was about to push the button on the jamb when the door itself swung open.

A table lamp deeper in the house turned her into a silhouette, the sheer body stocking the kind he'd seen only on women in mail-order catalogs.

"I've been waiting for you, Frank," said Lisa Doyle in a voice from one of his dreams.

IV

Wednesday morning, Frank Rossi couldn't believe how he felt, even just sitting in his bailiff's chair. Tingling all over, the way a real movie star must feel after a night with a starlet.

Only Lisa Doyle wasn't any kid, and she knew how to do everything perfectly. Not like the porn films he'd rented before growing tired of them, the bimbos looking like they were bored or faking or so obviously coked up it amounted to the same thing. No, Lisa was a . . . a sorceress, taking him to the top once, twice, and even Frank didn't believe the third time.

By the same token, there was no bullshit about her. He was going to enjoy her body and talents only until she got the money to pay him for killing her husband.

And Lisa Doyle had even come up with the perfect way to do that, Frank had to admit.

"So," she said as soon as he arrived for the second night, "let's run through it again."

Lisa had rearranged the dining room chairs in her living room, just like she'd shown him the prior evening. Four of the chairs outlined the courtroom's bar enclosure on either side of its center-aisle gate. One of the chairs represented the first gallery bench, where Lisa had sat throughout the trial, dabbing her eyes with that black hankie.

Now, in the beach house, she pointed to the small revolver she'd laid in Frank's hand. "Let's practice you passing it to me again."

He turned the gun over. "You sure the serial numbers are wiped off?"

"Positive. Dennis always said, 'You need a clean piece, this is the one you use.'"

Frank didn't think he wanted to know why Dennis the Menace would believe his wife might need a "clean piece."

Lisa said, "You've smuggled that through the employee entrance in the morning, where there's no metal detector and you're not searched.

In the locker room, when nobody's watching, you put the gun in the side pocket of your uniform pants with the black hankie around it. Now, go ahead."

"Go ahead what?"

Lisa took a small breath before smiling. "Put the gun in the hankie and everything in your right pocket. Good. Now, make like it's just before court starts. You walk around the chairs like they're that bar fence, and I'll turn away from the gate."

As he had the night before, Frank felt a little silly, but he moved along the two chairs as though they were actually the bar enclosure. Using his left hand, he pushed on the imaginary "gate," stepping into the "center aisle."

Over her shoulder, Lisa said, "That's when I'll turn back around and bump into you, so the gun already has to be in the black hankie and in your hand for me."

"What if I slip up and put a fingerprint on the gun by accident?"

"While it's in your pocket?"

"Or while I'm pulling it out."

"Then just be sure you're the first one to Dennis."

Frank pictured what she meant.

Lisa frowned. "You okay?"

"I'm okay."

"You look kind of—"

"I'm okay, all right? Now what?"

Lisa smiled again, that dreamy . . ."Just like we did last night."

Frank shook his head, but he moved through the living room as though he were walking down the center aisle. After six strides, he said, "Judge'll be out in a minute" to an imaginary person before turning and walking back.

Lisa frowned a little. "You'll look more natural in the real court-room, I think."

Frank "opened" the gate again and approached his usual "swivel chair" at the gallery end of the jury box.

"And besides," she waved at the surrounding walls, "there won't be any cameras to catch it anyway."

In the Doyles' living room, Frank sat down in the chair that was sup-posed to be his own.

"After that," said Lisa, "all we have to do is wait till the morning break, and—"

"Recess."

"What?"

"The morning recess, the judge calls it."

"Fine." That smile. "When she says it's time for the morning recess, you say 'All rise' like any other day. Then I lean over the bar rail to Dennis, and I push the gun into his hand."

"What if that Eddie guy is there?"

"Half the time he isn't."

"He might see you, though."

"Don't worry about it."

"Or Weinberg. He'll be right there, too."

"Frank," a little impatience maybe creeping through the smile. "I'll pass the thing so nobody sees me."

"But without leaving any prints on it."

"What the hankie's for, remember?" Lisa closed her eyes a moment. "That's when I scream, 'Dennis, no!'"

"And I yell 'Gun, gun, gun!'"

Lisa stopped, a hand rubbing the ear closest to Frank. "That's how you're going to do it, three times like that?"

"It's the way they trained us."

"Fine, so that's what you'll do. And then . . . ?"

"Then . . ." Frank hesitated until the dreamiest smile yet about melted him. "Then I pull my Glock and shoot him."

"Just 'shoot' him?"

Another hesitation. "Kill him."

"Say it again."

Frank cleared his throat. "I kill him."

"Try it three times, loud, like when you yell about the gun."

"I kill him, I kill him, I kill him!"

A different smile. "Now you've got the idea."

Afterward, in bed, Lisa said, "You probably should leave soon."

Frank spoke to the ceiling, the sheets still caked to him all over. "When?"

"Say ten minutes. You want to shower, it's—"

"No." Frank shifted a little, but didn't get any more comfortable. "I mean, when do you think we'll do it?"

"Pretty soon. Aaron says he doesn't see that whiny prosecutor having much more to throw at Dennis."

What Frank heard was the "Aaron" part again. "You trust him?"

"Who?"

"Your husband's lawyer."

A sigh. "You've probably seen him in action more than I have, but yeah, I trust his judgment on the trial stuff."

Frank couldn't bring himself to ask anything more about Weinberg.

"Frank?"

"Yeah?"

"Don't worry. You'll be a hero. Believe me, Dennis really killed that guy. Not to mention a dozen others."

Right then, Frank Rossi was thinking less about the people Dennis the Menace Doyle had shot and more about the ones Frank himself hadn't.

V

Thursday morning before court, Frank noticed that Eddie wasn't in the gallery. Doyle himself almost lounged in his chair at the defense table, joking with Aaron Weinberg like a salesman knowing he was going to close a big deal. At the first recess, Frank did a dryrun with Lisa, not actually bumping her in the center aisle, but feeling out the distances and timing.

When the trial resumed, Weinberg started hammering at a Commonwealth "earwitness," as Frank liked to call people who heard something about a crime but didn't actually see the thing go down. By the time Doyle's attorney was done, the witness looked battered, and dumpy Ellen Duchesne looked beaten.

Lisa, on the other hand, looked beautiful. Just before lunch, she acted like she had something in her eye, using the hankie to hide her giving Frank a wink.

And that's when he knew for sure he was going to do it. All the doubts he'd felt—qualms, his late mother would have called them—just seemed to slide away inside his chest, and Frank genuinely relaxed in the swivel chair.

He was going to do it. Less for the money and more for Lisa, to get her free of that arrogant pig.

In fact, you look at it the right way, you're kind of *her* hero, solving this problem she has.

Thursday night, when Lisa opened the front door of the beach house for Frank, she had on a dress instead of lingerie, but it was a different kind of dress than the quiet business ones she wore to court for her husband's trial. This was kind of skimpy, plain black and a little shiny, too. Like silk, maybe.

When Frank stepped into the foyer, he could see the dining room chairs arranged again in the living room. "We gonna do another rehearsal?"

"Passing the gun, you mean?"

"Yeah."

"Later."

"Later?"

"After we go upstairs. I have a treat for you."

Frank could actually feel his knees shaking from excitement as he climbed the steps behind her.

Once in the bedroom, Lisa turned to him. The sheets were already pulled down, the lights muted. Frank kind of liked that she'd dimmed the lights because he knew he didn't have the greatest physique in the world, nothing like a male version of the body on her.

Lisa gave him the dreamy smile, her teeth the brightest things in the room. "Tear off my dress."

That stopped him, but excited him, too. "What?"

"Tear off my dress. "

"I . . . I don't get . . ."

"Frank," reaching for his hand, "you've been a good guy through this so far, and I want you to have something special out of it tonight." She brought his hand up to her neckline. "I want you to tear this thing off me, get to see what I'm wearing underneath."

Frank could feel the silky material, could feel himself swelling below his belt buckle, bigger than he'd ever—

"Come on, Frank. I want you to."

And suddenly, irresistibly, he wanted to as well. He ripped the dress down the side of her body, then across, like a huge letter "L" with the foot kind of diagonal instead of straight.

Which was when he could see that what she was wearing underneath was nothing at all.

"It's tomorrow, right?"

After Frank had spoken the words to the ceiling, he turned away from Lisa and stared at her torn dress on the bedroom carpet.

"How did you know?" she said.

He turned back to the ceiling. "Because after it happens, we don't see each other again except for you giving me the money, and tonight felt kind of like . . ."

"A going-away present?"

Lisa's voice sounded thick to Frank, almost as if she was going to cry.

He said, "Something like that, yeah."

Her voice steadied. "Aaron told us today he doesn't think he has to put on much of a defense case, and for sure not call Dennis to the stand as a witness himself."

"So, if we don't do it at the morning recess—"

"We may not get another chance."

Frank could see it, feel it. Lisa was right.

In an even steadier voice, she said, "Tomorrow you're going to be a hero, Frank. And a week later, you'll be rich to boot."

Frank Rossi was conscious of hearing both things Lisa Doyle told him, but he realized it was only the first part that he cared about.

VI

At five minutes to the morning recess, Eddie the number-two guy still hadn't shown up in the courtroom, and Frank let himself breathe a little easier in his swivel chair. It'd been a piece of cake getting the snubbie revolver wrapped in Lisa's handkerchief through the employee's entrance and, at his locker, into the side pocket of his uniform pants. And Frank had passed it to Lisa at the center aisle so smoothly, he'd felt like a feather as he floated down the aisle, exchanged a stupid crack with another bailiff at the rear of the room, and then walked back to his chair.

When the judge announced the morning recess, Frank stood quickly. Calling out, "All rise," he was aware of everybody else getting to their feet. But then the rest of it played out in a kind of slow motion, like one of those shoot-'em-up scenes from a spaghetti western.

Lisa, her hankie between her hands, leaning over the gallery rail to Dennis Doyle, like she always did. Him taking both of her hands in his, again like always.

Then Lisa jumping back as the two bailiffs casually approached the defendant, her mouth opening, her words splitting the air.

Somewhere between "Dennis" and "no!," Frank was bringing the Glock out of his holster, the two bailiffs jumping back themselves from Lisa's scream. Frank bellowed the magic word "Gun!" three times as he opened fire, the shots making his ears ring.

The first slug struck Dennis Doyle square in the chest, just as the man was looking down at the revolver in his own hand. The second caught him near the left shoulder, knocking the mobster off-center. The third bullet punched Doyle in the throat, carrying him back over his chair and onto the defense table. By now, everybody in the room except for Frank had dropped to their haunches, yelling like they were real excited about looking for a contact lens on the floor.

And then there was nothing but the smell of cordite hanging heavy around him, every living eye staring up at the hero near the gallery end of the jury box.

Funny, the thing you think will be the worst part turns out to be the easiest.

Passing that revolver to Lisa without fumbling it out of the hankie or putting a fingerprint on the frame was what had occupied Frank the most, but the thing he'd really worried about was the shooting itself. With a real human being in his sights, would he be able to pull the trigger?

But, turned out, everything felt exactly the way it did on the firing range. Frank had found himself not so much aiming as just pointing and squeezing off the rounds, seeing the little puffs of cloth and blood come up as the slugs impacted their target. There was no video of the scene to play back, of course, except the one in his head, which improved slightly each time Frank revisited it during his week's paid leave of absence from the job.

He'd also worried some about the Shoot Team interrogation, but that proved to be so routine he was almost embarrassed to answer their questions. The guys who really drew the heat were the two bailiffs who supposedly checked the defendant carefully each time they brought him into the courtroom, because—after all—that little snubbie had to come from *some*where.

Frank was less concerned about Aaron Weinberg. The defense attorney immediately told the press that there was "absolutely no reason" Dennis Doyle would have thought he needed to shoot his way out of the charge against him, especially given Weinberg's confidence "in the jury's eventual verdict." Obviously, Lisa had done a nice job of shielding the gun from her husband's lawyer.

In fact, as things unfolded, the biggest pain in the ass for Frank was all the fuss the media made over him. He stopped clipping the newspaper headlines—or even taping the broadcast stuff with his V.C.R.—by the end of the second day. The fucking jackals, they camped outside his apartment around the clock, just waiting for him to go buy a loaf of bread or a sixpack of beer to pump him for "additional comments" or "after-shock feelings" on the incident which had made him "The Dirty-Harry Hero."

At least, Frank conceded, they'd gone with a movie he liked.

In the end, though, it wasn't till the fifth day—when two state troopers brought down a drive-by shooter after a high-speed chase— that the media picked up stakes and moved their circus to somebody else's front yard. Frank telephoned his superior, saying he figured he could come back in to work then, but still was told to wait until after the weekend.

Which washed fine with Frank. After the days he'd had with the media—not to mention the nights with Lisa before that—he could use the rest. He began to spend his time more normally, going out for a few beers, the hero stuff still there but starting to slack off in the bars. The way Frank saw it, he was getting his life back on track.

But what had happened in Lisa's bedroom and the courtroom had been a part of his life, too. And, starting up the old Buick to drive to her house for his money, Frank Rossi realized that he had no regrets about having lived those parts—and having been her hero—for real.

"It's open," was Lisa Doyle's muffled answer to his knock on the front door.

Frank entered the foyer, noticing that all the furniture from the dining room had been moved back to where it belonged.

"I'm upstairs."

He climbed the steps, thinking how differently he'd felt every other time he'd done so.

"My bedroom, Frank," in the dreamy voice.

The tantalizing thought of a "bonus" went through his head, and he walked a little faster to the open door of the room Frank associated with the best hours he'd ever lived.

Before what he saw stopped him dead.

"God, Frank, don't be shy now."

On the bed, a briefcase lay open like a clamshell, cash stacked inside it. Lisa stood next to the bed, fanning a pack of greenbacks with her left thumb, the right hand behind her, like she was pregnant and resting it on her butt.

But Lisa wore the silky black dress from their last night together. The torn one, only with a bra and panties clearly visible underneath.

Frank said, "I don't . . ."

"I thought it might be kind of fun to do it one last time." She gestured with the cash in her left hand. "On the bed, but with your money spread all around us."

Frank just stared.

Lisa took two steps toward him. "Come on, what do you say?"

He couldn't say anything, truth to tell, but he swallowed hard and began walking toward her.

When Frank was about an arm's length away—like they'd been that first time after she'd yelled to him on the street—Lisa Doyle brought her right hand out from behind her back and fired the gun in it three times.

Frank thought somebody had hit him in the chest with a sledgehammer. Then the walls and ceiling began to switch places. He felt the back of his head bounce off the floor, but somehow it didn't hurt.

Which seemed kind of funny, you know?

Stretched out flat, staring at the ceiling from a different perspective than he'd gotten those nights from her bed, Frank heard other footsteps and saw two faces superimpose themselves on the ceiling, looking down on him now. Lisa's, right side up and . . .

Eddie's, upside down?

Sure, thought Frank. Because he's standing behind you.

"I didn't kill him?" from Lisa's face.

"The fucking whale's got to bleed out," from Eddie's. "Way it's going, shouldn't take too long."

Your eyes and ears still work, but so hard to . . . breathe.

Lisa's face said, "Should I shoot him again?"

"No. Lab stuff from the cops wouldn't look right, the sex-crazed hero gets shot on the floor after you already popped him for tearing your dress off to rape you."

Frank wanted to say something, but could only burble out some . . . spit?

She turned away. "Jesus, he's trying to talk."

"I'll give you this, Lise," said Eddie. "The fucking guy never knew we were setting him up."

Coming from a new direction, Lisa's voice sounded bitter. "We wouldn't have had to, you'd done the frame on Dennis right from the start."

"Yeah, well, I didn't," said Eddie's face, grinning down at Frank. "Every day of that trial, the boss had me hustling my ass all over the fucking place, trying to find out who'd fingered him. But, once Weinberg got Dennis off in court, the boss would have figured why I was coming up empty."

"And figured us," from Lisa.

"Hey." Eddie looked away now. "Make sure you don't smear the whale's fingerprints on that fucking dress."

Lisa Doyle's face loomed back into Frank's vision, and he tried to muster a smile to thank her for the sight.

She spoke with those eyes as well as her mouth. "Sorry, Frank, but I needed you to make this thing work. Do you understand?"

Frank Rossi tried to remember which movie that reminded him of, but there wasn't quite . . . enough time . . . to . . .

Ro Erg

Robert Weinberg

THE CLOCK IN THE HALLWAY was striking eight o'clock as Ronald Rosenberg opened the door to his house. With a wan smile he nodded to himself. *On time as usual.* Slowly, he removed his coat and hat, unwound the wool scarf from his neck, and hung them up neatly in the nearby closet. By then his wife Marge's voice was drifting out of the kitchen.

"Is that you, honey?" she asked. Always the same question, night after night, month after month, year after year. Asked without thinking, without considering the foolishness of the remark. As if a burglar might answer otherwise. It was part of their daily routine. Their unchanging, uninspiring, dull, and predictable life together.

"Yes, dear," he said, mentally sighing, "it's me."

Once, just once, he wanted to say, "No, it's a fuckin' crook, come to steal your money and smash your skull, you dumb bitch." But he knew better. The harsh words would upset Marge, and then he'd be forced to spend the entire evening apologizing, repeating over and over again how he shouldn't make such cruel remarks. Listening to her tell him how hard she slaved keeping his life running smoothly and how he didn't appreciate her efforts. Experience had taught him to keep such errant thoughts to himself.

"Dinner will be ready in five minutes," Marge called. "It's one of your favorites, beef stew and potatoes."

Ron nodded, a resigned expression on his face. Thursday was always beef stew night. Just like Tuesday was always spaghetti and Friday was always chicken. Marge did everything strictly by routine. Organization was her life. Once she settled on a menu, she stuck to it for months at a time. The only variety in their meals was Sunday, when they went out for dinner. And even then, no matter what restaurant they visited, Marge consistently ordered the roast turkey dinner. With dressing, sweet potatoes, and salad. One glass of white wine. And apple pie for dessert.

Everything in Marge's life was planned, programmed, and perfect. She knew what she liked and how she liked it. Deviation from the norm was wrong, observing a schedule was right. Even their sex life was governed by a complicated series of rules and regulations, designed, Ron was secretly convinced, to make sure he did not receive more than a moment's worth of satisfaction from the act. More than once he had asked himself if he had married a woman or a robot.

With a shrug of his shoulders, he picked up the mail Marge had left on the lamp table in the hall. As per usual, she had sliced open all the letters but then placed them there for him to sort through. The mail was his job. Business for men, household duties for women. Marge was definitely not a feminist.

Most of the letters—advertisements, junk mail, and sincerely worded pleas asking for donations to one charity or another—went into the nearby garbage can. A short note from his brother complaining about his latest money problems Ron read twice, frowning as he did so. Chris was an inept businessman and a spendthrift. That he was in a deep financial hole was no surprise. That he also expected Ron to help him out of the jam was equally no surprise. Ron tucked the letter in his shirt pocket, vowing to call his brother after dinner.

The gas bill and electric bill followed into the same pocket. They would go on his dresser, to be paid tomorrow morning. Though Ron hated to admit it, in many ways he was just as much a creature of habit and routine as his wife.

One letter remained. He looked at it curiously. It was from a credit card company. Something about receiving a new charge card without having to do anything more than sign the enclosed application. Ron already had Visa and MasterCard and American Express. He saw no reason for another piece of plastic. Why would they even bother to ask?

Searching the front of the envelope for an explanation, he noted in annoyance that the application wasn't even addressed to him. It was for a Mr. RO ERG. His eyes narrowed as he stared at the letter. The address was right. It was his. But the name was definitely wrong. No one named RO ERG lived in this house. Then, in a sudden flash of insight, he understood.

He was RO ERG. The computer at the credit card company offices had somehow taken the front two letters of his first name and final three letters of his last name to form this new person. Quite out of character, he grinned. The name RO ERG had a certain wild, untamed ring to it. He liked it. He liked it a lot. Uncertain of exactly why, Ron Rosenberg slipped the application to Ro Erg into his pocket behind the bills.

"Dinner's ready," declared his wife, interrupting his wandering thoughts. "Come and get it while it's hot."

The form remained untouched the rest of the evening. Until, late at night, when Marge's steady, deep breathing indicated she was fast asleep. Quietly, Ron slipped out of their bed. Not that it mattered. He was the one who was a light sleeper. A million minor annoyances and worries kept him awake for hours. Marge dismissed as unimportant anything that wasn't an immediate threat. An earthquake wouldn't disturb her slumber.

Sitting in the bathroom, Ron carefully opened the envelope and studied the application within. It was exactly as he had suspected. The request was a mail-merge letter, generated by an unthinking computer program. In three different places he was referred to as "Mr. Erg." Ron found the missive unintentionally hilarious when they commended Ro Erg on his outstanding credit record. Though he prided himself on never retaining a balance on any of his charge cards, Ron had never expected his frugality would entitle an imaginary entity to a $10,000 line of credit.

"Ten thousand bucks," he whispered aloud, the numbers suddenly dancing through his head. That was a lot of money, a real lot of money. He closed his eyes, feeling strange. Feeling . . . excited. "Ten thousand bucks."

Ron was extremely cautious with his finances. After all, he had to support his wife, pay the mortgage on their house, and make the payments on their two cars. As well as save for the future. There usually wasn't much money left from his paycheck at the end of the month. Not that Marge believed in going out on the town anyway. Renting a movie on videotape was her notion of an exciting evening.

His face burning with suppressed excitement, Ron headed for the kitchen. All his life he had done what was right, what was proper. Now, for a change, he could do something crazy and no one else would know. The plastic card meant nothing. He would never use it. But just sending away for it was a small but still important act of rebellion. That was what mattered.

Grabbing a magnetic pen off the refrigerator, Ron scribbled "Ro Erg" on the signature line of the document. Quickly, before he could change his mind, he placed the acceptance card into the postage-paid envelope and put it with the rest of the mail.

"Can't do any harm," he murmured to himself as he settled back into bed. "I'm just sending it in to see if they're stupid enough to follow through with the offer. That's the reason. The only reason."

And though he continued to whisper that line until he finally drifted off into slumber, deep inside he knew all the while he was lying.

The card arrived two weeks later. It came complete with a ten-thousand-dollar credit limit and a promise of a PIN number to follow within a few days so that he could draw cash advances from ATMs. Casually, Ron tucked the charge card in his wallet and hid the page of terms beneath a stack of old bills in his files. He had never considered the possibility of a PIN number. And cash advances. Suddenly, his minor act of rebellion took on a whole new life of its own.

The identification number came three days later. Three long days, one of which made infinitely longer by his brother's monthly visit. Tall and handsome, with broad shoulders and a winning smile, Chris always made Ron extremely uncomfortable when he was around. His sibling was everything that Ron was not. Chris was wild and carefree and extremely charming. He was also as dumb as a rock and proud of it.

Chris treated money as something to be spent as quickly as possible.

It was an attitude that drove Ron crazy. Though they were brothers, Ron found his brother insufferable.

Annoyingly enough, Marge thought Chris was cute and only needed some time to "mature." It was Marge who continually insisted that Ron lend Chris money—money that disappeared without a trace and never a word about repayment. His wife, Ron had concluded long ago, was an easy mark.

Fortunately, Chris always arrived in the afternoon when Ron was still at work and departed right after dinner. Taking along with him another $100 of his brother's hard-earned cash.

"Damned bloodsucker," said Ron as his brother drove off in a much nicer car than the one Ron owned.

"Ronald," said Marge, her voice sharp. "He's your brother. Give Chris a chance. Be patient. I'm sure he'll pay you back someday."

Sure. When hell freezes over, thought Ron. But he knew better than to say the words aloud. That would only start them arguing. Ron hated fights. They gave Marge headaches and then they didn't have sex that night. And to Ron sex was one of the few things that made life bearable.

All was quickly forgotten the next night when Ron found the latest letter addressed to RO ERG waiting for him in the evening mail. Ripping open the envelope, he quickly scanned the enclosed letter and accompanying card. It was his Personal Identification Number and instructions for its use.

He chuckled with a combination of joy and relief. His brother's visit had been the final straw. There was a limit to how much badgering he could take. Before, RO ERG had been nothing more than a test of the credit card company's intelligence. The PIN card put a whole new spin on the game. For once Ron could outdo Chris at his own game. And he intended to do exactly that.

"Good news, honey?" asked Marge from the kitchen.

"Yes, dear," answered Ron, "very good news."

The next afternoon, he called Marge and sadly informed her that he would be late for dinner. Extra work at the office, he explained, that had to be cleared up before he could leave for home. Ron was confident his wife wouldn't suspect a thing. In the past he often had stayed late at work. There was no reason she would suspect today it wasn't the truth. She didn't.

Informing his supervisor he needed the afternoon off to visit a friend in the hospital, Ron headed straight for the nearest cash station. Nervously, he inserted the RO ERG card and punched in the correct numbers for a thousand-dollar cash advance. The entire transaction took less than a minute. Feeling slightly dazed, Ron stumbled away from the ATM with ten hundred-dollar bills crammed into his pockets.

"A thousand smackers," he muttered to himself, walking down the street. "All mine, just by pushing some buttons!"

It was then that he had his first revelation about modern life. Society no longer cared about your background. People moved from one location to another so often that no one had real roots in their community. Relatives, schools, old friends, meant nothing. You were no longer defined by your past. Instead, the only thing that really mattered was the name of your credit cards. Those little pieces of plastic provided you with all the history you needed.

Dozens of people at work and in his neighborhood knew him as Ron Rosenberg. But the bank teller processing his charge receipt, the credit card employee handling his account, the postal worker sorting the mail, they knew him as Ro Erg. He was no longer merely one person. He was two separate entities sharing the same body—Ron Rosenberg and Ro Erg.

Shaken by his new grasp of reality, Ron tried to focus his thoughts on more immediate concerns. He had to consider what to do with the cash. If he brought the money home, Marge was sure to discover it. And thus learn about Ro Erg.

Ron couldn't let that happen. Ro Erg was his secret. And he meant to keep it that way. Anxiously, he hailed a cab. He needed a drink. But not in this neighborhood, close to his office where someone he knew might spot him.

"Take me to the airport," he commanded the cabdriver, his voice shaking slightly. "There's a bar up there. I forget the name. You know the one I mean. It's a quiet place. Where a guy can get a drink and be alone with his thoughts."

"Sure, buddy," said the cabbie with a laugh. "I know the place. Max's joint. Right?"

"Right," said Ron, settling back in the seat. "That's the one."

Max's place was The Red Garter and it was a dump. Dimly lit, with a dozen wooden booths hugging the far wall, its only saving grace was that it lacked a jukebox. Except for an old man whispering to a much younger woman at the end of the bar, there were no other customers. It was exactly the type of place Ron wanted.

"Scotch, on the rocks," he told the lone bartender. "Make it a double."

Without thinking, Ron paid for the drink with a crumpled hundred pulled out of his pocket. The bartender stared at the bill for a moment, then with a loud cough and a shrug of his shoulders made change. It was as if he was trying to attract someone's attention to the money.

Lost in his thoughts about the meaning of identity, Ron hardly noticed when, a few minutes later, the old man at the end of the bar half fell off his chair and staggered out of the tavern, muttering obscenities the whole time under his breath. Nor did he give much thought to the man's female companion. Until she sat down in the chair next to him.

"Buy a girl a drink?" she asked in a soft voice.

"Sure," he said with a shrug. The scotch had made him somewhat dizzy and a little light-headed. "Whatever you want."

"Gin," said the woman to the bartender. "Straight up."

"Another scotch for me," said Ron, gesturing to the cash still on the bar. "Take it out of there."

"My name's Ginger," said the woman, sipping her drink. "What's yours?"

Suspiciously, Ron turned and stared at the woman. There was little question as to her profession. Ginger was dressed in a tight red dress that left nothing to the imagination. She wore black fishnet stockings and a pair of high-heeled black boots. The edge of her dress had ridden up to nearly the top of her thighs, but she made no effort to pull it down.

Her face was fairly attractive, though too much lipstick, blush, and eyeliner made her look cheap. And nothing could hide the hardness of her eyes.

Ron Rosenberg would have told her to stop bothering him. He was a married man and had no time for hookers. Ron never took chances, especially with women like Ginger. But it wasn't Ron who answered.

"I'm Ro," he said hesitantly. "Ro Erg."

"Glad to meet you, Ro," Ginger giggled, trying to sound seductive but not succeeding. She accepted his name without question. "You look lonely. Need somebody to talk to?"

"I'm trying to . . . ," began Ron, then paused, his words catching in his throat. Holding her drink in her right hand, Ginger had casually reached over with her left and placed it directly on his thigh. Smiling, she winked and gently squeezed her fingers.

Ron Rosenberg would have been panic-stricken. Aggressive women frightened him. But Ginger's hand wasn't resting on Ron's leg. Desperately, he clung to that thought. To the hooker he was Ro, not Ron. Ro Erg.

"My, my," she murmured a few seconds later as her wandering fingers encountered his growing erection, "you are a big one. How about if we retire to one of the booths in the back. We can *enjoy our conversation* without interruption back there."

Licking his lips, Ro nodded. He knew he was acting crazy, but he didn't care. Besides, no one would ever know. This wasn't happening to Ron Rosenberg. He was Ro Erg.

Leaving a five for the bartender, Ro scooped up the rest of the money and followed Ginger to the farthest booth. She gestured him in, so their backs were to the bar. "Nobody can see a thing from here," she whispered, sliding in next to him. "We're completely alone."

"But—but," protested Ron, a measure of sanity emerging from his befuddled brain, "the two of us are right out in the open. The bartender could come back here at any time."

"Harry?" laughed Ginger. "He knows what's going on. And he'll get his cut."

Giving him no time to protest further, Ginger swiftly reached out with both hands for his clothing. In seconds, she unbuckled Ron's pants and zipped down his fly. He groaned in excitement as she reached into his trousers and pulled out his already erect cock.

"Nice," she cooed, shifting slightly on the seat. The motion sent her dress riding up over her hips. Not surprisingly, she wasn't wearing anything underneath.

"Blow job costs fifty," she said matter-of-factly, her fingers expertly massaging his rock-hard organ. "If you want to fuck, it's a hundred. One twenty-five for both."

"This can't be real," said Ron, shaking his head in amazement. "It can't be."

"Wanna bet, sweetie?" said Ginger. Swiftly, she bent over and lightly placed her lips around the tip of his cock. Gently she sucked on the head. Once, twice, three times she flicked her tongue. She looked up at him and grinned. "This is sex. This is real. How much are you gonna pay?"

It was then, bedazzled from the whiskey and sex, that Ron experienced his second revelation. Money was all that mattered. Ginger didn't care if his name was Ron or Ro or mud. She was a tramp, looking to make a quick buck satisfying a john's lust. His name, personality, history, meant nothing to her. Married or single, rich or poor, saint or sinner, Ginger didn't mind. All that mattered was money. A piece of plastic gave Ro Erg identity. Money gave him power. Those were the basic truths, the only truths that mattered, of modern life.

Ron Rosenberg would have been too consumed by guilt, worried that somehow, someway, Marge would discover this encounter, to continue. But it hadn't been Ron who withdrew the thousand in cash. The money wasn't his. It belonged to Ro Erg. Ginger hadn't been talking to Ron. She had asked Ro. And Ro answered.

"I'll take it all," he declared, his voice thick with lust. He dug a wad of bills out of his pocket and handed Ginger a hundred and two twenties. "Make it last a long time," he said, and you can keep the change."

Satisfied he had made the right choice, Ro Erg settled back on the bench and let Ginger take over.

Ron Rosenberg, the practical, cautious planner, secured a safety deposit box and mailing address at a nearby rental depot. A hundred-dollar bill paid for the box and a place to receive mail. The cash remaining from Ro Erg's advance went into the box, along with a wallet containing the credit card. It was a lot safer here than at home, where it might be discovered by his wife.

After his encounter with Ginger, Ron knew there was no turning back. He was now a man with two identities—Ron Rosenberg and Ro Erg. Ron managed the important details while Ro enjoyed the results. It was a very satisfactory arrangement.

The new address for Ro proved important. Good news traveled fast in the credit card industry. A few months after activating his first charge card, Ro Erg received applications for two more. Again, each of them had ten-thousand-dollar limits, PIN numbers, and only required a signature for instant acceptance. He mailed in the documents for both.

Meanwhile, Ro learned the amazing truth about the power of plastic. Using the credit card as proof of his identity, he was able to obtain a charge card from a major department store. Using the two pieces of plastic, he was then able to get a new library card. With that and a mailing address, he was able to open a bank account. More chain store cards followed, as did further additions to his new identity. Day by day Ro Erg became more and more real. By year's end, Mr. Erg had a dozen charge cards and nearly $50,000 in credit.

Always careful with money, Ron made sure that Ro never strayed too far into debt. He juggled money and cash advances from one account to another. He borrowed cash from one card to pay the minimum due on the second. Then used his line of credit from his third card to pay off the minimum debt on the second. He owed all of the companies something, but he made sure that he didn't owe any of them too much. Whenever there was a shortage of funds, he slipped some cash from Ron Rosenberg's paycheck into Ro's cash accounts to help balance the books. It was an elaborate pyramid scheme, but one that Ron knew he could operate for years as long as his alter ego didn't spend too lavishly or run up any major charges.

In the meantime, Ro Erg emerged more and more as a full-fledged personality. He was Ron's wild side, his suppressed side, the part of him that urgently desired to drink deeply of life's pleasures without regard to right or wrong. It was the segment of his character that had been repressed and contained by his overbearing wife. But Marge Rosenberg meant nothing to Ro Erg.

At night, lying in bed awake, the two halves of his personality, Ron and Ro, would engage in long, meaningful debates. Mostly, these arguments centered on what to do next. Ron, careful and cautious, wanted to maintain life the way it was. Ro, wild and headstrong, hated Marge and the stability she represented. He wanted to make a complete break with the past. But Ron wouldn't let him. And, though Ro presented powerful grounds for change, Ron refused to let his darker side take control.

As the weeks stretched into months, the conflict between the two conflicting sides of his personality grew more intense. Ro Erg no longer seemed satisfied with being merely the untamed element of Ron's personality. He wanted to be in charge. Day after day Ro struggled to take control of their shared body.

A cheap apartment paid for in cash on a month-to-month basis served as their hideaway. It was here that Ro brought the hookers he picked up on the streets or in bars. Ginger was just the first of a long string of whores who provided him with sexual gratification. The one night a week that he had to work late stretched into two and sometimes even three. Marge never complained. If anything, she almost seemed pleased by his devotion to his work. Which should have made Ron suspicious. But it never did. He just could not imagine his plain, ordinary wife was any more than what he believed. It took a hooker to open his eyes.

"Wearing a wedding ring, I see," remarked Candy, a bleached blonde with huge breasts and a talented tongue, late one night as she collected her hundred bucks from Ro. "What's wrong, sweetie? Don't get enough from the wifey?"

"She's a cold, stupid bitch," said Ro. "Fucking for five minutes is a major effort for her."

"Maybe," said Candy with a nasty laugh. "But you should keep an eye on her. Lots of times, things ain't what you think. You positive she don't got a stud of her own on the side? It ain't unusual for straying husbands to find out their wives been doing the same. Plenty of my johns' wives get their lovin' from the milkman."

"We don't get our milk delivered," replied Ron indignantly. Then his eyes narrowed as a sudden thought struck him and raced through his mind. Trembling with rage, his fingers clenched into fists. The truth hit him like a hammer between the eyes.

"But," growled Ro Erg, "there is my fuckin' brother." Blood rushed to his face, turning his features bright crimson. Candy, licking her lips nervously, stepped back.

"Gotta leave, honey," she gasped and, grabbing her purse, fled the room. Ro hardly noticed.

"My lazy son of a bitch brother," snarled Ro. "Not enough for him to rip off my hard-earned money. He has to fuck my wife on the side."

Slowly, Ro shook his head from side to side in disbelief. Marge had ruined Ron's life for years with her control fetish. That she had been screwing his brother at the same time was beyond belief. But instinctively he knew the truth. The cold, unyielding truth. It was enough to drive a man insane.

"They'll learn," he swore, his voice thick with anger. "They'll find out soon enough you don't mess with Ro Erg."

Two days later, as Ron ate breakfast, Marge informed him that Chris would be stopping by for dinner. He nodded, smiling gently as if recalling some secret joke.

"I'll be home around seven," he promised as he dutifully kissed his wife on the cheek good-bye. "Have a good day."

"I'm sure I will," she replied cheerfully, the tone of her voice confirming his most sickening suspicions.

Ron Rosenberg left his house, burning with repressed fury. However, it was Ro Erg—cold, calm, collected—who stopped at the bar on the north side of town to pick up the black market .45 automatic he had ordered the other night.

"Fully loaded and ready for use," drawled the bartender, a big, bushy-bearded man named Jackson, as he handed over the weapon to Ro along with a box of shells. "You know how to use it?"

"I was in the army for two years," said Ro, checking the gun carefully. "I know how to use it just fine."

Then, as if seeking to deflect suspicion, he added, "I work in a dangerous neighborhood. There's been a lot of muggings lately. I don't intend to be worked over by some crackhead."

"Sure," said Jackson, the tone of his voice indicating he didn't care how Ro planned to use the automatic. "Stay cool."

"Thanks," said Ro, "I plan to."

He spent the rest of the morning and the early part of the afternoon drifting from one bar to another. A drink here, a drink there, staying calm, letting the anger simmer deep in his belly. Only occasionally did a spark of Ron Rosenberg emerge into his consciousness, asking the inevitable question. "Are you sure about this? Are you really convinced we're doing the right thing?"

"I'm positive," said Ro.

At two, after finishing a roast beef sandwich and plate of french fries, he drove home. Not unexpectedly, he spotted his brother's car parked in the driveway. Drawing in a deep breath, he left his own auto a block away and walked back to the house.

The front door was locked. Carefully, Ro turned his key, trying to make as little sound as possible. He needn't have worried. The hallway and living room were deserted. But he had no trouble pinpointing his brother's location. Chris's cries of pleasure, emanating from the bedroom, rocked the whole house.

Coldly, Ro pulled out his gun and checked it over one last time. Deep in his mind, Ron sobbed uncontrollably. Ro ignored the voice. There was no pity in him. Ron had let Marge ruin his life. Ro was not going to let her do the same to him.

Satisfied the automatic was ready, he silently tiptoed down the hall to the bedroom. The door was half closed, giving Ro full view of the room without revealing him to the pair inside. Even expecting the worst, he felt sick with anger as he gazed on the scene within.

Chris was naked sitting on the edge of the bed. His face was raised to the ceiling, eyes clenched tightly together. "Yes, yes, yes," he was screaming passionately, his hands wrapped around Marge's head. His fingers were curled in her hair, urging her on. His legs were spread wide open.

Crouched on her hands and knees in front of Chris was Marge. Also nude, she was busily sucking on her brother-in-law's engorged cock. Her whole body shook with the bobbing movement of her head as she forced more and more of his swollen organ into her mouth. Her ass, facing Ro, swayed to and fro wildly with her every motion.

Ro's head throbbed with incredible pain. It felt as if his skull was about to explode. Throughout her marriage Marge had continually refused to perform oral sex on Ron. More than once she had expressed her absolute and total revulsion of the act. And here she was, sucking on Chris's cock with an all-consuming mania.

Furious, Ro's gaze fastened on the full-length mirror on the closet door directly across from Marge. Every few seconds she glanced at it, caught sight of her swiftly moving head, and then, as if excited by watching herself in action, redoubled her efforts. The dual image of

Marge and her reflection both giving his brother a blow job wiped any possibility of mercy from Ro's thoughts.

"I'm close!" howled Chris, thrusting his groin forward so that the entire length of his organ disappeared into Marge's mouth. "Now, now, now!"

Chris screamed in wordless ecstasy. His fingers clenched Marge's head in place, holding her immobile as his body shook with the force of his climax. "I'm cuming, I'm cuming," he shrieked as Marge's eyes widened in sudden shock as his cock exploded in her mouth. Half moaning, half gagging, she struggled to swallow his ejaculation.

Enveloped in lust, neither of them noticed Ro step quietly into the room. Chris, his eyes clenched shut, giggled in pleasure as Marge continued to suck passionately on his now spent cock. His first indication of trouble was when Ro pressed the cold steel of the gun barrel against his forehead. Chris's eyes widened in panic, but before he could open his mouth to beg forgiveness, Ro pulled the trigger.

The roar of the automatic filled the bedroom. Chris's head exploded like a ripe pumpkin hit with an ax. Fired from point-blank range, the powerful .45 removed most of his skull and forehead. Blood, brains, and gore erupted across his body and Marge's, soaking the bedsheets and the carpet like bright red paint.

Marge, her eyes still glazed and bewildered, looked up at Ro. Mouth still sticky with cum, she screamed. But there was no one there to help her.

"Please, Ron," she cried. "Forgive me! Please!"

"Sorry, Marge, but you got the wrong man," declared Ro, pointing the automatic between her eyes and squeezing the trigger. He fired three times in succession, until there wasn't enough left of her face to be called a face.

Ro smiled. He felt good, real good. They deserved to die. Justice had been served. Now it was time for him to leave, before the police arrived.

He checked the room carefully. There was nothing here to connect him to the murders. Marge was Ron's wife, not his. Likewise, Chris was a total stranger. Ro Erg was in the clear. He had no motive for murder. No one had witnessed his crime.

It was then that he spotted Ron's face in the full-length mirror. Stared deep into Ron's eyes and saw the fear lurking within. Watched as

Ron glanced down at the two crumpled bodies on the floor and shuddered in revulsion. That's when Ro understood that he no longer could trust Ron. As long as he was around, Ro would never be safe. There was only one thing to do.

Slowly, methodically, Ro raised the gun he still clenched in his fist. Lifted it inch by inch, as Ron's face twisted in horror as he comprehended what Ro planned. But there was nothing Ron could do to stop him. With a nod of satisfaction Ro pressed the bloody nozzle of the gun to Ron's forehead. And pulled the trigger.

SAUCE FOR THE GOOSE

Gil Brewer

COUNTRY LIFE IS JUST THE THING, if you know how to live right, and if you really enjoy it. Sally and I had it made. For something over a year previous to the time I met her, I'd been clean. I'd been lucky, too. I never did time, and since I'd never packed any heat, I hadn't made the big error. Ever since I was a kid, I had fooled around with oil paints, taking correspondence lessons, and even before I left the rackets I was selling some commercial stuff. Finally I landed a few good magazine hook-ups and broke clean with the past and married Sally.

She never knew anything about what I'd been. I was just a struggling artist, so far as she was concerned, and I aimed to keep it that way. So we bought this place in the Adirondacks on what I had stashed away. It was a nice place, big and roomy, overlooking a lake.

"Chris," Sally said, "from now on I'm a happy girl. It's wonderful!"

She meant it. She got along with this sort of life, and I never wanted anything else. Just Sally. I had a big studio in the house, on the second floor. I worked hard, and like I said—it was the life. Sometimes when I had a big job to fill for some magazine, maybe a cover, I'd stick right in the studio, working and snatching sleep when I was too tired to go on. So when I came out, Sally hadn't been with me nights and it was really something. Like falling in love all over again. You know?

She was a honey. That's for sure. There's been a smattering of girls in my life, but they'd been mostly of a type.

Blonde, Sally was, really shaped-up, deep blue eyes, a sunny disposition and she possessed that ability to amuse herself no matter how dull life might seem to others. I'd be working, maybe, and look out the window and there she'd be, romping on the shore of the lake in her red bathing suit, her long smooth legs flashing in the afternoon sunlight. Even so, we had more or less decided to start having kids. It was time.

Anyway, everything was rosy, until that day I drove into town alone after some painting supplies. I needed a couple brushes and a tube of white. Normally I had the stuff shipped in, but I'd run short.

I came back to the car and I saw this blonde hair lying across the back of the front seat, and then the arm and the head and I thought What's Sally doing down here?

Only it wasn't Sally.

It was Gloria.

It was like being run over by a truck.

"Hi, there, Chris. How's tricks?"

"That's a question I might ask you."

"Let's not be nasty."

I stood there with the door open, staring at her. She grinned at me, and she looked even more luscious than I remembered. Gloria had always lived a fast life, but somehow it never showed much. Someday, maybe. But not yet. She was a great big bundle of over-ripe, overanxious, frank anticipation. Her hair was so soft it made you tingle just looking at it. She was wearing an aqua dress of soft silk that dripped and clung as if it were soaking wet.

"I look good, huh, Chris?"

"Yeah. You look good. Now, get. No explanation, no old times—just get. Come on."

I reached in and took hold of her arm. She went all loose, grinning that damned grin of hers. Dead weight and wetlipped.

I let go and laid the stuff I'd bought in the back seat.

"Gloria, I mean it. I don't want to know how come you're here I just want to see your tail switching around the corner."

She clucked her tongue. She wasn't moving. There was nothing to do. I went around and climbed in under the wheel and sat there, biting my lip. I could smell her and she moved a little on the seat.

"I'm your cousin, Chris."

"What?"

"That's right. I'm your cousin Gloria. My folks died and I haven't any place to stay. So I came up here. I'm going to live with you for a while. You don't mind, because we were always very close cousins." She slid across the seat until her hip was against me, and she leaned against me and laid one hand on my knee. "*Very close*. Right?" Her dress flowed up her thighs as she moved, clinging, past the smooth sheer nylon tops and I remembered and remembered.

It was a warm afternoon to begin with. I pushed her away.

"Spill," I said. "And make it quick."

"I just did." She leaned back against the door watching me from down under. Gloria had a down-under look that would put a practiced actress to shame. She didn't do anything with her skirt either. She just let it flow upstream. She had a gang of this heavy costume jewelry on one arm and it clanked when she moved. There were huge white buttons down the front of her dress. They were unbuttoned to her waist; that's the way the dress was built.

"I'm married, Gloria."

"I know. I think that's just ducky."

I looked at her, then out the windshield.

"Look, Chris," she said. "I'm tired. I've come a long way. From Chicago. I got a line on you through one of the girls you used to know. We read up on you in the papers. I even saw some of your paintings. You're not so hot, Chris."

"Quit playing critic."

"I'm tired. I need a place to stay for a while. You're it. You know you haven't any choice, darling. I'd bet my bottom dollar you've never told little Sally about us, Chris. Right? Sure, I'm right. And you won't tip the cops for your own sake. Besides, I'd still tell Sally. Wouldn't she like to know?"

"Damn you."

"Sure. So, look. You go ahead and drive home. I'll call you in two hours, to make it look good. Then I'll come out in a taxi."

"Gloria, for God's sake. Don't do this!"

"Nuts!" She skidded across the seat, grabbed my face in both hands.

Her palms were moist and so were her lips as she plastered them to mine. "Won't we have fun, Chris? I'm in the mood for fun."

"Get out!"

"Sure. And don't ask me what I'm running from. Let it lay, honey." She slid back across the seat, opened the door, and climbed out. She was something very nice to look at. "On second thought," she said, "after I phone, you come down and get me. It'll look better." She winked.

I started to say something, didn't. What use was there?

"Bye, now." She turned and walked away. I watched her.

It was too late, as usual. I hadn't told Sally. I knew I never could tell her. She wasn't the type to be told things like that. Some people just aren't, that's all. It's nothing against them. It's their bringing up. Sally was perfect in every respect, but if I told her about the old days she'd never be able to take it. It would be the merry end.

I drove home and I was as sick as a man can get.

"Somebody wants to speak to you on the phone, Chris."

"Oh?" I came down the hall. Sally handed me the phone, and started hugging me. She was wearing yellow shorts and she was hot from being out in the sun. She kissed my throat and Gloria spoke into my ear.

"Honey," she said. "I can't wait. Honest! Make with the talk, so it looks good—if your wife's around."

"Oh," I said. I went into a spiel. Sally was around all right, hanging onto me and half-hearing Gloria's voice. I tried to edge away from her, because Gloria was speaking loudly and what she said would fix everything. She was a great kidder.

I hung up, faced Sally's frown and told her the lie.

"But, Chris—you never mentioned a cousin."

I shrugged. "Just one of those things. The poor kid's got nothing. She's come all the way up here. What can I do?"

She looked at me, put her hands on her hips, rocked on her toes. She was wearing a yellow sweater to match the shorts.

"I think it's fine, Chris. Company will be good for a change. You've got a lot of work ahead of you, so it won't be any bother. I never see you, tucked away in your workroom, anyway."

"Yeah. I'll have to pick her up."

"Fine. I'll come with you."

"You better stay here. You know how it is. She might be embarrassed. Fix something good for dinner. She's probably starved. I won't be long."

"It's nice country," Gloria said, coming back through the hills. "Frankly I like town life, but this'll do for a while."

"A damned short while."

She chuckled. "Maybe Chris—maybe."

"Listen," I said. "That dress you're wearing. It's going to look bad, you walking in with that on. Believe me. Sally thinks you're down and out. Haven't you anything a bit—"

"Sure!" She turned and climbed over into the back seat, and started rummaging through her luggage. "Drive carefully," she said and started to strip. I turned the rearview mirror up, so I wouldn't be tempted.

"Got to stop for eggs, butter and milk at a farm near our place," I told her. "If Hewes comes out to the car, for God's sake act right."

Elmer Hewes took care of a fair-sized dairy farm and a sick wife, just over the hill from our house. He insisted on helping me carry the stuff to the car, and when he saw Gloria, his eyes kind of went bloodshot. She'd changed into a tight fawn-colored skirt, and a short-sleeved white blouse. She had the car door open, and was sitting there with her legs crossed. I introduced them, and he shook her hand, and held it for a time, and she grinned at him that way. Then I got out of there.

"Dairy farms are interesting," she'd told him.

"Why don't you come on over for a spell?" he told her. "I'd right like to show you around."

He was a big raw-boned husker, wearing a gray flannel shirt and levis. Gloria gave him the down-under and he reddened up a little.

Coming in our driveway, I warned her again.

"Just act right," I said. "I'm not saying any more."

"Honey, for you I'd act any damned way there is."

I parked the car and we got out. She went peddling right up to the front door and was talking with Sally, before I'd even got her bags out of the back seat.

There was a lot of gurgling in one of the bags. Gloria always kept herself well supplied with liquor. She was a dilly.

"I think she's very nice," Sally told me that night. We were in our bedroom. I wanted a good night's sleep before starting on a series of advertisements in the morning. I lay in bed and watched her undress and listened and heard Gloria taking a shower down the hall.

"Glad of that," I said. "I guess she's all right. Just a mixed-up kid."

"Well, I wouldn't exactly call her a kid, Chris. She certainly is—has— Well, you know what I mean. I mean, *really.*" Sally moved over by the bed, tying the little pink bow on her shorty nightgown. She sat down and I could feel her warmth through the blanket. "She told me not to say anything to you," Sally said. "It would embarrass her, thinking you knew. But she was married and her husband left her—took all their savings, everything. She ran away from her home town." Sally shook her head. "I feel sorry for her."

"Sure."

"But she'll make out. Soon as she gets on her feet."

I turned away and stared at the wall.

Five days later it was under way. Full steam. Gloria was a lounge lizard and an atom bomb, rolled into one. She could lounge around better than any woman I'd ever seen. It came natural with her. She'd take a pose on the couch that would make you froth. After the first day, she broke her bottles out and she stayed in a blue haze most of the time. Real dreamy.

One night at the dinner table Gloria made it a little plainer. Not that she wasn't outspoken all the time.

"Say, Chris," she said. "Don't you need anybody to pose for you?" She paused and smiled at Sally and Sally smiled back. "I can pose real swell, I bet."

"Sally usually—"

"Oh, but Sally's your wife, Chris. Wouldn't it be better if *I* posed?"

"I don't need any models right now."

"You know," she went on. "It would maybe change the appearance of your paintings a little. Put a kick into them." She grinned and Sally tried to grin, and I sat there. Gloria got up from the table and I saw she'd been hitting the nectar, just the way she moved.

"Look." She pranced out into the middle of the room, and hauled her skirt up. She had a way of doing it. You know? "How're my gams, Chris? Are they O.K.?"

"Yeah—uh—sure."

"I think they're very nice legs," Sally said, not looking at them even once. "Real sexy."

"You know it, hon," Gloria said. "And I thank you. There's lots more than just this. Don't you agree I'd make a nice ad?"

"For what?" I said.

Sally got up and went into the kitchen. Gloria looked at me and winked.

I went out into the kitchen.

Sally was standing by the refrigerator, staring at her thumbs.

"I'm sorry, honey," I said. "She's just—"

"Don't tell me. I know."

I sucked some air through my teeth. I tried to put my arms around her. She shrugged away. She was real irked.

I went back into the living room, and grabbed Gloria's arm, where she was sprawled on the couch. I marched her out onto the porch and down onto the lawn and stood there.

"Listen," I said. "You're going to have to leave. Tonight. If not tonight, in the morning."

"Chrissy," she said. "Good old Chrissy."

She grabbed me and hung on tight. I tried to get loose, and I heard the door slam on the porch and Sally was there, looking out toward us. I got loose. I wasn't sure she'd seen us.

"Chris?" Sally said.

"Be right in," I told her. "I'm just checking the lawn. Figure it'll need mowing tomorrow."

Gloria giggled. Sally turned and went back into the house and the door slammed. This was perfect.

"Is Chrissy worried?" Gloria said. "Poor Chrissy."

I left her standing out there. I didn't know what to do. To top it off, she was getting to me. I didn't want it that way, but there it was. I went on inside and found Sally in the kitchen again.

"Where's Gloria?" I said. "She go up to her room?"

"What are we going to do, Chris?"

"How you mean?"

She looked at me.

"How you mean?" I said.

"Oh, nothing—maybe it's nothing at all." She stepped over by me and put her arms around my waist. "What do you honestly think of Gloria, Chris?"

"She's young, see?" I said. "She's mixed up. She's been hitting that darned bottle. What can you do?"

"She's been hurt, too. I suppose she's taking it out on herself."

I felt better. Sally seemed to understand. Only that was as far as it went, because Gloria came out into the kitchen and it started again. Worse than ever.

I knew something had to be done.

"You've got to leave," I told her again, later that night. Sally was in bed and I'd been working until I couldn't stand it, thinking about this little pigeon any longer. I went down to Gloria's room and told her and she laughed.

"I'm not leaving, Chris. Maybe I'm going to be around for a good long while. What d'you think of that?"

I didn't say anything. I couldn't keep my eyes off her and she knew it and that was bad. It was driving me nuts. If she hung around any longer, I knew what was going to happen. And it would be wrong. Because I loved Sally and I wanted Sally to be happy, and God, I'd built all this up and now she had to come along.

"You know, and I know," Gloria said, lying in bed, propped over on one elbow, "what would happen if I told Sally the kind of guy you really are. A thief. A crook, and a lot of other things, too. Like with me. See?"

"Damn you. Why pick me? There's lot of other guys, other places to stay!"

"You've got the best place I know of—and I'm hot. I can't show myself, see?" She reached up for me.

"Cut it out!"

"I see I've made a connection. Right? You haven't forgot after all. Those lovely hours in Saskatchewan."

"Shut up!"

"Why don't you give mama a big kisso?"

I practically ran from the room, followed by her chuckle. She knew how I was feeling. There was nothing I could do.

Every damned thing I wanted out of life would go down the drain. If she told Sally, it was all over. If Gloria stayed, it was all over. Anyway you looked at it, I was messed up.

I began to think. Hard. To plan. There had to be a way, because where Gloria was concerned I was as weak as they come. I wanted that girl. Just the way it had been not too long ago.

And I loved Sally.

So two nights later I was sweating in the studio, trying to paint, and I looked out the window. I half had the bad thing in mind, the one way to get rid of her, when I saw her crossing the rear lawn. She cut through the fence and over toward the hill by the woods. Then I saw him.

It was old Hewes, as sure as hell. He met her on the edge of the woods in the moonlight, just above the highway. They grabbed each other and hung on, and started toward his place.

Well, it hit me hard. I had it clearly in mind; what I was going to do before they were even out of sight.

I watched for five nights. And five nights she met him. During the day I looked at her real wise, but I wouldn't say anything, because I had a plan. It seemed real neat.

Sally was really worried now. She tried not to show it, because she knew damned well I was fighting a battle. But the morning on the sixth day, she nailed me.

"You've got to ask her to go, Chris. I know it's rude, but I can't take this any more. And don't ask me what."

I didn't say anything.

Sally and I were in the kitchen and she came over and stood by me and when I reached for her, she backed away. Her eyes were tired and worried and her lower lip pouted.

"You going to ask her?" she said.

"Sure. Look, I think we've both got her all wrong," I said. "Honest, honey, She's just mixed up."

Sally turned and left the room.

I caught up with her. "Listen," I said. "I've got to make a little run into Buffalo. See? I'll be back tonight. We'll talk about it. O.K.?"

Sally shrugged and started clearing the table. Then she looked at me, real straight, between the eyes.

"Something's got to be done, Chris. I mean it."

It was like old times; the city streets and keeping an eye out all the time. I had a good bank account from the old days, when I'd played it smart, stashing it. I went down and located this guy, Gus, and Gus said if I wanted to see Pearly, I'd have to work it through Harry Strickens.

"Why Strickens?"

"He's handling the end I think you refer to," Gus said, Gus ran a garage for cover. "Things have changed, Chris, boy."

"Look," I said, "Gus."

He shook his head. He looked nice and grease-smeared for the trade, just the way he should. Which was for laughs, because Gus probably hadn't even learned how to pump gas yet. He had a guy working for him and Gus carried his end mostly by phone.

"All right, Gus." I handed him the hundred-dollar bill. "Now, I want to see this Pearly, I know it's Pearly, because I called Rogers the minute I got in town."

Gus shrugged, put the hundred away. "Rogers can't do it for you. It's still the same. You got to work through Strickens."

So I saw Strickens. He ran a bookstore, now. How things had changed. He asked me out back and we snuck out there and sat down and he handed me a paper cup and looked around, and closed the door and filled the cup with gin.

"Hurry up and drink," he said. "The bottoms fall out."

I tossed it off and waited. "Why all the burlesque?"

"You know how it is, Chris."

"You forget. I been away."

"Yeah. Well, how much?"

"How much what? Come off it. I want information first, then I want to see this Pearly, whoever the hell he is."

"It'll cost."

"I expect that."

"Like what?"

"Who was Gloria Sharn with on her last job? What was the job? I need it quick. I know she's hot, but I want the story."

"Gloria Sharn?"

"Milwaukee," I told him. "She said Chicago, but she's lying."

He made a motion with his fingers. I laid out two hundred, and he stared at it without moving his hands. I laid another hundred down. He stacked the bills, folded them, and put them under the desk blotter. "Just a minute, Chris."

I watched him leave the room. He was phoning out there somewhere, the son of a gun, selling one of the C-notes. Pretty soon he came back.

"Milwaukee was right," he said. "You keep on tap, don't you?" He came around and sat down and sighed. "It was a snatch job, Chris. Muffed all around. She was with Jimmy Driskton. He fell and she got away. He made a break for it from the town clink and they shot him down. She's hot. They got no line on her, though. She with you?"

"All right," I said. "I bought it. Now, is Pearly a real heavy?"

"He'll do."

"Sane?"

"Well, they're all nuts. You know that. Pearly's all right. Wife and kids, plays it tame."

"Where do I make contact?"

He sent me to this address on a street in Tonawanda. It was a barber shop. Pearly was in the back room dealing poker hands, all alone, waiting. I had expected the usual. Pearly wasn't exactly. He looked like your next-door neighbor, wearing rimless glasses, clean shaven, neatly dressed, steady in the eyes. But he had that damned look they all got.

He didn't say anything.

"We talk here?" I said.

He looked at me and smiled pleasantly and nodded.

"It's two," I said. "Not one. Two."

"One apiece," he said. "One extra. Three grand. All right?"

"I figured nothing like this."

"Times have changed. Listen I gotta meet the wife. Is it on?"

I dealt him half and started talking. You could hear the barber clipping away in the other room, and the baseball game was soft on the radio.

"About three, every morning. She comes out the back door, starts over the hill just above the highway. That's your best spot."

"I'll figure the best spot. You just talk."

"She meets him and they go into the woods. It'll have to be before they make the woods. It should be from the road. That's the way I'd like it, if it will be all right with you."

"Do I know her?"

"What difference?"

"I'll have to know that much," he said.

"You don't know her."

"Don't tell me anything else. I don't want to know her, nothing about her. All right. You're on."

"You think it's all right?"

"It stinks, but I'll look at it."

"When?"

"I'll let you know when. You can listen real careful."

"Good."

"Come on. The rest of the dough. I work all the way. You gamble, I gamble, we all gamble."

We looked at each other. I paid him.

"Don't ever come near me again," Pearly said. "I'll phone you. It won't be a week."

I had a haircut and headed for home.

I stretched out what work I had. If I went to bed with Sally, it was no good. I couldn't watch out the window and I was scared plenty Gloria would wear Hewes out and quit seeing him, or something. Two days went by and she met him every night, right on schedule.

But the fourth day, she went to work on me.

"We were always pals," Gloria said.

She'd come up to the studio that afternoon. Sally was downstairs. I could hear her running the vacuum cleaner on the rugs. I thought about her and looked at Gloria.

"Great pals," I said.

"You like my shorts?"

"They're swell."

They were black shorts, and I couldn't have done a better job with a paint brush, let me tell you. She looked absolutely vibrant. She was busting out all over with him. She came around the easel by me, breathing down my neck.

"Get out of here," I said.

"Put your arms around me, honey. Make it like Saskatchewan, huh?"

I turned and grabbed her. It was the end. She was sticky hot from the sunshine and our teeth clicked in a crazy kiss. I hated her. I wanted to sock her.

"Chris, baby. Why don't you ditch all this and start having fun again?"

I heard Sally in the hall. I gave Gloria a shove. She staggered back across the room and landed on the studio couch and Sally came in. Gloria was lying on her back, bicycling.

"Oh," Sally said. "I'm sorry."

I went after Sally, I tried to explain. It was no good. She was hopping mad. "Honey," I said. "I'm going to tell her she'll have to leave. I don't blame you, the way you feel."

"How do you know how I feel? You could never know."

"All right. She's my cousin. I was helping her out. I'll tell her."

Sally looked at me. "Thanks, Chris."

I held her, then, and she let me. She kissed me the way it should be.

"Can you blame me, really?" she said.

"No."

And that night Pearly called. "It's tonight," he said. "Goodbye, friend."

I locked myself in the studio and told Sally I had an all-night job. She said, "Did you tell her, yet?"

"The first thing in the morning. I've got to run into town, and she's going to make the first train out."

Sally was really happy. You could tell.

"God it'll be swell—just the two of us, again."

So I waited, and I couldn't any more touch the paints than take a smooth breath. And sure enough, at three a.m. out comes Gloria and away she goes. She's kind of running, even—the anxious, I-can't-wait type.

I stood by the window and watched. I was dripping sweat. She cut through the fence and started along the slope above the highway. Then Hewes stepped out of the shadows.

A car I hadn't seen started up and there was a hell of a roar from the road. Then another roar and a flash and I knew Pearly had used a shot-gun. It was like hunting season with the rabbits running, and that car was gone before you really knew it was there. No lights, running in the dark, and out there on the slope they lay together, bathed in the moon-light.

I lit out of the studio. Anybody would have heard the boom of that gun.

"Sally!" I called. "What's going on? You all right?"

I ran down the stairs thinking, Free. Free. It's all right now. I started through the hall past the closed bedroom doors.

Gloria stepped out of her room and looked at me.

"Chris," she said. "What's all the racket?"

I stopped running. I stood there and looked at her. She was wearing an orange pajama top, yawning and blinking. She was all frowzy, and hell, I knew. This was sweet.

"Chris," she said, real serious. "That sounded like a shotgun, I swear!"

"It was," I told her. "It was."

So I started walking steadily and Gloria tagged along. She kept saying my name and we walked out there through the fence and up the slope into the moonlight.

Sally and Hewes lay there together on the dew-wet, moon-white grass not far from the edge of the woods. They were in each others arms and she was wearing her pink shorty nightgown. They were a mess.

"Chris," Gloria said. "What is this?"

"Well," I said. "It's too late now, isn't it?" I sat down on the grass and looked over at the road. I'd worked too hard, that was it. I hadn't realized all the nights I'd left Sally alone, lately especially—watching out the window. Watching her run to meet Hewes. And she must have got to liking it fine. She'd wanted to get rid of Gloria, because she fig-ured maybe Gloria would wise up and tell me. Very nice.

Sally, Sally, I thought. I loved you for real.

"Chris, don't sit there. You know who they'll ticket for this? You know, don't you?"

"Yeah."

I knew, all right. They'd ticket me and little Gloria would be there, too. Because this was one rap I'd never beat.

EVERY MORNING

Richard Marsten

HE SANG SOFTLY TO HIMSELF as he worked on the long white beach. He could see the pleasure craft scooting over the deep blue waters, could see the cottony clouds moving leisurely across the wide expanse of sky. There was a mild breeze in the air, and it touched the wooly skullcap that was his hair, caressed his brown skin. He worked with a long rake, pulling at the tangled sea vegetation that the norther had tossed onto the sand. The sun was strong, and the sound of the sea was good, and he was almost happy as he worked.

He watched the muscles ripple on his long brown arms as he pulled at the rake. She would not like it if the beach were dirty. She liked the beach to be sparkling white and clean . . . the way her skin was.

"Jonas!"

He heard the call, and he turned his head toward the big house. He felt the same panic he'd felt a hundred times before. He could feel the trembling start in his hands, and he turned back to the rake, wanting to stall as long as he could, hoping she would not call again, but knowing she would.

"Jonas! Jo-naaaas!"

The call came from the second floor of the house, and he knew it came from her bedroom, and he knew she was rising, and he knew exactly what would happen if he went up there. He hated what was about to happen, but at the same time it excited him. He clutched the rake more tightly, telling himself he would not answer her call, lying to himself because he knew he would go if she called one more time.

"Jonas! Where the devil are you?"

"Coming, Mrs. Hicks," he shouted.

He sighed deeply and put down the rake. He climbed the concrete steps leading from the beach, and then he walked past the barbecue pit and the beach house, moving under the Australian pines that lined the beach. The pine needles were soft under his feet, and though he knew the pines were planted to form a covering over the sand, to stop sand from being tracked into the house, he still enjoyed the soft feel under his shoes. For an instant, he wished he were barefoot, and then he scolded himself for having a thought that was strictly "native."

He shook his head and climbed the steps to the screened back porch of the house. The hibiscus climbed the screen in a wild array of color, pinks and reds and orchids. The smaller bougainvillea reached up for the sun where it splashed down through the pines. He closed the door behind him and walked through the dim cool interior of the house, starting up the steps to her bedroom.

When he reached her door, he paused outside, and then he knocked discreetly.

"Is that you, Jonas?"

"Yes, Mrs. Hicks."

"Well, come in."

He opened the door and stepped into the bedroom. She was sitting in bed, the sheet reaching to her waist. Her long blond hair spilled over her shoulders, trailing down her back. She wore a white nylon gown, and he could see the mounds of her breasts beneath the gown, could see the erect rosebuds of her nipples. Hastily, he lowered his eyes.

"Good morning, Jonas," she said.

"Good morning, Mrs. Hicks."

"My, it's a beautiful morning, isn't it?"

"Yes, Mrs. Hicks."

"Where were you when I called, Jonas?"

"On the beach, Mrs. Hicks."

"Swimming, Jonas?" She lifted one eyebrow archly, and a tiny smile curled her mouth.

"Oh, no, Mrs. Hicks. I was raking up the . . ."

"Haven't you ever felt like taking a swim at that beach, Jonas?"

He did not answer. He stared at his shoes, and he felt his hands clench at his sides.

"Jonas?"

"Yes, Mrs. Hicks?"

"Haven't you ever felt like taking a swim at that beach?"

"There's lots of places to swim, Mrs. Hicks."

"Yes." The smile expanded. Her green eyes were smiling now, too. She sat in bed like a slender cat, licking her chops. "That's what I like about Nassau. There are lots of places to swim." She continued smiling for a moment, and then she sat up straighter, as if she were ready for business now.

"Well," she said, "what shall we have for breakfast? Has the cook come in, Jonas?"

"Yes, Mrs. Hicks."

"Eggs, I think. Coddled. And some toast and marmalade. And a little juice." He made a movement toward the door, and she stopped him with a wave of her hand. "Oh, there's no rush, Jonas. Stay. I want you to help me."

He swallowed, and he put his hands behind his back to hide the trembling. "Yes . . . Mrs. Hicks."

She threw back the sheet, and he saw her long legs beneath the hem of the short nightgown. She reached for her slippers on the floor near her bed, squirmed her feet into them, and then stood up. Luxuriantly, she stretched her arms over her head and yawned. The nightgown tightened across her chest, lifting is she raised her arms, showing more of the long curve of her legs. She walked to the window and threw open the blinds, and the sun splashed through the gown, and he saw the full outline of her body, and he thought: *Every morning, every morning the same thing.*

He could feel the sweat beading his brow, and he wanted to get out of that room, wanted to get far away from her and her body, wanted to escape this labyrinth that led to one exit alone.

"Ahhhhhhhhh." She let out her breath and then walked across the room to her dressing table. She sat and crossed her legs, and he could see the whiter area on her thigh that the sun never reached. And looking at that whiter stretch of flesh, his own skin felt browner.

"Do you like working for me?" she asked suddenly.

"Yes, Mrs. Hicks," he said quickly.

"You don't really, though, do you?"

"I like it, Mrs. Hicks," he said.

"I like you to work for me, Jonas. I wouldn't have you leave for anything in the world. You know that, don't you, Jonas?"

"Yes, Mrs. Hicks."

There has to be a way out, he thought. *There has to be some way. A way other than the one . . . the one . . .*

"Have you ever thought of quitting this job, Jonas?"

"No, Mrs. Hicks," he lied.

"That's sensible, you know. Not quitting, I mean. It wouldn't be wise for you to quit, would it, Jonas? Aside from the salary, I mean, which is rather handsome, wouldn't you say, Jonas?"

"It's a handsome salary," he said.

"Yes. But aside from that, aside from losing the salary if you quit. I wouldn't like you to quit, Jonas. I would let Mr. Hicks know of my displeasure, and my husband is really quite a powerful man, you know that, don't you?"

"Yes, Mrs. Hicks."

"It might be difficult for you to get work afterwards, I mean if you ever decided to leave me. Heaven knows there's not much work for Bahamians as it is. And Mr. Hicks is quite powerful, knowing the Governor and all, isn't that right, Jonas?"

When he did not answer, she giggled suddenly.

"Oh, we're being silly. You like the job, and I like you, so why should we talk of leaving?" She paused. "Has my husband gone to the club?"

"Yes, Mrs. Hicks."

"Good," she said. "Come do my hair, Jonas."

"I . . ."

"Come do my hair," she said slowly and firmly.

"Y . . . yes, Mrs. Hicks."

She held out the brush to him, and he took it and then placed himself behind her chair. He could see her face in the mirror of the dressing table, could see the clean sweep of her throat, and beneath that the first rise of her breasts where the neck of the gown ended. She tilted her head back and her eyes met his in the mirror.

"Stroke evenly now, Jonas. And gently. Remember. Gently."

He began stroking her hair. He watched her face as he stroked, not wanting to watch it, but knowing that he was inside the trap now, and knowing that he had to watch her face, had to watch her lips part as he stroked, had to watch the narrowing of those green eyes. Every morning, every morning the same thing, every morning driving him out of his mind with her body and her glances, always daring him, always challenging him, and always reminding him that it could not be. He stroked, and her breath came faster in her throat, and he watched the animal pleasure on her face as the brush bristles searched her scalp.

And as he stroked, he thought again of the only way out, and he wondered if he had the courage to do it, wondered if he could ever muster the courage to stop all this, stop it finally and irrevocably. She counted softly as he stroked, and her voice was a whisper, and he continued to think of what he must do to end it, and he felt the great fear within him, but he knew he could not take much more of this, not every morning, and he knew he could not leave the job because she would make sure there would never be work for him again.

But even knowing all this, the way out was a drastic one, and he wondered what it would be like without her hair to brush every morning, without the sight of her body, without the soft caress of her voice.

Death, he thought.

Death.

"That's enough, Jonas," she said.

He handed her the brush. "I'll tell the cook, Mrs. Hicks, to . . ."

"No, stay."

He looked at her curiously. She always dismissed him after the brushing. Her eyes always turned cold and forbidding then, as if she had had her day's sport and was then ready to end the farce . . . until the next morning. "I think something bit me yesterday. An insect, I think," she said. "I wonder if you'd mind looking. You natives . . . what I mean, you'd probably be familiar with it."

She stood up and walked toward him, and then she began unbuttoning the yoke neck of her gown. He watched her in panic, not knowing whether to flee or stand, knowing only that he would have to carry out his plan after this, knowing that she would go further and further unless it were ended, and knowing that only he could end it, in the only possible way for him.

He watched her take the hem of her gown in her fingers and pull it up over her waist. He saw the clean whiteness of her skin, and then she pulled the gown up over her back, turning, her breasts still covered, bending.

"In the center of my back, Jonas, don't you see it?"

She came closer to him, and he was wet with perspiration now. He stared at her back, and the fullness of her buttocks, the impression of her spine against her flesh.

"There's . . . there's nothing, Mrs. Hicks," he said. "Nothing."

She dropped the gown abruptly, and then turned to face him, the smile on her mouth again, the yoke of the gown open so that he could see her breasts plainly.

"Nothing?" she asked, smiling. "You saw nothing, Jonas?"

"Nothing, Mrs. Hicks," he said, and he turned and left her, still smiling, her hands on her hips.

He slit his wrists with a razor blade the next morning. He watched the blood stain the sand on the beach he'd always kept so clean, and he felt a strange inner peace possess him as the life drained out of him.

The native police did not ask many questions when they arrived, and Mrs. Hicks did not offer to show them her torn and shredded night-gown, or the purple bruises on her breasts and thighs.

She hired a new caretaker that afternoon.

I'M IN THE BOOK

Loren D. Estleman

WHEN I FINALLY GOT IN TO SEE ALEC WYNN of Reiner, Switz, Galsworthy, & Wynn, the sun was high over Lake St. Clair outside the window behind his desk and striking sparks off the choppy steel-blue surface with sailboats gliding around on it cutting white foam, their sharkfin sails striped in broad bright bikini colors. Wynn sat with his back to the view and never turned to look at it. He didn't need to. On the wall across from him hung a big framed color photograph of bright-striped sailboats cutting white foam on the steel-blue surface of Lake St. Clair.

Wynn was a big neat man with a black widow's peak trimmed tight to his skull and the soft gray hair at his temples worn long over the tops of his ears. He had on aviator's glasses with clear plastic rims and a suit the color and approximate weight of ground fog, that fit him like no suit will ever fit me if I hit the Michigan Lottery tomorrow. He had deep lines in his Miami-brown face and a mouth that turned down like a shark's to show a bottom row of caps as white and even as military monuments. It was a predator's face. I liked it fine. It belonged to a lawyer, and in my business lawyers mean a warm feeling in the pit of the bank account.

"Walker, Amos," he said, as if he were reading roll call. "I like the name. It has a certain smoky strength."

"I've had it a long time."

He looked at me with his strong white hands folded on top of his absolutely clean desk. His palms didn't leave marks on the glossy surface the way mine would have. "I keep seeing your name on reports. The Reliance people employ your services often."

"Only when the job involves people," I said. "Those big investigation agencies are good with computers and diamonds and those teeny little cameras you can hide in your left ear. But when it comes to stroking old ladies who see things and leaning on supermarket stock boys who smuggle sides of beef out the back door, they remember us little shows."

"How big is your agency?"

"You're looking at it. I have an answering service," I added quickly.

"Better and better. It means you can keep a secret. You have a reputation for that, too."

"Who told?"

"The humor I can take or let alone." He refolded his hands the other way. "I don't like going behind Reliance's back like this. We've worked together for years and the director's an old friend. But this is a personal matter, and there are some things you would prefer to have a stranger know than someone you play poker with every Saturday night."

"I don't play poker," I said. "Whoops, sorry." I got out a cigarette and smoothed it between my fingers. "Who's missing, your wife or your daughter?"

He shot me a look he probably would have kept hooded in court. Then he sat back, nodding slightly. "I guess it's not all that uncommon."

"I do other work but my main specialty is tracing missing persons. You get so you smell it coming." I waited.

"It's my wife. She's left me again."

"Again?"

"Last time it was with one of the apprentices here, a man named Lloyd Debner. But they came back after three days. I fired him, naturally."

"Naturally."

A thin smile played around with his shark's mouth, gave it up and went away. "Seems awfully Old Testament, I know. I tried to be modern about it. There's really no sense in blaming the other man. But I saw myself hiding out in here to avoid meeting him in the hall, and that would be grotesque. I gave him excellent references. One of our competitors snapped him up right away."

"What about this time?"

"She left the usual note saying she was going away and I was not to look for her. I called Debner but he assured me he hadn't seen Cecelia since their first—fling. I believe him. But it's been almost a week now, and I'm concerned for her safety."

"What about the police?"

"I believe we covered that when we were discussing keeping secrets," he said acidly.

"You've been married how long?"

"Six years. And, yes, she's younger than I, by fourteen years. That was your next question, wasn't it?"

"It was in there. Do you think that had anything to do with her leaving?"

"I think it had everything to do with it. She has appetites that I've been increasingly unable to fulfill. But I never thought it was a problem until she left the first time."

"You quarreled?"

"The normal amount. Never about that. Which I suppose is revealing. I rather think she's found a new boyfriend, but I'm damned if I can say who it is."

"May I see the note?"

He extracted a fold of paper from an inside breast pocket and passed it across the desk. "I'm afraid I got my fingerprints all over it before I thought over all the angles."

"That's okay. I never have worked on anything where prints were any use."

It was written on common drugstore stationery, tinted blue with a spray of flowers in the upper right-hand corner. A hasty hand full of sharp points and closed loops. It said what he'd reported it had said and nothing else. Signed with a C.

"There's no date."

"She knew I'd read it the day she wrote it. It was last Tuesday."

"Uh-huh."

"That means what?" he demanded.

"Just uh-huh. It's something I say when I can't think of anything to say." I gave back the note. "Any ideas where she might go to be alone? Favorite vacation spot, her hometown, a summer house, anything like that? I don't mean to insult you. Sometimes the hardest place to find your hat is on your head."

"We sublet our Florida home in the off-season. She grew up in this area and has universally disliked every place we've visited on vacation. Really, I was expecting something more from a professional."

"I'm just groping for a handle. Does she have any hobbies?"

"Spending my money."

I watched my cigarette smoke drifting toward the window. "It seems to me you don't know your wife too well after six years, Mr. Wynn. When I find her, if I find her, I can tell you where she is, but I can't make her come back, and from the sound of things she may not want to come back. I wouldn't be representing your best interests if I didn't advise you to save your money and set the cops loose on it. I can't give guarantees they won't give."

"Are you saying you don't want the job?"

"Not me. I don't have any practice at that. Just being straight with a client I'd prefer keeping."

"Don't do me any favors, Walker."

"Okay. I'll need a picture. And what's her maiden name? She may go back to it."

"Collier." He spelled it. "And here." He got a wallet-size color photograph out of the top drawer of the desk and skidded it across the glossy top like someone dealing a card.

She was a redhead, and the top of that line. She looked like someone who would wind up married to a full partner in a weighty law firm with gray temples and an office overlooking Lake St. Clair. It would be in her high school yearbook under Predictions.

I put the picture in my breast pocket. "Where do I find this Debner?"

"He's with Paxton and Ring on West Michigan. But I told you he doesn't know where Cecelia is."

"Maybe he should be asked a different way." I killed my stub in the smoking stand next to the chair and rose. "You'll be hearing from me."

His eyes followed me up. All eight of his fingers were lined up on the near edge of his desk, the nails pink and perfect. "Can you be reached if I want to hear from you sooner?"

"My service will page me. I'm in the book."

A Japanese accent at Paxton & Ring told me over the telephone that Lloyd Debner would be tied up all afternoon in Detroit Recorders Court. Lawyers are always in court the way executives are always in meetings. At the Frank Murphy Hall of Justice a bailiff stopped spitting on his handkerchief and rubbing at a spot on his uniform to point out a bearded man in his early thirties with a mane of black hair, smoking a pipe and talking to a gray-headed man in the corridor outside one of the courtrooms. I went over there and introduced myself.

"Second," he said, without taking his eyes off the other man. "Tim, we're talking a lousy twenty bucks over the fifteen hundred. Even if you win, the judge will order probation. The kid'll get that anyway if we plead Larceny Under, and there's no percentage in mucking up his record for life just to fatten your win column. And there's nothing saying you'll win."

I said, "This won't take long."

"Make an appointment. Listen, Tim—"

"It's about Cecelia Wynn," I said. "We can talk about it out here in the hall if you like. Tim won't mind."

He looked at me then for the first time. "Tim, I'll catch you later."

"After the sentencing." The gray-headed man went into the court-room, chuckling.

"Who'd you say you were?" Debner demanded.

"Amos Walker. I still am, but a little older. I'm a P.I. Alec Wynn hired me to look for his wife."

"You came to the wrong place. That's all over."

"I'm interested in when it wasn't."

He glanced up and down the hall. There were a few people in it, lawyers and fixers and the bailiff with the stain that wouldn't go away from his crisp blue uniform shirt. "Come on. I can give you a couple of minutes."

I followed him into a men's room two doors down. We stared at a guy combing his hair in front of the long mirror over the sinks until he put away his comb and picked up a brown leather briefcase and left. Debner bent down to see if there were any feet in the stalls, straightened, and knocked out his pipe into a sink. He laid it on a soap canister to cool and moved his necktie a centimeter to the right.

"I don't see Cecelia when we pass on the street," he said, inspecting the results in the mirror. "I had my phone number changed after we got back from Jamaica so she couldn't call me."

"That where you went?"

"I rented a bungalow outside Kingston. Worst mistake I ever made. I was headed for a junior partnership at Reiner when this happened. Now I'm back to dealing school board presidents' sons out of jams they wouldn't be in if five guys ahead of me hadn't dealt them out of jams just like them starting when they were in junior high."

"How'd you and Cecelia get on?"

"Oh, swell. So good we crammed a two-week reservation into three days and came back home."

"What went wrong?"

"Different drummers." He picked up his pipe and blew through it.

"Not good enough," I said.

He grinned boyishly. "I didn't think so. To begin with, she's a health nut. I run and take a little wheat germ myself sometimes—don't even have to point a gun at me—but I draw the line at dropping vitamins and herb pills at every meal. She must've taken sixteen capsules every time we sat down to eat. It can drive you blinkers. People in restaurants must've figured her for a drug addict."

"Sure she wasn't?"

"She was pretty open about taking them if she was. She filled the capsules herself from plastic bags. Her purse rattled like a used car."

A fat party in a gray suit and pink shirt came in and smiled and nodded at both of us and used the urinal and washed his hands. Debner used the time to recharge his pipe.

"Still not good enough," I said, when the fat party had gone. "You don't cut a vacation short just because your bedpartner does wild garlic."

"It just didn't work out. Look, I'm due back in court."

"Not at half-past noon." I waited.

He finished lighting his pipe, dropped the match into the sink where he'd knocked his ashes, grinned around the stem. I bet that melted the women jurors. "If this gets around I'm washed up with every pretty legal secretary in the building."

"Nothing has to get around. I'm just looking for Cecelia Wynn."

"Yeah. You said." He puffed on the pipe, took it out, smoothed his beard, and looked at it in the mirror. "Yeah. Well, she said she wasn't satisfied."

"Uh-huh."

"No one's ever told me that before. I'm not used to complaints."

"Uh-*huh*."

He turned back toward me. His eyes flicked up and down. "We never had this conversation, okay?"

"What conversation?"

"Yeah." He put the pipe back between his teeth, puffed. "Yeah."

We shook hands. He squeezed a little harder than I figured he did normally.

I dropped two dimes into a pay telephone in the downstairs lobby and fought my way through two secretaries before Alec Wynn came on the line. His voice was a full octave deeper than it had been in person. I figured it was that way in court too.

"Just checking back, Mr. Wynn. How come when I asked you about hobbies you didn't tell me your wife was into herbs?"

"Into *what*?"

I told him what Debner had said about the capsules. He said, "I haven't dined with my wife in months. Most legal business is conducted in restaurants."

"I guess you wouldn't know who her herbalist is, then."

"Herbalist?"

"Sort of an oregano guru. They tell their customers which herbs to take in the never-ending American quest for a healthy body. Not a few of the runaways I've traced take their restlessness to them first."

"Well, I wouldn't know anything about that. Trina might. She's at the house now."

"Would you call her and tell her I'm coming?"

He said he would and broke the connection.

* * *

It was a nice place if you like windows. There must have been fifty on the street side alone, with ivy or something just as green crawling up the brick wall around them and a courtyard with a marble fountain in the center and a black chauffeur with no shirt on washing a blue Mercedes in front. They are always washing cars. A white-haired Puerto Rican woman with muddy eyes and a faint moustache answered my ring.

"Trina?"

"Yes. You are Mr. Walker? Mr. Wynn told me to expect you."

I followed her through a room twice the size of my living room, but that was designed just for following maids through, and down a hall with dark paintings on the walls to a glassed-in porch at the back of the house containing ferns in pots and lawn chairs upholstered in floral print. The sliding glass door leading outside was ajar and strong chlorine stench floated in from an outdoor crescent-shaped swimming pool. She slid the door shut.

"The pool man says alkali is leaking into the water from an underground spring," she said. "The chlorine controls the smell."

"The rich suffer too." I told her what I wanted.

"Capsules? Yes, Mrs. Wynn has many bottles of capsules in her room. There is a name on the bottles. I will get one."

"No hurry. What sort of woman is Mrs. Wynn to work for?"

"I don't know that that is a good question to answer."

"You're a good maid, Trina." I wound a five-dollar bill around my right index finger.

She slid the tube off the finger and flattened it and folded it over and tucked it inside her apron pocket. "She is a good employer. She says please and does not run her fingers over the furniture after I have dusted, like the last woman I worked for."

"Is that all you can tell me?"

"I have not worked here long, sir. Only five weeks."

"Who was maid before that?"

"A girl named Ann Foster, at my agency. Multi-Urban Services. She was fired." Her voice sank to a whisper on the last part. We were alone.

"Fired why?"

"William the chauffeur told me she was fired. I didn't ask why. I have been a maid long enough to learn that the less you know the more you work. I will get one of the bottles."

She left me, returning a few minutes later carrying a glass container the size of an aspirin bottle, with a cork in the top. It was half full of gelatin capsules filled with fine brown powder. I pulled the cork and sniffed. A sharp, spicy scent. The name of a health foods store on Livernois was typewritten on the label.

"How many of these does Mrs. Wynn have in her bedroom?" I asked.

"Many. Ten or twelve bottles."

"As full as this?"

"More, some of them."

"That's a lot of capsules to fill and then leave behind. Did she take many clothes with her?"

"No, sir. Her closets and drawers are full."

I thanked her and gave her back the bottle. It was getting to be the damnedest disappearing act I had covered in a long, long time.

The black chauffeur was hosing off the Mercedes when I came out. He was tall, almost my height, and the bluish skin of his torso was stretched taut over lumpy muscle. I asked him if he was William.

He twisted shut the nozzle of the hose, watching me from under his brows with his head down, like a boxer. Scar tissue shone around his eyes. "Depends on who you might be."

I sighed. When you can't even get their name out of them, the rest is like pulling nails with your toes. I stood a folded ten-spot on the Mercedes' hood. He watched the bottom edge darken as it soaked up water. "Ann Foster," I said.

"What about her?"

"How close was she to Cecelia Wynn?"

"I wouldn't know. I work outside."

"Who fired her, Mr. or Mrs. Wynn?"

He thought about it. Watched the bill getting wetter. Then he snatched it up and waved it dry. "She did. Mrs. Wynn."

"Why?"

He shrugged. I reached up and plucked the bill out of his fingers. He grabbed for it but I drew it back out of his reach. He shrugged again, wringing the hose in his hands to make his muscles bulge. "They had a fight of some kind the day Ann left. I could hear them screaming at each other out here. I don't know what it was about."

"Where'd she go after she left here?"

He started to shrug a third time, stopped. "Back to the agency, maybe. I don't ask questions. In this line—"

"Yeah. The less you know the more you work." I gave him the ten and split.

The health foods place was standard, plank floor and hanging plants and stuff you can buy in any supermarket for a fraction of what they were asking. The herbalist was a small, pretty woman of about 30, in a gypsy blouse and floor-length denim skirt with bare feet poking out underneath and a bandana tied around her head. She also owned the place. She hadn't seen Mrs. Wynn since before she'd turned up missing. I bought a package of unsalted nuts for her trouble and ate them on the way to the office. They needed salt.

I found Multi-Urban Services in the Detroit metropolitan directory and dialed the number. A woman whose voice reminded me of the way cool green mints taste answered.

"We're not at liberty to give out information about our clients."

"I'm sorry to hear that," I said. "I went to a party at the Wynn place in Grosse Pointe about six weeks ago and was very impressed with Miss Foster's efficiency. I'd heard she was free and was thinking of engaging her services on a full-time basis."

The mints melted. "I'm sorry, Miss Foster is no longer with this agency. But I can recommend another girl just as efficient. Multi-Urban prides itself—"

"I'm sure it does. Can you tell me where Miss Foster is currently working?"

"Stormy Heat Productions. But not as a maid."

I thanked her and hung up, thinking about how little it takes to turn mint to acid. Stormy Heat was listed on Mt. Elliott. Its line was busy. Before leaving the office, I broke the Smith & Wesson out of the desk drawer and snapped the holster onto my belt under my jacket. It was that kind of neighborhood.

* * *

The outfit worked out of old gymnasium across from Mt. Elliott Cemetery, a scorched brick building as old as the eight-hour day with a hand-lettered sign over the door and a concrete stoop deep in the process of going back to the land. The door was locked. I pushed a sunken button that grated in its socket. No sound issued from within. I was about to knock when a square panel opened in the door at head level and a mean black face with a beard that grew to a point looked into mine.

"You've got to be kidding," I said.

"What do you want?" demanded the face.

"Ann Foster."

"What for?"

"Talk."

"Sorry." The panel slid shut.

I was smoking a cigarette. I dropped it to the stoop and crushed it out and used the button again. When the panel shot back I reached up and grasped the beard in my fist and yanked. His chest banged the door.

"You white—!"

I twisted the beard in my fist. He gasped and tears sprang to his eyes. "Joe sent me," I said. "The goose flies high. May the Force be with you. Pick the password you like, but open the door."

"Who—?"

"Jerk Root, the Painless Barber. Open."

"Okay, okay." Metal snapped on his side. Still hanging on to his whiskers, I reached down with my free hand and tried the knob. It turned. I let go and opened the door. He was standing just inside the threshold, a big man in threadbare jeans and a white shirt open to the navel Byron-fashion, smoothing his beard with thick fingers. He had a Colt magnum in his other hand pointed at my belt buckle.

"Nice," I said. "The nickel plating goes with your eyes. You got a permit for that?"

He smiled crookedly. His eyes were still watering. "Why didn't you say you was cop?" He reached back and jammed the revolver into a hip pocket. "You got paper?"

"Not today. I'm not raiding the place. I just want to talk to Ann Foster."

"Okay," he said. "Okay. I don't need no beef with the laws. You don't see nothing on the way, deal?"

I spread my hands. "I'm blind. This isn't an election year."

There was a lot not to see. Films produced by Stormy Heat were not interested in the Academy Award or even feature billing at the all-night grindhouses on Woodward Avenue. Its actors were thin and ferretlike and its actresses used powder to fill the cavities in their faces and cover their stretch marks. The lights and cameras were strictly surplus, their cables frayed and patched all over like old garden hoses. We walked past carnal scenes, unnoticed by the grunting performers or the sweat-stained crews, to a scuffed steel door at the rear that had originally led into a locker room. My escort went through it without pausing. I followed.

"Don't they teach you to knock in the jungle?"

I'd had a flash of a naked youthful brown body, and then it was covered by a red silk kimono that left a pair of long legs bare to the tops of the thighs. She had her hair cut very short and her face, with its upturned nose and lower lip thrust out in a belligerent pout, was boyish. I had seen enough to know she wasn't a boy.

"What's to see that I ain't already seen out on the floor?" asked the Beard. "Man to see you. From the Machine."

Ann Foster looked at me quickly. The whites of her eyes had a bluish tinge against her dark skin. "Since when they picking matinee idols for cops?"

"Thanks," I said. "But I've got a job."

We stared at the guy with the beard until he left us, letting the door drift shut behind him. The room had been converted into a community dressing room, but without much conviction. A library table littered with combs and brushes and pots of industrial strength make-up stood before a long mirror, but the bench on this side had come with the place and the air smelled of mildew and old sweat. She said, "Show me you're cop."

I flashed my photostat and honorary sheriffs star. "I'm private. I let Lothar out there think different. It saved time."

"Well, you wasted it all here. I don't like rental heat any more than the other kind. I don't even like men."

"You picked a swell business not to like them in."

She smiled, not unpleasantly. "I work with an all-girl cast."

"Does it pay better than being a maid?'

"About as much. But when I get on my knees it's not to scrub floors."

"Cecelia Wynn," I said.

Her face moved as if I'd slapped her. "What about her?" she barked.

"She's missing. Her husband wants her back. You had a fight with her just before you got fired. What started it?"

"What happens if I don't answer?"

"Nothing. Now. But if it turns out she doesn't want to be missing, the cops get it. I could save you a trip downtown."

She said, "Hell, she's probably off someplace with her lawyer boyfriend like last time."

"No, he's accounted for. Also she left almost all her clothes behind, along with the herbs she spent a small country buying and a lot of time stuffing into capsules. It's starting to look like leaving wasn't her idea, or that where she was going she wouldn't need those things. What was the fight about?"

"I wouldn't do windows."

I slapped her for real. It made a loud flat noise off the echoing walls and she yelled. The door swung open. Beard stuck his face inside. Farther down the magnum glittered. "What."

I looked at him, looked at the woman. She stroked her burning cheek. My revolver was behind my right hipbone, a thousand miles away. Finally she said, "Nothing."

"Sure?"

She nodded. The man with the beard left his eyes on me a moment longer, then withdrew. The door closed.

"It was weird," she told me. "Serving dinner this one night I spilled salad oil down the front of my uniform. I went to my room to change. Mrs. Wynn stepped inside to ask for something, just like you walked in on me just now. She caught me naked."

"So?"

"So she excused herself and got out. Half an hour later I was canned. For spilling the salad oil. I yelled about it, as who wouldn't? But it wasn't the reason."

"What was?"

She smoothed the kimono across her pelvis. "You think I don't know that look on another woman's face when I see it?"

We talked some more, but none of it was for me. On my way out I laid a twenty on the dressing table and stood a pot of mascara on top of it. I hesitated, then added one of my cards to the stack. "In case something happens to change your mind about rental heat," I said. "If you lose the card, I'm in the book."

Back in civilization I gassed up and used the telephone in the service station to call Alec Wynn at his office. I asked him to meet me at his home in Grosse Pointe in twenty minutes.

"I can't," he said. "I'm meeting a client at four."

"He'll keep. If you don't show you may be one yourself." We stopped talking to each other.

Both William the chauffeur and the Mercedes were gone from the courtyard, leaving only a puddle on the asphalt to reflect the window-studded facade of the big house. Trina let me in and listened to me and escorted me back to the enclosed porch. When she left I slid open the glass door and stepped outside to the pool area. I was there when Wynn came out five minutes later. His gray suit looked right even in those surroundings. It always would.

"You've caused me to place an important case in the hands of an apprentice," he announced. "I hope this means you've found Cecelia."

"I've found her. I think."

"What's that supposed to signify? Or is this the famous Walker sense of humor at work?"

"Save it for your next jury, Mr. Wynn. We're just two guys talking. How long have you been hanging on to your wife's good-bye note? Since the first time she walked out?"

"You're babbling."

"It worried me that it wasn't dated," I said. "A thing like that comes in handy too often. Being in corporate law, you might not know that the cops have ways now to treat writing in ink with chemicals that can prove within a number of weeks when it was written."

His face was starting to match his suit. I went on.

"Someone else knew you hadn't been able to satisfy Cecelia sexually, or you wouldn't have been so quick to tell me. Masculine pride is a strong motive for murder, and in case something had happened to her, you wanted to be sure you were covered. That's why you hired me, and that's why you dusted off the old note. She didn't leave one this time, did she?"

"You have found her."

I said nothing. Suddenly he was an old man. He shuffled blindly to a marble bench near the pool and sank down onto it. His hands worked on his knees.

"When I didn't hear from her after several days I became frightened," he said. "The servants knew we argued. She'd told Debner of my—shortcomings. Before I left criminal law, I saw several convictions obtained on flimsier evidence. Can you understand that I had to protect myself?"

I said, "It wasn't necessary. Debner was just as unsuccessful keeping her happy. Any man would have been. Your wife was a lesbian, Mr. Wynn."

"That's a damn lie!" He started to rise. Halfway up, his knees gave out and he sat back down with a thud.

"Not a practicing one. It's possible she didn't even realize what her problem was until about five weeks ago, when she accidentally saw your former maid naked. The maid is a lesbian and recognized the reaction. Was Cecelia a proud woman?"

"Intensely."

"A lot of smoke gets blown about the male fear of loss of masculinity," I said. "No one gives much thought to women's fears for their femininity. They can drive a woman to fire a servant out of hand, but she would just be removing temptation from her path for the moment. After a time, when the full force of her situation struck home, she might do something more desperate.

"She would be too proud to leave a note."

Wynn had his elbows on his knees and his face in his hands. I peeled cellophane off a fresh pack of Winstons.

"The cops can't really tell when a note was written, Mr. Wynn. I just said that to hear what you'd say."

"Where is she, Walker?"

I watched my reflection in the pool's turquoise-colored surface, squinting against the chlorine fumes. The water was clear enough to see through to the bottom, but there was a recessed area along the north edge with a shelf obscuring it from above, a design flaw that would trap leaves and twigs and other debris that would normally be exposed when the pool was drained. Shadows swirled in the pocket, thick and dark and full of secrets.

HELL ON WHEELS

Thomas S. Roche

THE CAR SHOULD HAVE SPELLED IT OUT FOR ME, EARLY ON. She drove a '56 Mercury Medalist, the 292 bored out to a 312 with a stock Holly Haystack carb and one fuck of a hot cam. Hell on wheels. It was the radials that really made the difference, though, they stuck to the road like bad news to an ex-con. She'd glued a plastic Jesus on the dash and hung a St Christopher medal from the rear-view, presumably in case the radials gave out.

Those goddamn radials. Not even a hint of scratch, just nothing but grip from the second you laid it down. That fucker could haul ass, go from zero to ninety in the time it took you to shit your pants and it didn't stop there while you pissed them, too. The 312 never even worked up a sweat.

Lady drives a car like that, she just ain't safe.

Then I should have known to back off when she said to meet her at the Hammerhead. A rich lady hangs out at the Hammerhead, something's wrong with her, she's got a thing for danger, or maybe a death wish. The Hammerhead is down by the water, out on the Delta. It's by the freeway so there's a weird mix there of bikers, killer truckers, freaks, and college kids. But not your normal college kids, it's kids buying speed, looking for trouble, that sort of thing. And not your average truckers—the kind of guys you figure are shipping human heads to some factory upstate. Or something. And freeway hookers looking for tricks. It's a nasty place, nasty things happen there. I saw this guy get cut up in there, seems someone didn't like his colors so they did that beer bottle trick you always see in movies but never seems to happen much in real life. Turned out later the biker who did the cutting had a knife in his back pocket, he just liked the idea of grinding that shattered beer bottle into the guy's face. He was laughing as the cops led him away. Still gives me bad dreams sometimes, on my bad days.

Me, I don't wear colors. Roxanne Ketchum, she wears black.

I don't expect her to show up, but sure enough the lady is a tramp. Ha ha ha. She slides into the bar, real cool, like she belongs there, clearing a path through the crowd of Angels. Whistles go up as she passes, and she ignores them. She's changed into a tight black skirt and a white T-shirt that shows just what it needs to show. She doesn't look anything like that bored, rich woman who had her Medalist fixed at my garage today, the one who was bossing me around, the one who gave me a goddamn *tip*, for Chrissake. She could even be a local trailer-park whore or something—only thing that gives her away are those boots, pointy-toed, black patent leather, knee-high, buckled. The sort you just can't get in a small town. That's City stuff—Haight-Ashbury, Nordstrom's.

Ketchum's up close to me in a second, against the bar, like she doesn't even need to know me to come on to me.

She leans up hard against me and asks what I'm drinking. *Jack and Ginger. That's a kid's drink*, she tells me, orders her Jack straight up.

We make some small talk, about cars mostly. She knows more about engines than any lady I've ever known. I tell her a thing or two about Mercs, but there isn't a lot she doesn't know. I tell her about the bored out 312 and the power transfer down the drive shaft. She seems impressed. Go figure. She tells me she's thinking of going home early, doesn't like to be out late and get a hangover. She wants to hit the sack by midnight. Now it's my turn to be impressed.

"You're a Mrs for a reason, right—*Mrs.* Ketchum?" I say.

"Everything that happens has a reason," she tells me, and gets down off the barstool, tossing a bill on the counter.

Five minutes after that we're in the Merc. My hand's on her thigh, and she isn't wearing anything under that skirt. But I don't get to find out what she does have under it—not yet, anyway, because before I know it she's got the Merc in gear and the radials grabbing pavement, not a hint of scratch, out of the parking lot, then slams the pedal down up the ramp, thirty, forty, forty-five, like it was nothing. She's going north on 99 and I watch the dial hit fifty, sixty, sixty-five. She lights a cigarette. Her hands are steady. Then, not seeming to think too much about it, she wriggles in the seat and pulls her skirt down as we level off at eighty. I did the right things with the Merc this afternoon. She's running like a dream, not a hint of rough stuff in the carb, listen to that engine, it's like a whisper on the edge of a growl.

I laugh and light up a Pall Mall, blowing the smoke out the window. She drives like a dream, like smooth velvet across flesh. She lets her right foot sink down a little bit, pretty soon we're doing 95 on the straightaway, inching toward 100 before we hit the curve near the Cuervo billboard. But I can't resist busting her balls. "Mrs. Ketchum, you drive like a city girl."

Ketchum draws deep on her cig, an expensive European brand, a Gitanes or something. She says coolly, "Oh yeah? Well, you kiss like a fucking redneck."

The mansion out on the delta has a big lawn and a remote-control iron gate outside, razorwire at the top.

She brakes hard into the turnabout, drops the keys on the car floor, pushes herself across the gearshift, crawls on top of me, pulls the door handle, shoves me out of the car. The two of us come down hard and roll onto the manicured lawn. The car door stays open as she rubs hard against me. Right there on the front lawn. Then her tongue's in my mouth and she's kneeling over me, getting my pants open.

She comes down harder than ever against me, if I didn't know better I'd say she was trying to kill me. We do it on the front lawn and it's like

I can't stop myself, Roxanne Ketchum has totally taken me over, all I want to do is make it with her in front of the whole world, the hot Central-Valley night blowing over us.

After, we just lay there on the expensive lawn and breathe hard for a while.

Finally, she gets up, gathers her clothes in a ball, walks to the front door fumbling with her keys. She's standing there at the door, stark naked in the security lights, except for the boots. She turns and looks back at me, her skin all unnaturally blue-white, like she doesn't give a damn what the neighbors see, which in this part of the state is more guts than most chicks have, but then why does that surprise me? She cocks her head at me.

"There's beer in the fridge, right through the first hallway," she says as she goes in. "Bedroom's at the top of the stairs, turn right."

Everything's packed in boxes from expensive stores. Roxy told me at the garage earlier today that they're just moving in. Seems weird to be fooling around in such a brand-new, empty house, with her fine China sealed in boxes.

She's waiting for me on the four-poster bed, boots off this time. Sprawled out like she owns the world. I take a plug from the bottle of Anchor Steam and join her.

Mr. Ketchum's off on business in New York until Tuesday. According to Roxy, that means balling young whores in skirts too short to properly be called garments. He has a recent taste for blondes. Roxy's hair is black, just inching toward grey.

"I heard some rumors about you," she tells me.

We're under the canopy in her four-poster bed, and it's four in the morning. She's tangled me up in black satin sheets and scattered dead rose petals around me. Candles fill the room, the light flickering and scattering through the white lace curtain.

I take a long pull off the warm Anchor. "Something bad?"

"Something real bad." No expression on her face.

"Worse than adultery?"

"You tell me."

"You're a big girl—you don't think it's that easy to find out a man's secrets, do you? Look, maybe I did something and maybe I didn't. What the fuck business is it of yours?"

"Maybe it is my business."

"You better have a good reason for asking, then."

Roxy presses against me and nuzzles my throat. Then she starts kissing me.

I almost forget what we were talking about by the time she tells me, long minutes later, "I got a reason. If you did it once, you'd do it again."

Sunday morning, Roxy and I miss church, I'll have to remember to mention it to my priest next time I go to confession, ha ha. We sit out on the balcony watching the smog settle in the Central Valley. Roxy's sent all the servants home so she cooks me breakfast. She pours out her whole sad story over Eggs Benedict, sautéed vegetables, fresh-squeezed juice, coffee. She's one hell of a cook. She tells me all her problems, and what she wants to do about them.

Sweet Roxy's horny hubby Roger Ketchum won't give her a divorce, not the kind she wants. And she's sick and tired of his habit of coming home with a different perfume every night. There's other shit, too, I guess he doesn't treat her so good. Roxy has scars across her back and a couple of bruises on her shoulder, old ones, at least a week, so they must have been pretty bad. Nothing makes me sicker than a guy who slaps his woman around like he owns her.

But it seems Roger and Roxy had a pre-nuptial agreement, so even though he's hitting the sack with nineteen-year-old cocktail waitresses, Roxy won't get a dime if she leaves her old man. Of course, while he's doing younger chicks she's making it with ex-con garage mechanics, but that's strictly a moral dilemma and way the fuck out of my territory. What's in my territory, is fifty grand, cash, small bills, non-consecutive serial numbers.

I get to thinking about old Luis Reyes as I lay there with Roxy Ketchum wrapped around me, sleeping restlessly. Reyes was a smartass college fuck, young and cocky, always talking shit. A little too smart for his own good, talking how he had money waiting for him in Frisco soon as he finished up at the State College. Liked to talk about rednecks and scumbags. Thought he was hot shit, some sort of business major, weekend saucier, wanted to go to chef school and open up a restaurant. One day he fucked with me a little, just a little, and it was the wrong day. I was pissed off and high on a little speed. I must have beat him pretty bad. Didn't mean to, but he had it coming. I did some time but it was my hometown and he was half spic, even if he was raised in Marin fucking County. I had this girlfriend, Annie, she had a little money, her nephew's college fund. She got me a slick City lawyer and I plea bargained down to manslaughter. I figure Annie'd wait for me, but fourteen months into my time in the joint she finds some other guy, and she hits the road with him. His name was Carver, ha ha. Poor Annie, she never did have the best judgement. She ended up face down in the Delta. Carver got off scot-free 'cause all the evidence is circumstantial and it's a capital offense. Explain that one to me. He was smart enough not to leave prints, smarter than me, I guess. It made the papers. Seems Carver was the wrong guy for poor Annie to run away with. Annie never did have any taste in men except for me.

It wasn't fair, that was for sure. The serial killer sex criminal weirdo never gets convicted. But I go up the river for teaching a college asshole some manners, which is why Carver could kill Annie, because if I'd been around he wouldn't have gotten near her. I never would have hurt Annie, even though I was pretty pissed when she stopped visiting me. I loved Annie like I loved nothing else in this world, except maybe that 289 I dropped into the Fairlane I had when I was 17. So I took care of things after I got out. Found Carver coming out of his house, just off of 99 by the interchange. I was on parole so I couldn't carry a gun. Bummer for Carver, he took a long time to die with that 2 x 4.

Just my luck that just as I finish him off a patrol car comes to pick the bastard up. Seems they've had complaints from PG & E linemen about the smell.

This time it was clearly self-defense. I should have been a damn hero, especially when they found that shit in the guy's basement. Fuck! It still weirds me out to think about it. The cops should have gotten on their knees and sucked my dick for what I did. Carver would have convinced a court his mama made him wear panties or something, and would have been living in a trailer park in Fresno in six years, carving up someone else's daughters and girlfriends.

But the pigs didn't see it that way, and this time I didn't have Annie's money, so I got a lousy Public Defender, the guy couldn't give a rat's ass whether I got the gas chamber or a room at the Ritz. He bargained me down to aggravated assault or something and I got two more years in the joint—hard time. That's where I learned about piano wire.

Reyes was just a stuck-up bastard, he deserved what he got. Carver was the fucking Devil's right hand as far as I'm concerned, the fucker still gives me nightmares when I think about that basement of his with that heater-pipe. The Governor should have given me a medal for killing the bastard. Manslaughter my ass. Aggravated assault my ass. Way I figure it I was the only guy around who was sane, both times.

"I'm not asking you to scare him," she tells me, her legs twined with mine. "I don't want you to beat him up or anything. I don't want a divorce—not now. I'm not trying to get rid of him. I tried to reason with him . . ."

He calls her from the car phone. She tells him she's sorry for the things she said, that she wants to show him how sorry she was. I sit there smoking a Pall Mall as she tells him all the things she's going to do to him, to make up for their fight.

Roxy lays down on the black velvet divan in the living room. Leaves the front curtains open, with the room lights down and candles lit behind her. So he'll see her right when he pulls up in the Jag.

When he comes in he isn't seeing anything except Roxy. He doesn't look behind the curtains on the side of the window.

He doesn't see much for long.

I take the Medalist out on 99, heading south. It's a crime to drive the thing at 65. But I can't take any chances. Even holding back like that, the thing's a dream, it makes me want to cry just hearing that 312 whisper-growl. It's a fucking beauty, it's like the chariot of the gods. I pull off down by the old power plant, near the drainage system, where they used to dump the toxic waste. I pop the trunk and get started. No one'll come here in a million years.

***

I learned things, in the joint. Besides cars. Of course, nothing's for sure—it never is. But if I did everything right, the cops won't find a thing. There isn't much left to find anyway. The only thing that spooks me is, he's not dead when I get him out of the trunk of the Medalist. All I can grab on short notice is the tire iron. I guess I didn't learn that first part right. I'll have to practice with the piano wire.

It kind of freaks me out, you know? I mean, don't get me wrong, I'm not getting religious on you. I just don't like it when you have to see their eyes. I'm not saying he didn't deserve it. I just don't like seeing his eyes.

Out on 99 again, Christ, now I can really lay it down. Clean. Smooth. Lush. The feeling of total power under my right foot. Driving with the window down, one hand on the wheel, blowing Pall Mall smoke—it's like a dream come true. I get it up to 95 in the straightaway, then push it just a little. One hundred. Beautiful.

Roxy's waiting for me in the bedroom. She has a bottle of champagne on ice. She's stretched out on the four-poster bed.

"Did you do it?" she asks, her voice a whisper on the edge of a growl. Her lips are painted red. She brushes her hair out of her face.

"Don't ask that," I tell her.

She looks me right in the eye. "I want to know everything," she says.

I don't like it at first, but I guess I don't take much convincing. And Roxy's a good talker. She wants to know it all.

Wants to know what he looked like when I opened the trunk. What kind of a knife I used to carve him up. Where I tossed the knife and the wire so the pigs wouldn't find them. She wants to know whether it made me hard when I did him. It didn't. She seems disappointed.

People watch too much TV these days. Turns them into fucking weirdos.

I don't like to think this, but it's gotta be pretty obvious by now. Roxy's some kind of a sex-kill freak, a weirdo like Carver. She wants me to tie her up and then she struggles, pulling hard against the ropes. Makes me tell her over and over again how I killed her husband, makes me give her every detail. Then she wants me to call her names.

I've never done this to a chick before. But it turns me on pretty hardcore, which freaks me out. I do her like there's nothing else either of us wants in the world, and she and I both come more times than I can count.

After, smoking a cigarette, I don't feel so good about what I did. Not the killing, that's OK. I mean what Roxy and me did. It seems too close to something I've seen before, something I see every night lately, something that hits me right where I live, in my nightmares.

I'd never kill a chick, that'd be fucking demented, but Roxy wants me to pretend like I would, and I do it better than I want to. I'm not sure I like that.

But I do what she wants me to do. It makes me kind of nauseous, but I do it. This chick is fucking scary.

Way I figure it, it's like she's slamming me right up face to face with my dark side or something, my evil twin serial killer. Making me become someone like Carver. Making me touch my own darkness. People see too many sex crime serial-killer movies these days on late-night cable and video. Makes them unable to deal with reality, as far as I'm concerned. Makes them crave violence like it was some sort of candy.

The Merc should have tipped me off. Woman drives a car like that, she's fucking slow dynamite, fuse in your mouth, gonna blow your head off. That's what I think.

It's definitely not right for a chick to get into a killing like this, any more than it was right for Carver. How long 'till Roxy decides she wants another corpse to hear about? Just for laughs?

How long till that's what I want? That's what really fucking bugs me about it.

By the time both of us fall asleep I've figured out that this is going to have to be a short-lived affair.

"Wake up," says Roxy softly.

Roxy's legs are spread around my torso and she has a pistol in my face.

It's a revolver—looks like a .357. Those things blow your head open like a melon. I try to stay calm.

"Jesus, Roxy, what the—"

"I called the cops. I'm just holding you till they get here. I called them from downstairs. They know everything."

"What the fuck?" I start to get up. Roxy's hand tightens on the gun, and I freeze. She's got her knees wedged on my wrists, holding me down. Maybe I could throw her off, take her down, get the gun away from her. But if I try that she just might do me. She lets the short barrel of the revolver creep closer to my face, until it almost touches my lips. I cross my eyes looking to see if it's loaded. It is. Six shells in six cylinders. Hell on wheels.

"Roxy," I say calmly. "When did you call the cops?"

"Just a few minutes ago," she tells me.

"There's still time to get away. We can get away together. We'll take some cash and run like hell, all right? Mexico or something. I've got a friend who grows weed down there, he's got connections."

Roxy looks me right in the eye.

"You ever make it down to Frisco?" She says it without emotion. She's flipping out, I figure. Reverting to childhood or something.

"Look, Roxy, you're hysterical—we've got to get out of here—"

"I asked you a question."

"No," I say, fighting hard not to lose my calm. I don't want to set her off. "I don't get to Frisco much. Been there a couple times. What the fuck is wrong with you?"

"Me and Luis wanted to open up a restaurant on Valencia. You know, around Twenty-fourth Street? A breakfast place. He made a hell of an omelet. Roger was going to finance it, before he found out about the affair I was having with Luis. I was slipping him money so he could do his time at the Culinary Academy. When Roger found out he pulled the rug on me. Kept track of all my cash. Threatened to have Luis killed. I couldn't give him money any more. So Luis had to transfer to the state school."

I hear the sirens in the distance.

"You are one crazy bitch," I say flatly.

I look into her eyes, and see him. See the memory, something she has held onto, kept close to her heart for three years, kept close and hard and tight, through years of her marriage—loveless, brutal, cruel.

"You're a three time loser. This time it's Murder One with extenuating circumstances. You know what that means, in California?"

I've got to kill some time so I can get my hand free, get the gun out of her hand. So I ask her a question I don't give a shit about. "Why not just kill me?"

I think I can get my hand out from under her knee.

"It wouldn't be right," she tells me. "That wouldn't be *justice*."

I'm playing her, getting her to talk to me so she won't notice I'm getting my wrist angled just right to pull it free. The barrel of the revolver is against my lips, I can taste the metal. Drool is running down the side of my face. "I'll tell the cops everything—"

"Tell 'em. Let's see who they believe. I put the fifty grand in the furnace. You did my man so you could have me to yourself. Sound reasonable?"

"Sounds like a *Matlock* episode, for Chrissake."

But I can see her wrists have raw, bloody, bruised lines where the ropes cut into her skin. "You even took Polaroids, you sick bastard. You're going straight to the gas chamber, and if the cops find out about the fifty grand, make it conspiracy to murder, that's one more count for you and maybe they haul me in too—you'll *still* get the chamber and I'll be out on parole in less than ten years. Your friendly Public Defender is going to plea bargain your three-time-loser ass up to mass murder and treason and conspiracy to sell the H-Bomb to Canada. Three strikes, asshole. You're out."

There's no emotion in her voice, and I know she's going to kill me if I don't do it right. But I move faster than she does. I yank my hand out from under her knee, grab the lamp off the nightstand before she can pull the trigger. I hit her hard with the base of the lamp, as hard as I can. It shatters across her skull, blood splattering into my eyes. The revolver smashes my lip, cutting it. Footsteps on the stairs. I wrestle the gun to the side and then everything's thunder, my ears explode and I can't hear a thing but this high-pitched whine, and everything's filmed in a white light. The side of my face burns like fuck and one eye seems seared shut. Feathers scatter about us, clogging my mouth, from where the bullet slammed into the satin feather pillow.

I twist, hard, with both hands, slamming the heel of my hand into her wrist so that I hear it cracking. But still Roxy doesn't let go. The barrel of the .357 is hovering in front of my face, ready to take me out. I try to peel her fingers back. I get hold of two of them and bend them back, fighting to keep the muzzle of the gun out of my face. I pull hard until I hear a crack. She rolls, screaming in pain, but still both her hands are wrapped around the butt of the gun. I get her off the bed and she hits the floor, hard, but she doesn't let go of the gun even after I land on her chest with my knee, all my weight in her solar plexus. Her face goes white and her eyes bulge, there's a weird puking sound deep in her throat, her eyes flood with red. I can hear her ribs crack. I get my hand around her wrist but even with her ribs and two fingers broken she's got a death-grip on the butt of the revolver. I hear the door splintering. She's got one finger, must be her middle, under the trigger guard of the .357. Everything opens up in a blaze of flame and heat. First bullet. Wall. Powder burning in my hair. Second bullet. Ceiling. Every breath burns.

Third bullet. Throat.

Blood covers both our faces in a fine spray. Roxy probably figures she can plea-bargain this one down to unlawful discharge.

I hit the floor trying to scream, not having much luck. Roxy's body is pressed up against me; her face is filmed with blood, her teeth pink. The cops are screaming at her to put the gun down. Sounds like there's a million of them. Roxy puts the Ladysmith under my chin.

A HANDGUN FOR PROTECTION

John Lutz

I HAD TO HAVE HER. Lani Sundale was her name, and for the past three Saturday nights I'd sat at the corner of the bar in the Lost Beach Lounge and listened to her talk to her friends—another girl, a blonde—and a tall, husky guy with graying hair and bushy eyebrows. Once there was an older woman with a lot of jewelry who acted like she was the gray haired guy's wife. They'd sit and drink and gab to each other about nothing in particular, and I'd sit working on my bourbon and water, watching her reflection in the back bar mirror.

It wasn't until the second Saturday night, when she got a telephone call, that I learned her name, but even before that I was—well, let's say committed.

Lani was a dark haired, medium-height, liquid motion girl, shapely and a little heavier than was the style, like a woman should be. But with her face she didn't need her body. She really got to me right off: high cheekbones, upturned nose, and slightly parted, pouty little red lips, as if she'd just been slapped. Then she had those big dark eyes that kind of looked deep into a guy and asked questions. And from time to time she'd look up at me in the mirror and smile like it just might mean something.

The fourth Saturday night she came in alone.

I swiveled on my bar stool with practiced casualness to face her booth. "Where's your friends?"

She shrugged and smiled. "Other things to do." Past her, outside the window, I could see the blank night sky and the huge Pacific rolling darkly on the beach.

"No stars tonight," I said. "You're the shiningest thing around."

"You're trying to tell me it's going to rain," she said, still with the smile. It was a kind of crooked, wicked little smile that looked perfect on her. "I drink whiskey sours."

I ordered her one, myself a bourbon and water, and sat down across from her in the soft vinyl booth. Two guys down the bar looked at me briefly with naked envy.

"Your name's Lani," I told her. She didn't seem surprised that I knew. "I'm Dennis Conners."

The bartender brought our drinks on a tray and Lani raised her glass. "To new acquaintances."

Three drinks later we left together.

It was about four when Lani drove me back to the Lounge parking lot to pick up my car. Hard as it was for me to see much in the dark, I knew we were in an expensive section of coast real estate where a lot of wealthy people had plush beach houses, like the beach house I'd just visited with Lani.

She drove her black convertible fast, not bothering to stop and put up the top against the sparse, cold raindrops that stung our faces. What I liked most about her then was that she didn't bother with the ashamed act, and when we reached the parking lot and the car had stopped, she leaned over and gave me a kiss with that tilted little grin.

"See you again?" she said as I got out of the car.

"We'll most likely run across one another," I said with a smile, slamming the heavy door.

I could hear her laughter over the roar and screech of tires as the big convertible backed and turned onto the empty highway. I walked back to my car slowly.

During the next two weeks we were together at the beach house half a dozen times. The place spelled money, all right. Not real big but definitely plush, stone fireplace, deep carpeting, rough sawn beams, modern kitchen, expensive and comfortable furniture. There was no place the two of us would rather have been, the way it felt with the heavy drapes drawn and a low fire throwing out its twisted, moving shadows. And the way we could hear that wild ocean curl up moaning on the beach, over and over again. It was a night like that, late, when she started talking about her husband.

"Howard's crippled," she said. "An automobile accident. He'll never get out of his wheelchair." She looked up at me as if she'd just explained something.

"How long ago?" I asked.

"Two years. It was his own fault. Drunk at ninety miles an hour. He can't complain."

"I've been drunk at ninety miles an hour myself."

"Oh, so have I." The shrug and tilted smile. "We all take our chances."

I wondered how much her husband knew about her. How much I knew about her. From time to time I'd marvelled at how skillfully she could cover up the bruises on her face and neck with makeup. She was all that mattered to me now, and it made me ache with a strange compassion for her husband, thinking how it would be watching her from a wheelchair.

"Let's get going," she said, standing and slipping into her suede high heeled shoes. "The fire's getting low."

I yanked her back by the elbow. Then I walked over and put another log on the fire.

Where I lived, at a motel in North Beach, was quite it comedown from the beach house love nest. During the long days of dwindling heat and afternoon showers I'd lie on my bed, sipping bourbon over ice and thinking about Lani and myself. I'm no kind of fool, and I knew what was happening didn't exactly tally. With her money and looks Lani could have had her choice of big husky young ones, her kind. I never kidded myself; I was over thirty-five, blond hair getting a little thin and once-athletic body now sporting a slight drinker's paunch. Not a bad looking guy, but not the pick of the litter. And my not-so-lucrative occupation of water skiing instructor during the vacation season would hardly have attracted Lani. I already owed her over five hundred dollars she never expected to get back.

Maybe any guy in my situation would have wondered how he'd got so lucky. I didn't know or really care. I only knew I had what I wanted most. And even during the day I could close my eyes and lean back in my bed five miles from sea and hear the tortured surf of the rolling night ocean.

"He has more money than he could burn," Lani said to me one night at the beach house.

"Howard?"

She nodded and ran her fingernails through the hair on my chest.

"You're his wife," I told her. "Half of all he owns is yours and vice versa."

"You're something I own that isn't half his, Dennis. We own each other. I feel more married to you than to Howard."

"Divorce him," I said. "You'd get your half."

She pulled her head away from me for a moment and looked incredulous.

"Are you kidding? The court wouldn't look too kindly on a woman leaving a cripple. And Howard's really ruthless. His lawyers might bring out something from my past."

"Or present."

She tried to bite my arm and I pulled her back by the hair. I knew what she'd been talking toward and I didn't care. I didn't care about anything but her. She was twisting her head all around, laughing, as I slapped her and shoved her away. She was still laughing when she said it.

"Dennis, there's only one—"

I interrupted her. "I'll kill him for you," I said.

We were both serious then. She sat up and we stared at each other. The twin reflections of the fire were tiny star-points of red light in her dark eyes. I reached for her.

The beach house was where we discussed the thing in detail, weighing one plan after another. We always met there and nowhere else. I'd conceal my old sedan in the shadows behind a jagged stand of rock and walk down through the grass and cool sand to the door off the wooden sun deck. She'd be waiting for me.

"Listen," she said to me one night when the sea wind was howling in gusts around the sturdy house, "why don't we use this on him?" She opened her purse and drew out a small, snub-nosed .32 caliber revolver.

I took it from her and turned it over in my hand. A compact, ugly weapon with an unusual eight shot cylinder, the purity of its flawless white pearl grips made the rest of it seem all the uglier.

"Whose?" I asked.

Lani closed her purse and tossed it onto the sofa from where she sat on an oversized cushion. "Howard gave it to me just after we were married, for protection."

"Then it can be traced to you."

She shook her head impatiently. "He bought it for me in Europe, when he was on a business trip in a communist block country. Brought it back illegally, really. I looked into this thing, Dennis. I know the police can identify the type and make weapon used from the bullet, only this make gun won't even be known to them. All they'll be able to say for sure is it was a .32 caliber."

I looked at her admiringly and slipped the revolver into my pants pocket. "You do your homework like a good girl. How many people know you own this thing?"

"Quite a few people were there when Howard gave it to me three years ago, but only a few people have seen it since. I doubt if anybody even knows what caliber it is. I know I can pretend I don't."

She was watching me closely as I thoughtfully rubbed the back of my hand across my mouth. "What happens if the police ask you to produce the gun? Nothing to prevent them from matching it with the murder bullet then."

Lani laughed. "In three years I lost it! Let them search for it if they want. It'll be at the bottom of the ocean where you threw it." She was grinning secretively, her dark hair hanging loose over one ear and the makeup under one eye smudged.

"Why not let me in on your entire plan?" I said. "The whole thing would come off better."

"I didn't mean to take over or anything. I just want it to be safe for you, baby, for both of us. So we can enjoy afterward together."

I wondered then if afterward would be like before.

"I know this gun is safe," Lani went on. "No matter where you got another one the police might eventually trace it. But with this one they can't."

"Is it registered or anything?"

"No, Howard just gave it to me."

"But the people who saw him give it to you, couldn't they identify it?"

"Not if they never saw it again." She took a sip of the expensive blended whiskey she was drinking from the bottle and looked up smiling at me with her head tilted back and kind of resting on one shoulder. "I think I've got an idea you'll like," she said. Her lips were parted wide, still glistening wet from the whiskey.

That's how three nights later I found myself dressed only in swimming trunks and deck shoes, seated uncomfortably in the hard, barnacle-clad wooden structure of the underside of the long pier that jutted out into the sea from Howard Sundale's private beach. To the right, beyond the rise of sand, I could see the lights of his sprawling hacienda style house as I kept shifting my weight and feeling the spray from the surf lick at my ankles. I'd always considered myself small time, maybe, not the toughest but smart, and here I was killing for a woman. There'd been plenty of passed up opportunities to kill for money. I knew it wasn't Lani's money at all; I'd have wanted her rich or poor.

I unconsciously glanced at my wrist for the engraved watch I'd been careful not to wear, and I cursed softly as the white foaming breakers surged out their rolling lives beneath me. It *had* to be ten o'clock!

Lani had guaranteed me that Belson, her husband's chauffeur and handyman, would bring Howard for his nightly stroll out onto the long pier at ten o'clock.

"Belson always wheels him there," she'd said. "It's habit with them. Only this time I'll call Belson back to the house for a moment and he'll leave Howard there alone—for you."

The idea then was simple and effective. I was to climb up from my hiding place, shoot Howard, strip him of ring, watch and wallet, then swim back along the shoreline to near where my car was hidden and drive for North Beach Bridge, where I'd throw the murder gun into deep water.

At first I'd been for just rolling Howard wheelchair and all into the ocean. But Lani had assured me it was better to make it look like murder and robbery for the very expensive ring he was known to wear. Less chance of a mistake that way, she'd argued, than if we tried to get tricky and outwit the police by faking an accident. And Howard's upper body was exceptionally strong. Even without the use of his legs he'd be able to stay afloat and make his way to shore.

So at last we'd agreed on the revolver.

I looked up from my place in the shadows. Something was passing between me and the house lights. Two forms were moving through the night toward the pier: Howard Sundale hunched in his wheelchair, and Belson, a tall, slender man leaning forward, propelling the chair with straight arms and short but smooth steps.

As they drew nearer I saw that the lower part of Howard's body was covered by a blanket, and Belson, an elderly man with unruly curly hair, was wearing a light windbreaker and a servant's look of polite blankness. They turned onto the pier and passed over me, and I crouched listening to the wheelchair's rubber tires' choppy rhythm over the rough planks.

A minute later I heard Lani's voice, clear, urgent. "Belson! Belson, will you come to the house for a minute? It's important!"

Belson said something to Howard I couldn't understand. Then I heard his hurried, measured footsteps pass over me and away. Then quiet. I drew the revolver from its waterproof plastic bag.

Howard Sundale was sitting motionless, staring seaward, and the sound of the rushing surf was enough to cover my noise as I climbed up onto the pier, checked to make sure Belson was gone, then walked softly in my canvas deck shoes toward the wheelchair.

"Mr. Sundale?"

He was startled as I moved around to stand in front of him. "Who are you?"

Howard Sundale was not what I'd expected. He was a lean faced, broad shouldered, virile looking man in his forties, keen blue eyes beneath wind-ruffled sandy hair. I understood now why Lani hadn't wanted me to risk pushing him into the sea. He appeared momentarily surprised, then wary when I brought the gun around from behind me and aimed it at him. His eyes darted for a moment in the direction of the distant house lights.

"For Lani, I suppose," he said. Fear made his voice too high.

I nodded. "You should try to understand."

He smiled a knowing, hopeless little frightened smile as I aimed for his heart and pulled the trigger twice.

Quickly I slipped off his diamond ring and wristwatch, amazed at the coolness of his still hands. Then I reached around for his wallet, couldn't find it, discovered it was in his side pocket. I put it all in the plastic bag with the revolver, sealed the bag shut, then slipped off the pier into the water. As I lowered myself I found I was laughing at the way Howard was sitting motionless and dead in the moonlight, still looking out to sea as if there was something there that had caught his attention. Then the cold water sobered me.

I followed the case in the papers. Murder and robbery, the police were saying. An expensive wristwatch, his wallet and a diamond ring valued at over five thousand dollars the victim was known always to wear were missing. At first Belson, the elderly chauffeur, was suspected. He claimed, of all things, that he'd been having an affair with his employer's wife and was with her at the time of the shooting. That must have brought a laugh from the law, especially with the way Lani looked and the act she was putting on. Finally the old guy was cleared and released anyway.

The month Lani and I let pass after the funeral was the longest thirty days of my life. On the night we'd agreed to meet, I reached the beach house first, let myself in and waited before the struggling, growing fire that I'd built.

She was fifteen minutes late, smiling when she came in. We kissed and it was good to hold her again. I squeezed the nape of her neck, pulled her head back and kissed her hard.

"Wait . . . Wait!" she gasped. "Let's have a drink first." There was a fleck of blood on her trembling lower lip.

I watched her walk into the kitchen to mix our drinks.

When she returned the smile returned with her. "I told you it would work, Dennis."

"You told me," I said, accepting my drink.

She saw the pearl handled revolver then, where I'd laid it on the coffee table. Quickly she walked to it, picked it up and examined it. There was surprise in her eyes, in the downturned, pouting mouth. "What happened?"

"I forgot to throw it into the sea, took it home with me by mistake and didn't realize it until this afternoon."

She put the gun down. "You're kidding?"

"No, I was mixed up that night. Not thinking straight. Your husband was the first man I ever killed."

She stood for a moment, pondering what I'd said. After a while she took a sip of her drink, put it down and came to me.

"Did the police question you about the gun?" I asked her.

"Uh-hm. I told them it was lost."

"I'll get rid of it tonight on my way home."

"Tomorrow morning," Lani corrected me as her arms snaked around my shoulders. "And we'll meet here again tomorrow night . . . and the night after that and after that . . ."

Despite her words her enthusiasm seemed to be slipping. That didn't matter to me.

Lani was the first one at the beach house the next evening. It was a windy, moon-bright night, only a few dark clouds racing above the yellow dappled sea at right angles to the surf, as she opened the door to my knock and let me in. Her first words were what I expected.

"Did you get rid of the gun?"

"No." I watched her eyes darken and narrow slightly.

"No? . . ."

"I'm keeping it," I said, "for protection."

"What do you mean, Dennis?" The anger crackled in her voice.

I only smiled. "I mean I have the revolver, and I've left a letter to be opened in the event of my death telling a lawyer where it's hidden."

Lani turned, walked from me with her head bowed then wheeled to face me. "Explain it! It doesn't scare me and I know it should."

"It should," I said, crossing the room and seating myself on the sofa with my legs outstretched. "I wiped the gun clean of prints when I brought it here, then lifted it by a pencil in the barrel when I left here after you last night. Your fingerprints are on it now, nice and clear."

She cocked her head at me, gave me a confused, crooked half-smile. "So what—it's my gun. My prints would naturally be on it."

"But yours are the *only* prints on it," I said. "No one could have shot Howard without erasing or overlapping them. Meaning that you had to have handled the weapon *after* the murder—or during. If that gun ever happened to find its way to the police . . ."

Her eyebrows raised.

"I could tell them I found it," she said with a try for spunk, "and then it was stolen from me."

"They wouldn't believe you. And it isn't likely that anyone would take the gun without smudging or overlapping your prints. What the law would do is run a ballistics test on it, determine it was the murder weapon then arrest you. What's your alibi?"

"Belson—"

"You'd be contradicting your own story. And I doubt if Belson would come to your defense now. No one would believe either of you anyway. Then there's that past you mentioned."

I grinned, watching the fallen, trapped expression on her pouting face. A bitter, resigned look widened her dark eyes. When I rose, still grinning, and moved toward her she backed away.

"You're crazy!" Fear broke her voice and she raised her hands palms out before her. "Crazy!"

"It's been said," I told her as calmly as I could.

I made love to her then, while the moon-struck ocean roared its approval.

Afterward she lay beside me, completely meek.

"We were going to be together anyway, darling, always," she whispered, lightly trailing her long fingernails over me. Her fingernails were lacquered pale pink, and I saw that two of them were broken. "It doesn't matter about the revolver. I don't blame you. Not for anything."

She'd do anything to recover the gun, to recover her freedom.

"I'm glad," I said, holding her tight against me, feeling the blood-rush pounding in her heart.

"It doesn't matter," she repeated softly, "doesn't matter."

That's when I knew the really deadly game was just beginning.

ALL THAT GLITTERS

Joan Hess

WELCOME TO THE HOME OF REMMINGTON BOLES and his mother, Audrey Antoinette (née Tattlinger) Boles. It is a small yet gracious house in the center of the historic district. At one time it was the site of fancy luncheons and elegant dinner parties. There have been no parties of any significance since the timely and unremarkable demise of Ralph Edward Boles. I believe this was in 1962, but it may have been the following year.

Remmington, who is called Remmie by his mother and few remaining relatives, is forty-one years old, reasonably tall, reasonably attractive. There is little else to say about his physical presence. It's likely you would trust him on first sight. He has never been unkind to animals or children.

Audrey is of an age that falls between sixty and seventy. She was once attractive in an antebellum sort of way. In her heyday thirty years ago, she was president of the Junior League and almost single-handedly raised the money for a children's cancer wing at the regional hospital.

At this moment, Audrey is in her bedroom at the top of the stairs. Although we cannot see her, we can deduce from her vaguely querulous tone that she is no longer in robust health.

"Remmie? Do you have time to find my slippers before you leave? It seems so damp and chilly this morning. I hope there's nothing wrong with the furnace."

Her son's voice is patient and, for the most part, imbued with affection. He is not a candidate for sainthood, but he is a good son.

"There's nothing wrong with the furnace," he says as he comes into her bedroom. "Let me raise the blinds so you can enjoy the sunshine."

He takes two steps, then pauses as he does every morning. The microdrama has been performed for many years. Very rarely does anything happen to disrupt it, and there is nothing in the air to lead Remmie to suspect this day will be extraordinary.

"No, leave them down. I can't tolerate the glare. Oh, Remmie, I pray every night that you'll never face the specter of blindness. It's so very frightening."

Two steps to her side; two squeezes of her hand. "Now, Mother, Dr. Whitbread found no symptoms of retinopathy, and he said you shouldn't worry. The ophthalmologist said the same thing only a few months ago."

Her eyes are bleached and rimmed with red, but they regard him with birdlike acuity. "You're so good to me. I don't know how I could ever get along without you."

"I'm late for work, Mother. Here are your slippers right beside the bed. I'll be home at noon to fix your lunch." He bends down to kiss her forehead, then waits to be dismissed.

"Bless you, Remmie."

Remmie Boles goes downstairs to the kitchen, rinses out his coffee cup, and props it in the rack, then makes sure his mother's tray is ready for her midmorning snack: tea bag, porcelain cup and saucer, two sugar cookies in a cellophane bag. The teapot, filled with a precise quantity of water, is on the back burner.

He enjoys the six-block walk to Boles Discount Furniture Warehouse, and produces a smile for his secretary, who is filing her fingernails. She is not overly bright, but she is very dependable—a trait much valued in small business concerns.

"Good morning, Ailene," Remmie says, collecting the mail from the corner of her desk.

"Some guy from your church called, Mr. Boles. He wants to know if you're gonna be on the bowling team this year. He says they'll take you back as long as you promise not to quit in the middle of the season like

you did last year." Having been an employee for ten years, she feels entitled to make unseemly comments. "You really should get out and meet
people. You're not all that old, you know, and kinda cute. There are a
lot of women who'd jump at the chance to go out with a guy like you."

"Please bring me the sales tax figures from the last quarter." Remmie
goes into his office and closes the door before he allows himself to
react.

Ailene has made a point. Remmie is not a recluse. He has dated over
the years, albeit infrequently and for no great duration. Alas, he has not
been out since the fiasco that was responsible for his abandonment of
the First Methodist Holy Rollers in midseason.

Yes, even Methodists can evince a sense of humor.

Lucinda was (and still is, as far as I know) a waitress at the bowling
alley. He'd been dazzled by her bright red hair, mischievous grin, and
body that rippled like a field of ripe wheat when she walked. She agreed
to go out for drinks. One thing had led to another, first in the front
seat of his car, then on the waterbed in her apartment.

The very idea of experiencing such sexual bliss every night left
Remmie giddy, and he found himself pondering marriage. After a series
of increasingly erotic encounters, he invited Lucinda to meet his mother.

It was a ghastly idea. Lucinda arrived in a tight purple dress that
scarcely covered the tops of her thighs, and brought a bottle of whiskey
as a present. In the harsh light of his living room, he could see the bags
under her eyes and the slackness of her jowls. Her voice was coarse, her
laugh a bray, her ripple nothing more than a cheap, seductive wiggle.
He quit the bowling team immediately.

Back to work, Remmie.

He ignores the message and settles down with the figures. At eleven,
he goes out to the showroom to make sure his salesmen aren't gossip-
ing in the break room. He is heading for the counter when a woman
comes through the main door and halts, her expression wary, as if she's
worried that ravenous beasts are lurking under oak veneer tables and
behind plaid recliners.

If Ailene hadn't made her presumptuous comments, perhaps Remmie
would not have given this particular customer more than a cursory
assessment. As it is, he notices she's a tiny bit plump, several inches
shorter than he, and of a similar age. Her hair, short and curly, is the

color of milk chocolate. She is wearing a dark skirt and white blouse, and carrying a shiny black handbag.

"May I help you?" he says.

"I'm just looking. It's hard to know where to start, isn't it?"

"Are you in the market for living room furniture? We have a good assortment on sale right now."

"I need all sorts of things, but I don't have much of a budget," she says rather sadly. "Then again, I don't have much of a house."

To his horror, her eyes fill with tears.

Remmie persuades her to accept a cup of coffee in his office, and within a half hour, possesses her story. Crystal Ambler grew up on the seedy side of the city, attended the junior college, and is now the office manager of a small medical clinic. A childless marriage ended in divorce more than five years ago. She spends her free time reading, gardening, and occasionally playing bridge with her parents and sister. She once had a cat, but it ran away and now she lives alone.

"Not very exciting, is it?" she says with a self-deprecatory laugh. "It's hard being single these days, and almost impossible to meet someone who isn't burdened with a psychosis and an outstanding warrant or two."

"Mr. Boles," Ailene says from the doorway, "your mother called to remind you to pick up syringes on your way home for lunch."

"Is your mother ill?" asks Crystal with appropriate sympathy.

"She was diagnosed with diabetes the year I graduated from college. It's manageable with daily insulin injections and a strict diet."

"It must be awfully hard on you and your wife," she begins, then gasps and rises unsteadily. "I'm sorry. It's none of my business and I shouldn't have—"

"It's perfectly all right." Remmie catches her hands between his and studies her contrite expression, spotting for the first time a little dimple on her chin. "I should be the one to apologize. You came here to look for furniture, and I've wasted your time with my questions. I do hope you'll allow me to help you find a bargain."

Crystal is amenable.

Remmie smiles thoughtfully as he walks home for lunch. There is something charmingly quaint about Miss Ambler. She is by no means a hapless maiden awaiting rescue by a knight; when she selected the sofa, she did so with no hint of indecision or tacit plea for his approval. But at the same time, she is soft-spoken and modest. He's certain she would never wear a tight purple dress or drink whiskey. He doubts she drinks anything more potent than white wine.

He's halfway across the living room when he realizes something is acutely wrong. His mother never fails to call his name when he enters the house. It is an inviolate part of their script.

"Mother?" he calls as he hurries upstairs to her bedroom. The room is dim; the television, invariably set on a game show, is silent. The figure on the bed is motionless. "Mother?" he repeats with a growing sense of panic.

"Remmie, thank God you're here. I feel so weak. I tried to call you, but I couldn't even lift the receiver."

"Shall I call for an ambulance?"

"No, I simply need something to nibble on to elevate my blood sugar. If it's not too much trouble, would you please bring the cookies from this morning?"

"You skipped your snack? Dr. Whitbread stressed how very vital it is that you stay on your schedule. Maybe I should call him."

"All I need are the cookies, Remmie." Despite her avowed weakness, she picks up the clock and squints at it. "My goodness, you're almost an hour late. Was there an emergency at the store?"

"A minor one," he murmurs.

Remmie calls Crystal that evening to make sure she is pleased with her selection. She shyly invites him to come by some time and see how well the sofa goes with the drapes. Remmie professes eagerness to do so, and suggests Saturday morning. Although Crystal sounds disappointed, she promises coffee and cake.

The week progresses uneventfully. Whatever has caused Audrey's bout of weakness has not recurred, although she has noticed a disturbing new symptom and broaches it after the evening news is over.

She holds out a hand. "Feel my fingers, Remmie. They're so swollen I haven't been able to wear any of my rings. Perhaps you should take all my jewelry down to the bank tomorrow morning and put it in the safe-deposit box. If it's not too much bother, of course. It's so maddening not to be able to do things for myself. I know I'm such a terrible burden on you."

"I'll do it Saturday morning," Remmie says. "I have some other errands, and I'll be in that neighborhood."

"Errands? I hate to think of you spending your weekend driving all over town instead of having a chance to relax around the house. You work so hard all week."

"I enjoy getting out." He picks up her tray and heads for the kitchen.

Saturday.

Remmie grimaces as he pulls into the driveway. His mother's jewelry is still in the glove compartment, and the bank closes at noon on Saturdays. His mother will spend the weekend fretting if she finds out about his negligence, but there's no reason why she will. A good son does not cause his mother unnecessary concern.

He sits in the car and replays his visit. Upon opening the door, Crystal hadn't thrown herself into his arms, but she'd held his hand several seconds longer than decorum dictates. Their conversation had been lively. They'd parted with yet another warm handshake.

He locks the glove compartment and goes inside. And freezes as he sees his mother slumped on the sofa, her hands splayed across her chest and her eyes closed.

"Mother!" he says as he sinks to her side. "Can you hear me?"

"I'm conscious," Audrey says dully. "I was on my way to the kitchen when I felt so dizzy I almost fell."

"Let me help you back to bed, and then I'll call the doctor." Remmie picks her up and carries her to her bedroom, settles her on the bed, and reaches for the telephone.

"No, don't disturb Dr. Whitbread. He's entitled to his weekends, just as you are. If I'm not better on Monday, you can call him then."

"Are you sure?" asks Remmie, alarmed at the thinness of her voice.

"It's very dear of you to be so concerned about me, Remmie. Most children put their ailing parents in nursing homes and try to forget about them. The poor old things lose what wits they have and spend their last days drooling and being tormented by sadistic nurses."

"This is your home, Mother. Why don't you take a little nap while I fix your lunch?"

"Bless you," she says with a sigh. He's almost to the door when she adds, "There was a call for you half an hour ago. A woman with a trailer park sort of name said you'd left your gloves at her house. I tried to catch you at the bank to relay the message, but they said you hadn't come in. I hope they weren't your suede gloves, Remmie. I ordered them from Italy, you know."

"I know." He urges himself back into motion. Had he subconsciously chosen to leave his gloves at Crystal's house so he'd have another excuse to call her? He ponders the possibility as he washes lettuce and slices a tomato.

Audrey is strangely quiet all afternoon and declines his offer to play gin rummy after dinner. Remmie finally breaks down and tells her about Crystal Ambler.

"She sounds very nice," says Audrey. "She lives in that neighborhood beyond the interstate, you said? Your father and I made a point of never driving through that area after dark, even if it meant going miles out of our way." She pauses as if reliving a long and torturous detour, then says, "What exactly does this woman do?"

Audrey listens as Remmie describes Crystal's job, her clean, if somewhat Spartan, house, her garden, even her new sofa. "She sounds very nice," is all she says as she limps across the dining room and down the hall. "Very nice."

Sunday, Sunday.
Remmie calls Crystal while his mother is napping. After he apologizes for leaving his gloves, he invites her to meet him after work on Monday for a glass of wine.

Monday.
Remmie tells his mother he'll be working late in preparation for the inventory-reduction sale. He uses the same excuse when he takes Crys-

tal to dinner later that week. On Saturday afternoon, he makes an ambiguous reference to the hardware store and takes Crystal for a drive in the country. Afterward, he feels foolish when Audrey not only brings up Crystal's name, but encourages him to ask her out. He admits they have plans.

"Dinner on Wednesday?" murmurs Audrey, carefully folding her napkin and placing it on the table. "What a lovely idea, Remmie. I'm sure she'll be thrilled to have a meal in a proper restaurant."

"Would you like me to see if Miss McCloud can sit with you while I'm out?"

"I wouldn't dream of bothering her. After all, I'm here by myself every day. I'm so used to being alone that I'll scarcely notice that you're out with this woman."

"I'd like to meet your mother," Crystal says as they dally over coffee in her living room. "You're obviously devoted to her."

"My father left a very small estate. My mother insisted on working at a clothing shop to put me through college, then used the last of the insurance money to finance the store. Before her illness grew more debilitating, she came down to the showroom at night and dusted the displays." Remmie smiles gently. "I'd like you to meet her. She's asked me all about you, and I think she's beginning to suspect I might be . . ."

"Be what?"

"Falling in love," he says, then leans forward and kisses her. When she responds, he slides his arm behind her back and marvels at the supple contours. Their kisses intensify, as do Remmie's caresses and her tiny moans. His hand finds its way beneath her sweater to her round breasts. His mind swirls with deliciously impure images.

Therefore, he's startled when she pulls back and moves to the far end of the sofa. For an alarming moment, she looks close to tears, but she takes a shuddery breath and says, "No, Remmie, I'm not going to have an affair. I shouldn't have gone out with you in the first place. I'm too old to get into another pointless relationship. I'd rather get a cat."

Remmie bites back a groan. "Crystal, darling, I'd never do anything to hurt you. I don't want a pointless relationship, either."

"Then take me home to meet your mother."

He frowns at the obstinate edge in her voice. "I will when the time's right. Mother's been fretting about her blood pressure lately, and I don't want to excite her more than necessary."

"Maybe you'd better go home and check on her," Crystal says as she stands up. However, rather than hurrying him out the door, she presses her body against his and kisses him with such fierce passion that he nearly loses his balance. "There'll be more of this when we're engaged," she promises in a warm, moist whisper. She goes on to describe what lies in store after they're married.

The constraints of the genre prevent me from providing details.

Time flies.

"Does your friend drive an old white Honda?" Audrey asks Remmie while he's massaging her feet to stimulate circulation.

He gives her a surprised look. "Why do you ask?"

"Someone who matches her description has driven by here several times. It most likely wasn't her, though. This woman had the predatory gleam of a real estate appraiser trying to decide how much our house is worth." Audrey manages a weak chuckle. "And of course I can barely see the street from my window these days. It's all a matter of time before I'm no longer a burden, Remmie, and you'll be free to get on with your life."

"Don't say that, Mother," he says as he strokes her wispy gray hair. A sudden vision of the future floods his mind: his mother's bedroom is unlit and empty, but farther down the hall, Crystal smiles from his bed, her arms outstretched and her breasts heaving beneath a silky black gown.

He realizes his mother is staring at him and wipes a sheen of perspiration off his forehead. "Don't say that," he repeats.

Several more weeks pass, and then back to Boles Discount Furniture Warehouse we go.

This morning Ailene is typing slowly but steadily. "Crystal called," she says without looking up. "She said to tell you that she can't go to the movies tonight."

"Did she say why?"

"Something about baby-sitting for her sister. Oh, and your mother called right before you got here. She wants you to pick up some ointment for her blisters. She said you'd know what kind and where to get it."

Remmie closes his office door, reaches for the telephone, and then lowers his hand. Crystal has made it clear that he's not to call her at the clinic. But this is the second time this week she's canceled their date to do a favor for her sister. Last week she met him at the door and announced she was going out with some friends from the clinic. Remmie had not been invited to join them.

Can he be losing her? When they're together on the sofa, her passion seems to rival his own. Although she continues to refuse to make love, she has found ways to soften his frustration. She swears she has never loved anyone as deeply.

He collapses in his chair, cradles his head in his hands, and silently mouths her name.

When Remmie comes into the living room, he is shocked. He is stunned, bewildered, and profoundly inarticulate. The one thing he is not prepared to see is his mother sitting at one end of the sofa and Crystal at the other. A tray with teacups and saucers resides on the coffee table, a few crumbs indicative that cookies have been consumed.

"Crystal," he gasps.

"Remmie, dear," his mother says chidingly, "that's no way to welcome a guest into our home. Have you forgotten your manners?"

Crystal's smile is as sweet as the sugar granules on the tray. "I was in the neighborhood, and it seemed like time to stop by and meet your mother. We've been having a lovely chat."

"Oh, yes," says Audrey. "A lovely chat."

Remmie sinks down on the edge of the recliner, aware his mouth is slack. "That's good," he says at last.

Audrey nods. "Crystal and I discovered a most amazing coincidence. It seems her mother used to clean house for Laetitia Whimsey, who was in my garden club for years."

"Amazing," Remmie says, glaring at Crystal. He's angry at her effrontery in coming, but she refuses to acknowledge him and listens attentively as Audrey reminisces about her garden club.

Out on the porch, however, Crystal crosses her arms and gazes defiantly at him. "This meeting was long overdue," she says, "and you've been stalling. Well, now I've met her. She seems to like me well enough, and I'm sure we'll get along just fine in the future. We do have a future, don't we?"

"Of course we do," he says, shocked by her vehemence. "I was only waiting until Mother . . ."

"Dies?"

Remmie steps back and clutches the rail. "Don't be ridiculous. She's experiencing numbness in her lower legs and feet, and the doctor recommended tests for arteriosclerosis. Mother is always distraught about going into the hospital."

"And then what, Remmie? Will she have problems with her kidneys? Will her blood pressure fluctuate?"

"I don't know, Crystal. Her condition is very delicate, but the doctor seems to feel that in general her prognosis is good."

"Then what's the delay?" she counters. "I believed you when you told me that you love me. Otherwise, I would have broken off our relationship long before I became emotionally involved. There are plenty of women who'll sleep with you, Remmie—if that's all you want."

He stares as she marches down the steps and across the street to her little white car. He remains on the porch even after she has driven away without so much as a glance in his direction.

"Remmie?" calls his mother. "Could you be a dear and help me upstairs? I wasn't expecting any visitors, and now I'm exhausted. There's no rush, of course. I'll just sit here in the dark until you have a moment."

January proves to be the cruelest month.

Crystal allows Remmie to take her out several times, and permits him a few more liberties on the sofa, for which he is grateful. On the other hand, he senses a reticence on her part to abandon herself to his embraces. They both avoid any references to Audrey, who continues to encourage him to go out with Crystal.

Remmie begins to feel as if he's losing his mind. He's obsessed with

Crystal; his waking hours are haunted by memories of how she feels in his arms. His dreams are so explicit that he awakens drenched with sweat and shivering with frustration.

The obvious question arises: Why does he not propose marriage? If he could answer this, he would. For the most part, Crystal is the girl of his dreams (if he and I may employ the cliché). She has shown a flicker of annoyance now and then, but she is quick to apologize and kiss away his injured feelings. She has joined his church. On two occasions she has brought Audrey flowers and perky greeting cards.

When Audrey mentions Crystal's name, Remmie listens intently for any nuances in her voice. He's perceptive enough to anticipate a petty display of jealousy, but thus far he has not seen it. Audrey maintains that she is fond of Crystal, that she enjoys their infrequent but pleasant conversations.

Why is he incapable of proposing?

Mercifully, January ends and we ease into February, a month fraught with significance for young and old lovers alike.

"Does Crystal have a brother?" asks Audrey one morning as Remmie is straightening her blanket.

"I don't think so."

"How odd," she says under her breath.

"Why would you think she has a brother, Mother?"

"It's so silly that I hate to confess." Audrey sighs and looks away, then adds, "I called her house yesterday morning to thank her for the romance novel she sent. A man answered the telephone, and I was so unnerved that I hung up without saying a word. It was quite early; you'd just left for work."

Remmie is aware that two days ago Crystal canceled their plans for dinner, saying that she needed to work on files from the clinic. He has not spoken to her since then, although he has left messages for her to call.

"It must have been a plumber," Audrey says dismissively. "Would you check the thermostat, dear? I can hardly wiggle my toes."

As Valentine's Day approaches, Remmie becomes more and more distracted. Crystal denies having a brother; he's too embarrassed to say anything further. He feels as if he's driving down a steep mountain road, tires skidding, brakes smoking and squealing, gravel spewing behind him.

He is staring at the calendar when Ailene comes into his office.

"Here's the candy," she says, putting down a plain white box that has come in the morning mail. "You should get a medal or something for going to all this trouble every year. It must cost twice as much as regular candy."

"It's one of our little traditions. I've told Mother she can have sugar-free chocolate all year, but she says it's sweeter because it's a Valentine's Day gift."

"You doing something special with Crystal?" asks Ailene, who has been monitoring the relationship with a healthy curiosity.

Remmie comes to a decision. "Yes, I am," he says without taking his eyes off the white box.

Late in the morning, he calls Audrey and tells her that he is unable to come home to prepare her lunch, citing the need to run errands. She wishes him a profitable hour and assures him she will have a nice bowl of soup.

Remmie goes to the bank and gains access to the safe deposit box. The jewelry is in a brown felt pouch. He spreads it open and finds the diamond engagement ring given to his mother fifty-odd years ago. If he wished, he could buy a bigger and more impressive one, but he hopes Crystal will accept this as a loving tribute to his mother.

At the drugstore, he buys two heart-shaped boxes of candy. One is red, the other white, and both have glittery bows. He finds a sentimental card for his mother, who will reread it many times before adding it to the collection in her dresser drawer.

When he returns to the office, he opens the white box and dumps the sumptuous chocolates on Ailene's desk. He then refills the box with the sugar-free chocolates made especially for diabetics, writes a loving message to his mother, and tucks the card under the pink ribbon.

Gnawing his lip, he dials the telephone number of a cozy country inn that is a hundred miles away. He makes reservations for dinner for the evening of February 14.

Despite a sudden dryness in his mouth, he also reserves a room with a fireplace and a double bed.

Crystal agrees to dinner. Remmie does not mention the room reservation. He will wait until they are sipping wine and savoring whatever decadently rich dessert the inn has prepared for the event, then slip the ring on her finger and ask her to marry him. He feels a warm tingle as he envisions what will follow.

"How romantic," murmurs Audrey as he describes the plans he has made, although he alludes only obliquely to what he hopes will transpire after his proposal. He's aware that she disapproves of sexual activity outside of wedlock, but he is over forty, after all.

He realizes he is blushing and wills himself to stop behaving like a bashful adolescent. "I'll call Miss McCloud and ask her to stay with you. That way, if you feel dizzy or need extra insulin, she'll be there to help you."

"Don't be absurd," she responds curtly.

"But I'll worry about you if you're here alone all night."

"I can take care of myself—and don't call her against my wishes. If she shows up at the front door, I'll send her away. Now please stop dithering and bring me another blanket. My feet feel as though they're frozen."

He goes to the linen closet in the hallway. As he takes a blanket from the shelf, he hears a peculiar thump. He dashes to his mother's bedroom and finds her lying on the floor like a discarded rag doll.

"Did she break any bones?" asks Crystal.

Remmie puts down his coffee cup and shrugs. "No, she just has some bad bruises. They kept her overnight at the hospital for observation, but Dr. Whitbread insisted she'd be more comfortable in her own bed. I took her home after I got off work."

"And left her alone?"

"Of course not," he says, appalled that she would even ask. "Miss McCloud stopped by with a plant, and I took the opportunity to come see you for a few minutes." He looks at his watch and stands up. "I'd better go."

Crystal stands up but does not move toward him. "Does this mean our Valentine dinner date is off? If you're afraid to leave your mother for more than thirty minutes, I'd like to know it right now. There's a new doctor at the clinic who's asked me out a couple of times. He's single, and he doesn't make plans around his mother."

"We're still going," he says hastily.

She goes to the door and opens it. "You'd better go home, Remmie. I hear your mother calling."

Oddly enough, Remmie almost hears her, too.

Audrey is unable to sleep because of her pain. At least once a night she calls out for Remmie, who hurries into her room with a glass of water and a white pill. Each time she apologizes at length for disturbing him.

"Do you know who Crystal reminds me of?" asks Audrey as Remmie pauses. He is reading the newspaper to her because her eyesight has worsened. It has become a new addition to their evening ritual.

"Who?"

"That woman from the bowling alley. They both have a certain hardness about their eyes. Not that Crystal is anything like . . . what was her name?"

"Lucinda," supplies Remmie. He zeroes in on a story concerning a charity fund-raiser and begins to read.

Too loudly, I'm afraid.

Valentine's Day.

Remmie hands his mother a notebook. Names and telephone numbers are written in a heavy black hand; surely she can make them out should an emergency arise. "It's not too late to call Miss McCloud, Mother. She said she will be delighted to stay with you. If you prefer, she can stay downstairs and you won't even know she's here."

"Absolutely not."

"If you're sure," he says. He has already made his decision, but it is not too late for Audrey to change the course of her destiny. He looks down at her. Her lower lip is extended and her jaw is rigid.

He realizes that when next he sees her, she will be at peace. Blinking back tears, he bends down to brush his lips across her forehead. "Good-bye, Mother," he whispers.

"Good-bye, Mrs. Boles," Crystal says from the doorway. She is holding something behind her back and scuffling her feet as if she were a small child. She gives Remmie a conspiratorial smile. "Aren't you forgetting to give your mother something?"

Remmie's face is bloodless as he takes the white heart-shaped box and presents it to Audrey. "I didn't forget," he says. "Special candy for a special person. Don't eat so much you get a tummyache."

"Don't condescend to me," Audrey says coldly, but her expression softens and she reaches up to squeeze his hand. "I love these chocolates almost as much as I love you, Remmie. One of these days you won't have to go to all the bother to order them just for me."

Remmie stumbles as he leaves the room, brushing past Crystal as if she were nothing more substantial than a shadow.

Unamused, she follows him downstairs to the kitchen, where a second box of chocolates sits on the table.

"Did you order them just for me?" she says, mimicking Audrey's simpery voice.

The trip has not started on a happy note, obviously. Remmie curses as he fights traffic until they are clear of the city, and only then does he loosen his grip on the steering wheel and glance at Crystal.

"You look nervous," he comments.

"So do you." She opens the box of chocolates and offers it to him.

He recoils, then regains control of himself. "Maybe later," he mumbles unhappily.

"Are you worried about your mother?"

"Of course I am. What if she has a dizzy spell and takes another fall? She could break her hip this time and be in such pain that she's unable to call for help."

"She'll be all right," Crystal says as she selects a chocolate and pops it in her mouth. A surprised expression crosses her face, but Remmie is in the midst of passing a truck and does not notice.

In fact, he is so distracted that he fails to respond when she comments on the scenery, and again when she cautions him to slow down as they approach a small town.

She finally taps him on the shoulder. "What's the matter with you, Remmie? Do you want to turn around and go home to check on your mother?"

Sweat dribbles down his forehead. His breathing is irregular, his lips quivering, his eyes darting, his hands once again gripping the steering wheel so tightly that his fingers are unnaturally pale.

"Remmie!" Crystal says, suddenly frightened. "What's wrong?"

He pulls to the shoulder, stops, and leans his head against the steering wheel. "I can't go through with it," he says with a whimper. "I thought I could, but I just can't do it. I'll have to find a telephone and call her before it's too late—even if it means she'll hate me for the rest of her life." He begins to cry. "How could I have betrayed her like this?"

"What are you talking about?"

"I switched the candy. The sugar will put her in a diabetic coma, and it's likely to be fatal unless she gets emergency treatment. I have to call her. If she doesn't answer, I'll call Dr. Whitbread and have him go to the house." He sits up and wipes his cheeks. "Maybe it's not too late. We've only been gone half—"

"It's not too late," Crystal snaps, "and you don't need to call anyone, especially this doctor. You'll be confessing to attempted murder. I doubt the jury will feel much sympathy."

"I don't deserve any sympathy, and I don't care what happens to me. We've got to find a telephone."

She reaches over to take the key from the ignition. After a moment of reflection, she says, "Your mother is not in danger. While I was waiting in the kitchen, I opened both boxes and figured out what you'd done. I switched them back, Remmie. Audrey is contentedly eating sugar-free chocolates."

"She is?" he says numbly.

Crystal's nod lacks enthusiasm and her smile is strained. "Yes, she sure is. I knew you couldn't live with yourself if you did something so terrible."

Remmie finally convinces himself that she is telling the truth and his mother is not in danger. "I suppose I'd better take you home."

"Why?"

"You must loathe me."

"I'll get over it," Crystal says, shrugging. "What I think we'll do is have our dinner and spend the night at this inn. Tomorrow morning we can go to the local courthouse to get a marriage license, and find a justice of the peace. Audrey will be surprised, of course, but she'll get over it more quickly if it's a done deal."

Remmie is more surprised than Audrey will ever be. "You want to get married—knowing that I tried to murder my mother? Don't you want some time to think about it?"

"I assumed you were going to propose this evening, and I'd decided to accept. I've already given my notice at the clinic so that I can stay home and take care of your mother."

Remmie attempts to decipher the odd determination in her voice, but finally gives up and leans over to kiss her. "I brought a ring to give you over dinner," he admits. "It's the one my father presented to my mother on their second date."

"How thoughtful," she says. "You really must call your mother as soon as we check in and reassure yourself that she's perfectly fine."

And so Remmie and Crystal dine by candlelight and make love under a ruffled canopy. The following morning, a license is procured and a justice of the peace conducts a brief ceremony. The witnesses find it remarkably romantic and are teary as the groom kisses the bride.

Only later, as Remmie catches sight of the white heart-shaped box on his mother's bedside table, does he ask himself the obvious question: how did Crystal know to switch back the chocolates?

He does not ask her, however. He is a good husband as well as a good son.

And there is always next year.

THE MAN WHO SHOT TRINITY VALANCE

Paul Bishop

TRINITY VALANCE WAS A MASTER ASSASSIN, one of the best in the game. The word on the street, for those who concerned themselves with such things, was that her prowess was second only to that of the enigma known as Simon.

Ever since the thrilling rush of completing her first crude hit, Trinity knew that she had found her true calling. She adopted the cover name of Starlight, and as her reputation grew, it rapidly became clear that killing was something at which she excelled. But for Trinity excelling wasn't good enough. She had to be the best.

To this end, Simon became an obsession with her.

Twice the two assassins had crossed swords while competing for the same open contract. And twice Simon had snatched the kill from directly in front of Trinity's proverbial gunsights. Even in her anger Trinity sensed that Simon had been playing cat and mouse with her, showing his disdain for her techniques of killing from a distance—through the use of booby traps—while he killed up close and person-ally—personally enough to feel the victim's fading heartbeat.

But while Simon's figurative laughter taunted Trinity, his true iden-tity eluded her.

Trinity took pride in achieving letter-perfect executions with a trade-mark touch of flair or panache. She had developed a delicious knack for choosing an intriguing location, or a difficult time when the victim was surrounded by a crowd, or a situation where both the trigger and the mark would be on the move when the hit went down, or anything else that would add to the challenge and heighten the rush.

However, even though she planned each of her hits down to the finest detail, Trinity still felt that Simon was always a step ahead of her, mocking her, constantly letting her know that she wasn't quite good enough to be the best, to be considered numero uno.

As Trinity soaked in the bathtub, hot water channeled a thin, sensual canal between the swells of full breasts turned lobster red by the heat. Tendrils of blond hair, having rebelled at being confined in a bun on the top of her head, hung limply with the steam rising off the water.

Running a soft sponge down her body, she glanced up at the eight-by-ten glossy taped to the fogged bathroom mirror. Tonight, she thought, tonight the kill would be different. Tonight she would be inside the kill zone, and all of her senses would be alive with the thrill.

But the biggest rush of all tonight would come in her snatching the mantle of superiority from Simon's goading shoulders.

Trinity had accepted this new assignment immediately upon the successful completion of her last score. Normally she would have taken a break before making her next move, but this next time she had been instantly infatuated by the face of her target. It was as if there already existed a link between the executioner and her intended victim, a link that ran beyond mere fate and into the sensual.

The features in the photo were hollowed almost to the point of being considered gaunt. The sharp cheekbones and neatly clipped beard served only to emphasize the pointed chin and cadaverous cheeks. The eyes, however, that peered out from below heavy brows seemed to hold a Santa Claus twinkle that was immediately betrayed by the cruel line of the lips. Trinity considered that the sparkle in the eyes was really nothing more than a trick of the photographer's flash, whereas the draw of the lips perhaps exposed a true glimpse of the inner man.

Whenever she looked up at the photo, Trinity felt the butterflies of anticipation change their direction of flight as they fluttered through her stomach. For the first time a contract was becoming very personal, touching her for some reason at the core of her sexuality. She longed for the kill, lusted for the sexual release of it, and knew that this time she needed to be close enough to touch, smell, and taste the target, to feel the tingle in her loins when she pulled the trigger.

In her bath her fingers were drawn inexorably downward across her abdomen as she closed her eyes and opened her mind to the fantasy.

Professor Royce Kilpatrick rested his large-boned hands on the padded steering wheel as he guided the snowy white Lincoln Town Car through the heat of the desert that was Las Vegas. He had always admired his hands, and he stared at them now as he drove, drawing comfort from their perfection. The tendons and veins that ran across their backs looked almost sculpted, and his long fingers had character etched into each individual knuckle and smoothly polished fingernail.

He knew that in the Old West hands like his would have been referred to as gambler's hands: hands best suited to dealing or double dealing cards, shuffling, cutting, nimbly and invisibly snatching cards from the bottom, middle, or top of the deck, hands that could make you rich or make you dead, with either option being better than poor. Royce cherished that image because he was by nature a gambler and cards were his natural vice.

He took one of his long-fingered hands off the steering wheel to smooth his beard across hollowed cheeks. His job as a professor of English at the University of Nevada Las Vegas didn't pay nearly enough to cover the style of living that he strove to maintain. Items like the leased Town Car he was driving and the expensive but out-of-date clothes covering his body did not come cheaply, and they were well beyond his professor's salary. Still, there were other ways to make money.

Recently, however, his losses had been higher at the gambling tables than usual. His touch for the cards seemed to have deserted him. He knew it would only be a little while before he managed to get back on track again, but until then he knew he had to keep hustling, not just with cards but with the dice, the sports books, the ponies, or even how hot the temperature would be the next day. Experience had taught him that if he could just get enough balls up in the air, something would come through. He secretly loved the rush he got from it all. Anything that smacked of a game of chance pumped his blood like a fire hose turned on full blast.

He'd been in gambling trouble like this once before—way in over his head, watching out for leg breakers at every turn, living life on the cutting edge of the envelope—but that time he'd scammed his way to safety by riding a fixed horse race that gave the bookies a bath and had given him enough ready cash to pay off his markers, renew his lifestyle, and begin to work his way back into the hole again.

Royce had been one of the small fish in that scam, a bottom feeder who sucked up a diamond by pure luck, and as such he'd been ignored by the heavy mob that were sent after the players who pulled the coup. Royce figured it was because he was a sharp operator. The fact was that the big boys knew he'd be back. There was no way somebody like Royce stayed away. And there was no way he'd get away again.

If he'd been honest with himself, delving beyond the arrogant facade of education that he used to keep his students in line, Royce would have realized that this latest streak of bad luck was taking him down a long tunnel where the light at the end was nothing more than an onrushing train.

Every once in a while a worry would sneak into his conscious mind, but it was more a worry about finding a casino that would still let him play than about the markers that were piling up like a child's block tower. If the thought of how much he owed ever battled through his defenses long enough to be recognized, he shoved it casually aside. The big boys didn't kill anyone over being in debt. They wouldn't kill the golden goose. If he were dead, how the hell would they ever get their money? How the hell would he ever get even again?

Nah, the big boys wouldn't kill you for just being in debt.

Would they?

The first time Royce saw the intriguing blonde in the hot red convertible was in his rearview mirror as she roared up behind his cruising Town Car entering the outskirts of Las Vegas. The red convertible pulled to the left and blasted past in a flash of color. All Royce could see of the blonde was a mass of flying hair and a glimpse of a red choker around a long, elegant neck. Watching her, Royce felt primal male instincts move within him, as if he were an old lion intrigued by a lioness from another pride.

Off the highway and driving along the Strip heading for downtown he saw the blonde again. There were faster ways to get to the downtown area of Vegas, but Royce enjoyed driving along the the Strip with its crush of tourists and its flashing lights coming to life in the early-evening dusk. The Strip never failed to energize him, to build up his anticipation for the evening ahead, an effect like that of a lover's foreplay.

Stopped behind the limit line at a traffic light, Royce heard an engine revving quietly next to him. Looking over, he was surprised to see the blonde in the red convertible who had blown past him as they came into town.

In profile, without her hair blowing in the wind, he could see that she was cast from the mold of the classic beauties. This time he could see that the bloodred choker matched the color of both her lipstick and her perfect fingernails, which tapped a beat across the convertible's black steering wheel. Even in the deepening dusk it was easy to see that the color perfectly offset the blonde's pale, flawless skin.

As if she knew Royce was staring at her, the blonde turned her eyes toward him, smiled briefly in acknowledgment of her own beauty, and then left him standing flatly at the light as she accelerated away. A horn sounding from behind brought Royce back to reality, and he fumbled to pull away from the light himself.

The evening did not start out well for Royce. The first two casinos he entered had security moving immediately. Royce knew all about the overhead cameras and other techniques used by the casinos to keep undesirables at a distance and to make sure that the majority of the chips stayed on the right side of the table.

In the Empress Royce was frozen out immediately at the cashier's window when he tried to exchange a chunk of ready cash he'd picked up earlier in the day from a hot tip on a horse in the fourth at Holly-wood Park. He had a cash-and-carry deal with the bookie he used for the bet, and it was one of the few resources he hadn't tapped out.

Now, at the Empress cashier's window, he was approached by the floor manager, who told him he would have to make a payment on his credit line before he would be allowed to play further. The cash burning a hole in Royce's pocket wouldn't go very far if he tried paying off debts at this point. He had to parlay it, make it into a sizable chunk before he paid off on past miscalculations. And to do that, he had to get on to the tables.

At the Golden Nugget Royce got as far as sitting down at the blackjack table before trouble brewed. He was three hands into the shoe— two wins and a loss—when he saw Benny Harrington moving toward him. Royce felt a stab of panic lance through his chest. If ex-Mr. Universe Benny Harrington was around, then his twin brother, Billy Harrington, also an ex-Mr. Universe, couldn't be far behind.

Benny and Billy were a tag team of leg breakers. They enjoyed their work. For them a gambler past his credit limit was a rawhide chew bone to be abused by two bull mastiffs in a tug-of-war. Royce scooped his chips from the table and fled. It wasn't cool, but it was smart.

There was something more to the unpleasant start to the evening however. Ever since the blonde had roared away from him at the traffic light on the Strip, Royce had found thoughts of her popping in and out of his mind. Royce never had much trouble seducing women, as several of the female staff and female student body at the university could attest; it was just that sex never did as much for him as gambling. For some reason, though, the brief glimpses he'd had of the blonde in the red convertible had set his hormones racing. As a result, the unrequited sexual lust was taking the luster off the usually arousing prospect of the slap of the cards.

Royce managed to get into a poker game in the Pacifica, but he soon ran through the majority of his collateral and was forced to withdraw when no credit was forthcoming.

Making his way back to the center of the Strip, he entered the Citadel casino. He hadn't been in the Citadel for a while and hoped that he might find a friendlier reception there. He decided to try his luck and approached the cashier's window to see about extending his credit line.

"No problem," said the clerk, after consulting her computer screen.

Surprised, Royce quickly drew out a thousand dollars in chips before the clerk changed her mind or realized the computer had made a mistake. With a bounce in his step and an immediately growing confidence, he made his way to the playing floor.

And then he saw her.

A brief flash of bloodred around a long, pale neck.

He brought his attention back to the craps table and saw the blonde from the red convertible as she placed a stack of chips on the green baize. The shooter fired out the dice to the admiration of the small crowd, which "ooohed" and "ahhhed" over the result. The blonde was cool as the stickman pushed a stack of chips in her direction.

Royce felt a stirring as he took in the blonde's complete package: white sequined dress over red seamed hose and bloodred high heels. She was broader through the shoulders than most women, as if she had been a competitive swimmer at some time, but slim and flat through the hips. She was tall, just below six feet, and her legs seemed to go on forever.

As he watched the blonde, Royce's pulse rate increased in anticipation. Never one to turn down a long-odds proposition, he made his way over to the table and into an open position next to the blonde. She looked at him and smiled. It wasn't a dazzler, full of perfectly capped teeth and Pepsodent, but it was more of a seduction, a mocking acceptance of Royce's motives for standing where he did.

"Hello," he said, in response to her look.

The blonde nodded casually and returned her attention to the table. She took several chips from the stack in front of her and placed them on the baize. Without hesitating, Royce placed his chips next to hers.

Even before the shooter rolled the dice, Royce felt his luck click back into place. It was almost a physical sensation, a trilling of the nerve endings. The dice tumbled and bounced, but Royce didn't even bother to watch them. He knew he was going to turn up a winner. And indeed, he did.

Double sixes, boxcars, showed their faces when the dice came to rest, and there were Royce's chips sitting sweetly on the number 12, next to the blonde's.

As their winnings were pushed across the table, the blonde looked at Royce again. "It appears as if I'm good luck for you," she said.

"It certainly does," he replied.

The blonde extended her right hand. "Trinity Valance," she said, introducing herself.

Royce took her hand. Like the blonde's disposition, it was cool and dry, her fingers lingering in his grasp for the extra second that determines the difference between friendly and sensuous. "Royce Kilpatrick," he said.

"And a fine Irish name it is, too," said Trinity. Her voice was throaty with promise, the sound of silk sliding down a willing thigh.

Royce laughed. "And your name?" he asked. "Any relation to Liberty Valance?"

"Let's put it this way," Trinity said, her heart pounding at being this close to her quarry. "The name of John Wayne is never mentioned at any of my family reunions." She smiled, and this time it was a dazzler.

This is it. The thought raced silently through Royce's mind and rapidly became a belief. Lucky streak city.

The rest of the evening and night passed in a whirlwind. There was no game that could not be bowed before the combination of Royce's skill and Trinity's luck. They laughed, touched, and gathered in their chips: intimate strangers riding a bullet train from which there was no getting off.

Trinity was thrilling to the sensations of being so close to a man she was about to kill. She had known of Royce's gambling problems and had arranged on her own account for the extension of credit to him at the Citadel. She was extremely pleased with the way she had picked Royce up while leaving him with the feeling that he was the one doing the picking.

The cat and mouse overtones of the whole hit appealed to her, making her feel vibrant and sexy. For her, death had become so close to sex in so many ways that she understood why the French referred to orgasm as "the little death."

From the gaming tables Trinity deftly moved Royce away and into a darkened lounge in one corner of the vast casino. It was just after midnight, and the room was populated by couples swaying to a live samba beat across the dance floor.

Royce knew he was being led but was loving every second of it. Under normal conditions he would have stayed at the table as long as he was winning, a slave to the drug of gambling that always promised the next score would be the big one, the one that would give you enough "screw you" money to walk away for good. But nobody ever did, because there was not enough "screw you" money in the world to keep a true addict away from the rush of the risk.

Royce also knew, however, that the current circumstances weren't normal. Trinity Valance was a wild card that could make every hand a winner, and her spell was stronger than that of any game of chance. Somehow she had turned up in the hand he'd been dealt, and Royce could do nothing but play her out.

Moving into his arms, Trinity guided Royce out onto the dance floor. The beat had become slow and sultry, the lighting a subdued hue of blue tinged with red edges. The combo on the small stage was unknowingly caught up in Trinity's seduction.

As she leaned against the wiry muscles of the body next to her, Trinity's breath took on a ragged edge, and she truly realized for the first time why Simon had always laughed at her. He had always known the intensity of life that came from making death personal, the power of being right there next to the target and knowing that you could snatch his very breath away any second you desired.

Trinity leaned hard into Royce, her lips next to his ear. She nipped his earlobe hard with her small white teeth, and when he didn't pull away, she whispered, "I have a room upstairs."

He squeezed her tightly, and by mutual consent they moved off the dance floor, out of the lounge, and toward the elevators. Alone, inside the small boxlike projectile, Trinity wrapped herself around Royce. Their mouths met, lips full and open, tongues intertwining and darting away as if they were birds executing a mating ritual. Royce's hands moved up to cup Trinity's braless breasts. Her nipples were already as hard as nailheads, and she moaned through their kiss.

They broke their clinch as the elevator doors opened and moved with the speed of desire down the long corridor to Trinity's room. She fumbled to unlock the door as Royce ran his hands all over her from behind, biting at her neck and eliciting a jealous "Disgusting!" from a pair of passing matrons.

The couple tumbled into the room and fell onto the deep pile carpet. They pulled at each other's clothing, animal passion taking over from human compassion. Naked, except for the bloodred choker around Trinity's neck, they made a halfhearted move for the sheets and comfort of the turned-down bed but didn't make it. Still on the floor, they embraced—killer and quarry—their metaphysical beings separated only by the physical barriers of skill, bone, blood, and muscle.

Bloodred nails scrabbled against taut back muscles. Long fingers entwined in masses of blond hair. Pelvic movements sought each other and joined in a ritual as old as animalkind.

The heat and the passion burned brightly from one completion to the next, and the next, until Royce lay exhausted, his eyes closed as he savored the last lingering sensations of his giving. Beside him, Trinity breathed deeply, trembling on the edge of consciousness.

In time Royce drew himself up, and Trinity heard him enter the bathroom and close the door. There was the rush of water as the shower came to life. Deep within her, Trinity felt the quiver of the final orgasm that she had been holding back, nurturing, denying herself the pleasure of its release until the right moment.

Pulling her legs underneath her, Trinity stood up and moved in naked beauty to the bed. Leaning over, she pulled open the night side table and withdrew her gun. She checked the load for the hundredth time and turned toward the bathroom.

In a soft voice she crooned the perverted mantra from which she took her work name. "Star light. Star bright. First star I see tonight. I wish I may, I wish I might, kill myself a man tonight."

Silently she twisted the bathroom door handle and pushed it inward, to be met by clouds of steam. Blood was screaming through her veins, bringing her closer and closer to the ultimate climax with every passing millisecond, the gun in her feminine right hand becoming the ultimate extension of male sexuality.

Simon. Simon. Simon was right. Every fiber of her being trembled.

She moved forward, slid open the opaque shower door with a violent shove, and thrust her gun hand into the billowing steam.

For a moment her orgasm froze as she stared into the empty stall, and then she felt the ice-cold ring of a gun muzzle as it pressed into the back of her pale, swanlike neck. Above the noise of the running water, she heard the gentle laughter that had haunted her dreams.

Royce's voice seemed to reach her from a long way off. "Simon says, you lose."

Her orgasm and the assassin's gun at her neck both shattered time and existence together.

* * *

The following Monday morning Trinity Valance ducked out of her humanities class at the University of Nevada Las Vegas and made her way quickly across the campus quad to a scheduled meeting with Professor Royce Kilpatrick. At the Student Union she stepped through the open double doors and saw him waiting for her in front of a large portable bulletin board. Standing next to him was a petite blonde who was scribbling violently in a shorthand notebook.

"Trinity! Over here," Royce called out, waving when he spotted her. When she was close enough, he drew her to him with an arm around her shoulders and introduced her to the smaller blonde. "This is Lynn Berkster," he said. "She's a reporter for the local rag." The two women nodded at each other in the assessing way that instant rivals have. "It seems," Royce continued, oblivious of the antagonism, "that the university's staff have been causing the usual ruckus over our annual Killer tournament. Lynn has come out to cover the action. I was just showing her the obituary board."

Royce, alias Simon, took his arm away from Trinity's shoulders and turned to examine the board behind them. "You see, Lynn," he said in his best professor's mode. Trinity could see, however, that the reporter wasn't impressed; that raised Lynn several notches in Trinity's estimation. "Trinity is proof that women can be very good at this game. This was her first tournament, and she took second place. I was really amazed."

Trinity cringed. Amazed, was he? She was going to amaze him all right. The fact that he had beaten her was bad enough, but his chauvinistic, condescending attitude was far too much of a goad to swallow. She refused to be considered second best.

The bulletin board held twenty eight-by-ten glossies. Royce's picture, a duplicate of the one that had been taped to Trinity's bathroom mirror, was at the top with Trinity's right below it. All the photos except Royce's had the word "deceased" stamped in red across the subject's features.

"Killer is simply a role-playing game acted out on a life-size scale." Royce continued his lecture. "It's harmless. A modern version of cowboys and Indians, or James Bond versus the bad guys, for adults using confetti bombs, or starter pistols, or other harmless devices. Each player chooses a secret identity and is then given an assignment to assassinate another one of the group who is also trying to assassinate another player. Once a hit has been successful, the killed player turns his assignment over to the player who bumped him off. In this way the tournament is a virtually self-destructing circle, leaving only one player to be the top assassin at the end of play. Participants know only the code names of the other players but not their true identities. Trinity is in one of my lecture classes on campus—and doing very well, I might say—but neither of us knew the other was involved in the role playing when the tournament started. Part of the role-playing game, however, is using your own devious methods to discover the true identities of the other players, as I did with Trinity. That way you can bump them off before they can get a crack at you."

Oh, you smug bastard, Trinity steamed silently. Her stomach churned as she thought about what a fool she'd been. She'd thought she was leading her target along when all the time the target was leading her, smirking at her, laughing up his sleeve at her.

Royce had learned her true identity and then played with her, watching as she prepared to "assassinate" two of her Killer targets and then beating her to the punch by "assassinating" them himself. She was embarrassed by the memory of how she'd been manipulated, and humiliated by the way she'd fallen for Royce, allowing her to learn of his real-life gambling problems in order to lure her into his web.

Damn! She was angry.

"Players also don't know how close to the top of the obituary board they are getting." Royce continued his explanation. "That side of things is run by a gamemaster who oversees all the action and is the final judge when rulings are needed. In order to keep players from learning their competitors' identities too easily, the gamemaster keeps the obituary board a secret until the end of the tournament.

"This year I took the code name Simon and came out numero uno. Trinity, here"—Royce patted his rival— "was known as Starlight. She did a fine job but wasn't quite good enough to beat the best." He laughed softly, and fingers of anger and humiliation again wrapped themselves around Trinity's spine at the familiar, taunting sound.

Berkster looked up from her notebook long enough to pose a question. "The university staff is worried not only about a game which could be construed as morally repulsive but also about a player who might blur the line between fantasy and reality. How do you feel about that proposition?"

Royce laughed softly again. "Come on. We're all adults here just having a little fun. There are worrywarts everywhere who still think rock 'n' roll will destroy the world, that children's cartoons will pervert the masses, and that superhero comic books will corrupt the next generation. All of them are full of hot air.

"Playing Killer no more distorts the line of reality than playing Battleship or reenacting historical battles with tin soldiers. Or live ones in dress-up, for that matter. I'll tell you what, why don't you come along to the celebration beer bust tonight and talk to some of the other players? You'll see that Killer is no more harmful than swallowing goldfish, cramming students into a phone booth, or any other college fad."

"That's what they said about college hazing," the reporter replied. "But I'll come and talk to the others." She stuffed her notebook away.

"Good," said Royce. "We'll see you there." He put his arm around Trinity, but it was obvious his sexual antenna was pointing in another direction.

"Oh, just one thing," Trinity said, breaking away from Royce. "You might need this for protection." From her purse she withdrew the starter pistol she'd used in the Citadel's hotel room and tossed it to the reporter with a grin.

Smiling, she moved back into the curve of Royce's arm. The purse that she'd slung back over her shoulder was only slightly lighter. It was still comfortably weighted by the bulk of the brand-new fully loaded .38 Smith & Wesson nestled inside.

For Trinity reality and fantasy did blur on occasion, and soon she would show everyone who was really the best. Numero uno. Number one with a bullet.

THE AGE OF DESIRE

Clive Barker

THE BURNING MAN PROPELLED HIMSELF DOWN THE STEPS of the Hume Laboratories as the police car—summoned, he presumed, by the alarm either Welles or Dance had set off upstairs—appeared at the gate and swung up the driveway. As he ran from the door the car screeched up to the steps and discharged its human cargo. He waited in the shadows, too exhausted by terror to run any farther, certain that they would see him. But they disappeared through the swing doors without so much as a glance toward his torment. Am I on fire at all? he wondered. Was this horrifying spectacle—his flesh baptized with a polished flame that seared but failed to consume—simply a hallucination, for his eyes and his eyes only? If so, perhaps all that he had suffered up in the laboratory had also been delirium. Perhaps he had not truly committed the crimes he had fled from, the heat in his flesh licking him into ecstasies.

He looked down his body. His exposed skin still crawled with livid dots of fire, but one by one they were being extinguished. He was going out, he realized, like a neglected bonfire. The sensations that had suffused him—so intense and so demanding that they had been as like pain as pleasure—were finally deserting his nerve endings, leaving a numbness for which he was grateful. His body, now appearing from beneath the veil of fire, was in a sorry condition. His skin was a panic-map of scratches, his clothes torn to shreds, his hands sticky with coagulating blood; blood, he knew, that was not his own. There was no avoiding the bitter truth. He *had* done all he had imagined doing. Even now the officers would be staring down at his atrocious handiwork.

He crept away from his niche beside the door and down the driveway, keeping a lookout for the return of the two policemen. Neither reappeared. The street beyond the gate was deserted. He started to run. He had managed only a few paces when the alarm in the building behind him was abruptly cut off. For several seconds his ears rang in sympathy with the silenced bell. Then, eerily, he began to hear the sound of heat—the surreptitious murmuring of embers—distant enough that he didn't panic, yet close as his heartbeat.

He limped on to put as much distance as he could between him and his felonies before they were discovered. But however fast he ran, the heat went with him, safe in some backwater of his gut, threatening with every desperate step he took to ignite him afresh.

It took Dooley several seconds to identify the cacophony he was hearing from the upper floor now that McBride had hushed the alarm bell. It was the high-pitched chattering of monkeys, and it came from one of the many rooms down the corridor to his right.

"Virgil," he called down the stairwell. "Get up here."

Not waiting for his partner to join him, Dooley headed off toward the source of the din. Halfway along the corridor the smell of static and new carpeting gave way to a more pungent combination: urine, disinfectant and rotting fruit. Dooley slowed his advance. He didn't like the smell any more than he liked the hysteria in the babble of monkey voices. But McBride was slow in answering his call, and after a short hesitation, Dooley's curiosity got the better of his disquiet. Hand on truncheon, he approached the open door and stepped in. His appearance sparked off another wave of frenzy from the animals, a dozen or so rhesus monkeys. They threw themselves around in their cages, somersaulting, screeching and berating the wire mesh. Their excitement was infectious. Dooley could feel the sweat begin to squeeze from his pores.

"Is there anybody here?" he called out.

The only reply came from the prisoners: more hysteria, more cage rattling. He stared across the room at them. They stared back, their teeth bared in fear or welcome; Dooley didn't know which, nor did he wish to test their intentions. He kept well clear of the bench on which the cages were lined up as he began a perfunctory search of the laboratory.

"I wondered what the hell the smell was," McBride said, appearing at the door.

"Just animals," Dooley replied.

"Don't they ever wash? Filthy buggers."

"Anything downstairs?"

"Nope," McBride said, crossing to the cages. The monkeys met his advance with more gymnastics. "Just the alarm."

"Nothing up here either," Dooley said. He was about to add, "*Don't do that*," to prevent his partner putting his finger to the mesh, but before the words were out one of the animals seized the proffered digit and bit it. McBride wrested his finger free and threw a blow back against the mesh in retaliation. Squealing its anger, the occupant flung its scrawny body about in a lunatic fandango that threatened to pitch cage and monkey alike onto the floor.

"You'll need a tetanus shot for that," Dooley commented.

"Shit!" said McBride, "what's wrong with the little bastard anyhow?"

"Maybe they don't like strangers."

"They're out of their tiny minds." McBride sucked ruminatively on his finger, then spat. "I mean, look at them."

Dooley didn't answer.

"I said, *look* . . ." McBride repeated.

Very quietly, Dooley said: "Over here."

"What is it?"

"Just come over here."

McBride drew his gaze from the row of cages and across the cluttered work surfaces to where Dooley was staring at the ground, the look on his face one of fascinated revulsion. McBride neglected his finger sucking and threaded his way among the benches and stools to where his partner stood.

"Under there," Dooley murmured.

On the scuffed floor at Dooley's feet was a woman's beige shoe; beneath the bench was the shoe's owner. To judge by her cramped position she had either been secreted there by the miscreant or dragged herself out of sight and died in hiding.

"Is she dead?" McBride asked.

"Look at her, for Christ's sake," Dooley replied, "she's been torn open."

"We've got to check for vital signs," McBride reminded him. Dooley made no move to comply, so McBride squatted down in front of the victim and checked for a pulse at her ravaged neck. There was none. Her skin was still warm beneath his fingers however. A gloss of saliva on her check had not yet dried.

Dooley, calling in his report, looked down at the deceased. The worst of her wounds, on the upper torso, were masked by McBride's crouching body. All he could see was a fall of auburn hair and her legs, one foot shoeless, protruding from her hiding place. They were beautiful legs, he thought. He might have whistled after such legs once upon a time.

"She's a doctor or a technician," McBride said. "She's wearing a lab coat." Or she had been. In fact the coat had been ripped open, as had the layers of clothing beneath, and then, as if to complete the exhibition, the skin and muscle beneath that. McBride peered into her chest. The sternum had been snapped and the heart teased from its seat, as if her killer had wanted to take it as a keepsake and been interrupted in the act. He perused her without squeamishness; he had always prided himself on his strong stomach.

"Are you satisfied she's dead?"

"Never saw deader."

"Carnegie's coming down," Dooley said, crossing to one of the sinks. Careless of fingerprints, he turned on the tap and splashed a handful of cold water onto his face. When he looked up from his ablutions McBride had left off his tête-à-tête with the corpse and was walking down the laboratory toward a bank of machinery.

"What do they do here, for Christ's sake?" he remarked. "Look at all this stuff."

"Some kind of research facility," Dooley said.

"What do they research?"

"How the hell do I know?" Dooley snapped. The ceaseless chatterings of the monkeys and the proximity of the dead woman made him want to desert the place. "Let's leave it be, huh?"

McBride ignored Dooley's request; equipment fascinated him. He stared entranced at the encephalograph and electro-cardiograph; at the printout units still disgorging yards of blank paper onto the floor; at the video display monitors and the consoles. The scene brought the *Marie Celeste* to his mind. This was like some deserted ship of science—still humming some tuneless song to itself as it sailed on, though there was neither captain nor crew left behind to attend upon it.

Beyond the wall of equipment was a window, no more than a yard square. McBride had assumed it let on to the exterior of the building, but now that he looked more closely he realized it did not. A test chamber lay beyond the banked units.

"Dooley . . . ?" he said, glancing around. The man had gone, however, down to meet Carnegie presumably. Content to be left to his exploration, McBride returned his attention to the window. There was no light on inside. Curious, he walked around the back of the banked equipment until he found the chamber door. It was ajar. Without hesitation, he stepped through.

Most of the light through the window was blocked by the instruments on the other side; the interior was dark. It took McBride's eyes a few seconds to get a true impression of the chaos the chamber contained: the overturned table; the chair of which somebody had made matchwood; the tangle of cables and demolished equipment—cameras, perhaps, to monitor proceedings in the chamber?—clusters of lights which had been similarly smashed. No professional vandal could have made a more thorough job of breaking up the chamber than had been made.

There was a smell in the air which McBride recognized but, irritatingly, couldn't place. He stood still, tantalized by the scent. The sound of sirens rose from down the corridor outside; Carnegie would be here in moments. Suddenly, the smell's association came to him. It was the same scent that twitched in his nostrils when, after making love to Jessica and—as was his ritual—washing himself, he returned from the bathroom to bedroom. It was the smell of sex. He smiled.

His face was still registering pleasure when a heavy object sliced through the air and met his nose. He felt the cartilage give and a rush of blood come. He took two or three giddy steps backward, thereby avoiding the subsequent slice, but lost his footing in the disarray. He fell awkwardly in a litter of glass shards and looked up to see his assailant, wielding a metal bar, moving toward him. The man's face resembled one of the monkeys; the same yellowed teeth, the same rabid eyes. "*No!*" the man shouted, as he brought his makeshift club down on McBride, who managed to ward off the blow with his arm, snatching at the weapon in so doing. The attack had taken him unawares but now, with the pain in his mashed nose to add fury to his response, he was more than the equal of the aggressor. He plucked the club from the man, sweets from a babe, and leaped, roaring, to his feet. Any precepts he might once have been taught about arrest techniques had fled from his mind. He lay a hail of blows on the man's head and shoulders, forcing him backward across the chamber. The man cowered beneath the assault and eventually slumped, whimpering against the wall. Only now, with his antagonist abused to the verge of unconsciousness, did McBride's furor falter. He stood in the middle of the chamber, gasping for breath, and watched the beaten man slip down the wall. He had made a profound error. The assailant, he now realized, was dressed in a white laboratory coat. He was, as Dooley was irritatingly fond of saying, on the side of the angels.

"Damn," said McBride, "shit, hell and damn."

The man's eyes flickered open, and he gazed up at McBride. His grasp on consciousness was evidently tenuous, but a look of recognition crossed his wide-browed, somber face. Or rather, recognition's absence.

"You're not him," he murmured.

"Who?" said McBride, realizing he might yet salvage his reputation from this fiasco if he could squeeze a clue from the witness. "Who did you think I was?"

The man opened his mouth, but no words emerged. Eager to hear the testimony, McBride crouched beside him and said: "Who did you think you were attacking?"

Again the mouth opened; again no audible words emerged. McBride pressed his suit. "It's important," he said, "just tell me who was here."

The man strove to voice his reply. McBride pressed his ear to the trembling mouth.

"In a pig's eye," the man said, then passed out, leaving McBride to curse his father, who'd bequeathed him a temper he was afraid he would probably live to regret. But then, what was living for?

***

Inspector Carnegie was used to boredom. For every rare moment of genuine discovery his professional life had furnished him with, he had endured hour upon hour of waiting for bodies to be photographed and examined, for lawyers to be bargained with and suspects intimidated. He had long ago given up attempting to fight this tide of ennui and, after his fashion, had learned the art of going with the flow. The process of investigation could not be hurried. The wise man, he had come to appreciate, let the pathologists, the lawyers and all their tribes have their tardy way. All that mattered, in the fullness of time, was that the finger be pointed and that the guilty quake.

Now, with the clock on the laboratory wall reading twelve fifty-three a.m., and even the monkeys hushed in their cages, he sat at one of the benches and waited for Hendrix to finish his calculations. The surgeon consulted the thermometer, then stripped off his gloves like a second skin and threw them down onto the sheet on which the deceased lay. "It's always difficult," the doctor said, "fixing time of death. She's lost less than three degrees. I'd say she's been dead under two hours."

"The officers arrived at a quarter to twelve," Carnegie said, "so she died maybe half an hour before that?"

"Something of that order."

"Was she put in there?" he asked, indicating the place beneath the bench.

"Oh certainly. There's no way she hid herself away. Not with those injuries. They're quite something, aren't they?"

Carnegie stared at Hendrix. The man had presumably seen hundreds of corpses, in every conceivable condition, but the enthusiasm in his pinched features was unqualified. Carnegie found that mystery more fascinating in its way than that of the dead woman and her slaughterer. How could anyone possibly enjoy taking the rectal temperature of a corpse? It confounded him. But the pleasure was there, gleaming in the man's eyes.

"Motive?" Carnegie asked.

"Pretty explicit, isn't it? Rape. There's been very thorough molestation; contusions around the vagina; copious semen deposits. Plenty to work with."

"And the wounds on her torso?"

"Ragged. Tears more than cuts."

"Weapon?"

"Don't know." Hendrix made an inverted U of his mouth. "I mean, the flesh has been *mauled*. If it weren't for the rape evidence I'd be tempted to suggest an animal."

"Dog, you mean?"

"I was thinking more of a tiger," Hendrix said.

Carnegie frowned. "Tiger?"

"Joke," Hendrix replied, "I was making a joke, Carnegie. My Christ, do you have *any* sense of irony?"

"This isn't funny," Carnegie said.

"I'm not laughing," Hendrix replied with a sour look.

"The man McBride found in the test chamber?"

"What about him?"

"Suspect?"

"Not in a thousand years. We're looking for a *maniac*, Carnegie? Big, strong. Wild."

"And the wounding? Before or after?"

Hendrix scowled. "I don't know. Postmortem will give us more. But for what it's worth, I think our man was in a frenzy. I'd say the wounding and the rape were probably simultaneous."

Carnegie's normally phlegmatic features registered something close to shock. "Simultaneous?"

Hendrix shrugged. "Lust's a funny thing," he said.

"Hilarious," came the appalled reply.

As was his wont, Carnegie had his driver deposit him half a mile from his doorstep to allow him a head-clearing walk before home, hot chocolate and slumber. The ritual was observed religiously, even when the Inspector was dog-tired. He used to stroll to wind down before stepping over the threshold. Long experience had taught him that taking his professional concerns into the house assisted neither the investigation nor his domestic life. He had learned the lesson too late to keep his wife from leaving him and his children from estrangement, but he applied the principle still.

Tonight, he walked slowly to allow the distressing scenes the evening had brought to recede somewhat. The route took him past a small cinema which, he had read in the local press, was soon to be demolished. He was not surprised. Though he was no cineaste the fare the flea pit provided had degenerated in recent years. The week's offering was a case in point: a double bill of horror movies. Lurid and derivative stuff to judge by the posters, with their crude graphics and their unashamed hyperbole. "*You May Never Sleep Again!*" one of the hook titles read; and beneath it a woman—very much awake—cowered in the shadow of a two-headed man. What trivial images the populists conjured to stir some fear in their audiences. The walking dead; nature grown vast and rampant in a miniature world; blood drinkers, omens, fire walkers, thunderstorms and all the other foolishness the public cowered before. It was all so laughably trite. Among that catalogue of penny dreadfuls there wasn't one that equaled the banality of human appetite, which horror (or the consequences of same) he saw every week of his working life. Thinking of it, his mind thumbed through a dozen snapshots: the dead by torchlight, face down and thrashed to oblivion; and the living too, meeting his mind's eye with hunger in theirs—for sex, for narcotics, for others' pain. Why didn't they put *that* on the posters?

As he reached his home a child squealed in the shadows beside his garage; the cry stopped him in his tracks. It came again, and this time he recognized it for what it was. No child at all but a cat, or cats, exchanging love calls in the darkened passageway. He went to the place to shoo them off. Their venereal secretions made the passage stink. He didn't need to yell; his footfall was sufficient to scare them away. They darted in all directions, not two, but half a dozen of them. A veritable orgy had been underway apparently. He had arrived on the spot too late however. The stench of their seductions was overpowering.

Carnegie looked blankly at the elaborate setup of monitors and video recorders that dominated his office.

"What in Christ's name is this about?" he wanted to know.

"The video tapes," said Boyle, his number two, "from the laboratory. I think you ought to have a look at them, sir."

Though they had worked in tandem for seven months, Boyle was not one of Carnegies favorite officers; you could practically smell the ambition off his smooth hide. In someone half his age again such greed would have been objectionable. In a man of thirty it verged on the obscene. This present display—the mustering of equipment ready to confront Carnegie when he walked in at eight in the morning—was just Boyle's style: flashy and redundant.

"Why so many screens?" Carnegie asked acidly. "Do I get it in stereo, too?"

"They had three cameras running simultaneously, sir. Covering the experiment from several angles."

"*What* experiment?"

Boyle gestured for his superior to sit down. Obsequious to a fault aren't you? thought Carnegie; much good it'll do you.

"Right," Boyle instructed the technician at the recorders, "roll the tapes."

Carnegie sipped at the cup of hot chocolate he had brought in with him. The beverage was a weakness of his, verging on addiction. On the days when the machine supplying it broke down he was an unhappy man indeed. He looked at the three screens. Suddenly, a title.

"*Project Blind Boy*," the words read. "*Restricted.*"

"*Blind Boy?*" said Carnegie. "What, or *who*, is that?"

"It's obviously a code word of some kind," Boyle said.

"*Blind Boy. Blind Boy.*" Carnegie repeated the phrase as if to beat it into submission, but before he could solve the problem the images on the three monitors diverged. They pictured the same subject—a bespectacled male in his late twenties sitting in a chair—but each showed the scene from a different angle. One took in the subject full length and in profile; the second was a three-quarter medium-shot angled from above; the third a straightforward close-up of the subject's head and shoulders, shot through the glass of the test chamber and from the front. The three images were in black and white, and none were completely centered or focused. Indeed, as the tapes began to run somebody was still adjusting such technicalities. A backwash of informal chatter ran between the subject and the woman—recognizable even in brief glimpses as the deceased—who was applying electrodes to his forehead. Much of the talk between them was difficult to catch; the acoustics in the chamber frustrated microphone and listener alike.

"The woman's Doctor Dance," Boyle offered. "The victim."

"Yes," said Carnegie, watching the screens intently, "I recognized her. How long does this preparation go on for?"

"Quite a while. Most of it's unedifying."

"Well, get to the edifying stuff, then."

"Fast forward," Boyle said. The technician obliged, and the actors on the three screens became squeaking comedians. "Wait!" said Boyle. "Back up a short way." Again, the technician did as instructed. "There!" said Boyle. "Stop there. Now run on at normal speed." The action settled back to its natural pace. "This is where it really begins, sir."

Carnegie had come to the end of his hot chocolate. He put his finger into the soft sludge at the bottom of the cup, delivering the sickly-sweet dregs to his tongue. On the screens Doctor Dance had approached the subject with a syringe, was now swabbing the crook of his elbow, and injecting him. Not for the first time since his visit to the Hume Laboratories did Carnegie wonder precisely what they did at the establishment. Was this kind of procedure *de rigueur* in pharmaceutical research? The implicit secrecy of the experiment—late at night in an otherwise deserted building—suggested not. And there was that imperative on the title card—"*Restricted.*" What they were watching had clearly never been intended for public viewing.

"Are you comfortable?" a man off camera now inquired. The subject nodded. His glasses had been removed and he looked slightly bemused without them. An unremarkable face, thought Carnegie; the subject— as yet unnamed—was neither Adonis nor Quasimodo. He was receding slightly, and his wispy, dirty-blond hair touched his shoulders.

"I'm fine, Doctor Welles," he replied to the off-camera questioner.

"You don't feel hot at all? Sweaty?"

"Not really," the guinea pig replied, slightly apologetically. "I feel ordinary."

That you are, Carnegie thought; then to Boyle: "Have you been through the tapes to the end?"

"No, sir," Boyle replied. "I thought you'd want to see them first. I only ran them as far as the injection."

"Any word from the hospital on Doctor Welles?"

"At the last call he was still comatose."

Carnegie grunted and returned his attention to the screens. Following the burst of action with the injection the tapes now settled into nonactivity: the three cameras fixed on their shortsighted subject with beady stares, the torpor occasionally interrupted by all inquiry from Welles as to the subject's condition. It remained the same. After three or four minutes of this eventless study even his occasional blinks began to assume major dramatic significance.

"Don't think much of the plot," the technician commented. Carnegie laughed; Boyle looked discomforted. Two or three more minutes passed in a similar manner.

"This doesn't look too hopeful," Carnegie said. "Run through it at speed, will you?"

The technician was about to obey when Boyle said: "*Wait*."

Carnegie glanced across at the man, irritated by his intervention, and then back at the screens. Something *was* happening. A subtle transformation had overtaken the insipid features of the subject. He had begun to smile to himself and was sinking down in his chair as if submerging his gangling body in a warm bath. His eyes, which had so far expressed little but affable indifference, now began to flicker closed, and then, once closed, opened again. When they did so there was a quality in them not previously visible, a hunger that seemed to reach out from the screen and into the calm of the inspector's office.

Carnegie put down his chocolate cup and approached the screens. As he did so the subject also got up out of his chair and walked toward the glass of the chamber, leaving two of the cameras' ranges. The third still recorded him, however, as he pressed his face against the window, and for a moment the two men faced each other through layers of glass and time, seemingly meeting each other's gaze.

The look on the man's face was critical now, the hunger was rapidly outgrowing sane control. Eyes burning, he laid his lips against the chamber window and kissed it, his tongue working against the glass.

"What in Christ's name is going on?" Carnegie said.

A prattle of voices had begun on the soundtrack. Doctor Welles was vainly asking the testee to articulate his feelings while Dance called off figures from the various monitoring instruments. It was difficult to hear much clearly—the din was further supplemented by an eruption of chatter from the caged monkeys—but it was evident that the readings coming through from the man's body were escalating. His face was flushed, his skin gleamed with a sudden sweat. He resembled a martyr with the tinder at his feet freshly lit, wild with a fatal ecstasy. He stopped French-kissing the window, tearing off the electrodes at his temples and the sensors from his arms and chest. Dance, her voice now registering alarm, called out for him to stop. Then she moved across the camera's view and out again crossing, Carnegie presumed, to the chamber door.

"Better not," he said, as if this drama were played out at his behest, and at a whim he could prevent the tragedy. But the woman took no notice. A moment later she appeared in long shot as she stepped into the chamber. The man moved to greet her, throwing over equipment as he did so. She called out to him—his name, perhaps. If so, it was inaudible over the monkeys' hullabaloo. "Shit," said Carnegie, as the testee's flailing arms caught first the profile camera, and then the three-quarter medium-shot. Two of the three monitors went dead. Only the head-on shot, the camera safe outside the chamber, still recorded events, but the tightness of the shot precluded more than an occasional glimpse of a moving body. Instead, the camera's sober eye gazed on, almost ironically, at the saliva-smeared glass of the chamber window, blind to the atrocities being committed a few feet out of range.

"What in Christ's name did they give him?" Carnegie said, as somewhere off camera the woman's screams rose over the screeching of the apes.

Jerome woke in the early afternoon feeling hungry and sore. When he threw the sheet off his body he was appalled at his state. His torso was scored with scratches, and his groin region was red-raw. Wincing, he moved to the edge of the bed and sat there for a while, trying to piece the previous evening back together again. He remembered going to the laboratories, but very little after that. He had been a paid guinea pig for several months, giving of his blood, comfort and patience to supplement his meager earnings as a translator. The arrangement had begun courtesy of a friend who did similar work, but whereas Figley had been part of the laboratories' mainstream program, Jerome had been approached after one week at the place by Doctors Welles and Dance, who had invited him—subject to a series of psychological tests—to work exclusively for them. It had been made clear from the outset that their project (he had never even been told its purpose) was of a secret nature, and that they would demand his total dedication and discretion. He had needed the funds, and the recompense they offered was marginally better than that paid by the laboratories, so he had agreed, although the hours they had demanded of him were unsociable. For several weeks now he had been required to attend the research facility late at night and often working into the small hours of the morning as he endured Welles's interminable questions about his private life and Dance's glassy stare.

Thinking of her cold look, he felt a tremor in him. Was it because once he had fooled himself that she had looked upon him more fondly than a doctor need? Such self-deception, he chided himself, was pitiful. He was not the stuff of which women dreamed, and each day he walked the streets reinforced that conviction. He could not remember one occasion in his adult life when a woman had looked his way, and kept looking; a time when an appreciative glance of his had been returned. Why this should bother him now he wasn't certain. His loveless condition was, he knew, commonplace. And nature had been kind. Knowing, it seemed, that the gift of allurement had passed him by, it had seen fit to minimize his libido. Weeks passed without his conscious thoughts mourning his enforced chastity.

Once in a while, when he heard the pipes roar, he might wonder what Mrs. Morrisey, his landlady, looked like in the bath; might imagine the firmness of her soapy breasts, or the dark divide of her rump as she stooped to put talcum powder between her toes. But such torments were, blissfully, infrequent. And when his cup brimmed he would pocket the money he had saved from his sessions at the laboratories and buy an hour's companionship from a woman called Angela (he'd never learned her second name) on Greek Street.

It would be several weeks before he did so again, he thought. Whatever he had done last night, or, more correctly, had done to him, the bruises alone had nearly crippled him. The only plausible explanation—though he couldn't recall any details—was that he'd been beaten up on the way back from the laboratories. Either that, or he'd stepped into a bar and somebody had picked a fight with him. It had happened before, on occasion. He had one of those faces that woke the bully in drunkards.

He stood up and hobbled to the small bathroom adjoining his room.

His glasses were missing from their normal spot beside the shaving mirror and his reflection was woefully blurred, but it was apparent that his face was as badly scratched as the rest of his anatomy. And more: a clump of hair had been pulled out from above his left ear; clotted blood ran down to his neck. Painfully, he bent to the task of cleaning his wounds, then bathing them in a stinging solution of antiseptic. That done, he returned into his room to seek out his spectacles. But search as he might he could not locate them. Cursing his idiocy, he rooted among his belongings for his old pair and found them. Their prescription was out of date—his eyes had worsened considerably since he'd worn them—but they at least brought his surroundings into a dreamy kind of focus.

An indisputable melancholy had crept up on him, compounded of his pain and those unwelcome thoughts of Mrs. Morrisey. To keep its intimacy at bay he turned on the radio. A sleek voice emerged, purveying the usual palliatives. Jerome had always had contempt for popular music and its apologists, but now, as he mooched around the small room, unwilling to clothe himself with chafing weaves when his scratches still pained him, the songs began to stir something other than scorn in him. It was as though he were hearing the words and music for the first time, as though all his life he had been deaf to their sentiments. Enthralled, he forgot his pain and listened. The songs told one seamless and obsessive story: of love lost and found, only to be lost again. The lyricists filled the airwaves with metaphor—much of it ludicrous, but no less potent for that. Of paradise, of hearts on fire; of birds, bells, journeys, sunsets; of passion as lunacy, as flight, as unimaginable treasure. The songs did not calm him with their fatuous sentiments. They flayed him, evoking, despite feeble rhyme and trite melody, a world bewitched by desire. He began to tremble. His eyes, strained (or so he reasoned) by the unfamiliar spectacles, began to delude him. It seemed as though he could see traces of light in his skin, sparks flying from the ends of his fingers.

He stared at his hands and arms. The illusion, far from retreating in the face of this scrutiny, increased. Beads of brightness, like the traces of fire in ash, began to climb through his veins, multiplying even as he watched. Curiously, he felt no distress. This burgeoning fire merely reflected the passion in the story the songs were telling him. Love, they said, was in the air, around every corner, waiting to be found. He thought again of the widow Morrisey in the flat below him, going about her business, sighing, no doubt, as he had done; awaiting her hero. The more he thought of her the more inflamed he became. She would not reject him, of that the songs convinced him. Or if she did he must press his case until (again, as the songs promised) she surrendered to him. Suddenly, at the thought of her surrender, the fire engulfed him. Laughing, he left the radio singing behind him and made his way downstairs.

It had taken the best part of the morning to assemble a list of testees employed at the laboratories. Carnegie had sensed a reluctance on the part of the establishment to open their files to the investigation despite the horror that had been committed on its premises. Finally, just after they had presented him with a hastily assembled who's who of subjects, four and a half dozen *in toto*, and their addresses. None, the offices claimed, matched the description of Welles's testee. The doctors, it was explained, had been clearly using laboratory facilities to work on private projects. Though this was not encouraged, both had been senior researchers, and allowed leeway on the matter. It was likely, therefore, that the man Carnegie was seeking had never even been on the laboratories' payroll. Undaunted, Carnegie ordered a selection of photographs taken off the video recording and had them distributed—with the list of names and addresses—to his officers. From then on it was down to footwork and patience.

Leo Boyle ran his finger down the list of names he had been given. "Another fourteen," he said. His driver grunted, and Boyle glanced across at him. "You were McBride's partner, weren't you?" he said.

"That's right," Dooley replied. "He's been suspended."

"Why?"

Dooley scowled. "Lacks finesse, that Virgil. Can't get the hang of arrest technique."

Dooley drew the car to a halt.

"Is this it?" Boyle asked.

"You said number eighty. This is eighty. On the door. Eight. Oh."

"I've got eyes."

Boyle got out of the car and made his way up the pathway. The house was sizeable, and had been divided into flats. There were several bells. He pressed for J. Tredgold—the name on his list—and waited. Of the five houses they had so far visited, two had been unoccupied and the residents of the other three had born no resemblance to the malefactor.

Boyle waited on the step a few seconds and then pressed the bell again; a longer ring this time.

"Nobody in," Dooley said from the pavement.

"Looks like it." Even as he spoke Boyle caught sight of a figure flitting across the hallway, its outline distorted by the cobblestone glass in the door. "Wait a minute," he said.

"What is it?"

"Somebody's in there and not answering." He pressed the first bell again, and then the others. Dooley approached up the pathway, flicking away an overattentive wasp.

"You sure?" he said.

"I saw somebody in there."

"Press the other bells," Dooley suggested.

"I already did. There's somebody in there and they don't want to come to the door." He rapped on the glass. "Open up," he announced. "Police."

Clever, thought Dooley; why not a loudspeaker, so heaven knows too? When the door, predictably, remained unanswered, Boyle turned to Dooley. "Is there a side gate?"

"Yes, sir."

"Then get around the back, pronto, before he's away."

"Shouldn't we call—?"

"Do it? I'll keep watch here. If you can get in the back come through and open the front door."

Dooley moved, leaving Boyle alone at the front door. He rang the series of bells again and, cupping his hand to his brow, put his face to the glass. There was no sign of movement in the halfway. Was it possible that the bird had already flown? He backed down the path and stared up at the windows; they stared back vacuously. Ample time had now passed for Dooley to get around the back of the house, but so far he had neither reappeared nor called. Stymied where he stood, and nervous that his tactics had lost them their quarry, Boyle decided to follow his nose around the back of the house.

The side gate had been left open by Dooley. Boyle advanced up the side passage, glancing through a window into an empty living room before heading around to the back door. It was open. Dooley, however, was not in sight. Boyle pocketed the photograph and the list and stepped inside, loath to call Dooley's name for fear it alert any felon to his presence, yet nervous of the silence. Cautious as a cat on broken glass he crept through the flat, but each room was deserted. At the apartment door, which let on to the hallway in which he had first seen the figure, he paused. Where had Dooley gone? The man had apparently disappeared from sight.

Then, a groan from beyond the door.

"Dooley?" Boyle ventured. Another groan. He stepped into the hallway. Three more doors presented themselves, all were closed; other flats, presumably. On the coconut mat at the front door lay Dooley's truncheon, dropped there as if its owner had been in the process of making his escape. Boyle swallowed his fear and walked into the body of the hall. The complaint came again, close by. He looked around and up the stairs. There, on the half-landing, lay Dooley. He was barely conscious. A rough attempt had been made to rip his clothes. Large portions of his flabby lower anatomy were exposed.

"What's going on, Dooley?" Boyle asked, moving to the bottom of the stairs. The officer heard his voice and rolled himself over. His bleary eyes, settling on Boyle, opened in terror.

"It's all right," Boyle reassured him. "It's only me."

Too late, Boyle registered that Dooley's gaze wasn't fixed on *him* at all, but on some sight over his shoulder. As he pivoted on his heel to snatch a glance at Dooley's bugaboo a charging figure slammed into him. Winded and cursing, Boyle was thrown off his feet. He scrabbled about on the floor for several seconds before his attacker seized hold of him by jacket and hair and hauled him to his feet. He recognized at once the wild face that was thrust into his—the receding hairline, the weak mouth, the *hunger*—but there was much too he had not anticipated. For one, the man was naked as a babe, though scarcely so modestly endowed. For another, he was clearly aroused to fever pitch. If the beady eye at his groin, shining up at Boyle, were not evidence enough, the hands now tearing at his clothes made the assailant's intention perfectly apparent.

"Dooley!" Boyle shrieked as he was thrown across the hallway. "In Christ's name! Dooley!"

His pleas were silenced as he hit the opposite wall. The wild man was at his back in half a heartbeat, smearing Boyle's face against the wallpaper. Birds and flowers, intertwined, filled his eyes. In desperation Boyle fought back, but the man's passion lent him ungovernable strength. With one insolent hand holding the policeman's head, he tore at Boyle's trousers and underwear, leaving his buttocks exposed.

"God . . ." Boyle begged into the pattern of the wallpaper. "Please God, somebody help me . . ." But the prayers were no more fruitful than his struggles. He was pinned against the wall like a butterfly spread on cork, about to be pierced through. He closed his eyes, tears of frustration running down his cheeks. The assailant left off his hold on Boyle's head and pressed his violation home. Boyle refused to cry out. The pain he felt was not the equal of his shame. Better perhaps that Dooley remained comatose; that this humiliation be done and finished with unwitnessed.

"Stop," he murmured into the wall, not to his attacker but to his body, urging it not to find pleasure in this outrage. But his nerve endings were treacherous; they caught fire from the assault. Beneath the stabbing agony some unforgivable part of him rose to the occasion.

On the stairs, Dooley hauled himself to his feet. His lumbar region, which had been weak since the car accident the previous Christmas, had given out almost as soon as the wild man had sprung him in the hall. Now, as he descended the stairs, the least motion caused excruciating agonies. Crippled with pain he stumbled to the bottom of the stairs and looked, amazed, across the hallway. Could this be Boyle—he the supercilious, he the rising man, being pummeled like a street kid in need of dope money? The sight transfixed Dooley for several seconds before he unhinged his eyes and swung them down to the truncheon on the mat. He moved cautiously, but the wild man was too occupied with the deflowering to notice him.

Jerome was listening to Boyle's heart. It was a loud, seductive beat, and with every thrust into the man it seemed to get louder. He wanted it: the heat of it, the life of it. His hand moved around to Boyle's chest and dug at the flesh.

"Give me your heart," he said. It was like a line from one of the songs.

Boyle screamed into the wall as his attacker mauled his chest. He'd seen photographs of the woman at the laboratories; the open wound of her torso was lightning-clear in his mind's eye. Now the maniac intended the same atrocity. *Give me your heart.* Panicked to the ledge of his sanity he found new stamina and began to fight afresh, reaching around and clawing at the man's torso. Nothing—not even the bloody loss of hair from his scalp—broke the rhythm of his thrusts, however. In extremis, Boyle attempted to insinuate one of his hands between his body and the wall and reach between his legs to unman the bastard. As he did so, Dooley attacked, delivering a hail of truncheon blows upon the man's head. The diversion gave Boyle precious leeway. He pressed hard against the wall. The man, his grip on Boyle's chest slicked with blood, lost his hold. Again, Boyle pushed. This time he managed to shrug the man off entirely. The bodies disengaged. Boyle turned, bleeding but in no danger, and watched Dooley follow the man across the hallway, beating at his greasy blond head. He made little attempt to protect himself however. His burning eyes (Boyle had never understood the physical accuracy of that image until now) were still on the object of his affections.

"Kill him!" Boyle said quietly as the man grinned—grinned!—through the blows. "Break every bone in his body!"

Even if Dooley, hobbled as he was, had been in any fit state to obey the imperative, he had no chance to do so. His berating was interrupted by a voice from down the hallway. A woman had emerged from the flat Boyle had come through. She too had been a victim of this marauder, to judge by her state. But Dooley's entry into the house had clearly distracted her molester before he could do serious damage.

"Arrest him!" she said, pointing at the leering man. "He tried to rape me!"

Dooley closed in to take possession of the prisoner, but Jerome had other intentions. He put his hand in Dooley's face and pushed him back against the front door. The coconut mat slid from under him; he all but fell. By the time he'd regained his balance Jerome was up and away. Boyle made a wretched attempt to stop him, but the tatters of his trousers were wrapped about his lower legs and Jerome, fleet-footed, was soon halfway up the stairs.

"Call for help," Boyle ordered Dooley. "And make it quick."

Dooley nodded and opened the front door.

"Is there any way out from upstairs?" Boyle demanded of Mrs. Morrisey. She shook her head. "Then we've got the bastard trapped, haven't we?" he said. "Go on, Dooley!" Dooley hobbled away down the path. "And you," he said to the woman, "fetch something in the way of weaponry. Anything solid." The woman nodded and returned the way she'd come, leaving Boyle slumped beside the open door. A soft breeze cooled the sweat on his face. At the car outside Dooley was calling up reinforcements.

All too soon, Boyle thought, the cars would be here, and the man upstairs would be hauled away to give his testimony. There would be no opportunity for revenge once he was in custody. The law would take its placid course, and he, the victim, would be only a bystander. If he was ever to salvage the ruins of his manhood, *now* was the time. If he didn't—if he languished here, his bowels on fire—he would never shrug off the horror he felt at his body's betrayal. He must act now— beat the grin off his ravisher's face once and for all—or else live in self-disgust until memory failed him.

The choice was no choice at all. Without further debate, he got up from his squatting position and began up the stairs. As he reached the half-landing he realized he hadn't brought a weapon with him. He knew, however, that if he descended again he'd lose all momentum. Prepared, in that moment, to die if necessary, he headed on up.

There was only one door open on the top landing. Through it came the sound of a radio. Downstairs, in the safety of the hall, he heard Dooley come in to tell him that the call had been made, only to break off in mid-announcement. Ignoring the distraction, Boyle stepped into the flat.

There was nobody there. It took Boyle a few moments only to check the kitchen, the tiny bathroom and the living room. All were deserted. He returned to the bathroom, the window of which was open, and put his head out. The drop to the grass of the garden below was quite manageable. There was an imprint in the ground of the man's body. He had leaped. And gone.

Boyle cursed his tardiness and hung his head. A trickle of heat ran down the inside of his leg. In the next room, the love songs played on.

For Jerome, there was no forgetfulness, not this time. The encounter with Mrs. Morrisey, which had been interrupted by Dooley, and the episode with Boyle that had followed, had all merely served to fan the fire in him. Now, by the light of those flames, he saw clearly what crimes he had committed. He remembered with horrible clarity the laboratory, the injection, the monkeys, the blood. The acts he recalled, however (and there were many), woke no sense of sinfulness in him. All moral consequence, all shame or remorse, was burned out by the fire that was even now licking his flesh to new enthusiasms.

He took refuge in a quiet cul-de-sac to make himself presentable. The clothes he had managed to snatch before making his escape were motley but would serve to keep him from attracting unwelcome attention. As he buttoned himself up—his body seeming to strain from its covering as if resentful of being concealed—he tried to control the holocaust that raged between his ears. But the flames wouldn't be dampened. His every fiber seemed alive to the flux and flow of the world around him. The marshaled trees along the road, the wall at his back, the very paving stones beneath his bare feet were catching a spark from him and burning now with their own fire. He grinned to see the conflagration spread. The world, in its every eager particular, grinned back.

Aroused beyond control, he turned to the wall he had been leaning against. The sun had fallen full upon it, and it was warm; the bricks smelled ambrosial. He laid kisses on their gritty faces, his hands exploring every nook and cranny. Murmuring sweet nothings, he unzipped himself, found an accommodating niche, and filled it. His mind was running with liquid pictures: mingled anatomies, female and male in one undistinguishable congress. Above him, even the clouds had caught fire. Enthralled by their burning heads he felt the moment rise in his gristle. Breath was short now. But the ecstasy? Surely that would go on forever.

Without warning a spasm of pain traveled down his spine from cortex to testicles and back again, convulsing him. His hands lost grip of the brick and he finished his agonizing climax on the air as he fell across the pavement. For several seconds he lay where he had collapsed, while the echoes of the initial spasm bounced back and forth along his spine, diminishing with each return. He could taste blood at the back of his throat. He wasn't certain if he'd bitten his lip or tongue, but he thought not. Above his head the birds circled on, rising lazily on a spiral of warm air. He watched the fire in the clouds gutter out.

He got to his feet and looked down at the coinage of semen he'd spent on the pavement. For a fragile instant he caught again a whiff of the vision he'd just had; imagined a marriage of his seed with the paving stone. What sublime children the world might boast, he thought, if he could only mate with brick or tree. He would gladly suffer the agonies of conception if such miracles were possible. But the paving stone was unmoved by his seed's entreaties. The vision, like the fire above him, cooled and hid its glories.

He put his bloodied member away and leaned against the wall, turning the strange events of his recent life over and over. Something fundamental was changing in him, of that he had no doubt. The rapture that had possessed him (and would, no doubt, possess him again) was like nothing he had hitherto experienced. And whatever they had injected into his system, it showed no signs of being discharged naturally; far from it. He could feel the heat in him still, as he had leaving the laboratories, but this time the roar of its presence was louder than ever.

It was a new kind of life he was living, and the thought, though frightening, exulted him. Not once did it occur to his spinning, eroticized brain that this new kind of life would, in time, demand a new kind of death.

Carnegie had been warned by his superiors that results were expected. He was now passing the verbal beating he'd received to those under him. It was a line of humiliation in which the greater was encouraged to kick the lesser man, and that man, in turn, his lesser. Carnegie had sometimes wondered what the man at the end of the line took his ire out on; his dog presumably.

"This miscreant is still loose, gentlemen, despite his photograph in many of this morning's newspapers and an operating method which is, to say the least, insolent. We *will* catch him, of course, but let's get the bastard before we have another murder on our hands—"

The phone rang. Boyle's replacement, Migeon, picked it up, while Carnegie concluded his pep talk to the assembled officers.

"I want him in the next twenty-four hours, gentlemen. That's the time scale I've been given, and that's what we've got. Twenty-four hours."

Migeon interrupted. "Sir? It's Johannson. He says he's got something for you. It's urgent."

"Right." The inspector claimed the receiver. "Carnegie."

The voice at the other end was soft to the point of inaudibility. "Carnegie," Johannson said, "we've been right through the laboratory, dug up every piece of information we could find on Dance and Welles's tests—"

"And?"

"We've also analyzed traces of the agent from the hypo they used on the suspect. I think we've found the *Boy*, Carnegie."

"What boy?" Carnegie wanted to know. He found Johannson's obfuscation irritating.

"*The Blind Boy*, Carnegie."

"And?"

For some inexplicable reason Carnegie was certain the man *smiled* down the phone before replying: "I think perhaps you'd better come down and see for yourself. Sometime around noon suit you?"

Johannson could have been one of history's greatest poisoners. He had all the requisite qualifications. A tidy mind (poisoners were, in Carnegie's experience, domestic paragons), a patient nature (poison could take time) and, most importantly, an encyclopedic knowledge of toxicology. Watching him at work, which Carnegie had done on two previous cases, was to see a subtle man at his subtle craft, and the spectacle made Carnegie's blood run cold.

Johannson had installed himself in the laboratory on the top floor, where Doctor Dance had been murdered, rather than use police facilities for the investigation, because, as he explained to Carnegie, much of the equipment that the Hume organization boasted was simply not available elsewhere. His dominion over the place, accompanied by his two assistants, had, however, transformed the laboratory from the clutter left by the experimenters to a dream of order. Only the monkeys remained a constant. Try as he might Johannson could not control their behavior.

"We didn't have any difficulty finding the drug used on your man," Johannson said, "we simply cross-checked traces remaining in the hypodermic with materials found in the room. In fact, they seem to have been manufacturing this stuff, or variations on the theme, for some time. The people here claim they know nothing about it, of course. I'm inclined to believe them. What the good doctors were doing here was, I'm sure, in the nature of a personal experiment."

"What sort of experiment?"

Johannson took off his spectacles and set about cleaning them with the tongue of his red tie. "At first, we thought they were developing some kind of hallucinogen," he said. "In some regards the agent used on your man resembles a narcotic. In fact—methods apart—I think they made some very exciting discoveries. Developments which take us into entirely new territory."

"It's not a drug then?"

"Oh, yes, of course it's a drug," Johannson said, replacing the spectacles, "but one created for a very specific purpose. See for yourself."

Johannson led the way across the laboratory to the row of monkeys' cages. Instead of being confined separately, the toxicologist had seen fit to open the interconnecting doors between one cage and the next, allowing the animals free access to gather in groups. The consequence was absolutely plain—the animals were engaged in an elaborate series of sexual acts. Why, Carnegie wondered, did monkeys perpetually perform obscenities? It was the same torrid display whenever he'd taken his offspring, as children, to Regent's Park Zoo; the ape enclosure elicited one embarrassing question upon another. He'd stopped taking the children after a while. He simply found it too mortifying.

"Haven't they got anything better to do?" he asked of Johannson glancing away and then back at a menage à trois that was so intimate the eye could not ascribe member to monkey.

"Believe me," Johannson smirked, "this is mild by comparison with much of the behavior we've seen from them since we gave them a shot of the agent. From that point on they neglected all normal behavior patterns. They bypassed the arousal signals, the courtship rituals. They no longer show any interest in food. They don't sleep. They have become sexual obsessives. All other stimuli are forgotten. Unless the agent is naturally discharged, I suspect they are going to screw themselves to death."

Carnegie looked along the rest of the cages. The same pornographic scenes were being played out in each one. Mass rape, homosexual liaisons, fervent and ecstatic masturbation.

"It's no wonder the doctors made a secret project of their discovery," Johannson went on. "They were on to something that could have made them a fortune. An aphrodisiac that actually works."

"An aphrodisiac?"

"Most are useless, of course. Rhinoceros horn, live eels in cream sauce: symbolic stuff. They're designed to arouse by association."

Carnegie remembered the hunger in Jerome's eyes. It was echoed here in the monkeys'. Hunger, and the desperation that hunger brings.

"And the ointments too, all useless. *Cantharis vesticatora*—"

"What's that?"

"You know the stuff as Spanish fly, perhaps? It's a paste made from a beetle. Again, useless. At best these things are irritants. But this . . ." He picked up a vial of colorless fluid. "*This* is damn near genius."

"They don't look too happy with it to me."

"Oh, it's still crude," Johannson said. "I think the researchers were greedy and moved into tests on living subjects a good two or three years before it was wise to do so. The stuff is almost lethal as it stands, no doubt of that. But it *could* be made to work, given time. You see, they've sidestepped the mechanical problems. This stuff operates directly on the sexual imagination, on the libido. If you arouse the *mind*, the body follows. That's the trick of it."

A rattling of the wire mesh close by drew Carnegie's attention from Johannson's pale features. One of the female monkeys, apparently not satisfied with the attentions of several males, was spread-eagled against her cage, her nimble fingers reaching for Carnegie. Her spouses, not to be left loveless, had taken to sodomy. "*Blind Boy?*" said Carnegie. "Is that Jerome?"

"It's Cupid, isn't it?" Johannson said:

"Love looks not with the eyes but with the mind,
And therefore is winged Cupid painted blind.

It's *Midsummer Night's Dream."*

"The bard was never my strongest suit," said Carnegie. He went back to staring at the female monkey. "And Jerome?" he said.

"He has the agent in his system. A sizeable dose."

"So he's like this lot!"

"I would presume—his intellectual capacities being greater—that the agent may not be able to work in quite such an *unfettered* fashion. But, having said that, sex can make monkeys out of the best of us, can't it?" Johannson allowed himself a half-smile at the notion. "All our so-called higher concerns become secondary to the pursuit. For a short time sex makes us obsessive. We call perform, or at least *think* we can perform, what with hindsight may seem extraordinary feats."

"I don't think there's anything so extraordinary about rape," Carnegie commented, attempting to stem Johannson's rhapsody. But the other man would not be subdued.

"Sex without end, without compromise or apology," he said. "Imagine it. The dream of Casanova."

The world had seen so many Ages: the Age of Enlightenment; of Reformation; of Reason. Now, at last, the Age of Desire. And after this, an end to Ages; an end, perhaps, to everything. For the fires that were being stoked now were fiercer than the innocent world suspected. They were terrible fires, fires without end, which would illuminate the world in one last, fierce light.

So Welles thought as he lay in his bed. He had been conscious for several hours, but had chosen not to signify such. Whenever a nurse came to his room he would clamp his eyes closed and slow the rhythm of his breath. He knew he could not keep the illusion up for long, but the hours gave him a while to think through his itinerary from here. His first move had to be back to the laboratories. There were papers there he had to shred, tapes to wipe clean. From now on he was determined that every scrap of information about *Project Blind Boy* exist solely in his head. That way he would have complete control over his masterwork, and nobody could claim it from him.

He had never had much interest in making money from the discovery, although he was well aware of how lucrative a workable aphrodisiac would be; he had never given a fig for material wealth. His initial motivation for the development of the drug—which they had chanced upon quite by accident while testing an agent to aid schizophrenics—had been investigative. But his motives had matured through their months of secret work. He had come to think of himself as the bringer of the millennium. He would not have anyone attempt to snatch that sacred role from him.

So he thought, lying in his bed, waiting for a moment to slip away.

As he walked the streets Jerome would have happily affirmed Welles's vision. Perhaps he, of all men, was most eager to welcome the Age of Desire. He saw its portents everywhere: on advertising billboards and cinema marquees, in shop windows, on television screens—everywhere, the body as merchandise. Where flesh was not being used to market artifacts of steel and stone, those artifacts were taking on its properties. Automobiles passed him by with every voluptuous attribute but breath—their sinuous bodywork gleamed, their interiors invited plushly. The buildings beleaguered him with sexual puns: spires, passageways, shadowed plazas with white-water fountains. Beneath the raptures of the shallow—the thousand trivial distractions he encountered in street and square—he sensed the ripe life of the body informing every particular.

The spectacle kept the fire in him well stoked. It was all that will power could do to keep him from pressing his attention on every creature that he met eyes with. A few seemed to sense the heat in him and gave him wide berth. Dogs sensed it too. Several followed him, aroused by *his* arousal. Flies orbited his head in squadrons. But his growing ease with his condition gave him some rudimentary control over it. He knew that to make a public display of his ardor would bring the law down upon him, and that in turn would hinder his adventures. Soon enough, the fire that he had begun would spread. *Then* he would emerge from hiding and bathe in it freely. Until then, discretion was best.

He had on occasion bought the company of a young woman in Soho; he went to find her now. The afternoon was stiflingly hot, but he felt no weariness. He had not eaten since the previous evening, but he felt no hunger. Indeed, as he climbed the narrow stairway up to the room on the first floor which Angela had once occupied, he felt as primed as an athlete, glowing with health. The immaculately dressed and wall-eyed pimp who usually occupied a place at the top of the stairs was absent. Jerome simply went to the girl's room and knocked. There was no reply. He rapped again, more urgently. The noise brought an early middle-aged woman to the door at the end of the landing.

"What do you want?"

"The woman," he replied simply.

"Angela's gone. And you'd better get out of here too in that state. This isn't a flophouse."

"When will she be back?" he asked, keeping as tight a leash as he could on his appetite.

The woman, who was as tall as Jerome and half as heavy again as his wasted frame, advanced toward him. "The girl won't *be* back," she said, "so you get the hell out of here, before I call Isaiah."

Jerome looked at the woman. She shared Angela's profession, no doubt, if not her youth or prettiness. He smiled at her. "I can hear your heart," he said.

"I told you—"

Before she could finish the words Jerome moved down the landing toward her. She wasn't intimidated by his approach, merely repulsed.

"If I call Isaiah, you'll be sorry," she informed him. The pace of her heartbeat had risen, he could hear it.

"I'm burning," he said.

She frowned. She was clearly losing this battle of wits. "Stay away from me," she told. "I'm warning you."

The heartbeat was getting more rapid still. The rhythm, buried in her substance, drew him on. From that source: all life, all heat.

"Give me your heart," he said.

"Isaiah!"

Nobody came running at her shout, however. Jerome gave her no opportunity to cry out a second time. He reached to embrace her, clamping a hand over her mouth. She let fly a volley of blows against him, but the pain only fanned the flames. He was brighter by the moment. His every orifice let onto the furnace in belly and loins and head. Her superior bulk was of no advantage against such fervor. He pushed her against the wall—the beat of her heart loud in his ears—and began to apply kisses to her neck, tearing her dress open to free her breasts.

"Don't shout," he said, trying to sound persuasive. "There's no harm meant."

She shook her head and said, "I won't," against his palm. He took his hand from her mouth and she dragged in several desperate breaths. Where was Isaiah? she thought. Not far, surely. Fearing for her life if she tried to resist this interloper—how his eyes shone!—she gave up any pretense to resistance and let him have his way. Men's supply of passion, she knew from long experience, was easily depleted. Though they might threaten to move earth and heaven too, half an hour later their boasts would be damp sheets and resentment. If worst came to worst, she could tolerate his inane talk of burning; she'd heard far obscener bedroom chat. As to the prong he was even now attempting to press into her, it and its comical like held no surprises for her.

Jerome wanted to touch the heart in her, wanted to see it splash up into his face, to bathe in it. He put his hand to her breast and felt the beat of her under his palm.

"You like that, do you?" she said as he pressed against her bosom. "You're not the first."

He clawed her skin.

"Gently, sweetheart," she chided him, looking over his shoulder to see if there was any sign of Isaiah. "Be gentle. This is the only body I've got."

He ignored her. His nails drew blood.

"Don't do that," she said.

"Wants to be out," he replied digging deeply, and it suddenly dawned on her that this was no love-game he was playing.

"*Stop it*," she said, as he began to tear at her. This time she screamed.

Downstairs, and a short way along the street, Isaiah dropped the slice of *tarte française* he'd just bought and ran to the door. It wasn't the first time his sweet tooth had tempted him from his post, but—unless he was quick to undo the damage—it might very well be his last.

There were terrible noises from the landing. He raced up the stairs. The scene that met his eyes was in every way worse than that his imagination had conjured. Simone was trapped against the wall beside her door with a man battened upon her. Blood was coming from somewhere between them, he couldn't see where.

Isaiah yelled. Jerome, hands bloody, looked around from his labors as a giant in a Savile Row suit reached for him. It took Jerome vital seconds to uproot himself from the furrow, by which time the man was upon him. Isaiah took hold of him, and dragged him off the woman. She took shelter, sobbing, in her room.

"Sick bastard," Isaiah said, launching a fusillade of punches. Jerome reeled. But he was on fire, and unafraid. In a moment's respite he leaped at his man like an angered baboon. Isaiah, taken unawares, lost balance, and fell back against one of the doors, which opened inward against his weight. He collapsed into a squalid lavatory, his head striking the lip of the toilet bowl as he went down. The impact disoriented him, and he lay on the stained linoleum groaning, legs akimbo. Jerome could hear his blood, eager in his veins; could smell sugar on his breath. It tempted him to stay. But his instinct for self-preservation counseled otherwise; Isaiah was already making an attempt to stand up again. Before he could get to his feet Jerome turned about and made a getaway down the stairs.

The dog day met him at the doorstep, and he smiled. The street wanted him more than the woman on the landing, and he was eager to oblige. He started out onto the pavement, his erection still pressing from his trousers. Behind him he heard the giant pounding down the stairs. He took to his heels, laughing. The fire was still uncurbed in him, and it lent speed to his feet. He ran down the street not caring if Sugar Breath was following or not. Pedestrians, unwilling in this dispassionate age to register more than casual interest in the blood-spattered satyr, parted to let him pass. A few pointed, assuming him an actor perhaps. Most took no notice at all. He made his way through a maze of back streets, aware without needing to look that Isaiah was still on his heels.

Perhaps it was accident that brought him to the street market; perhaps, and more probably, it was that the swelter carried the mingled scent of meat and fruit to his nostrils and he wanted to bathe in it. The narrow thoroughfare was thronged with purchasers, sightseers and stalls heaped with merchandise. He dove into the crowd happily, brushing against buttock and thigh, meeting the plaguing gaze of fellow flesh on every side. Such a day! He and his prick could scarcely believe their luck.

Behind him he heard Isaiah shout. He picked up his pace, heading for the most densely populated area of the market, where he could lose himself in the hot press of people. Each contact was a painful ecstasy. Each climax—and they came one upon the other as he pressed through the crowd—was a dry spasm in his system. His back ached, his balls ached. But what was his body now? Just a plinth for that singular monument, his prick. Head was *nothing*; mind was *nothing*. His arms were simply made to bring love close, his legs to carry the demanding rod any place where it might find satisfaction. He pictured himself as a walking erection, the world gaping on every side. Flesh, brick, steel, he didn't care—he would ravish it all.

Suddenly, without his seeking it, the crowd parted, and he found himself off the main thoroughfare and in a narrow street. Sunlight poured between the buildings, its zeal magnified. He was about to turn back to join the crowd again when he caught a scent and sight that drew him on. A short way down the heat-drenched street three shirtless young men were standing amid piles of fruit crates, each containing dozens of baskets of strawberries. There had been a glut of the fruit that year, and in the relentless heat much of it had begun to soften and rot. The trio of workers was going through the baskets, sorting bad fruit from good, and throwing the spoiled strawberries into the gutter. The smell in the narrow space was overpowering, a sweetness of such strength it would have sickened any interloper other than Jerome, whose senses had lost all capacity for revulsion or rejection. The world was the world was the world; he would take it, as in marriage, for better or worse. He stood watching the spectacle entranced: the sweating fruit sorters bright in the fall of sun, hands, arms and torsoes spattered with scarlet juice; the air mazed with every nectar-seeking insect; the discarded fruit heaped in the gutter in seeping mounds. Engaged in their sticky labors, the sorters didn't even see him at first. Then one of the three looked up and took in the extraordinary creature watching them. The grin on his face died as he met Jerome's eyes.

"What the hell?"

Now the other two looked up from their work.

"Sweet," said Jerome. He could hear their hearts tremble.

"Look at him," said the youngest of the three, pointing at Jerome's groin. "Fucking exposing himself."

They stood still in the sunlight, he and they, while the wasps whirled around the fruit and, in the narrow slice of blue summer sky between the roofs, birds passed over. Jerome wanted the moment to go on forever; his too-naked head tasted Eden here.

And then, the dream broke. He felt a shadow on his back. One of the sorters dropped the basket he was sorting through; the decayed fruit broke open on the gravel. Jerome frowned and half-turned. Isaiah had found the street. His weapon was steel and shone. It crossed the space between him and Jerome in one short second. Jerome felt an ache in his side as the knife slid into him.

"*Christ*," the young man said and began to run. His two brothers, unwilling to be witnesses at the scene of a wounding, hesitated only moments longer before following.

The pain made Jerome cry out, but nobody in the noisy market heard him. Isaiah withdrew the blade; heat came with it. He made to stab again but Jerome was too fast for the spoiler. He moved out of range and staggered across the street. The would-be assassin, fearful that Jerome's cries would draw too much attention, moved quickly in pursuit to finish the job. But the tarmac was slick with rotted fruit, and his fine suede shoes had less grip than Jerome's bare feet. The gap between them widened by a pace.

"No you don't," Isaiah said, determined not to let his humiliator escape. He pushed over a tower of fruit crates—baskets toppled and strewed their contents across Jerome's path. Jerome hesitated, to take in the bouquet of bruised fruit. The indulgence almost killed him. Isaiah closed in, ready to take the man. Jerome, his system taxed to near eruption by the stimulus of pain, watched the blade come close to opening up his belly. His mind conjured the wound: the abdomen slit—the heat spilling out to join the blood of the strawberries in the gutter. The thought was so tempting. He almost wanted it.

Isaiah had killed before, twice. He knew the wordless vocabulary of the act, and he could see the invitation in his victim's eyes. Happy to oblige, he came to meet it, knife at the ready. At the last possible moment Jerome recanted, and instead of presenting himself for slitting, threw a blow at the giant. Isaiah ducked to avoid it and his feet slid in the mush. The knife fled from his hand and fell among the debris of baskets and fruit. Jerome turned away as the hunter—the advantage lost—stooped to locate the knife. But his prey was gone before his ham-fisted grip had found it; lost again in the crowd-filled streets. He had no opportunity to pocket the knife before the uniform stepped out of the crowd and joined him in the hot passageway.

"What's the story?" the policeman demanded, looking down at the knife. Isaiah followed his gaze. The bloodied blade was black with flies.

In his office Inspector Carnegie sipped at his hot chocolate, his third in the past hour, and watched the processes of dusk. He had always wanted to be a detective, right from his earliest rememberings. And, in those rememberings, this had always been a charged and magical hour. Night descending on the city; myriad evils putting on their glad rags and coming out to play. A time for vigilance, for a new moral stringency.

But as a child he had failed to imagine the fatigue that twilight invariably brought. He was tired to his bones, and if he snatched any sleep in the next few hours he knew it would be here, in his chair, with his feet tip on the desk amid a clutter of plastic cups.

The phone rang. It was Johannson.

"Still at work?" he said, impressed by Johannson's dedication to the job. It was well after nine. Perhaps Johannson didn't have a home worth calling such to go back to either.

"I heard our man had a busy day," Johannson said.

"That's right. A prostitute in Soho, then got himself stabbed."

"He got through the cordon, I gather?"

"These things happen," Carnegie replied, too tired to be testy. "What can I do for you?"

"I just thought you'd want to know: the monkeys have started to die."

The words stirred Carnegie from his fatigue-stupor. "How many?" he asked.

"Three from fourteen so far. But the rest will be dead by dawn, I'd guess."

"What's killing them? Exhaustion?" Carnegie recalled the desperate saturnalia he'd seen in the cages. What animal—human or otherwise—could keep up such revelry without cracking up?

"It's not physical," Johannson said. "Or at least not in the way you're implying. We'll have to wait for the dissection results before we get any detailed explanations—"

"Your best guess?"

"For what it's worth . . ." Johannson said, ". . . which is quite a lot: I think they're going *bang*."

"What?"

"Cerebral overload of some kind. Their brains are simply giving out. The agent doesn't disperse you see. *It feeds on itself.* The more fevered they get, the more of the drug is produced; the more of the drug there is, the more fevered they get. It's a vicious circle. Hotter and hotter, wilder and wilder. Eventually the system can't take it, and suddenly I'm up to my armpits in dead monkeys." The smile came back into the voice again, cold and wry. "Not that the others let that spoil their fun. Necrophilia's quite the fashion down here."

Carnegie peered at his cooling hot chocolate. It had acquired a thin skin which puckered as he touched the cup. "So it's just a matter of time?" he said.

"Before our man goes for bust? Yes, I'd think so."

"All right. Thank you for the update. Keep me posted."

"You want to come down here and view the remains?"

"Monkey corpses I can do without, thank you."

Johannson laughed. Carnegie put down the receiver. When he turned back to the window, night had well and truly fallen.

In the laboratory Johannson crossed to the light switch by the door. In the time he'd been calling Carnegie the last of the daylight had fled. He saw the blow that felled him coming a mere heartbeat before it landed; it caught him across the side of his neck. One of his vertebrae snapped and his legs buckled. He collapsed without reaching the light switch. But by the time he hit the ground the distinction between day and night was academic.

Welles didn't bother to check whether his blow had been lethal or not; time was at a premium. He stepped over the body and headed across to the bench where Johannson had been working. There, lying in a circle of lamplight as if for the final act of a simian tragedy, lay a dead monkey. It had clearly perished in a frenzy. Its face was knitted up; mouth wide and spittle-stained; eyes fixed in a final look of alarm. Its fur had been pulled out in tufts in the throes of its copulations. Its body, wasted with exertion, was a mass of contusions. It took Welles half a minute of study to recognize the implications of the corpse, and of the other two he now saw lying on a nearby bench.

"Love kills," he murmured to himself philosophically and began his systematic destruction of *Blind Boy*.

I'm dying, Jerome thought. I'm dying of *terminal joy*. The thought amused him. It was the only thought in his head which made much sense. Since his encounter with Isaiah and the escape from the police that had followed, he could remember little with any coherence. The hours of hiding and nursing his wounds—of feeling the heat grow again, and of discharging it—had long since merged into one midsummer dream, from which, he knew with pleasurable certainty, only death would wake him. The blaze was devouring him utterly, from the entrails out. If he were to be eviscerated now, what would the witnesses find? Only embers and ashes.

Yet still his one-eyed friend demanded *more*. Still, as he wove his way back to the laboratories—where else for a made man to go when the stitches slipped but back to the first heat?—still the grids gaped at him seductively, and every brick wall offered up a hundred gritty invitations.

The night was balmy: a night for love songs and romance. In the questionable privacy of a parking lot a few blocks from his destination he saw two people having sex in the back of a car, the doors open to accommodate limbs and draft. Jerome paused to watch the ritual, enthralled as ever by the tangle of bodies and the sound—so loud it was like thunder—of twin hearts beating to one escalating rhythm. Watching, his rod grew eager.

The female saw him first and alerted her partner to the wreck of a human being who was watching them with such childish delight. The male looked around from his gropings to stare. Do I burn, Jerome wondered? Does my hair flame? At the last, does the illusion gain substance? To judge by the look on their faces, the answer was surely no. They were not in awe of him, merely angered and revolted.

"I'm on fire," he told them.

The male got to his feet and spat at Jerome. He almost expected the spittle to turn to steam as it approached him but instead it landed on his face and upper chest as a cooling shower.

"Go to hell," the woman said. "Leave us alone."

Jerome shook his head. The male warned him that another step would oblige him to break Jerome's head. It disturbed our man not a jot; no words, no blows, could silence the imperative of the rod.

Their hearts, he realized, as he moved toward them, no longer beat in tandem.

Carnegie consulted the map, five years out of date now, on his office wall to pinpoint the location of the attack that had just been reported. Neither of the victims had come to serious harm, apparently. The arrival of a carload of revelers had dissuaded Jerome (it was unquestionably Jerome) from lingering. Now the area was being flooded with officers, half a dozen of them armed. In a matter of minutes every street in the vicinity of the attack would be cordoned off. Unlike Soho, which had been crowded, the area would furnish the fugitive with few hiding places.

Carnegie pinpointed the location of the attack and realized that it was within a few blocks of the laboratories. No accident, surely. The man was heading back to the scene of his crime. Wounded, and undoubtedly on the verge of collapse—the lovers had described a man who looked more dead than alive—Jerome would probably be picked up before he reached home. But there was always the risk of his slipping through the net and getting to the laboratories. Johannson was working there, alone. The guard on the building was, in these straitened times, necessarily small.

Carnegie picked up the phone and dialed through to Johannson. The phone rang at the other end but nobody picked it up. The man's gone home, Carnegie thought, happy to be relieved of his concern. It's ten-fifty at night and he's earned his rest. Just as he was about to put the receiver down, however, it was picked up at the other end.

"Johannson?"

Nobody replied.

"Johannson? This is Carnegie." And still, no reply. "Answer me, damn it. Who is this?"

In the laboratories the receiver was forsaken. It was not replaced on the cradle but left to lie on the bench. Down the buzzing line, Carnegie could clearly hear the monkeys, their voices shrill.

"Johannson?" Carnegie demanded. "Are you there? Johannson?"

But the apes screamed on.

Welles had built two bonfires of the *Blind Boy* material in the sinks and then set them alight. They flared up enthusiastically. Smoke, heat and ashes filled the large room, thickening the air. When the fires were fairly raging he threw all the tapes he could lay hands upon into the conflagration, and added all of Johannson's notes for good measure. Several of the tapes had already gone from the files, he noted. But all they could show any thief was some teasing scenes of transformation. The heart of the secret remained his. With the procedures and formulae now destroyed, it only remained to wash the small amounts of remaining agent down the drain and kill and incinerate the animals.

He prepared a series of lethal hypodermics, going about the business with uncharacteristic orderliness. This systematic destruction gratified him. He felt no regret at the way things had turned out. From that first moment of panic, when he'd helplessly watched the *Blind Boy* serum work its awesome effects upon Jerome, to this final elimination of all that had gone before had been, he now saw, one steady process of wiping clean. With these fires he brought an end to the pretense of scientific inquiry. After this he was indisputably the Apostle of Desire, its John in the Wilderness. The thought blinded him to any other. Careless of the monkeys' scratchings he hauled them one by one from their cages to deliver the killing dose. He had dispatched three, and was opening the cage of the fourth, when a figure appeared in the doorway of the laboratory. Through the smoky air it was impossible to see who. The surviving monkeys seemed to recognize him, however. They left off their couplings and set up a din of welcome.

Welles stood still and waited for the newcomer to make his move.

"I'm dying," said Jerome.

Welles had not expected this. Of all the people he had anticipated here, Jerome was the last.

"Did you hear me?" the man wanted to know.

Welles nodded. "We're *all* dying, Jerome. Life is a slow disease, no more nor less. But such a *light*, eh? in the going."

"You *knew* this would happen," Jerome said. "You knew the fire would eat me away."

"No," came the sober reply. "No, I didn't. Really."

Jerome walked out of the door frame and into the murky light. He was a wasted shambles, a patchwork man, blood on his body, fire in his eyes. But Welles knew better than to trust the apparent vulnerability of this scarecrow. The agent in his system had made him capable of superhuman acts. He had seen Dance torn open with a few nonchalant strokes. Tact was required. Though clearly close to death, Jerome was still formidable.

"I didn't intend this, Jerome," Welles said, attempting to tame the tremor in his voice. "I wish, in a way, I could claim that I had. But I wasn't that farsighted. It's taken me time and pain to see the future plainly."

The burning man watched him, gaze intent.

"Such fires, Jerome, waiting to be lit."

"I know . . ." Jerome replied. "Believe me . . . I know."

"You and I, we are the end of the world."

The wretched monster pondered this for a while, and then nodded slowly. Welles softly exhaled a sigh of relief. The deathbed diplomacy was working. But he had little time to waste with talk. If Jerome was here, could the authorities be far behind?

"I have urgent work to do, my friend," he said calmly. "Would you think me uncivil if I continued with it?"

Without waiting for a reply he unlatched another cage and hauled the condemned monkey out, expertly turning its body around to facilitate the injection. The animal convulsed in his arms for a few moments then died. Welles disengaged its wizened fingers from his shirt and tossed the corpse and the discharged hypodermic on to the bench, turning with an executioner's economy to claim his next victim.

"Why?" Jerome asked, staring at the animal's open eyes.

"Act of mercy," Welles replied, picking up another primed hypodermic. "You can see how they're suffering." He reached to unlatch the next cage.

"Don't," Jerome said.

"No time for sentiment," Welles replied. "I beg you, an end to that."

Sentiment, Jerome thought, muddily remembering the songs on the radio that had first rewoken the fire in him. Didn't Welles understand that the processes of heart and head and groin were indivisible? That sentiment, however trite, might lead to undiscovered regions? He wanted to tell the doctor that, to explain all that he had seen and all that he had loved in these desperate hours. But somewhere between mind and tongue the explanations absconded. All he could say, to state the empathy he felt for all the suffering world, was: "*Don't*," as Welles unlocked the next cage. The doctor ignored him and reached into the wire-mesh cell. It contained three animals. He took hold of the nearest and drew it, protesting, from its companions' embraces. Without doubt it knew what fate awaited it; a flurry of screeches signaled its terror.

Jerome couldn't stomach this casual disposal. He moved, the wound in his side a torment, to prevent the killing. Welles, distracted by Jerome's advance, lost hold of his wriggling charge. The monkey scampered away across the benchtops. As he went to recapture it the prisoners in the cage behind him took their chance and slipped out.

"Damn you," Welles yelled at Jerome, "don't you see we've no *time*? Don't you understand?"

Jerome understood everything, and yet nothing. The fever he and the animals shared he understood; its purpose, to transform the world, he understood too. But why it should end like this—that joy, that vision—why it should all come down to a sordid room filled with smoke and pain, to frailty, to despair? *That* he did not comprehend. Nor, he now realized, did Welles, who had been the architect of these contradictions.

As the doctor made a snatch for one of the escaping monkeys Jerome crossed swiftly to the remaining cages and unlatched them all. The animals leaped to their freedom. Welles had succeeded with his recapture, however, and had the protesting monkey in his grip, about to deliver the panacea. Jerome made toward him.

"Let it be," he yelled.

Welles pressed the hypodermic into the monkey's body, but before he could depress the plunger Jerome had pulled at his wrist. The hypodermic spat its poison into the air and then fell to the ground. The monkey, wresting itself free, followed.

Jerome pulled Welles close. "I told you to *let it be*," he said.

Welles's response was to drive his fist into Jerome's wounded flank. Tears of pain spurted from his eyes, but he didn't release the doctor. The stimulus, unpleasant as it was, could not dissuade him from holding that beating heart close. He wished, embracing Welles like a prodigal, that he could ignite himself, that the dream of burning flesh he had endured would now become a reality, consuming maker and made in one cleansing flame. But his flesh was only flesh; his bone, bone. What miracles he had seen had been a private revelation, and now there was no time to communicate their glories or their horrors. What he had seen would die with him, to be rediscovered (perhaps) by some future self, only to be forgotten and discovered again. Like the story of love the radio had told; the same joy lost and found, found and lost. He stared at Welles with new comprehension dawning, hearing still the terrified beat of the man's heart. The doctor was *wrong*. If he left the man to live, he would come to know his error. They were not presagers of the millennium. They had both been dreaming.

"Don't kill me," Welles pleaded. "I don't want to die."

More fool you, Jerome thought, and let the man go.

Welles's bafflement was plain. He couldn't believe that his appeal for life had been answered. Anticipating a blow with every step he took he backed away from Jerome, who simply turned his back on the doctor and walked away.

From downstairs there came a shout, and then many shouts. Police, Welles guessed. They had presumably found the body of the officer who'd been on guard at the door. In moments only they would be coming up the stairs. There was no time now for finishing the tasks he'd come here to perform. He had to be away before they arrived.

On the floor below Carnegie watched the armed officers disappear up the stairs. There was a faint smell of burning in the air. He feared the worst.

I am the man who comes after the act, he thought to himself. I am perpetually upon the scene when the best of the action is over. Used as he was to waiting, patient as a loyal dog, this time he could not hold his anxieties in check while the others went ahead. Disregarding the voices advising him to wait, he began up the stairs.

The laboratory on the top floor was empty but for the monkeys and Johannson's corpse. The toxicologist lay on his face where he had fallen, neck broken. The emergency exit, which let on to the fire escape, was open; smoky air was being sucked out through it. As Carnegie stepped away from Johannson's body officers were already on the fire escape calling to their colleagues below to seek out the fugitive.

"Sir?"

Carnegie looked across at the mustachioed individual who had approached him.

"What is it?"

The officer pointed to the other end of the laboratory, to the test chamber. There was somebody at the window. Carnegie recognized the features, even though they were much changed. It was Jerome. At first he thought the man was watching him, but a short perusal scotched that idea. Jerome was staring, tears on his face, at his own reflection in the smeared glass. Even as Carnegie watched, the face retreated with the gloom of the chamber.

Other officers had noticed the man too. They were moving down the length of the laboratory, taking up positions behind the benches where they had a good line on the door, weapons at the ready. Carnegie had been present in such situations before; they had their own, terrible momentum. Unless he intervened, there would be blood.

"No," he said, "hold your fire."

He pressed the protesting officer aside and began to walk down the laboratory, making no attempt to conceal his advance. He walked past sinks in which the remains of *Blind Boy* guttered, past the bench under which, a short age ago, they'd found the dead Dance. A monkey, its head bowed, dragged itself across his path, apparently deaf to his proximity. He let it find a hole to die in, then moved on to the chamber door. It was ajar. He reached for the handle. Behind him the laboratory had fallen completely silent; all eyes were on him. He pulled the door open. Fingers tightened on triggers. There was no attack however. Carnegie stepped inside.

Jerome was standing against the opposite wall. If he saw Carnegie enter, or heard him, he made no sign of it. A dead monkey lay at his feet, one hand still grasping the hem of his trousers. Another whimpered in the corner, holding its head in its hands.

"Jerome?"

Was it Carnegie's imagination, or could he smell strawberries?

Jerome blinked.

"You're under arrest," Carnegie said. Hendrix would appreciate the irony of that, he thought. The man moved his bloody hand from the stab wound in his side to the front of his trousers and began to stroke himself.

"Too late," Jerome said. He could feel the last fire rising in him. Even if this intruder chose to cross the chamber and arrest him now, the intervening seconds would deny him his capture. *Death was here.* And what was it, now that he saw it clearly? Just another seduction, another sweet darkness to be filled up, and pleasured and made fertile.

A spasm began in his perineum, and lightning traveled in two directions from the spot, up his rod and up his spine. A laugh began in his throat.

In the corner of the chamber the monkey, hearing Jerome's humor, began to whimper again. The sound momentarily claimed Carnegie's attention, and when his gaze flitted back to Jerome the short-sighted eyes had closed, the hand had dropped, and he was dead, standing against the wall. For a short time the body defied gravity. Then, gracefully the legs buckled and Jerome fell forward. He was, Carnegie saw, a sack of bones, no more. It was a wonder the man had lived so long.

Cautiously, he crossed to the body and put his finger to the man's neck. There was no pulse. The remnants of Jerome's last laugh remained on his face, however, refusing to decay.

"Tell me . . ." Carnegie whispered to the man, sensing that despite his preemption he had missed the moment; that once again he was, and perhaps would always be, merely a witness of consequences. "Tell me. *What was the joke?*"

But the blind boy, as is the wont of his clan, wasn't telling.

SPEAKING OF LUST

Lawrence Block

"I DEALT, DIDN'T I?" THE SOLDIER SAID. He looked at his cards, shook his head. "What do you figure I had in mind? I pass."

The policeman, sitting to the dealer's left—East to his South—nodded, closed his eyes, opened them, and announced: "One club."

"Pass," said the doctor.

The priest said, "You bid a club, partner?" And, without waiting for a response, "One heart."

The soldier passed. You could tell he was a soldier, as he wore the dress uniform of a brigadier general in the United States Army.

"A spade," the policeman said. He too was in uniform, down to the revolver on his hip and the handcuffs hanging from his belt.

The doctor, wearing green scrubs, looked as though he might have just emerged from the operating room. He was silent, looking off into the middle distance, until the priest stared at him. "Oh, sorry," he said. "I pass."

"Two spades," said the priest, with a tug at his Roman collar.

"Pass," said the soldier.

"Four spades," the policeman said, and glanced around the table as if to confirm that the bidding was over. The doctor and priest and soldier dutifully passed in turn. The doctor studied his cards, frowned, and led the nine of hearts. The priest laid down his cards—four to the king in the trump suit, five hearts to the ace-jack—and sat back in his chair. The policeman won the trick with the ace of hearts from dummy and set about drawing trump.

Play was rapid and virtually silent. A fire crackled on the hearth, and the clock on the mantel chimed the quarter hour. Smoke drifted to the high ceiling—from the doctor's cigar, the priest's cigarette, the soldier's stubby briar pipe. Books, many of them bound in full leather, filled the shelves on either side of the fireplace, and one lay open in the lap of the room's only other occupant, the old man who sat by the fire. He had been sitting there when the four began their card game, the book open, his eyes closed, and he was there still.

"Four spades bid, five spades made," the policeman said, gathering the final trick. The priest took up his pencil and wrote down the score. The policeman shuffled the cards. The soldier cut them, and the policeman scooped them up and began to deal. He opened the bidding with a diamond, and the doctor doubled. The priest looked at his cards for a long moment.

"Lust," he said.

The others stared at him. "Is that your bid?" his partner said. "Lust?"

The priest stroked his chin. "Did I actually say that?" he said, bemused. "I meant to pass."

"Which made you think of making a pass," the doctor suggested, "and so you spoke as you did."

"Hardly that," the priest said. "I was thinking of lust, but I assure you I entertained no lustful thoughts. I was thinking of lust in the abstract, the sin of lust."

"Lust is a sin, is it?" said the soldier.

"One of the seven cardinal sins," the priest said.

"Lust is desire, isn't it?"

"A form of desire," the priest said. "A perversion of desire, perhaps. Desire raised to sinful proportions."

"But it's a desire all the same," the soldier insisted. "It's not an act, and a sin ought to be an act. Lust may prompt a sinful act, but it's not a sin in and of itself."

"One can sin in the mind," the policeman pointed out. "On the other hand, you can't hang a man for his thoughts."

"Hanging him is one thing," said the doctor. "Sending him to Hell is another."

"The seven deadly sins are all in the mind," the priest explained. "Pride, avarice, jealousy, anger, gluttony, sloth, and lust."

"Quite a menu," the soldier said.

"Sin is error," the priest went on. "A mistake, a tragic mistake, if you will. Out of pride, out of anger, out of gluttony, one commits an action which is sinful, or, if you will, entertains a sinful thought. Thus any sinful act a man might commit can be assigned to one of these seven categories."

"Without a certain amount of lust," the doctor said, "the human race would cease to exist."

"You could make the same argument for the other six sins as well," the priest told him, "because what is any of them but a distortion of a normal and essential human instinct? There is a difference, I submit, between the natural desire of a man for a maid and what we would label as sinful lust."

"What about the desire of a man for a man?" the doctor wondered. "Or a maid for a maid?"

"Or a farmer's son for a sheep?" The priest sat back in his chair. "We call some desires normal, others abnormal, and much depends on who's making the call."

The discussion was a lively one, and ranged far and wide. At length the policeman held up a hand. "If I may," he said. "Priest, you started this. Unintentionally, perhaps, by voicing a thought when you only meant to pass. But you must have had something in mind."

"An altar boy," suggested the doctor. "Or an altered boy."

"Nun of the above," the soldier put in.

"You should show the cloth a measure of respect," the priest said. "But I did have something in mind, as a matter of fact. Something that came to me, though I couldn't tell you why. Rather an interesting incident that took place some years ago. But we're in the middle of a game, aren't we?"

A gentle snore came from the old man dozing beside the fire. The four card players looked at him. Then the policeman and the doctor and the soldier turned their gaze to the priest.

"Tell the story," the policeman said.

* * *

Some years ago (said the priest) I came to know a young couple named William and Carolyn Thompson. I say a young couple because they were slightly younger than I, and I was not quite forty at the time, which now seems to me to be very young indeed. Let's say that he was thirty-six when I met them, and she thirty-eight. I may be off slightly in their ages, but not in the age difference between them. She was just two years the elder.

They were an attractive couple, both of them tall and slender and fair, with not dissimilar facial features—long narrow noses and penetrating blue eyes. I've noticed that couples grow to resemble one another after they've been together a long time, and I suspect this is largely the result of their having each learned facial expressions from the other. The same thing happens on a larger scale, doesn't it? The French, say, shrug and grimace and raise their eyebrows in a certain way, and their faces develop lines accordingly, until a national physiognomy emerges. Have you observed how older persons will look *more* French, or Italian, or Russian? It's not that the genes thin out in the younger generations. It's that the old have had more time to acquire the characteristic look.

The Thompsons had been married for a decade and a half, long enough, certainly, for this phenomenon to transpire. And, spending as much time as they did together (living in a small house in one of the northwestern suburbs, working side by side in their shop) they'd had ample opportunity to mirror one another. Still, the resemblance they bore was more than a matter of shared attitudes and expressions. Why, they looked enough alike to be brother and sister.

As indeed they were.

William and Carolyn attended my church, though not with great regularity. I'd heard their confessions from time to time, and neither of them disclosed anything remarkable. I didn't really get to know them until Bill and I were brought into contact in connection with a community action project. We got accustomed to having a few beers after a meeting, and we became friends.

One afternoon he turned up at the rectory and asked if we could talk. "I don't want to make a formal confession," he said. "I just need to talk to someone, but it has to be confidential. If we just go over to Paddy Mac's and have a beer or two, could our conversation still be bound by the seal of the confessional?"

I told him I didn't see why not, and that I would certainly consider myself to be so bound.

The tavern we went to, a busy place in the evening, was dark and quiet of an afternoon. We sat off by ourselves, and Bill told me his story.

He grew up in another city on the other side of the country. He had an older sister—Carolyn, of course, but that revelation was to come later—and lived with her and his mother and father in a pre-war brick house in one of the older suburbs. He and his sister took after their mother, who was tall and blond. Their father was tall, too, but dark-complected, and heavily built.

His sister taught him to dance, took him shopping, and clued him in on all the things a young boy was supposed to learn. She comforted him, too, when he got a beating from their father. The man was a drinker, he said, and sometimes when he drank Bill would piss him off without knowing what he'd done wrong. Then he'd catch it.

One night when he was thirteen years old he did or said something to upset the man and got a few whacks with a belt for it. Afterward, his sister came to his room. He had been crying, and he was a little ashamed of that, too, and she told him he'd had a punishment he hadn't deserved, so now he was going to get a reward. Just as she'd taught him how to dance, now she would teach him how to kiss.

"So you'll know what to do when you're out with a girl," she said.

She sat next to him on his bed and they kissed. They'd kissed each other before, of course, but this was entirely different. You know how an unexciting activity may be said to be "like kissing your sister?" Well, this was not like kissing your sister.

Over the next several months, the kissing lessons continued. She always initiated them, coming into his room when he was doing his homework, closing the door, sitting on his bed with him. This was very exciting for him, especially when she let him touch her breasts, first through her clothing, then with his hand inside her blouse. When she would leave his room, finally, he would relieve himself.

He was so occupied one day when, having recently left his room, she returned to it, opening his door without knocking and catching him in the act. He covered himself at once, but she had seen him, and she asked him what he had been doing.

"Nothing," he said.

"You were touching yourself," she said. "Right? But you shouldn't have to do that, Billy."

He said he couldn't help it. He knew it was wrong, but he couldn't help it.

"I'm not saying it's wrong," she said, "but you shouldn't have to do it *yourself*."

She did it for him. And, from then on, that was how their sessions concluded, with her hand doing what his hand had previously done, and making a far more satisfying job of it. When they hadn't had time together during the day, she would make a point of slipping into his room at night after he'd gone to bed. He would usually pretend to sleep, and without a word she would satisfy him with her hands and return just as silently to her own room.

One night she used her mouth. The next day he asked her if she would do that again, and she said, "Oh, you mean you weren't really sleeping?"

Their play continued, and over time she led him on a veritable Cook's tour of sexuality, which eventually included every act either of them could think of short of actual coitus. Their pleasure was hampered only by the fear of discovery, and on more than one occasion they narrowly escaped having a parent walk in on them. Thus they limited themselves to relatively brief encounters, and had to avoid crying out in fulfillment. Quick and quiet, that was the nature of their coupling.

Not surprisingly, they dreamed of being able to spend an entire night together in safety and privacy. The sister raised the subject often, telling him just what she would like to do to him, and what she would have him do to her.

"Maybe when we're older," she said. "When we're both out of the house. Unless you find somebody else by then."

But there would never be anybody else, he assured her. She was the only one he wanted.

What she didn't point out in response, and what he knew without being told, was that what he wanted, what they both wanted, could never be. They were brother and sister. They could never be man and wife.

He couldn't imagine himself with anyone else, couldn't bear the thought of her in someone else's arms. She was his and he was hers.

How could he marry another woman, a stranger?

"I thought of becoming a priest," he told me. "If I couldn't have her, then it would be easier if I never had to have anyone. Then the absurdity of the notion struck me. I was in bed with my sister, I was committing all kinds of sins with her, and the fact that I wouldn't be able to go on committing them forever made me think I had a vocation. But I swear it seemed perfectly logical to me at the time."

One day she had an idea. He was still a member of a Boy Scout troop, although he'd become less active. The troop had a camping weekend scheduled. Suppose he signed up for it? And suppose she drove to the encampment and picked him up down the road around the time the troop's bugler blew taps and turned in for the night? They could go to a motel—she'd take care of booking a room—and they could have a whole night together and get him back to camp before reveille.

That's what they did. On Friday night, he waited until his tent mate was sleeping, then slipped out and trotted down the road to where she was waiting. It was all set for the following night, she told him. The room was booked, and she'd bought some massage oil and something provocative to wear. She wished they could go there now, but she had to get home. She had an excuse lined up for her absence the following night, but not tonight, and she had to get home.

They got into the back of the car and she brought him off quickly with her lips and fingers. Then he went back to his tent and lay grinning in the darkness, thinking of his tent mate and the other boys, thinking what they were missing.

The following night, Saturday night, he feigned sleep himself so that his tent mate would finally shut up, and then had to lie there listening while the other boy brought himself to lonely fulfillment. Then, when the boy's breathing deepened in sleep, he crept out and hurried to the appointed spot. The car wasn't there waiting for him, and he worried that she wasn't coming, worried that she'd come and gone, worried that something somehow had gone wrong.

Then the car appeared, and minutes later they were at the motel. She had already checked in, signing a false name on the register and paying in cash. She drove straight to the unit, unlocked the door, and led him inside.

She apologized for having been late. "Mama wanted help folding laundry," she said, "and I told her I was expected at Sandy's, and she said Sandy could wait. And then *he* came home, and the two of them started going at it, and that gave me a chance to slip out. Oh, but I don't want to waste time talking. I want to do everything. We don't have to be quiet for once and I want to make noise. I want to make you scream."

They both made noise, although no one screamed. They made love with the tireless enthusiasm of youth, and toward dawn she sighed and swore she couldn't help herself and threw herself astride him and took him deep within herself.

Years later he would recall thinking that this was it, that they'd crossed a line. Up until then they had done "everything but," and now they had done it all.

Before the sun was up she dropped him off where she'd picked him up, then headed for her friend's house. "Sandy thinks I'm at a motel with a frat boy," she said. "Little does she know. But she'll let me in, and cover for me."

His tent mate stirred when he returned, wanted to know where he's been. The latrine, he said. The other boy went back to sleep.

He lay there and watched through the tent flap as dawn broke.

He was a boy—fourteen now, he'd had a birthday since that first kissing lesson—but he felt like a man. *I just got laid*, he told himself. *I fucked my sister*. A man, yes, and a sinner.

He wondered what his punishment would be.

Within hours, he found out.

Shortly after breakfast, after they'd divided into groups for morning activities, a sheriff's car pulled into the camp grounds. A tall man wearing sunglasses got out and talked to the scoutmaster. Then the two men walked to where Billy was sitting, trying to undo a bad knot in the lanyard he was making. It was kid stuff, entwining the plastic lacing to make a lanyard, and pretty tame compared to fucking your sister in a motel room, but if you were going to do it you might as well get it right.

The scoutmaster hunkered down beside him, his red face troubled, the perspiration beading on his large forehead. The sheriff, or whoever he was, stood up straight as a ramrod. And the scoutmaster explained that there had been some trouble, that Billy was an orphan now, that both of his parents were dead.

Of course he couldn't take it in. He was numb with shock. How could they be dead? He found out gradually, with no one eager to tell him too much too soon. They were shot, he learned, his mother three times, twice in the chest and once in the face, his father once, the bullet entering his open mouth and exiting through the back of his skull. Death for both was virtually instantaneous. They didn't suffer, he was told.

And finally he was told who had done it. His father had come home drunk, and evidently there had been an argument. (He nodded as he took this in, nodded unconsciously, because this was something he already knew. But he wasn't supposed to know it, because who could have told him? He'd been at the camp the whole time.)

The person who told him made nothing of the nod. Maybe it only indicated that this was nothing uncommon, that his father often came home drunk, that his parents often argued.

But this argument had an atypical ending, because Billy's father had concluded it by taking a handgun from his desk drawer and putting three bullets into Billy's mother and, in remorse or anger or God knows what, blowing out his own brains.

The boy knew whose fault it was. It was his—his and his sister's. While they were crossing the last barrier, their father was murdering their mother, then sinning against the Holy Ghost by taking his own life.

As he remembered it, the ensuing days and weeks passed in a blur. While the authorities tried to find a relative who could take them in, Billy and Carolyn went on living in the house where their parents had died. No agreeable relative emerged, and the two were of an inconvenient age, too young to be on their own, too old to be placed in foster care. The officials shuffled papers and forgot about them, and they stayed where they were. Carolyn did the shopping and prepared the meals, Billy cut the grass and raked the lawn and shoveled the walk.

A week after the tragedy, they resumed sleeping together.

"All we've got is each other," she told him. "What happened's not our fault. I'll tell you something, it was going to happen sooner or later, and if we'd been home that night we'd have wound up dead, too. The way he drank, the way he got when he drank? And the way she provoked him? 'Man Kills Wife and Self.' If we had been home, it would have been 'Man Kills Wife, Two Children, and Self.' That's the only difference."

He knew she was right.

All they had was each other, and they loved each other. Socially, they withdrew further into themselves. For a year or two, this was unremarkable, a natural consequence of the family tragedy they had endured. Then, shortly after her eighteenth birthday, she announced that a boy had asked her on a date and she had agreed to go with him.

"People get suspicious. 'What's wrong with her that she never goes out with anybody?' They think I'm pretty, I ought to be interested in boys."

"Let them think you're a lesbian."

"Believe me, some of them already do. I've had some long looks from a couple members of the sisterhood, and one of them asked me if I'd like to come over to her house and watch the last round of the LPGA. Why would anyone want to watch golf, whether it was men or women playing? And why would I want to go over to her house anyway?"

"I wish you didn't have to go out with some guy," he said.

"You're jealous?"

"I guess so."

"I'm not going to let him do anything, Billy. But I think it makes sense to go out with him. And you're going to have to start going out with girls."

"Or they'll think I'm a fag?"

"Or a retard."

"I don't care what they think," he said, but of course he did. Later he told her he wished they could be where nobody knew anything about them.

"I've been thinking about that," she said.

They put the house on the market and sold it, rented an apartment in a college town a few hundred miles away. She'd been given her mother's maiden name as a middle name, and now she dropped her surname, and they lived together as William Thompson and Carolyn Peyton. She built up a collection of identification in that name, and enrolled at the college, and a year later so did he. The money from the house, supplemented by their earnings from part-time jobs, covered their tuition and expenses, and they had both always been good students. He took an accelerated program and they graduated together, four years after they'd sold the house.

Neither had made a single close friend during those four years. Neither had gone out on a date, or shown any interest in a member of the opposite sex. All they wanted was to be together, and they were confident their feelings were not going to change.

They got married. "We could just say we were married," she told him. "When does anyone ask to see a marriage license? And I already feel married to you. More than married to you. But I want to do it all the same."

"And have kids?"

"A baby with two heads," she said. "That's what you get if you sleep with your brother. Remember how kids used to think that? I've done some research, and it doesn't necessarily work out that way. There's a chance, though, that there might be something abnormal about the child."

"I don't really want kids, anyway."

"Neither do I," she said, "but that might change, for one or both of us. If it does—"

"We could take our chances," he said. "Or adopt."

"But for now," she said, "all I want is you."

And so they got married, and Carolyn Peyton legally changed her name again, back to Carolyn Peyton Thompson. And, as man and wife, they moved to the city where I came to know them. They went into business together, made a success of it, bought a house, and, well, lived happily ever after. They postponed the decision about children until they realized it had resolved itself; they were a complete unit now, they had been a complete unit from that first kissing lesson, and a child would be an unwelcome extra presence in their home.

Legally married, they came to feel less as though they had something to hide. So they were more inclined to make friends, more prepared to play an active role in the life of the community. They were, in everybody's eyes, a decent and charming couple, attractive and personable and very much in love. And you could see at a glance that they belonged together. Why, they even looked alike. If you didn't know better, you'd take them for brother and sister.

***

"And that's it?" said the soldier.

The priest nodded. "More or less," he said.

"More or less," echoed the doctor. "Is it more or is it less? Never mind. Lust, eh? Well, I suppose it was lust that got them started, but it sounds to me more like a love story than one of unbridled sexual passion. It's not lust that keeps two people together for—what did you say? A decade and a half? No, that's how long they were married. He was thirteen when she gave him his first kissing lesson and thirty-six or so when he told you about it, so that's twenty-three years. If there's some kind of lust that lasts for twenty-three years, I'd like a case of it sent to my quarters."

"And I'm not sure where the sin comes in," the soldier said. "Unless the incest itself is the sin, and I suppose your church might call it that, but I don't know that I would. Whom did they harm? And where's the dissolute life to which sin's presumed to lead? They became model citizens, from the sound of things. They had a secret, but what couple doesn't have a few secrets, and who's to say they do them any harm?"

A snore came from the old man seated by the fire.

"My sentiments exactly," said the doctor. "What I can't figure out is why the fellow had that conversation with you. Incidentally, is it all right for you to recount it to us? You told him you'd consider yourself bound by the seal of the confessional."

"As you three don't know the people involved," the priest said, "and as I've changed their names, I don't feel I've violated a confidence. The Church might see it differently, but I've long since ceased to be bound by what the Church thinks. My own conscience is clear on this subject, if on few others." He turned to the policeman. "You haven't said anything," he said.

"It's a good story," the policeman said. "There's one question that occurs to me, though, but you may not know the answer."

"Ask it."

"I was wondering," the policeman said, "whether anybody ever gave that girl a paraffin test."

The priest smiled.

On the eve of their wedding (the priest continued) Carolyn cooked an elaborate dinner. Afterward they sat with cups of strong coffee, and she said she had something to tell him, something she was afraid to tell him. "If you're going to marry me," she said, "you should know this."

From the time she was eleven years old, she said, their father had taken to coming into her room while she was sleeping. He initiated a pattern of sexual abuse which progressed gradually from inappropriate touches and caresses while she slept, or feigned sleep, to acts which required her to be awake and an active participant. For the last three years of the man's life, the repertoire included sexual intercourse, and the man did not use a condom. She lived in fear that he would make her pregnant, but he managed on each occasion to withdraw in time, depositing his sticky gift on her belly.

Toward the end, though, he seemed to be considering impregnating her, and more than once said he wondered what kind of a mommy she'd make.

She hated him, and wanted to kill him. She hated her mother as well. Early on she had told the woman that he was coming to her room, that he was touching her. The woman refused to take it in. He's your father, she was told. He loves you. You're imagining things.

And so, on that Saturday night, while her father sat in front of the television set in a drunken slack-jawed stupor, she got the handgun from the drawer where he kept it, thrust the barrel into his open mouth, and pulled the trigger. When her mother came in to see what had happened, she leveled the gun and shot the woman three times. Then she wiped her own fingerprints from the gun, placed it in her father's dead hand, and curled his fingers around it.

Then she went off to meet her brother, and arrived just a few minutes late. And, having just committed a double murder, and sure she'd be found out and sent to prison, she blotted it all from her mind and gave herself over to a last night of joy and consummation with her beloved brother.

But of course she was never found out. The murder-suicide scene she'd staged was good enough to pass muster, and no one ever took a good hard look at her alibi. Her friend, Sandy, kept her secret; it wouldn't do to let out that Carolyn had been out cavorting with a boyfriend, nor would Sandy's parents be comfortable with the knowledge that their daughter had facilitated such deception. So why not keep that little secret? Carolyn surely had enough tragedy in her life, with her father having killed her mother and himself. She didn't need to have her sex life exposed to public scrutiny.

Nor did Billy's alibi get much attention. He crawled into his tent after taps and crawled out of it at reveille. Case closed.

And so, on the eve of his wedding, William Thompson learned for the first time that his father was not a murderer and that his sister was.

The following day they were married.

"And lived happily ever after," said the doctor. "A curious business, incest. More common, it turns out, than we used to think. No end of fathers, it turns out, lurch into their daughters' beds. And they're not always hillbillies or immigrants or welfare cases, either. It happens, as they say, in the best of families. As for brothers and sisters, well, what's that but a childhood game carried to its logical conclusion?"

"Playing doctor," the soldier said.

"Quite so. It must happen often, and who'd ever report it? If the two are close in age, if there's no force or intimidation involved, where's the abuse? It may be forbidden, they may be transgressors, but what's the harm?"

"I wonder how often they actually marry," the policeman said.

"Not too often," the doctor said. "I can't imagine marrying my sister, but then I can't imagine fucking her, either. Truth to tell, I can't imagine *anyone* fucking her."

"If you had a better-looking sister. . ."

"Then it might be a different story," the doctor allowed. "Speaking of stories, that's a good one, Priest. How did it turn out?"

"I don't know that it did," the priest said. "Two years or so after our conversation, Carolyn gave birth to a daughter. I christened the child, and she certainly looked like her parents, for all that you can tell when they're that small."

"So they rolled the dice," the soldier said. "Although I suppose someone else might have been the father. Artificial insemination and all that."

"Or else they'd have been swimming in the shallow end of the gene pool," said the doctor, "and that's dangerous, but not always disastrous. On the one hand you've got the Jukes and the Kallikaks, those horrible examples they tell you about in high school biology class, and on the other hand you've got all the crowned heads of Europe."

"When we have more time," the policeman said, "you can tell me which is worse. Any more to the story, Priest?"

The priest shook his head. "I was transferred shortly thereafter," he said, "and lost track of them. I hope things turned out well for them. I liked them."

"And I like your story," the policeman said. "Lust. I could tell a story about lust."

The others sat back, waiting.

I'm not much of a storyteller (said the policeman) and I don't know much about sin. Not that I'm free from it myself, but that I was not trained to think in those terms. My frame of reference is the law, the criminal code specifically. I can tell you whether or not an act is lawful, and, if it's not, I can correctly label it a violation or a misdemeanor or a felony. And even then my classification will not apply universally, but only in the jurisdiction where I lived and worked.

Determining what is or is not a criminal act is difficult enough. Determining whether or not an act is sinful, well, I wouldn't want to touch that with a stick.

Lust . . .

When I was still a young man, I was partnered with an older man, named—well, let me choose a name for him, as the priest chose a name for his young couple. And I ought to be able to come up with something a little more distinctive and imaginative than William Thompson, don't you think? Michael Walbeck, that's what we'll call my partner. Michael J. Walbeck, and the J stands for John. No, make it Jonathan. Michael Jonathan Walbeck, and everybody called him Mike, except for his mother, who still called him Mickey, and his wife, who called him Michael.

She was a beauty, his wife. Her hair was a heap of black curls that spilled down over her shoulders, and her face was heart-shaped, with dark almond-shaped eyes and a lush mouth. Walbeck was jealous of her. He'd call her eight or ten times a day, just to make sure he knew where she was. As far as I knew, Marie never gave him cause for jealousy, outside of always looking like she just hopped out of bed, and like she was ready at a moment's notice to hop back in again. But he didn't need cause. He was just a jealous man.

Meanwhile, he was running around on her. Here he was, talking about how he'd kill her if he ever caught her with another guy, and how he'd kill the guy, too, and at the same time he always had something going on the side, and sometimes more than one thing.

You've heard of guys who go through life following their dick around—that was Walbeck. He said himself that he'd screw a snake if somebody would hold its head, and I'm not entirely certain he was exaggerating. He'd roust hookers and let them off in return for a quick blow job—it's safe to say he wasn't the first cop who thought of that one—but his real specialty was the wives and girlfriends of criminals.

That's a little harder than getting a hooker to go down on you, but not by much. The first time I saw Mike in action, we had busted a guy who was cooking crank in his double-wide out on the edge of town. That's methamphetamine, also known as speed, and it's about as tricky to make as chili con carne. And cooking it's a felony in fifty states, and we had this poor bastard dead to rights. His rights were what Mike was reading him, as a matter of fact, but he stopped mid-sentence when he got a look at Cheryl.

I don't know if she was his wife or his girlfriend, and I don't remember her name, so for all I know it could have been Cheryl. Doesn't matter. She was a blowzy girl, and in a few years she'd be a real porker, but now she was in her early twenties and she looked hot and sluttish. She had a wrapper on, I remember, and it needed laundering, and you could pretty much tell she wasn't wearing anything under it.

"Nice looking girl," Walbeck told the mope. "You know, I wonder if there's a way we can work something out."

The guy got it before it touched the ground. "You see anything you like," he said, "it's yours."

"She's got to do us both," Walbeck said. "Me and my partner here."

"You got it."

"Eddie—" the girl said, whining.

"Shut up," he told her. "Like you're gonna miss it?"

"She's got some shape on her," Walbeck said. "She does us both, including we get to fuck her in the ass."

"No way," the girl said.

"I said shut up," Eddie said. "You do that, I get to keep the stuff."

"The crank."

"The crank and the money both. You don't confiscate nothing, and I walk, and for that you can fuck her anywhere you want. Cut a hole in her chest and fuck her in the heart, all I care."

"Eddie!"

"Deal," Walbeck said. He asked me if I wanted to go first. I shook my head and waited outside with Eddie, who professed not to care what was going on inside the trailer. I noticed, though, that he lit one cigarette off the butt of another, and smoked as if he wanted to burn up the whole cigarette in one furious drag.

"He's a prick," he said. "That partner of yours." I said something to the effect that nobody'd forced him to go for the deal. "Oh, it's a good deal," he said. "Don't get me wrong. She ain't gonna miss another slice off the loaf, and who gives a shit about her anyway? But he's still a prick."

Walbeck was in there long enough for Eddie to smoke three cigarettes, and he was zipping his pants as he came down the trailer steps. "Nice," he said, grinning. "I can see why you keep her around. You're up, partner."

You pass in a situation like that, you make trouble in your partnership. Like if you bend the rules for a storekeeper on your beat, let his suppliers park illegally when they're making their deliveries, and he slips you a few bucks out of gratitude. If one partner takes it and the other won't accept his cut, how are they going to get along?

So I managed a grin of my own and went up the steps and into the trailer. I wasn't really in the mood, so I figured I'd just sit around long enough for the guy outside to suck down a few more cigarettes while Walbeck broke his balls some more. But I figured without the woman. I got one look at her, sitting on the edge of the bed with her soiled wrapper hanging open in front, her face and attitude showing vulnerability and sluttishness in equal proportion, and just like that I wanted her. My head thought I ought to be above such things, but my dick had a mind of its own.

She gave me a sad smile and took off the wrapper, and that settled that. I got out of my clothes, and she looked at me and her face clouded. "Jesus," she said, "you're about twice as big as your friend. I hope you don't want to stick it the same place he did."

I told her the conventional route would do.

"You're nice," she said. "Go slow so I can really get into it, and you'll be glad you did."

Afterward, we stopped at a pay phone and Walbeck called his house. He talked to his wife, but that wasn't enough reassurance, and he insisted we take a run past his house to see if there was a strange car in the driveway. There wasn't, but two doors down on the other side of the street he spotted a car he didn't recognize, and right away he called a guy he knew at DMV and ran the plate. The car was registered to a man named Shoenstahl, with a residence listed across town, but there was a family on Walbeck's street with the same name, so it was probably a relative, and not some bastard nailing Walbeck's wife.

"You can't trust them," he told me. "Look at that choice specimen of trailer trash we were just with. Once you get past the surface, they're all like that."

I could have put in for a transfer, but Walbeck wasn't the worst partner in the world. The tail-chasing and the jealousy weren't endearing traits, but in other respects he was a fairly decent cop, and not as much of a pain in the ass to be harnessed with as some of them. I got used to him, and then he took the whole thing to another level when he met a woman I'll call Joanie.

I was with him when he first caught sight of her. It was at a basketball game. Someone had given him tickets and he invited me to come along. I didn't much like to hang out with Walbeck, I got enough of him on the job, but I like basketball and these were good seats. A few minutes into the first period he elbowed me and pointed. "The redhead," he said. "Third row up and on the aisle."

"What about her?"

"I gotta have her," he said.

She was a striking woman, with a lush body and strong facial features. Flaming red hair, and that pale skin redheads have, the ones that don't have freckles. I admired her myself, but it wasn't a matter of admiration with Walbeck. He took one look at her and decided he had to have her.

"If I don't get to fuck her," he said, "I'll fucking die."

She was sitting alone, with an empty seat next to her, and he was on the point of going over and taking the empty seat and hitting on her, when her companion turned up—her husband, although we didn't find that out until later. He was a tall man with a mustache and a sport jacket that looked like it was made from a horse blanket, and he was carrying a tray with a couple of hot dogs and beers. He sat down next to the redhead, and before he sat down he looked over in our general direction.

"He looks wrong," I said, meaning he looked like a lawbreaker. Hard to say what makes a guy look right or wrong, but a cop gets so he knows. Unconsciously he's adding up a whole batch of signs and mannerisms, and he knows.

"He damn well ought to look wrong," Mike Walbeck said. "That's Harv Jellin. He's got a sheet, he's done state time. Now how in the hell does a skell like Harv Jellin get a broad like that?"

I shrugged and turned my attention back to the game, but Walbeck was lost for the evening, his attention taken up entirely by the redhead and the man beside her. "You know what I wonder?" he said. "I wonder just what Harv Jellin was doing two weeks ago Saturday."

"Two weeks ago—"

"Two weeks ago Saturday," he said, "which was the night a couple of mopes knocked off the Cutler warehouse. All of a sudden I like Harv for that one. I like him a whole lot."

God knows we didn't have anything like a lead in the warehouse robbery, and there was plenty of pressure to solve it, because the perps had left a body behind—the night watchman, dead from a single blow to the head. Within a few days we'd made an arrest, picking up a three-time loser named O'Regan.

"We know you were just along to keep Harv Jellin company," Walbeck told him. "He's the one who set up the job and he's definitely the one who hit the watchman over the head. You'd never do a thing like that, would you? Hit an old guy over the head, crack his skull like an eggshell."

"I wasn't even there," O'Regan said.

"We got you dead to rights," Walbeck said, "and the only question is what kind of time you do. You roll over on your pal Jellin and you get the minimum. You hold out and you're in the joint the rest of your life."

"I hardly know Jellin," the mope said.

"Then you don't owe him a thing, do you? And he's your Get Out Of Jail Free card, so you better remember how well you know him."

"It's coming back to me," O'Regan said.

Between O'Regan's testimony and some artfully manufactured and planted evidence, Harvey Jellin didn't stand a chance. His lawyer convinced him to plead to robbery and manslaughter, arguing that otherwise a murder conviction was a foregone conclusion.

When you enter a guilty plea, you have to stand up in court and say what happened. I was there, and you could see how it infuriated Jellin to have to perjure himself in order to dodge a life sentence. "I only hit him once," he said of the dead watchman, "and I never meant to hurt him."

He got ten-to-twenty. The watchman's daughter told a reporter that was far too lenient, but it didn't seem all that lenient to me, given that the sonofabitch hadn't done anything.

Not that I wasted any tears on him. Jellin had done plenty of other things we hadn't been able to hang on him, and it was common knowledge that he'd killed a man in a bar fight, and probably one or two others as well. He went off to serve his time, and Walbeck got busy putting the moves on Joanie.

The wives of convicted felons are easy game, same as recent widows. They're made-to-order for cops, and Walbeck wasn't the first police officer to move in on a woman after sending her husband to the Joint. He might have had a harder time if the redhead had known he'd framed Jellin, but she didn't have a clue. Jellin had protested all along that he was being framed, or at least until he'd taken the plea, but criminals say that all the time, in and out of prison.

It took Walbeck a while, but he got her. And then he was stuck, because he couldn't get enough of her.

"She's in my blood," he said. "The woman's a fucking virus."

I'd never seen him like this before. It stopped him from chasing tail, because Joanie Jellin got all his attention. He didn't turn down what came along—I don't think he was capable of turning anything down in that department—but he quit seeking it out. And he spent every spare moment he could with the redhead.

The prison that housed her husband has an enlightened administration, and prisoners with good conduct privileges were able to receive monthly conjugal visits. The prisoner and his spouse would repair to a small house trailer, known inevitably as the Fuck Truck, where they could enjoy a romantic interlude of no more than an hour.

At first Walbeck didn't want her to go, but he had to agree that her absence would make Jellin suspicious. So he took to going with her, and he would make an expedition out of it, inventing some pretext to explain his overnight absence to his wife, and switching shifts with other cops or, more often, getting me to sign him in and out.

The evening before a conjugal visit, Walbeck and Joanie Jellin would drive to the town where the prison was situated and check in at a motel with waterbeds and porn videos. ("This is where they ought to have the goddam visits," Joanie told him. "This beats the hell out of the Fuck Truck.") With a fifth of vodka and one or another illegal substance to keep the party lively, the two would screw themselves silly all night long.

Then, in the morning, Joanie would drive to the prison to meet her husband.

Walbeck tried to get her to skip her morning shower. "You gotta be crazy," she told him. "You want to get me killed? He smells you on me, he breaks my neck right there in the Fuck Truck. What's he care, they tack a few more years on his sentence?"

She won that argument. But she didn't argue when he wanted to take her straight to bed the minute she returned from the prison visit. While he embraced her, he would make her tell him in detail what she and her husband had just done.

"I don't know," she said. "Sometimes I get the feeling you're queer for Harv."

"I'm queer for you," he said. "I can't get enough of you. I could kill you, I could cook you and eat you, and I still couldn't get enough."

"Don't talk that way."

"I could suck the marrow out of your bones. Still wouldn't be enough."

The more time he spent with Joanie Jellin, the more certain he grew that Marie was having an affair. "He's nailing her," he told me, "and he's doing it right in my own house. I walk in there and I can feel it. The air's thick and heavy, like he's still there in spirit."

"You like getting Joanie right after Harv's done with her," I pointed out. "Maybe you should tell Marie to skip her shower after."

I was joking, but he didn't see the humor, and I thought he was going to lose it altogether. "She's my wife," he said. "Somebody touches my wife, I rip his fucking heart out. I cut his dick off, stuff it down her throat and let her fucking choke on it."

He became convinced not only that Marie had a lover, but that the man coordinated his visits to coincide with his own overnight stays with Joanie. He set a trap, telling Marie the same thing he told her whenever Jellin had a conjugal visit scheduled. He had to escort a prisoner who'd been extradited to another state, he told her, and he'd be gone overnight.

Then he staked out his own house, waiting. And of course he never saw a single suspicious car. Marie never left the house, and no one came to visit her.

The next morning, when he walked into his house, he was utterly certain someone had been with her. "Who was it?" he shouted at her. "Tell me who it was!"

"I've been here all night," she said, looking at him like he was crazy. "Alone, in a robe, watching TV. And then I went to bed. Michael, don't they have somebody you can see? Like a psychiatrist? Because I think you should seriously consider it."

"He must have seen my car," he told me. "Must have parked around the block, sneaked through the yards and went in the back door, then got out the same way."

"Maybe you're imagining things, Mike."

"I don't think so. Partner, you gotta help me out. Tuesday, when Harv has his next visit? What I want you to do is check my block. He won't recognize your car."

"I don't know what you've got planned for this guy," I said, "but I don't want to be a part of it."

"Believe me," he said, "I want him all for myself. All I want from you is a plate number. I can take it from there."

He drove off on Tuesday, and when I met him Wednesday afternoon he looked like he was running on empty. "Too much bed and not enough sleep," he said. "Remember the first time I laid eyes on Joanie? That was all it took for me to know what was waiting there for me. She's amazing."

"Maybe you could divorce Marie," I suggested. "Marry Joanie, have her all for yourself."

He looked at me as if I'd taken leave of my senses. "Number one," he said, "Marie's my wife. That makes her mine forever. Number two, why would I want to marry Joanie? There's the kind of women you marry and the kind you don't, and she's definitely one you don't." He shook his head at my naiveté. "If you were married yourself," he said, "you'd know what I was talking about. Listen, did you do what I asked you to do? Did you find out anything?"

I lowered my eyes. "Bad news," I said.

"I knew it!"

"She had a visitor."

"I fucking knew it. At the house?"

I nodded. "He was there for two hours. Then I had to leave, but he was still there when I checked back around dawn."

"The son of a bitch."

"I ran his plate," I said. "I got a name and address."

"You're a pal," he said. "You didn't have to do that."

"I wanted to," I told him. "Waiting out there, thinking about what was going on inside your house, I started getting mad at him myself. I don't know what you've got planned for him, and I don't want to horn in on it, but I think I ought to be there to watch your back."

"Let's go," he said, then stopped himself. "Maybe I should stop home first," he said. "Light her up a little, then drop in on lover boy."

"Of course, if you can tell her how you've already gone and cleaned his clock . . ."

"You're right," he said. "Cut off his dick, walk in and tell her I brought her a present. Maybe I'll put it in a box and giftwrap it so I can get a look at her face when she opens it. 'What's this, Michael? It looks familiar. . . .'"

"Be something to see," I agreed.

I made a phone call and we got in the squad car. On our way he said, "You're a damn good friend, you know that? And you know what I'm gonna do? I'm gonna get her to fuck you."

For a second I thought he meant his wife.

"She'll do anything I tell her to do," he said. "Crazy bitch is wild. We'll team up on her, turn her every way but loose."

I didn't know what to say.

We drove across town to a dead-end street in the old Tannery district.

It was a bad block, and the address I had wasn't the best house on it. It was a little square box of a house, with some of the windowpanes broken and weeds poking up through the litter on the front lawn. The paint job was so far gone it was hard to say what color it was.

"Better Homes and Gardens," Walbeck said. "I can see why he likes to spend the night at my place, the son of a bitch."

"That's his car," I said, pointing to a Chevrolet Monte Carlo with a crumpled fender and a busted taillight.

"He parked that piece of shit on my street? You'd think he would have been ashamed."

He led the way, marched right up to the front door. He put a hand on the butt of his service revolver and made a fist of the other. "Police!" be bellowed, as he pounded on the door. Then, before anyone could open it, he drew back his foot and kicked it in.

The shotgun blast picked him up and blew him back onto the front porch.

I was standing to the side when the gun went off, and I already had my own revolver drawn. The weasel-faced little guy in the broken-down armchair had triggered both barrels, and I didn't give him time to reload. I put three slugs in his chest, and they told me later that two of them got the heart and the third didn't miss it by much. He was dead before the shots quit echoing.

I knelt down beside my partner. He was still breathing, but he's taken a double load of buckshot and he was on his way out. But it was important to tell him this before he was gone.

"I'm the one," I said. "I've been dicking your wife for months, you dumb shit. It was fun, putting one over on you, but finally we both got sick of having you around."

I was looking at his eyes as I spoke, and he got it, he took it in. But he didn't hang on to it for long. A moment later his eyes glazed and he was gone.

For a long moment the room was silent, but for the crackling of the fire and an impressive rumbling from the bowels of the old man dozing over his book. "There's a metaphor," the doctor said. "Life is just one long dream, punctuated by the occasional fart."

"That's quite a story, Policeman," the soldier said. "Quite a story to tell on yourself."

"It happened a long time ago," the policeman said.

"And you set the whole thing up. Who was the man with the shotgun?"

"He was wanted in three states," the policeman said, "for robbery and murder, and he'd sworn he would never be taken alive. One of my snitches told me where he was holed up."

"And the rest of it was your doing," the priest said.

The policeman nodded. "Mea culpa, Priest. The call I made before we rolled was to the station, to let them know we were investigating a tip on a fugitive. I let the perp gun down Walbeck, and then I took him out before he could do the same to me."

"And made sure to tell your partner what had happened."

"I wanted him to know," the policeman said.

"And it was true, what you said? You'd been with his wife for months?"

"For a few months, yes. Not as long as he'd been suspicious of her. His suspicions were groundless at first, but I was intrigued, and filled with some sort of righteous indignation at the way he was treating her. I'd have been less outraged, I'm sure, if I hadn't deep down wanted to have her myself."

"And how long did you have her, Policeman?"

"When I set up her husband," he said, "I thought I'd wait a decent interval and marry her. But over the next several weeks I came to see why Walbeck cheated on her. It turned out the woman was a pain in the ass. The affair ran its course and ended, and she married someone else."

"And you didn't worry she would let slip how you'd arranged her husband's death?"

"She never knew," the policeman said. "As far as she was concerned, it was a death in the line of duty. He got a medal awarded posthumously and she got a generous widow's pension."

"Because she was such a generous widow," the doctor suggested. "Did the old fellow fart again?"

"I think that was the fire."

"I think it was the man himself," the doctor said. "And what did you get, Policeman? A citation for bravery?"

"A commendation," the policeman said, "and a promotion not long thereafter."

"Virtue rewarded. And the other lady? Joanie Jellin, the convict's wife?"

"I consoled her," the policeman admitted. "And once again came to appreciate my late partner's point of view. The woman did kindle the flames of lust. But I just spent a few afternoons with her and bowed out of the picture."

"No keeping her company on conjugal visits?"

"None of that, no."

"The flames of lust," the soldier said, echoing the phrase the policeman had used. "They cast a nasty yellow glow, don't they? Lust ruled your partner, ran his life and ran him out of it, but wasn't it lust that drove all the parties in your story? You, certainly, and both of the women."

"It was the story that came to mind," the policeman said, "when the conversation turned to lust."

"Lust," the soldier mused. "Is it always about the sexual impulse? What about the lust for power? The lust for gold?"

"Metaphor," the priest said. "If I am said to have a lust for gold, the man who so defines me is saying that my desire for gold has the urgency of a sexual urge, that I yearn for it and seek after it in a lustful manner."

"And what of blood lust?" The soldier cleaned the dottle from his pipe, filled the bowl from his calfskin pouch, struck a wooden match and lit his pipe. "Is that a metaphor, or is it indeed sexual? I can think of an incident that suggests the latter." He drew on his pipe. "I wonder if I should recount it. It's not my story, not even in the sense that the priest's story was his. That was told to him by one of the tale's principals. Mine came to me by a less direct route."

They considered this in silence, a silence broken at length by a low rumbling from the hearthside.

"Was that another fart?" the doctor wondered. "No, I believe it was a snore. The old man's a whole impolite orchestra, isn't he?" He sighed. "Tell your story, Soldier."

I believe it was Robert E. Lee (said the soldier) who expressed the thought that it was just as well war was so horrible, or else we would like it too much. But it seems to me that we already like it to a considerable degree. Who doesn't recall George Patton proclaiming his love for combat. "God help me, I love it!" he cried.

Or at least George C. Scott did, in his portrayal of Patton. Was that accurate, or do we owe some Hollywood screenwriter for the creation of this myth?

I'm not sure it matters. It's clear Patton loved it, whether he ever said so or not. And, while it's quite appropriate that he was played by Scott rather than, say, Alan Alda, I'm sure the man was not entirely lacking in sensitivity. He may have loved war, but he was very likely aware that he shouldn't.

But people do, don't they? Otherwise we wouldn't have so many wars. They seem to retain their popularity down through the centuries, and for all that they grow ever more horrible, we do go on having them. Old men make wars, we are occasionally told, and young men have to fight them. The implication is that older men, safely lodged behind desks, feel free to make decisions that cost the unwilling lives of the young.

But does anyone genuinely think there would be fewer wars fought if younger men were their nations' leaders? The reverse, I think, is far more likely. The young are more reckless, with others' lives as well as their own. And it is indeed they who fight the wars, and die in them, because they are often so eager to do so.

I am not wholly without experience here. I saw combat in one war, and ordered men about in others. War is awful, certainly, but it is also quite wonderful. The two words once had the same meaning, did you know that? Awful and wonderful. The former we reserve now for that which we regard as especially bad, the latter for what seems especially good, yet they both have the same root meaning. Full of awe, full of wonder.

War's all of that and more.

It is exciting, for one thing. Not always, as the monotony of it can be excruciating, but when it ceases to be boring it becomes very exciting indeed, and that excitement is heightened by the urgency of it all. One might be killed at any moment, so how can the body fail to be in a state of excitement? That, after all, is what adrenaline is for.

And there's the camaraderie. Men working together, fighting together, united not merely in a common cause but in a matter of life and death. To do so seems to satisfy a fundamental human urge.

On top of that, there's the freedom. Does that strike you as strange? I can see that it might, as there's no one less at liberty in many ways than a soldier. His every action is in response to an order, and to defy a direct order is to court severe punishment. Yet this apparent slavery is freedom of a sort. One is free of the obligation to make decisions, free too of the past and the future. One's family, one's career, what one is going to do with one's life—all of this disappears as one follows orders and gets through the day.

And, of course, there's the chance to kill.

I wonder how many soldiers ever kill anybody. Relatively few have the opportunity. In any war, only a fraction of enlisted troops ever see combat, and fewer still ever have the enemy in their sights. And only some of those men take aim and pull the trigger. Some, it would appear, are reluctant to take the life of someone they don't even know.

Others are not. And there are those who find they like it.

Lucas Hallam, if I may call him that, was to all appearances entirely normal prior to his service in the armed forces. He grew up in a small Midwestern town, with three brothers (two older than himself) and a younger sister. Aside from the usual childhood and adolescent stunts (throwing snowballs at cars, smoking in the lavatory) he was never in trouble, and in school he was an average student, in athletics an average participant. There are three childhood markers for profound antisocial behavior, as I understand it, and Luke, as far as anyone knew, had none of them. He did not wet the bed, he did not set fires, and he did not torture animals. (The pathological implications of the latter two are not hard to infer, but what has bedwetting to do with anything? Perhaps the doctor will enlighten me later.)

After graduating from high school, Luke looked at the vocational opportunities open to him, thought unenthusiastically of college, and joined the army. There was no war on when he enlisted, but there was by the time he finished basic training. He was a good soldier, and his eyesight was excellent and his hand-eye coordination superb. On the firing range he qualified as an Expert Rifleman, and he was assigned to a platoon of combat infantry and shipped overseas.

At the end of his hitch he was rotated back to the States, and eventually discharged. But by then he had been in combat any number of times, and had had enemy soldiers in his sights on innumerable occasions. He had no difficulty pulling the trigger, and his skills were such that he generally hit what he aimed at.

He liked it, liked the way it felt. It gave him an enormous feeling of satisfaction. He was doing his job, serving his country, and saving his own life and the lives of his buddies by killing men who were trying to kill him. Take aim, squeeze off a shot, and you canceled a threat, took off the board someone who otherwise might take you or someone you cared about off the board. That was what he was supposed to do, what they'd sent him over there to do, and he was doing it well, and he felt good about it.

The first time he did it, actually saw his shot strike home, saw the man on the other side of the clearing stumble and fall, he was too busy sighting and shooting and trying to stay behind cover to notice how he felt. The action in a full-blown firefight was too intense for you to feel much of anything. You were too busy staying alive.

Later, remembering, he felt a fullness in his chest, as if his heart was swelling. With pride, he supposed.

Another time, they were pinned down by a sniper. He advanced, and when someone else drew the sniper's fire, he was able to spot the man perched in a tree. He got him in his sights and felt an overall excitement, as if all his cells were more intensely alive than before. He fired, and the man fell from the tree, and a cheer went up from those of his buddies who had seen the man fall. Once again he felt that fullness in his chest, but this time it wasn't only his heart that swelled. He noted with some surprise that there was a delicious warmth in his groin, and that he had a powerful erection.

Well, he was nineteen years old, and it didn't take a great deal to give him an erection. He would get hard thinking about girls, or looking at sexy pictures, or thinking about looking at sexy pictures. A ride in a Jeep on a rough road could give him an erection. He thought it was interesting, getting an erection in combat, but he didn't make too much of it.

Later, when they got back to base, he went drinking and whoring with his buddies. The sex was sweeter and more intense than ever before, but he figured it was the girl. She was, he decided, more attractive than most of them, and hot.

From that point on, sexual excitement was a component of every firefight he was in. Killing the enemy didn't carry him to orgasm, although there was at least one occasion when it didn't miss by much.

It did render him powerfully erect, however, and, when he was able to be with a girl afterward, the union was intensely satisfying. The girl didn't have to be spectacularly good-looking, he realized, or all that hot. She just had to be there when he was back from a mission on which he'd blown away one or more enemy troops.

As I said, his tour of duty concluded and he returned to the States. The war receded into memory. Back in his hometown, in the company of people who'd shared none of his military experiences, he let it all exist as a separate chapter of his life—or, perhaps more accurately, as another volume altogether, a closed book he didn't often take down from the shelf.

He found work, he dated a few local girls, and within a year or so he found one who suited him. In due course they were engaged, and then married. They bought a modest home and set about starting a family.

Now and then, when he was making love to his wife, wartime images would intrude. They came not as flashbacks of the sort common to victims of post-traumatic stress syndrome, but as simple memories that slipped unbidden into his consciousness. He recalled sex acts with the native prostitutes, and this made him guilty at first, as if he were cheating on his wife by having another woman's image in mind during their lovemaking.

He dismissed the guilt. After all, you couldn't hang a man for his thoughts, could you? And, if a memory of another woman enriched the sexual act for himself and his wife, where was the harm? He didn't seek to summon up such memories, but if they came he allowed himself to enjoy them.

There were other memories, though. Memories of drawing a bead on a sniper in a tree, holding his breath, squeezing off the shot. Seeing the man fall in delicious slow motion, seeing him fall never to rise again.

He didn't like that, and it bothered him a little. He found he could will such thoughts away, and did so as quickly as they came. Then he could surrender to the delight of the moment, untroubled by recollections of the past. That, after all, was over and done with. He didn't hang out at the Legion post, didn't pal around with other vets, didn't talk about what he'd seen and done. He barely thought about it, so why should he think of it now, at such an intimate moment?

Never mind. You couldn't help the thoughts that came to you, but you didn't have to entertain them. He blinked and they were gone.

After his second child was born, Luke's sex life slowed down considerably. The pregnancy had been a difficult one, and when he and his wife attempted to resume relations after the birth, they were not terribly successful. She was willing enough but not very receptive, and he had difficulty becoming aroused and further difficulty in bringing his arousal to fulfillment.

He'd never had this problem before.

It was normal, he told himself. Nothing to worry about. It would work itself out.

He tried mental tricks—thinking of other women, using memory or fantasy as an erotic aid. This worked some of the time, but not always, and never as well as he would have liked.

Then one day he used a fantasy about a woman at work to help him become erect, and, during the act, he tried to extend the fantasy to reach a climax. But instead it winked out like a spent lightbulb, and what replaced it was an involuntary memory of a firefight. This time he didn't blink it away, but let himself relive the fight, the aiming, the firing, the bodies falling in obedience to his will.

His orgasm was powerful.

If it troubled him at all to have used memories of killing, any disquiet he felt was offset by the height of his excitement and the depth of his satisfaction. Henceforth he employed memories and fantasies of killing as he had previously used memories and fantasies of other women, and to far greater advantage. His ardor had waned somewhat even before the second pregnancy, as is hardly uncommon after a few years of marriage; it now returned with a vengeance, and his wife caught a little of his own renewed enthusiasm. It was, she told him, like a second honeymoon.

That set his mind entirely to rest. It was good for both of them, he realized, and if what he did in the privacy of his own mind was a little kinky, even a little unpleasant, well, who was harmed?

Memories would take him only so far. You used them up when you replayed them over and over. Fantasies, though, were pretty good. He would think of someone he'd noticed at work or on television, and he would imagine the whole thing, stalking the person, making the kill. He would spend time with the fantasy, living it over and over in his mind each time he and his wife made love, refining it until it was just the way he wanted it.

And then, perhaps inevitably, there came a time when he found himself thinking about bringing one of his fantasies to life. Or, if you prefer, to death.

"Hunting," the policeman said. "Soldier, why the hell didn't the poor sonofabitch try hunting? No safer outlet for a man who wants to kill something. You get up early in the morning and go out in the woods and take it out on a deer or a squirrel."

"I wonder," said the priest. "Do you suppose that's why men hunt? I thought it was for the joy of walking in the woods, and the satisfaction of putting meat on one's table."

"Meat's cheaper in a store," the policeman said, "and you don't need to pick up a gun to take a walk in the woods. Oh, I'm sure there are other motives for hunting. It makes you feel resourceful and self-reliant and manly, fit to hang out with Daniel Boone and Natty Bumppo. But when all's said and done you're out there killing things, and if you don't like killing you'll find some other way to pass the time."

"He'd hunted as a boy," the soldier said. "You'd be hard put to avoid it if you grew up where he did. His brother took him out hunting rabbits, and he shot and killed one, and it made him sick."

"What did he get, tularemia?" the doctor wondered. "You can get it from handling infected rabbits."

"Sick to his stomach," the soldier said. "Sick inside. Killing an animal left him feeling awful."

"He was a boy then," the policeman said. "Now he was a man, and one who'd killed other men and was thinking about doing it again. You'd think he'd go out in the woods, if only for curiosity."

"And he did," said the soldier.

* * *

He thought along the very lines you suggested (continued the soldier), and he went out and bought a rifle and shells, and one crisp autumn morning he shouldered his rifle and drove a half hour north, where there was supposed to be good hunting. The deer season wouldn't open for another month, but all that meant was that the woods wouldn't be swarming with hunters. And you didn't have to wait for deer season to shoot varmints and small game.

He walked around for an hour or so, stopped to eat his lunch and drink a cup of coffee from the Thermos jug, got up and hefted his gun and walked around some more. Early on he spotted a bird on a branch, greeting the dawn in song. He squinted through the scope and took aim at the creature, not intending to shoot. What kind of person would gun down a songbird? But he wondered what it would feel like to have the bird in his sights, and was not surprised to note that there was no sense of excitement whatsoever, just a queasy sensation in the pit of his stomach.

Later he took aim at a squirrel and had the same reaction, or non-reaction. Hunting, he could see, was not an answer for him. He was if anything somewhat relieved that he hadn't had to shoot an animal to establish this.

He unloaded his rifle and walked some more, enjoying the crunch of fallen leaves under his feet, the sweetness of the air in his lungs. And then he came to a clearing, and in an old orchard across the way he saw a woman on a ladder, picking apples.

His pulse quickened. Without thinking he slipped into the shadows where he'd be invisible. He stood there, watching her, and he was excited.

She was pretty, or at least he thought she was. It was hard to tell at this distance. He should have brought binoculars, he thought, so he could get a better look.

And he remembered that the gun's telescopic sight would work as well.

He spun around, walked back the way he'd come. He was not going to look at the woman through a rifle sight. That was not what he was going to do.

He walked around for another hour and wound up right back where he'd seen the woman. Probably gone by now, he told himself. But no, there she was, still in the orchard, still up on the ladder. She was working a different tree now, and he could get a better look at her. Earlier her back had been toward him, but now had a frontal view, and he could see her face.

Not very well, though. Not from that far away.

He took the rifle from his shoulder, looked at her through the scope. Very pretty, he saw. Auburn hair—without the scope it had just looked dark—and a long oval face, and breasts that swelled the front of her plaid shirt.

He had never been so excited in his life. He unzipped his pants, freed himself from his underwear. His cock was huge and fiercely erect.

He touched himself, then returned his hand to the rifle. His finger curled tentatively around the trigger.

He thought he must be trembling too much to take aim, but his excitement was all within him, and his stance was rock-solid, his hands sure and skilled. He aimed, and drew a breath, and held the breath.

And squeezed the trigger.

The bullet took her in the throat. She hung on the ladder for a moment, blood gouting from the wound. Then she fell.

He stared through the scope while his seed sprang forth from his body and fell upon the carpet of leaves.

He was shocked, appalled. And, of course, more than a little frightened. He had taken life before, but that involved killing the enemy in time of war. He had just struck down a fellow citizen engaged in lawful activity on her own property, and for no good reason whatsoever. His sharpshooting overseas had won him medals and promotions; this would earn him—what? Life in prison? A death sentence?

He left the woods, and on the way home he dropped his rifle in the river. No one would note its absence. He'd purchased it without mentioning it to his wife, and now it was gone, and as if he'd never owned it.

But he had in fact owned it, and as a result a woman was dead.

The story was in the papers for days, weeks. A woman had been struck down by a single shot from a high-powered rifle. The woman's estranged husband, who was questioned and released, had been arrested twice on drug charges, and police theorized that her death was some sort of warning or reprisal. Another theory held that mere bad luck was to blame; a hunter, somewhere in the woods, had fired at a squirrel and missed, and the bullet, still lethal at a considerable distance, had flown with unerring aim at an unintended and unseen target.

Luke waited for some shred of evidence to materialize and trip him up. When that didn't happen, he realized he was in the clear. He could do nothing for the woman, but he could put the incident out of his mind and make certain nothing like it ever happened again.

He could, as it turned out, do neither. The incident returned to his mind, its memory kindling a passion that heightened his relations with his wife a hundredfold. And he found, after his initial fear and shock had dissipated, that he felt no more remorse for the woman's death than he had for those enemy soldiers he'd gunned down. If anything, what he felt for her was a curious gratitude, gratitude for being an instrument of pleasure for him. Every time he thought of her, every time he relived the memory of her murder, she furnished pleasure anew.

You can probably imagine the rest. He went to a nearby city, and in a downtown motel room he mounted a hollow-eyed whore. While she toiled beneath him, he whipped out a silenced small-caliber pistol and held it to her temple. The horror in her eyes tore at him, but at the same time it thrilled him. He held off as long as he could, then squeezed the trigger and spurted into her even as the life flowed out of her.

He picked up a hitchhiker, raped her, then killed her with a knife. Two states away, he picked up another hitchhiker, a teenage boy. When he stopped the car and drew a gun, the boy, terrified, offered sex. Luke was aroused and accepted the offer, but his ardor wilted the moment the boy took him in his mouth. He pushed the youth away, then pressed the gun to his chest and fired two shots into his heart.

That excited him, but he walked away from the death scene with his passion unspent and found a prostitute. She did what the boy had attempted to do, and did it successfully as his mind filled with memories of the boy's death. Then, satisfied, he killed the woman almost as an afterthought, taking her from behind and snapping her neck like a twig.

He was clever, and it was several years before they caught him. Although the impulse to kill, once triggered, was uncontrollable, he could control its onset, and sometimes months would pass between episodes. His killing methods and choice of victims varied considerably, and he traveled widely when he hunted, so no pattern became evident. Nowadays there may be a national bank of DNA evidence, evidence that would have established that the semen in the vagina of a runaway teen in Minneapolis was identical to that left on the abdomen of a housewife in Oklahoma. But no such facility existed at the time, and his killings were seen as isolated incidents.

And in some cases, of course, the bodies he left behind were never found. Once he managed to get two girls at once, sisters. He killed one right away, raped the other, killed her, and withdrew from her body in order to have his climax within the first victim. He threw both bodies down a well, where they remained until his confession led to their discovery.

A stupid mistake led to his arrest. He'd made mistakes before, but this one was his undoing. And perhaps he was ready to be caught. Who can say?

In his jail cell, he wrote out a lengthy confession, listing all the murders he had committed—or at least as many as he remembered. And then he committed suicide. They had taken his belt and shoelaces, of course, and there was nothing on the ceiling from which one could hang oneself with a braided bedsheet, but he found a way. He unbolted a metal support strip from his cot, honed it on the concrete floor of his cell until he'd fashioned a half-sharp homemade knife. He used it to amputate his penis, and bled to death.

"What a horrible story," the policeman said.

"Dreadful," the priest agreed, wringing his hands, and the doctor nodded his assent.

"I'm sorry," said the soldier. "I apologize to you all. As I said, it wasn't my own story, for which I must say I'm heartily grateful, nor was it a story I heard directly, and I daresay I'm grateful for that as well. It may have been embroidered along the way, before it was told to me, and I suspect I added something in the telling myself, inferring what went through the poor bastard's mind. If I were a better storyteller I might have made a better story of it. Perhaps I shouldn't have told it in the first place."

"No, no!" the doctor cried. "It wasn't a *bad* story. It was gripping and fascinating and superbly told, and whatever license you took for dramatic purposes was license well taken. It's a wonderful story."

"But you said—"

"That it was horrible," the priest said. "So Policeman said, and I added that it was terrible."

"You said dreadful," said the doctor.

"I stand corrected," the priest said. "Horrible, dreadful—both of those, to be sure, and terrible as well. And, as you said in your prefatory remarks, awful and wonderful. What do you make of young Luke, Soldier? Was he in fact a casualty of war?"

"We gave him a gun and taught him to kill," the soldier said. "When he did, we pinned medals on his chest. But we didn't make him like it. In fact, if his instructor had suspected he was likely to have that kind of a visceral response to firing at the enemy, he might never have been assigned to combat duty."

The doctor raised an eyebrow. "Oh? You find a lad who qualifies as Expert Rifleman and you shunt him aside for fear that he might enjoy doing what you've just taught him to do, and do so well? Is that any way to fight a war?"

"Well, perhaps we'd have taken a chance on him anyway," the soldier conceded. "Not so likely in a peacetime army, but with a war going on, yes, I suppose we might have applied a different standard."

"What passes for heroism on the battlefield," said the priest, "we might otherwise label psychosis."

"But the question," the soldier said doggedly, "is whether he'd have found the same end with or without his military service. The bullet that killed that first sniper put him on a path that led to the jail cell where he emasculated himself. But would he have gotten there anyway?"

"Your lot didn't program him," the policeman said. "You didn't have a surgeon implant a link between his trigger finger and his dick. The link was already in place and the first killing just activated it. Hunting hadn't activated it, though who's to say it wouldn't have if he got a cute little whitetail doe in his sights?"

The priest rolled his eyes.

"Sooner or later," the policeman said, "he'd have found out what turned him on. And I have to say I think he must have at least half-known all along. You say he didn't have sadistic sexual fantasies before the first killing, but how can any of us know that was the case? Did he state so unequivocally in this confession he wrote out? And can we take his word? Can we trust his memory?"

"Sooner or later," the doctor said, "his marital sex life would have slowed, for one reason or another."

"Or for no reason at all," the policeman said.

"Or for no reason at all, none beyond familiarity and entropy. And then he'd have found a fantasy that worked. And someone some day would have paid a terrible price."

"And the origin of it all?" the soldier wondered.

"Something deep and unknowable," the doctor said. "Something encoded in the genes or inscribed upon the psyche."

"Or the soul," the priest suggested.

"Or the soul," the doctor allowed.

There was a rumbling noise from the direction of the fireplace, and the doctor made a face. "There he goes again," he said. "I suppose I should be tolerant of the infirmities of age, eh? Flatulent senescence awaits us all."

"I think that was the fire," the policeman said.

"The fire?"

"An air pocket in a log."

"And the, ah, bouquet?"

"The soldier's pipe."

The doctor considered the matter. "Perhaps it is a foul pipe I smell," he allowed, "rather than an elderly gentleman's foul plumbing. No matter. We've rather covered the subject of lust, haven't we? And I'd say our stories have darkened as we've gone along. I've lost track of the hand. Shall we gather the cards and deal again?"

"We could," the priest said, "but have you nothing to offer on the subject, Doctor?"

"The subject of lust?"

The priest nodded. "One would think your calling would give you a useful perspective."

"Oh, I've seen many things," said the doctor, "and heard and read of many others. There's nothing quite so extraordinary as human behavior, but I guess we all know that, don't we?"

"Yes," said the priest and the policeman, and the soldier, busy lighting his pipe, managed a nod.

"As a matter of fact," the doctor said, "there was a story that came to mind. But I can't say it's the equal to what I've heard from the rest of you. Still, if you'd like to hear it . . ."

"Tell it," said the priest.

As a medical man (said the doctor) I have been privy to a good deal of information about people's sex lives. When I entered the profession, I was immediately assumed to know more about human sexuality than the average layman. I don't know that I actually did. I didn't know much, but then it's highly probable my patients knew even less.

Still, one understands the presumption. A physician is taught a good deal about anatomy, and the average person knows precious little about his or her own anatomical apparatus, let alone that of the opposite sex. Thus, to the extent that sex is a physiological matter, a doctor might indeed be presumed to know something about it.

So much of it, though, is in the mind. In the psyche or in the soul, as we've just now agreed. There may well be a physical component that's at the root of it, a wayward chromosome, a gene that leans to the left or to the right, and a new generation of doctors is almost certain to know more than we did, but will they be revered as we were?

I doubt it. For years people gave us more respect than we could possibly deserve, and now they don't give us nearly enough. They see us as mercenary pill-pushers who do what the HMOs tell us to do, no less and no more. Lawyers sue us for malpractice, and we respond by ordering unneeded tests and procedures to forestall such lawsuits. Every time a fellow physician anesthetizes a pretty patient and gives her a free pelvic exam, why, the whole profession suffers, just as every cleric gets a black eye when one of the priest's colleagues is caught playing Hide the Host with an altar boy.

Lust. That's our subject, isn't it? And do you suppose there's a physiological explanation for one's tendency to natter on and on in one's senior years? Is there a gene that turns us into garrulous old farts?

My point, to the extent that I have one, is this: As a physician, as a trusted medical practitioner, as a putative authority on matters of the human anatomy, I was taken into the confidence of my patients and thus made more aware than most people of the infinite variety and remarkable vagaries of human sexuality. I saw more penises than Catherine the Great, more vaginas than Casanova. Saw them up close, too, with no fumbling around in the dark. Told husbands how to satisfy their wives, women how to get pregnant.

Why, I knew an older man who had a half dozen women, widows and spinsters, who came to him once a month on average to be masturbated. The old duffer didn't call it that, and I don't even know if he thought of it in those terms. He was treating them, he confided, for hysteria, and the treatment employed an artificial phallus hygienically hooded with a condom. He wore rubber gloves, this doctor did, and seemed genuinely offended at the hint that he might be getting more than a fee for his troubles. As to my suggestion that he might send them home with dildoes and a clue as to how best to employ them, he grimaced at the very idea. "These are decent women," he told me, as if that explained everything. And perhaps it did.

I have become inclined, through observation both personal and professional in nature, to grant considerable respect to the sex drive. The urgency of its imperative is undeniable, the variety of its manifestation apparently infinite. I will furnish but one example of the latter: one patient of mine, a lesbian, married another woman in a ceremony which, if unsanctioned by the state, was nevertheless as formal a rite as any I've attended. My patient wore a white gown, her spouse a tuxedo.

After a few years they parted company, without having to undergo the legal rigors of a divorce. My patient began living as a man, and eventually took hormone treatments and counseling and underwent sex-change surgery. And so, quite unbeknownst to her, did her former marriage partner. They are now pals, working out at the gym together, going to ball games together, and looking for nice feminine girls to hook up with and marry.

Infinite variety . . .

But, entertaining as their saga may be, I wouldn't call it lust. Lust is desire raised to a level that prompts unacceptable behavior—how's that for a definition? And I can think of no clearer example of that than a fellow I'll call Gregory Dekker.

Dekker was a serial rapist. That's spelled with an S, not a C, lest you imagine some lunatic having it off with a bowl of Cream of Wheat, or working his way one by one through a box of Cheerios. His sexual desire was strong, though probably not abnormally so, and he satisfied it in one of two ways—by rape or by masturbation. And, when he masturbated, the images in his mind were rape fantasies.

Rape, we are often assured, is not truly sexual in nature. Rape is a violent expression of hostility toward women, and has nothing at all to do with desire. The rapist is wielding his phallus as a weapon—a sword, a club, a gun that fires seminal bullets. He is getting even with his mother for real or imagined abuse.

What crap.

Oh, surely hostility may play a part in his makeup. And surely there are some rapists who are acting out their primal dramas. But, if the chief aim of the act is to inflict pain and damage, why choose such an uncertain weapon? Why reach for a gun so apt to jam or misfire?

Rape, you see, requires an erect penis. And a successful rape culminates in orgasm and ejaculation. And who would imagine that all of this takes place in the absence of sexual desire?

Rape, I submit, is often nothing more or less than the sexual activity of a sociopath, a man lacking conscience who, as he might tell you, quite sensibly seeks to satisfy himself sexually without having to resort to candy or flowers, sweet words and false promises. He doesn't have to take his chosen partner to dinner or a movie, doesn't have to feign interest in her conversation, doesn't even have to tell her she looks nice. Why, he proves she looks good to him, good enough to throw down and ravish. Isn't that compliment enough?

I've no clear idea what makes a person grow up sociopathic. Is it in the genes? The upbringing? I don't have the answer. Nor, in fact, do I know much about Gregory Dekker in particular. He was never a patient of mine.

Susan Trenholme was, however.

She was a remarkably ordinary young woman, neither beautiful nor plain. Her hair was light brown, not quite blond, and her figure was womanly, and fuller than she'd have preferred; she was always trying new diets and over-the-counter appetite suppressants, all in an effort to lose five pounds over and over again. She was, I suppose, no more neurotic in this area than most young women; if they were as obsessed about their height, they'd all put on weighted boots and suspend themselves from the ceiling.

Susan met a young man in college and lived with him for two years. They drifted apart, and she was twenty-six years old and living alone when Gregory Dekker caught up with her in the parking lot of her apartment complex, knocked her to the ground, fell on her, and told her not to struggle or make a sound or he'd kill her.

Looking into his eyes, she knew he was serious. And she became convinced that, whether she cried out or remained silent, whether she struggled or acquiesced, her fate was sealed. He would kill her anyway once he'd had his pleasure with her.

In fact she had grounds for this assessment, beyond what she was able to read in his eyes. A rapist whose description matched her assailant had committed a string of rapes in the area within the past several months, and had left his two most recent victims for dead; one recovered, one was dead on arrival at a nearby hospital. Unlike the monster in your story, Soldier, Gregory Dekker was not given to lust-murder; he killed only to avoid being caught.

And he would have been easy to pick out of a lineup. If Susan Trenholme looked ordinary, Gregory Dekker surely did not. Whatever the cause —a drunken obstetrician misusing his forceps, a mother who dropped him on his face in infancy—Dekker was an heroically ugly young man. His schoolmates, perhaps inevitably, called him Frankenstein, and they had reason. Extensive facial and dental surgery would have helped, no doubt, but his parents couldn't have afforded it, if they even thought of it.

Dekker probably assumed he could never have a woman other than by force. He was almost certainly wrong in that assessment. Some women find ugly men particularly attractive, and others respond to qualities other than appearance. I knew one woman, for example, who held that there was no such thing as an ugly millionaire.

Well, Dekker was no millionaire, nor did he have other attractive qualities, so perhaps rape was a sound choice for him. In any event, it worked. When he wanted a woman, he took her. Sometimes this happened in the course of his work, which was burglary; he broke into homes and offices, grabbed cash or something readily converted thereto, and fled. If there was a woman on the premises, and if he liked her looks, he would take her as automatically as he would take her jewelry.

In Susan's case, he saw her at a supermarket, followed her to her car, then tailed her in his car and assaulted her, as I've said, in her parking lot. And would very likely have left her there, dead or dying, if she hadn't taken action.

She didn't resist, didn't cry out. On the contrary, she did everything she could to make things easier for him, and, after he had entered her, she wriggled beneath him and began uttering little moans and yelps of pleasure.

And she proceeded to do what countless of her sisters have done, not on the gritty pavement of a parking lot but in the sweet embrace of the marriage bed. To wit, she faked an orgasm.

It must have surprised the daylights out of her partner. I don't know what sort of fantasy life Gregory Dekker may have led, but he wouldn't have been the first rapist to persuade himself that a potential victim actually longed for his embrace, that a woman taken initially by force might be rendered passionate by his lovemaking, and might enjoy it as much as he did. None had shown any sign of enjoying his attentions in the past, but who was to say that his luck might not change?

If he'd entertained such fancies, he must have thought he'd died and gone to heaven. Because here was this creature, moaning and twisting in his arms, and ultimately wrapping her legs around him and crying out *Yes!* and telling him, as he lay exhausted in her arms, what a great lover he was and how she'd always dreamed of a man like him and a moment like this.

Did it enter his mind that she was putting on an act? Even if he believed her, wouldn't it be safer in the long run to bash her head in or break her neck?

He may have thought so, but she tried not to give him time for thought. She kept cooing at him, telling him how wonderful he was, talking about the extent of her excitement and satisfaction, running a loving hand over his distorted features, raising her head to kiss his misshapen mouth.

And then, as if unable to help herself, she fell upon him and behaved, well, like an impressionable White House interne.

By the time she was finished, she had effectively saved her life. Dekker believed what she wanted him to believe—that he'd excited and satisfied her and left her begging for more. And beg she did, wanting to know if she would see him again, if they could do this with some frequency. And wouldn't it be even more wonderful in a bedroom, with the lights lowered and soft music playing, and the comfort of a mattress and clean cotton sheets?

They made a date for the following night. He was to come to her apartment at nine. He got there at eight and rang her bell at ten, confident by then that she hadn't set up a police ambush. She met him with a drink in hand and soft music playing, telling him truthfully enough that she'd been worried he wasn't going to come.

He made an excuse, but later, at the evening's end, he told her how he'd staked out her building to see if any cops showed. "Just give me a minute," he told her, "and I'll hook your phone lines up again. I pulled them before I came in, in case you were planning to make a call."

"I wouldn't do that," she said.

"Well, I know that now," he said. "But I had to be sure."

Before he left she made him a cup of cocoa. After he left she stood at the sink, rinsing the cup, and pondering the curious situation she was in. Her rapist was her lover, and she was fixing cocoa for him.

He saw her the next night, and the night after that. When he came over the following day he had a sheepish expression on his face. She wanted to ask him what was the matter, but she waited, and he got around to it on his own.

"I may not be much good to you tonight," he said. "On account of what came up this afternoon."

"Oh?"

He was working, he said, prowling apartments, seeing what he could pick up, and this woman walked right in on him. "Last thing I wanted," he said, "but there she was, you know?" And he got this little-boy smirk on his face.

She let her excitement show in her face. "Tell me," she said.

"Well, I did her," he said.

"Tell me!"

"What, you want the gory details? You know something, Susie? You're as bad as I am. What I did, I was behind the bedroom door, you know, waiting for her, and she walks through and bingo, I got one hand over her mouth and the other grabbing her tits. Little tits, way smaller than yours, but they were nice."

The room was dark, the curtains drawn, and the woman never got a look at his face. "So I didn't have to, you know, do her."

"Kill her."

"Like you have to do if they get a good look at you. But it was dark, and I got some tape over her eyes before they got used to the dark. So she never saw my face and she never saw my dick, so what's she gonna tell them? What it felt like?" He laughed, and she laughed with him. "There's guys who get a kick out of, you know, finishing 'em off. Personally, I think that's sick. Waste of good pussy, you know?"

"But sometimes you don't have a choice," she said.

"That's it exactly. Sometimes you don't have a choice. And if I got to do it, well, it doesn't bother me. You do what you gotta do. Anyway, who told her to come home in the middle of the goddam afternoon? She's supposed to be working, so what's she doing at home?"

"She deserved it," she said.

"Probably half-wanted it," he said. "Like you the first time. Except this one wasn't like you, she was crying and making a fuss. Nice, though." He chucked her under the chin. "When I was done with her," he said, "I thought, oh shit, I'm not gonna be much good to Susie. She finds out, she's gonna be pissed."

"I'm not, though. It's exciting. Tell me what you did."

The report included anal intercourse, and she pouted when he told her. "We never tried that," she said.

"Well, most women don't like it."

"I'm not most women," she said. "Oh, what have we here? It looks as though you're going to be able to do something after all. My goodness!"

He left finally, after downing a cup of cocoa to soothe his stomach. His stomach had been bothering him lately, and he agreed that the cocoa would probably help.

Two nights later, she told him how it excited her to think of him raping another woman. "I only wish I could have been there," she said.

"You're some crazy dame," he said admiringly. "What would you do? Watch?"

She nodded, moistened her upper lip with the tip of her tongue.

"Maybe help," she added.

"Help?"

"I could hold her hands," she said. "Or . . ."

"Or what?"

"I don't know. Maybe do stuff."

"Like fool around with her?"

"Maybe."

"Like how?"

"Oh, I don't know," she said. "Maybe, you know, touch her. Do things to her."

"You ever been with a woman?"

"No."

"But you've been thinking about it."

"Well," she said, "if she couldn't do anything, you know. Like if she was tied up? And I was in control?"

"You are one crazy bitch," he said.

"Well."

"Man," he said, "now you got me going. Maybe we could, you know, pick somebody out, follow her home. Or if I was working and I found somebody, like, I could call you. Or . . ."

She had a better idea. There was this woman she knew, a former co-worker. A honey blonde, creamy skin, good breasts.

"You're hot for her," he said.

The woman was attractive, she allowed. And she knew how they could decoy the woman to a motel, where he could have a room booked. And they'd be waiting for her, and when she came in. . .

He helped her plan it out. "One thing," he said. "This broad knows you. And she'll know who lured her to the place, and anyway she'll see you when we do her, she'll see both of us. Unless you're telling me she's gonna like it?"

"No," she said. "She's not going to like it."

"Well then," he said. "You got to realize what's gonna have to happen when we're done. When the party's over, she ain't gonna turn into a pumpkin."

"I know."

"What I mean, I'll have to do her."

"We'll both do her."

He shook his head. "I don't mean do her like have sex with her. I mean do her so she's done. Finish her, is what I'm saying."

"I know."

"And you're okay with that?"

"Maybe I'll help," she said.

A few days later they were driving around, and she pointed out the woman she had described. He was excited and wanted to take their victim immediately, decoy her into the car, take her out into the woods and leave her there when they were finished. "It's better if we let her come to us," she insisted. "We set a trap and she walks right into it. And we can take our time, and do everything we want."

"Right now's when I'm horny," he said.

She grinned. "I can take care of that," she said.

On the appointed evening, he was waiting at the motel room when she arrived. "We've got half an hour before she gets here," she said. "Did I tell you she's selling real estate now? She thinks we're a nice sweet couple, we want her to show us some houses. Well, we're not that sweet, and we'll be showing her more than she shows us. Honey, are you as excited as I am?"

"Take a look."

"Oh God," she said. "I can't wait to see that going in and out of her." They talked some about what they would do to the blond, and then she said, "Oh, before I forget," and took a small unlabeled bottle from her purse. "For your stomach," she said. "Is it still bothering you?"

"Off and on. It's worse at night."

"'Intermittent pain, worse in the evening,'"she said. "I have this herbal doctor, I started to tell him about it and he was finishing my sentences for me. If you drink this it should cure it completely."

"What is it?"

"A mixture of Chinese herbs, and it doesn't taste great. But if you can get it down your troubles are over."

He took the bottle from her. "How much are you supposed to take?"

"All of it, if you can."

He uncapped the bottle, shrugged, tipped it up and drained it. His face twisted. "Jesus, that's terrible," he said. "Anything tastes that bad, it must be great for you."

"He said it tasted pretty bad."

"Well, he got that right."

"And at first it may make you feel worse," she said. "That's a sign that it's working. But after fifteen minutes you should feel great, so by the time our little blond friend gets here . . ."

"She's not so little. Pretty big in the tits department."

"Well, you'll be ready for her."

"I'm ready for her right now," he said. "Oh, shit."

"What's the matter?"

"I think this shit is working, that's all." He clutched his middle. "Oh, shit, that's pretty bad. What'd you say it had in it? Chinese herbs?"

"That's what he said."

"Jesus, if chop suey tasted like this nobody'd eat it. I fucked a Chinese girl once, did I ever tell you about her? She was so scared I thought she was gonna have a heart attack. And it ain't sideways, in case you were wondering."

"What's not sideways?"

"Her pussy. That's what they say about Chinese women. You never heard that? Anyway, her pussy was the same as anybody else's. Oh, Jesus, that's bad." He sprawled on the bed, rolling from side to side, wracked with spasms. "Jesus, it's working. You sure I'm gonna be all right by the time the blond cunt gets here?"

"She's not coming."

"Huh? What do you mean?"

"She was just a woman I pointed out to you," she said. "I don't even know her name. She's not coming. It's just the two of us."

"What are you—"

"And that wasn't Chinese herbs in the bottle. It was the same thing you've been getting in your cocoa every night, and it came out of a bottle marked 'Rat Poison.'"

He stared at her. She forced herself to meet his gaze. "I was giving you small doses," she said, "but this is one big dose, enough to kill a hundred rats. But all it has to kill is one big rat, and you can puke your guts out but it's too late now. It's in your system. You'll be dead in fifteen minutes, half an hour tops."

"Where are you going?"

"I'm not going anywhere," she said. "I'm just getting comfortable. You can't even get off the bed, can you? So I don't have anything to worry about. You're dying, and I'm going to stick around and see the show."

"Susie . . ."

"Maybe I'll touch myself," she said. "Maybe I'll make myself come while you're busy dying. You want to watch me? Do you think you'd like that? Maybe it'll take your mind off what's happening to you. Maybe it'll get you hot."

The policeman was the first to speak. "I suppose she got away with it," he said.

"She was never apprehended," said the doctor. "Never even questioned by the authorities. No one could connect her to Dekker, and the only risk she ran, aside from being discovered in the act, lay in the possibility that he'd left something incriminating among his effects. A diary, for instance, with entries detailing their relationship and their planned rendezvous at the motel. But that seemed unlikely, the man was functionally illiterate, and in the event nothing turned up to draw her into what investigation there was. And that was minimal, as you might suppose. Gregory Dekker's death was ruled a suicide."

"A suicide?"

"He checked in alone at a rundown motel and drank a bottle of rat poison. His prints were on the bottle, you know, and while it was unlabeled, one couldn't down it thinking it was a fine Cabernet just reaching its prime. The stuff tasted like poison. Dekker, of course, thought it tasted like medicine."

"She planned it," the soldier mused, "from the first cup of cocoa. It masked the taste of the non-lethal doses she fed him, which gave him the stomach aches."

"And probably accumulated in the soft tissues," the doctor said, "if the lethal ingredient was in fact arsenic, as I suspect it was. And the stomach aches made him quick to down a larger dose of the poison, in the hope of a cure. Oh, yes, I'd say she planned it. And got away with it, if in fact anybody ever gets away with anything. That would be more in your line, Priest."

The priest stroked his chin. "An undiscovered sin is a sin nevertheless," he said. "One is hardly absolved by the temporal authority's failure to uncover the sin and punish the sinner. Repentance is a prerequisite of absolution, and to repent is to acknowledge that one has not gotten away with it. So no, Doctor, I would hold that no one gets away with anything."

"A thoughtful answer, Priest."

"Long-winded, at least," the priest said. "But I find myself with a question of my own. Yours, like all our stories, is a story of lust, and the lust would seem to be that of the ill-favored young man, whom you call Gregory Dekker. And Susan Trenholme's sin, if we call her a sinner, would be a sin of wrath or anger. Blood lust, if you will. And yet . . ."

"Yes?"

"I wonder," he said. "When did she decide to kill her rapist?"

"When?"

"After the initial act, certainly," the priest said. "But would it have been before or after she arranged a second meeting? Did she at first plan to call the police and trap him, or did she know all along that she meant to kill him herself?"

The doctor smiled. "You have an interesting mind," he said. "But who can say exactly when the idea presented itself? Her first concern was self-preservation. She feigned a physical response to save her own life, then made a date with him to give him further reason to let her live. At first she must have thought she'd have policemen at hand when he came knocking on her door, but somewhere along the way she changed her mind. Why, if she reported the crime at all, she'd have no end of unwelcome attention, and there was even the chance the man would evade justice. And, as she planned her revenge, yes, we can say that blood lust came into it."

"And was that the only sort of lust she felt?" The priest put his palms together. "She faked one orgasm to save her life," he said, "but when she determined to punish the man herself, she drew up a scenario that called for her to engage in a variety of sex acts, and to simulate passion on several more occasions, and to fake a good number of orgasms. And was that passion simulated? Were those orgasms counterfeit?"

"What a subtle mind you have," said the doctor. "That's what bothered her, you know. That's what led her to tell me the story. In the parking lot, with his foul breath in her face and his body upon and within her, all she felt was revulsion. Her response was a triumph of an acting ability she had never dreamed she possessed, in or out of bed.

"He never doubted the sincerity of her response. He thought he had indeed turned her on. But he hadn't—she had turned herself on, and the experience, while profoundly disgusting to her on one level, was undeniably exciting on another."

"Awful and wonderful," murmured the policeman.

"Later, when she weighed her options, she knew that she would have to repeat her performance if she were to seek her own revenge. And the idea was at once distasteful and appealing. She had sex with him that second time, in her own apartment, in her own bed, and if anything she loathed him more than before. But it was not difficult to pretend to be aroused, and in fact she found she was genuinely aroused, though far more by her own performance and her own plans than by anything he was doing to her."

"And did she fake that orgasm, too?" the soldier wondered.

"I can't answer that," the doctor said, "because she didn't know herself. Where does performance leave off and reality begin? Perhaps she faked that orgasm, but faked it with her own being, so that he was not the only one taken in by her performance." The doctor shrugged. "From that point on, however, her response was unequivocal. She looked forward to his visits. She was excited by their lovemaking, if it's not too perverse to call it that. She was excited by him, and her excitement grew even as her hatred for him deepened. By the time she killed him, her sole regret was that she would no longer have him as a sexual partner."

"But that didn't stop her."

"No," the doctor said. "No, she wanted the pleasure of his death more than the pleasure of his embrace. But afterward she was appalled by what she'd done, and even more by what she'd become. Had she turned into a monster herself?"

"And had she?"

The doctor shook his head. "No, not at all. She did not find herself ruled by her passions, nor did an element of sadism become a lasting part of her sexual nature. It was not long before a boyfriend came into her life, and their relationship and others that were to follow were entirely normal."

"So she was unchanged by the experience?"

"Is one ever entirely unchanged by any experience? And could anyone remain unchanged by such an extraordinary experience? That said, no surface change was evident. Oh, sex was a little more satisfying than it had been in the past, and she was a bit less inhibited, and a bit more eager to try new acts and postures."

They fell silent, and the room grew very still indeed. The fire had burned down to coals, and had long since ceased to crackle. The silence stretched out.

And then it was broken by the fifth man in the room.

"That's very interesting," said the old man from his chair by the fireside.

The four cardplayers exchanged glances. "You're awake," the priest said. "I hope we didn't disturb you."

"You didn't disturb me," said the old man, his voice like dry leaves in the wind, thin and wispy, yet oddly penetrating for all that. "I fear I may have disturbed you, by breaking wind from time to time."

The doctor colored. "I was impolite enough to remark upon it," he said, "and for that I apologize. We had no idea you were awake."

"When one has reached my considerable age," the old man said, "one is never entirely asleep, and never entirely awake, either. One dozes through the days. But is that state of being the exclusive property of the aged? All my long life, I sometimes think, I have never been entirely awake or entirely asleep. Consciousness is somewhere between the two, and so is unconsciousness."

"Food for thought," the soldier said.

"But thinner gruel than the food for thought you four have provided. Lust!"

"Our topic," the priest said, "and it did set the stories rolling."

"How I lusted," said the old man. "How I longed for women. Yearned for them, burned for them. Of course those days of longing are long gone now. Now I sit by the fire, warming my old bones, neither awake nor asleep. I don't long for women. I don't long for anything."

"Well," the policeman said.

"But I remember them," the old man said.

"The women."

"The women, and how I felt about them, and what I did with them. I remember the ones I had, and there's not one I regret having. And I remember the ones I wanted and didn't have, and I regret every one of those lost chances."

"We most regret what we've left undone," said the priest. "Even the sins we left uncommitted. It's a mystery."

"In high school," the old man said, "there was a girl named Peggy Singer. How I longed for her! How she starred in my schoolboy fantasies! She was my partner for a minute or two at a school dance, before another wretched boy cut in. I couldn't possibly remember the clean smell of her skin, or the way she felt in my arms. But it seems to me that I do."

The doctor nodded, at a memory of his own.

"After graduation," the old man said, "I lost track of her entirely. Never learned what became of her. Never forgot her, either. And now my life is nearing its end, and when I add the plusses and minuses, they cancel each other out until I'm left with one unreconcilable fact. God help me, I never got to fuck Peggy Singer."

"Ah," the soldier said, and the policeman let out a sigh.

"Women," the old man said. "I remember what I did with them, and what I wanted to do, and what I hardly dared to dream of doing. And I remember how it felt, and the urgency of my desire. I remember how important it all was to me. But do you know what I don't remember, what I can't understand?"

They waited.

"I can't understand what was so *important* about it," the old man said. "Why did it matter so? Why? I've never understood that."

He paused, and the silence stretched as they waited for him to say more. Then the sound of his breathing deepened, and a snore came from the chair beside the fireplace.

"He's sleeping," the priest said.

"Or not," said the doctor. "Neither asleep nor awake, even as you and I."

"Well," said the policeman.

"Does anyone remember who's deal it is?" the soldier wondered, gathering the cards.

No one did. "You go ahead, Soldier," said the doctor, and the soldier shuffled and dealt, and the game resumed.

And the old man went on dozing by the fire.

AUTHORS' BIOGRAPHIES

Lawrence Block has come to dominate the contemporary mystery scene with two equally popular series. Brooding investigator Matt Scudder, who last appeared in *Everybody Dies*, isn't even a shirttail relative of droll gentleman thief Bernie Rhodenbarr, but they are both rendered with the same style and grace in every book or short story he writes. He also has a series character, the philosophic hit man known only as Keller, whose exploits were recently collected in the anthology *Hit Man* and who is now starring in his first feature-length novel, *Hit List*.

James W. Hall is one of a sudden swarm of authors who is writing about that world-within-a-world: South Florida. But where other authors end, he is just getting started, combining one-of-a-kind characters with plots that could exist only in the multicultural melting pot of the Florida panhandle. His novels include *Body Language*, *Red Sky at Night*, *Mean High Tide*, *Buzz Cut*, and his latest, *Rough Draft*. Every time you think he's exhausted his bag of tricks, he pulls out another surprise that leaves you breathless and gasping. An original in a field that is becoming more rapidly crowded each year, his books always stand out. Recently he left Florida, and now lives in North Carolina.

Simon Brett is adept at both the traditional mystery novel as well as the historical. His recent novels include *Mrs. Pargeter's Point of Honor* and *The Body on the Beach: A Fethering Mystery*. He's also quite accomplished in the short form as well, with stories appearing in the Malice Domestic series, as well as the anthologies *Once Upon a Crime* and *Funny Bones*. A winner of the Writer's Guild of Great Britain award for his radio plays and the Broadcasters Press Guild award, he has also written non-fiction books and edited several volumes in the Faber series, including *The Faber Book of Useful Verse* and *The Faber Book of Parodies*. He lives in Burpham, England.

Marthayn Pelegrimas is the author of numerous short stories in horror and western genres, including her appearances in *Borderlands 3*, *Till Death Do Us Part*, and *American Pulp*. Her first mystery novel was written under pseudonym "Christine Matthews" and is called *Murder Is the Deal of the Day*. She is also an editor, most notably credited with the audio anthology *Hear the Fear*. Currently she is at work on her next novel. She lives with her husband, fellow author Robert J. Randisi, in St. Louis, Missouri.

If versatility is a virtue then **Ed Gorman** is virtuous indeed. He has written steadily in three different genres, mystery, horror and westerns, for almost twenty years. He has also written a large number of short stories, with six of his collections of wry, poignant, unsettling fiction in print in the USA and UK. Kirkus said, "Gorman is one of the most original crime writers around," taking particular note of his Sam McCain-Judge Whitney series, which is set in small-town Iowa in the 1950s, and winning rave reviews from coast-to-coast. It is no surprise that he captures the essence of life in the Midwest, since he lives in Cedar Rapids, Iowa. As for the wealth of detail he brings to every novel and story he writes, well, he's been there and back again, and the observations he shares about life, love, and loss make his books all the richer. His most recent novel is *Will You Still Love Me Tomorrow?*, the third Sam McCain book.

Julian Symons (1912-1994) began his mystery-writing career with the novel *The Immaterial Murder Case*, which was written as part of an elaborate practical joke and sat in a drawer for six years before being submitted to publishers. Before that, he had worked primarily as a critic and book reviewer, writing critical books on Charles Dickens, Thomas Carlyle, Edgar Allan Poe, and historical accounts of the events in England in the 1930s, such as the General Strike of 1926 and the Gordon Relief Expedition. He was the author of the Inspector Bland series, which at the time of his death spanned more than twenty-five novels, including *The Broken Penny*, *Death's Darkest Foe*, and *The Man Who Lost His Wife*. He was honored with the Crime Writers Association award, the Cartier Diamond Dagger award, Mystery Writers of America Edgar Allan Poe award and Grand Master award. He also served as chairman of Crime Writers Association from 1969–1971.

James Crumley is the creator of two different series featuring private investigators in Montana. His first, Milo Milodragovitch, is sliding down a long path of self-destruction with the help of cocaine and alcohol. His second series is about C. W. Sughrue, an ex-Army spy who also has a drinking problem. The two characters meet up in the wild novel *Bordersnakes*. He earned a Masters of Fine Arts degree from the University of Iowa, and spent the next twenty years teaching English at several universities before turning to writing. Currently he lives in Missoula, Montana.

Joyce Carol Oates is widely regarded as one of America's premier authors and leading literary critics. Her articles have appeared in *The New York Times Review of Books* and other prestigious literary forums. Her novels and short stories deconstruct modern life as we know it, magnifying seemingly inconsequential events and showing the motives and rationalizations behind it all. She can make everyday life seem horrifying, and when she writes suspenseful fiction, there are few who are her equal. Currently the Roger S. Berlind Distinguished Professor at Princeton University, the awards she has received for her fiction and critical writing are numerous, including a National Endowment for the Arts grant, Guggenheim fellowship, the O'henry award, the National Book award, the Horror Writers of America Stoker award for Lifetime Achievement, and the Walt Whitman award. Recent books include *Blonde*, which is being developed into a film in Hollywood, and *Solstice*.

Jeremiah Healy is one of the private-eye writers who helped change a moribund mystery field in the eighties. A former professor at the New England School of Law, his debut novel about private detective John Francis Cuddy, *Blunt Darts,* announced that here was a wise new kid on the block. Since then he has written more than a dozen novels featuring his melancholy P.I., and his books and stories have done nothing but enhance his reputation as an important and sage writer whose work has taken the private-eye form to an exciting new level. Winner of the Shamus award in 1986 for *The Staked Goat,* he is one of those writers who packs the poise and depth of a good mainstream novel into an even better genre novel. Recent books include *The Stalking of Sheilah Quinn* and the latest Cuddy mystery *The Only Good Lawyer.*

Robert Weinberg has spent the last thirty-five years ensuring that the thousands of pulp stories published in the first half of the century remain in print today. In his spare time, he writes in all genres of fiction, appearing in the anthologies *Legends: Tales from the Eternal Archives, Dark Love, Miskatonic University* and *David Copperfield's Tales of the Impossible.* He is also scripting the Cable comic book series for Marvel Comics. In 1999 his science fiction novel *The Termination Node,* co-authored with Lois Gresh, was shortlisted for the Nebula award. A former two-time vice-president for the Horror Writers of America, he lives with his family in Oak Forest, Illinois.

Gil Brewer (1922-1983) was one of the mainstays of the Gold Medal line of pulp novels, with his books *13 French Street* and *A Killer Is Loose* selling hundreds of thousands of copies during pulp's 1950s heyday. His non-Fawcett novels are also excellent, in particular *The Red Scarf* and *Nude on Thin Ice.* Tragically, he fought alcoholism throughout his career, and died in the early 1980s, after several failed attempts to restart his writing career. But during those wild years when the pulps were king, he ruled the suspense fiction landscape with his noir tales of bad men and women, double-crosses, and danger.

There's no denying that **Evan Hunter**—a/k/a Ed McBain, Richard Marsten, and other pseudonyms—has amassed a body of work that stuns the senses when one sits down to reckon with it. That so much of it is excellent, and that some of it is possessed of true genius, and that every single piece of it makes for enjoyable reading is a testament to the man's prowess as an author. Because of such bestsellers as *The Blackboard Jungle* and *A Matter of Conviction*, Hunter's early fame was for his mainstream novels. But over the years he became better known for the 87th Precinct series. It's impossible to choose the "best" of the 87th books—there are just too many good ones—but one might suggest a peek at *He Who Hesitates* (1965), *Blood Relatives* (1975), *Long Time No See* (1977), and *The Big Bad City* (1999). He wrote the screenplay of *The Birds* for Alfred Hitchcock and his powerful novel *Last Summer* became one of the seminal films of the seventies. His recent novels include *The Last Dance: A Novel of the 87th Precinct* and *Candyland: A Novel of Obsession.*

Loren D. Estleman has distinguished himself in a number of literary fields including mainstream, western, private eye and thriller. His critically acclaimed fictionalized history series known as the Detroit Chronicles includes *Whiskey River, Motown, Jitterbug,* and *The Pontchartrain Club.* He has been nominated for the Pulitzer Prize and won a couple of shelves of literary awards. Everybody from John D. MacDonald to the reviewers at *People* magazine have showered him with the kind of adjectives writers like to keep in their wall safes at home. Because he started so young, his list of novels and story collections is not only long but luminous with style, innovation and a particular love of all things American. Well, most things American. His series characters, Detroit private investigator Amos Walker, has appeared in more than a dozen novels, the latest being *A Smile of the Face of the Tiger.*

Thomas S. Roche's stories have appeared in a wide variety of magazines and Web sites, as well as horror, crime and erotica anthologies. His books include the Noirotica series of erotic crime-noir anthologies and the short story collection *Dark Matter*. He lives and writes in San Francisco, California.

The old-fashioned private eye just plumb wore out back in the seventies. It was at this time that a few gifted writers, such as **John Lutz**, took a look at the genre and said, This has got to change. Alo Nudger was Lutz's first entry in the neo-private eye sweepstakes and boy was he a good one. Alo doesn't try to conquer life's vicissitudes with swill and swagger; he simply hopes to survive them—with a lot of help from his endless supply of Tums. Fred Carver came along after that. Fred is a kind of James Joycean p.i., Portrait of A Middle-Aged Shamus. He is all the things a private eye isn't supposed to be, generally confused, frequently unnerved, unfailingly in need of donuts, sympathy and various kinds of medication for his various physical ailments. All this is rendered in very nice prose, and with a worldview that occasionally reads like St. Francis of Assisi with a hangover. Lutz is also a true short story master. He has an Edgar and a Shamus award to prove it, and even if he didn't, this story, like dozens of others, would say it just as clearly. His short story "SWF Seeks Same" was the basis for the movie *Single White Female*.

Joan Hess, on or off the page, is funny. Off the page that's great. On the page, that's not always so good. At least not when reviewers, trained to look for Deep Meanings, look over her books. Nothing this enjoyable, they seem to think, can possibly have real merit. Not true, as she continues to demonstrate in novel after novel. Hess' spirited takes on her home state of Arkansas combines the cozy form with her own version of black comedy—domestic comedy that is set down with the same neurotic glee one finds in the stories of Anne Beatty. Whether she's writing about Clare Malloy, her young widow who runs a book store, or Arly Hanks, who is police chief of Maggody, Arkansas, Hess' two series are engaging but quite serious takes on relationships, middle-age, parental duties, and life in small-town America. Recent novels include Claire Malloy's latest appearance in *A Conventional Corpse* and Arly Hanks' newest mystery in *Murder@Maggody.com*. She lives with her family in Fayetteville, Arkansas.

Paul Bishop divides his time between writing bestselling mystery novels and heading up the Sex Crimes and Major Assault Crimes departments of the Los Angeles police department. During his twenty-year tenure, he has worked on a federal task force which coordinated with the L.A. Sheriff's Department, the FBI, CIA, and the Secret Service. Although his main series character is a female homicide detective named Fey

Croaker, he also writes about a one-eyed ex-soccer goalie turned private eye. His latest book is a collection of his short fiction entitled *Patterns of Behavior*. He lives in Camarillo, California.

Clive Barker first gained prominence in the horror/dark fantasy genre with the publication of his seminal six-volume short story series The Books of Blood. He followed that up with a series of novels, including *Weaveworld, Imajica,* and *Sacrament,* which blurred the line between literary fiction, imaginative fantasy, and outright horror. He has been honored with British and World Fantasy awards and a nomination for the Booker Prize (one of Britain's highest literary honors). His body of work in film is no less impressive, and includes the classic horror film *Hellraiser, Candyman,* and the distinguished semi-autobiographical film about the life of director James Whale, *Gods and Monsters.*